MIDDLE OF KNIGHT

JEWEL E ANN

Copyright © 2015 by Jewel E. Ann

Second Print Edition

ISBN: 978-1-7359982-5-1

Cover Designer: Jenn Beach

To women over forty. We've still got it!

CHAPTER ONE
KNIGHT

THE SIGNS WERE EVERYWHERE. That twenty-twenty hindsight was an evil, gloating bitch. What incentive was there to ponder a question that had already been answered? The PTSD *was* a catch-all. AJ knew it. Jillian dismissed it. Fate seized it.

I love you. Why would he say those words? Jillian Knight pondered that question while her brother, Jackson, drove her home from the hospital.

"So you just ran out?" Jackson asked, making a quick sideways glance.

"Walked. I walked out. I told AJ I needed to do something."

"And what was that?"

"I needed to get the hell out of there."

"Why?"

"He said ... 'I love you.'"

"I see ... Actually, I don't. You're going to have to help me out on this one."

"Why would he say that? Was his accident some near-death experience that brought about this rush of irrational feelings? And it wasn't just that he said it. It was the way he said it. It's like someone had a gun to his head."

"Do you love him?"

"No ... I-I don't know. That's just it. What was I supposed to say? *Thank you,* or *I'd rather you wouldn't?*"

"So what now?"

She sighed. "I don't know. Food, beer, and then I'll face him tomorrow."

By eleven o'clock that night, with the help of four bottles of Heineken, Jillian had an epiphany. It was a new record for her. Most epiphanies didn't happen until the end of the sixth bottle of Heineken.

"Jackie?" she whispered, opening Jackson's bedroom door.

"What the hell did you call me?" he grumbled with his head buried in his pillow, the bed sheet draped low on his waist.

Jillian giggled, then hiccupped. "Jackie ... I figured it out."

He flipped over, raising up on his elbows, eyes squinted against the hall light. "Call me that again and I'll knock you out before the beer gets to it."

"Scooch over." She stumbled to his bed.

"I'm naked."

"So ... scooch." Jillian wedged her way into his bed.

Jackson retreated to the other side, securing the sheet around his waist.

"I've decided to love AJ."

"Decided?"

Jillian rolled onto her side facing Jackson with her cheek rested on her folded hands. "Yes. Why not? Right? He's mature, and good in bed, and he gets me, and he's good in bed. He's strong and grumpy, which I find oddly sexy. Oh ... did I mention he's good in bed?"

Jackson stared at the ceiling. "Yes, you mentioned that." He chuckled. "Sex doesn't mean love."

"I never said that. God ... all you guys think about is sex." She slurred each word. "I'm serious. He's my chance. You're going to find that happily ever after, and she's not going to want me living with you forever. AJ will take me."

"God, you're so drunk right now. That's it, huh? You can just decide to love him, like love's a choice? And you're basing this deep emotion on the possibility that he 'gets' you, or even more pathetic ... that he'll 'take' you. You're making yourself sound like a stray dog. You need to get off the booze. It's beginning to rob you of your self-esteem."

"It doesn't matter. I'd rather he love me than hate me. He's had a vasectomy so he's not looking for a baby mama, and he's definitely not clingy so in some ways he's the perfect guy. And I have these feelings for him and maybe they're love. I'm not going to lose him because my head is messed up. When Cage called and said AJ had been in an accident, I swear my heart stopped. It has to be love."

Jackson rubbed his eyes. "You're thirty years old and just like that you're making the decision that you don't want a family?"

Jillian tried to roll her eyes, but it was hard to do behind heavy eyelids. "That makes no sense coming from my twin brother that doesn't want children."

"I never said that."

"You said you don't like kids."

"Misquoting once again. I don't like other people's kids. *My* kids will be awesome."

"*Will be?*"

"Yes. The whole slew of them. My wife is going to be so

hot I won't be able to keep my dick out of her. She'll be knocked up all the time."

Jillian laughed. "I can't wait to see that. My nieces and nephews ... not your dick in my sister-in-law."

"If you don't want to see my dick then get the hell out of here."

"Fine. Good night." Jillian bumped into the nightstand and then the wall, trying to maneuver her drunk self out of Jackson's room.

MORNING DIDN'T CARE that Jillian had too much to drink the previous night. Neither did the incessant knocking at the door.

"Jackson!" she called.

Nothing.

Unaware of the time—fifteen minutes after noon—Jillian grumbled about the poor etiquette of someone knocking on the door so early. She winced at the throbbing side effect of too much Heineken as she shuffled her bare feet to the front door.

"Cage, hey." The morning sun burned her retinas as her nipples saluted the crisp morning breeze.

Cage cleared his throat, forcing his eyes to stay on hers instead of her barely covered body.

"Uh ... hey. I just brought my dad home from the hospital. He wants to see you. I have to get back to campus, but I'll be back this weekend."

"Yeah ... I ... um, yeah." She nodded through her rambling of nothing that made any sense. "I'll shower and be over."

She started to close the door.

"Jillian?"

"Hmm?"

"Thank you."

She narrowed her eyes. "For what?"

"For being here and putting up with him. Even if he doesn't say it. I know he appreciates it. But mainly for me. It eases my mind to know that someone is ... looking out for him."

"Oh ... sure." She shrugged it off. "How's he doing today?"

"Fine. I think. He's quiet. Seems a little distracted. I think the accident really shook him up, which is a little weird because he's been in crashes, around gun fire, and even ejected from a plane that was shot down."

Jillian frowned. Cage confirmed her earlier suspicions that AJ wasn't quite right. "I'll talk to him. Drive safely back to campus."

"Thanks. I will."

After a long, procrastinating shower that included a review of the previous night's declaration made under the heavy influence of alcohol, Jillian slipped on a yellow sundress several shades brighter than her mood, red rain boots, and her best smile to mask the courage she struggled to muster. She considered taking him something to eat, but decided one near-death incident that week was enough.

"AJ?" Jillian called, letting herself in his house.

"On the couch."

She peeked around the corner to the great room. The closed blinds on every window rejected the light as the stagnant air leadened her lungs with doom. "Hey," she said, her voice unusually small. Damn nerves. "Are you drinking? Before five?"

AJ tipped back a bottle of beer. Just the sight of it caused Jillian's stomach to roil.

"Yeah, why not?" He flipped off the TV.

She slipped off her boots and sat on the opposite end of the couch, lifting his feet up to sit and resting them back on her lap.

He nursed his beer, staring at her, but not saying anything.

"About yesterday—"

He shook his head. "Don't worry about it."

"I'm not ... or I was, but I'm not now."

"Doesn't matter. Just forget about it."

Jillian traced her finger along the serpent tattoo on his leg. "What if I don't want to forget about it?"

"I don't give a fuck what you do."

She glanced up at him, lips parted, eyes wide. "Do you need a minute to rethink that?"

He took another pull. "Nope."

"Would you like me to come back later?"

"You don't need to come back at all. That's all I wanted to tell you."

The twenty-four-hour whiplash left quite a sting. Especially since she'd prepared to reciprocate his expression of feelings. Those feelings had taken a backseat to his anger.

"Are you having a moment or is this about me leaving yesterday?"

"Don't be so fucking condescending with me. I'm not having a *moment,* and I told you to forget about yesterday."

Scooting out from under his legs, she stood. "Call me if you need anything." He didn't deserve another glance as she pulled on her boots and walked to the door.

"I won't—" His voice slurred.

She turned. "AJ!"

He shook, tumbling from the sofa with a *thunk*.

"Oh my God!"

A seizure racked his body, stealing him from consciousness.

Jillian grabbed his cell phone off the sofa table and dialed 9-1-1. They talked her through it and sent an ambulance. She followed it to the hospital, leaving a message on Jackson's phone, but waited to call Cage, assuming it was most likely a side effect of his accident and the concussion.

They treated him in the ER, but no one would give her any information because she wasn't family. An hour later they let her see him.

"Why are you still here?" His words hung heavy with defeat as she entered the room.

"Because I love you, you idiot." It's not how she'd planned on telling him, but it came out and she couldn't stop it. The word didn't feel right, but it didn't feel wrong either. It just felt like a word.

He closed his eyes and turned his head side to side. "Don't."

She sat on the edge of his bed. "I shouldn't have left yesterday, and I'm sorry. What you said scared me. I don't feel worthy of that kind of love and—"

"Stop ... just stop." He opened his eyes. "I meant it when I said it doesn't matter."

"What doesn't matter?" Jillian's voice escalated. "Me? Us? Your love for me? Mine for you?"

"All of it," he said in a monotone voice.

"It mattered yesterday. You said—"

"You didn't let me finish!"

Jillian jumped.

AJ sighed. "You didn't let me finish yesterday. You left too soon."

She shook her head. "I don't understand."

"I needed you to know that I love you, but then I was going to tell you that I can't be with you anymore."

"Yeah, that makes perfectly no sense whatsoever. You need help. I know you don't want to talk about the PTSD, but it's eating you up inside. You may not think anyone can help you, but maybe you just need another opinion." She refused to back down, refused to be kicked to the curb like an old sofa up for grabs. He could be harsh and hurtful, but she could deal with it.

"Goodbye, Jillian." He looked away.

"I'm not leaving, you stubborn SOB." She grabbed his face and forced him to look at her. He was it—her last chance at love and she was determined to take it. Her past had taken too much already. It wasn't deserving of him too. He was her future—a future she would fight for.

"Is this a bad time?"

Jillian turned.

A doctor in a white lab coat stood at the door.

"No ... sorry, come in." She smiled past her anger and released AJ's face as if she hadn't just manhandled a patient.

He nodded, walking toward them. "I'm Dr. Rinehart from oncology."

Every last bit of air evaporated from the room. Jillian couldn't find a single breath.

"Doctor." AJ nodded. "This is my friend, Jillian."

Jillian looked at AJ, not Dr. Rinehart. "W-why do you need an oncologist?"

"Tell her, Doc. Why do I need you?"

Dr. Rinehart gave Jillian a regretful smile. "AJ has a brain tumor. It was discovered on his MRI after his accident yesterday."

The air. Where was all the fucking air? The migraines, the personality that flipped without warning, the PTSD pigeonholing for everything ... how could everyone have missed it?

"Cancer?" she whispered.

"We're not sure," Dr. Rinehart replied.

"When will you know?"

Dr. Rinehart looked at AJ.

"When I'm dead and an autopsy confirms it."

Jillian turned, glaring at AJ. It wasn't the time to be mad at him, but she was. How could he say that? Why would he say that?

"You're not dying!" She looked to Dr. Rinehart for confirmation.

"I've consulted with the neurologist that saw AJ yesterday. The tumor may be inoperable."

"But ... you can do radiation or chemotherapy or something else, right?"

"Yes, there are other options."

"But the neurologist confessed that the success rate is lower with tumors like mine. And I'm sure as hell not going to be a guinea pig, so—"

"So what?" Jillian snapped at AJ. "You're just going to do nothing? Wait until your headaches get even worse? Wait until you're having seizures every day? Wait until you —" The familiar pain in her chest crashed like a wrecking ball. She didn't notice the tears streaming down her cheeks until she tasted their salty presence.

"Die?" AJ grabbed her hand and squeezed it so hard that pain in her chest exploded into something irreversibly destructive. "Yes, Jillian. I'm going to die."

CHAPTER TWO

THERE WAS nothing and yet everything to say, but the nothing won over. AJ left the hospital with a grim nod from the doctor and a handful of medications to help with the migraines and lessen his chances of having seizures. Jillian opened her mouth to speak at least a dozen times on the way home, but nothing came out.

"Thanks for the ride." AJ mumbled, getting out of her car.

"Have you told Cage or your parents?" She jumped out and chased him toward his door.

He shook his head and kept walking.

"Don't shut me out." Raw emotion bled from her words. Everything had happened so fast she couldn't process it.

The man that dared anyone to cross him stood in defeat at his door with his back to her, head bowed, hands on his hips. "Why? You shut me out all the time."

"I don't—"

He turned. "You do. You're orphaned Jillian from New York. You have a sick need to make men bleed. You're thirty and your greatest skill is selling sex toys. That's so fucking

10

pathetic. Yet somewhere along the way, I bought into all of it. Part of me loves you, but I don't know how and I sure as hell don't know why, because I don't really even know you!"

Her teeth clenched. "You didn't want to know. You said it yourself."

"Well I do now."

"Well I ... can't," she whispered, shaking her head.

"Why not?"

"I just can't." She would never be able to make him understand. "I don't want you to die."

Why couldn't he see the pleading in her eyes that said everything she couldn't?

"Tell me what happened to you. Tell me and I'll make an appointment with the oncologist on Monday."

"That's not fair."

"I have a goddamn tumor in my head. Life's not fair!"

She continued to shake her head. It was a nightmare. Eventually she would have to wake up. "You're black-mailing me with your fucking life? What's wrong with you? You have a son and parents who love you."

"You don't trust me." He narrowed his eyes then turned toward the door.

"It's not about trust!" She grabbed his arm. "Just..." the anger and desperation pulled the pin to another grenade inside her chest "...forget it ever happened. Please."

He laughed. He actually laughed. Her anger held back the tears.

"Forget what? The biting and clawing? The broken nose? The fact that we can't sleep in the same bed?"

"Yes," she whispered, closing her eyes as shame stole the last bit of fight she had left.

He pulled away from her. "I can't."

As she pushed open the front door, feeling weak with defeat, her phone vibrated with a text message.

Hebrews 9:22

"How's he doing?"

The thundering of her pulse muffled the sound of Jackson's voice. Some fucker kept vying for her attention, trying to cripple her with fear, when AJ's doctors had already given her an overdose of it.

"He has a brain tumor."

"Jill ..." He pulled her into his arms, but still no tears, just a cold numbness. "Cancer?"

"They're not sure yet, but it seems inoperable and AJ doesn't want treatment." She stepped back, laughing at the morbidity of the situation. "Let me rephrase that ... he'll agree to treatment if I tell him about my past."

"Oh ... you're not thinking of—"

"No, I'm not going to tell him." She shrugged. "What's one more death to my name?"

"It's not your fault."

Shaking her head, she held up her phone. "Doesn't matter anyway. I'll probably die before him."

Jackson plucked it from her hand. A squint of confusion etched along his forehead. He searched for its meaning. *"Indeed, under the law almost everything is purified with blood, and without the shedding of blood there is no forgiveness of sins."*

"What if it's him?"

Jillian narrowed her eyes. "Who?"

"AJ."

"Not funny."

"I'm not trying to be funny."

"Jesus, Jackson! Did you hear me say he has a brain tumor? It gives him migraines, and seizures, it's probably the reason his personality flips without a moment's notice, but he's not a stalker."

"Maybe one of his personalities is."

"It's not."

"Nothing else makes sense. Trigger and Four are dead. If it were the people responsible for Mom and Dad, they wouldn't play this cat and mouse game ... we'd simply be dead."

Jillian put her hands over her face and sighed with a little grumble. "Tell Knox to get me a new phone. I'm going to bed ... for the next month. Don't wake me."

<hr>

THE OVERPROTECTIVE AND sometimes doting brother hated being the bastard, but someone had to be. After three days of Jillian leaving her bedroom only for water, Jackson yanked her from the black hole.

"Time's up. I'll give you five seconds to get out of bed before I start your intervention."

"Touch me and I'll kill you," Jillian warned from under her rat's nest of covers.

"I welcome the challenge. At this point I'd welcome any sign of life from you. Maybe you need a good ass-kicking."

"Jackson!" she yelled and flailed as he heaved her over his shoulder and carried her to the bathroom. Depositing her stubborn ass in the shower, he turned the lever until an icy stream of water rained on her.

She clawed at the walls and slipped along the floor like a drowning cat.

"Wash up. You stink."

An hour later she emerged from her room with clean clothes and wet hair. "He loves me. And he's dying. That's messed up, right?" She looked at Jackson through vacant eyes.

He could confirm AJ's impending death, but not from his tumor. "He's not dying, not today anyway. I'd call it shock. Once he accepts the reality of his situation, he'll man up, let them fry half his brain with some experimental treatment, and live happily ever after with his psychotic neighbor."

"Not funny."

Jackson cradled her face then sighed at her lifelessness. "I'll never stop reminding you that *you* are the strongest person I have ever known because when you hit the lowest depths of hell, you choose to claw your way out every time. It's not what you do ... it's who you are. You're a survivor."

The bravest woman alive sucked in a shaky breath. "I'm not. *You* ... I'd die without you."

He hugged her. "You wouldn't. I think a meteor could hit Earth and wipe out the human population with the exception of you."

She grunted. "I'm not invincible."

Jackson kissed the top of her head. She encompassed his world. "You are to me."

Even the protector of this brave woman lived with his own demons. Had he followed his instincts, he could have saved Claire's life and in turn, his sister's. Instead he waited for their dad to get home nearly twenty-four hours later.

Twenty-four hours too late.

He never told his sister that, and he swallowed the guilt

every day of his life. Nothing but more pain could come from what-ifs.

"I have a lesson in two hours and I have a few errands to run. So eat something and call Dodge and Lilith. They've been worried about you."

Jillian nodded.

"And ice your eyes or something ... your face just looks all kinds of wrong right now."

"Thanks for that."

"Anytime."

<hr>

Jillian forced down a piece of dry toast then lay down with teabags on her eyes. The man who would always have her heart was alive, but she would never see him again. The man who made her think love was possible without said heart was right next door, but he was on a cruel suicide mission and eventually he would die and she would *never see him again.*

Maybe she *would* be the last person standing. It was just her and life—both equally crazy.

The doorbell rang. Tossing the teabags in the trash, she shuffled her bare feet to the door.

"Hi." Jillian mustered a smile at the woman standing on her stoop.

"Hi, sorry to bother you. I'm Ryn Middleton. I clean AJ's house." She pointed next door. "There's usually a key under his planter, but it's not there. And the garage code doesn't work either. I tried his cell phone but it goes straight to voicemail."

Jillian laughed a little. She had no doubt that AJ was trying to keep someone out of his house, but it wasn't Ryn.

"He's had some *issues* lately. I'm sure it's just an oversight on his part."

Ryn wrinkled her nose a bit. "I don't want to make you uncomfortable or get you in trouble, but would you happen to have a spare key to his place? I've been cleaning his house for over five years so I'm not a thief or anything. I just have a really full schedule, so if I don't clean for him today he'll have to wait another two weeks."

Jillian smiled. "I do actually." She held up a finger. "Just let me grab it."

The woman, to whom the rules did not apply, returned with a small black box. Ryn raised a brow.

"I'll open it for you. I'm Jillian, by the way."

Ryn followed as Jillian's boots squeaked with each step through the dewy grass to AJ's front door. "Uh ... that doesn't look like a key,"

"It's a universal key. Comes in quite handy. You should think about getting one. I'm sure this isn't the first house you've been locked out of."

Ryn replied with a nervous laugh. "I'm not sure what the neighbors would think of me using a lock-picking set to open a client's door."

"They'd think you're ingenious." Jillian turned the handle and the door opened. "Well, at least that's what I'd think if I saw you doing it." She returned the picks to the box and closed it.

"What if he asks how I got in?"

Jillian grinned with pride. "Tell him I let you in. It's the truth, and trust me, he won't ask you any more questions after that."

Ryn gave her an easy nod. "Thanks. I'd better get to work."

Jillian smiled, took a few steps toward home, then turned. "Are you taking new clients?"

Ryn grabbed two buckets of supplies from the back of her car. "I could probably take on one more, but it would have to be a weekly client. I have a two hour slot on Tuesday afternoons, but it's not enough time for a bi-weekly job. More dirt. More time."

"My brother and I could use someone to do some light cleaning, if you're interested."

"Your brother?"

Jillian laughed. "Yes. My roommate happens to be my brother, for now. We just moved here."

"Well, yeah ... if you want Tuesdays I could put you on my schedule. When I'm done here, I can come over and give you an estimate if you'll still be home."

Jillian didn't really need an estimate, but it seemed like the normal thing to expect so she went with it. "Sure. If I'm not home Jackson will be. And, just a fair warning ... he's going to like you." She winked at Ryn.

An uneasy smile formed along her lips. "Excuse me?"

"Just ignore everything he says or does. He's taken a vow of celibacy. Some days are easier than others."

<hr>

"We hired AJ's cleaning lady to clean this pit on Tuesdays, and she'll be dropping by to give an estimate when she's done with his place. So be nice and keep your dick in your pants. I'm going to watch Lilith." Jillian pulled her hair back into a ponytail.

"*We* hired her?" He loved how his sister made decisions for both of them without consulting him.

"Yes."

"And *why* do you think my dick will wander from my pants?"

She insulted him with her lack of trust. He was a changed man.

Her answer began with a sigh. "Because she's older than you—maybe late thirties, early forties. And she's pretty."

Jackson crossed his arms. "Elaborate on pretty."

"She's most likely married with kids, two fish, and a dog, so I don't know why it matters."

"Elaborate on pretty." He held firm.

"Five-seven, a hundred and thirty pounds, shy smile, an inverted bob cut with wavy shades of blond, light blue eyes, and freckles. Bye." She shut the door.

After piecing all the descriptives into a mental image, he looked down at his crotch. "Yeah, buddy, this could be a problem."

Several hours later, while in the middle of his lesson, a few soft taps rapped on the door.

"Keep playing. I'll only be a minute."

He opened the door. "Hello." The smile that curled along his lips continued to grow as he stole a few extra seconds to just look. It didn't hurt to look. "You must be AJ's housekeeper."

"Yes. Ryn Middleton." She strained her neck to the side. "Sorry, am I interrupting?"

"I'm in the middle of a lesson, but Jillian said you'd be coming by. Come in. Feel free to scope out the place. You won't bother us."

A nice smile, indeed shy but genuine, graced her mesmerizing face as she nodded. Although, it was her eyes that held his attention, a stark change from his past. He usually couldn't remember a woman's name, let alone her eye color. The exception, however, stood in front of him with the most brilliant blue eyes that faded to icy blue halos right next to her pupils. They drew him in like a hypnotic spiral—an idiot just staring at her.

"Oh..." he moved to the side and grinned "...yes, come in."

"Thanks," she whispered.

His student continued to kill his piano by playing her own made-up chords that had him dreaming of physically harming her. Ryn didn't need to whisper. Her voice offered an angelic reprieve from the musical massacre going on in the background.

The distracted piano teacher, with his head in the gutter, sat back down by his student while Ryn surveyed their place. No wedding band shackled her finger, but it was possible she didn't wear one while cleaning. Five or so minutes later she paused near the front door, writing something on a pad of paper.

"Play that song again," he told his student. His mind screamed, *Get out! And never touch Black Beauty again.*

Jackson's new obsession smiled as he approached her. "Here's the estimate."

"Great. So I'll see you Tuesday."

Her brow furrowed a bit. "You..." she gestured to the piece of paper "...didn't even look at it."

Jackson looked at it for two quick seconds. "Great. So I'll see you next Tuesday."

Ryn chuckled. "Twelve-thirty."

He nodded. "If you need to discuss that time with your *husband* and call us back that's fine."

Ryn peaked a single brow. "I'm pretty sure women asking their husbands' permission to schedule work went out of style a couple generations ago. Twelve-thirty on Tuesday."

A terrible answer. What was he supposed to deduce from that? A simple "I'm not married" or "I don't need my husband's permission" were the acceptable answers. At least they would have been clear answers; the only acceptable answer was the first one.

SHIT. Shit. Shitty. Shit. Shit. That pretty much summed up Ryn's thoughts on her new clients, specifically the tattooed sex-on-a-stick that taught piano lessons. Guys that looked like that did not teach piano lessons. Then there were those geeky glasses with the white tape on the bridge. Was it wrong that within thirty seconds of him answering the door her mind had him crawling up her body wearing nothing but those glasses? Probably.

Damn hormones.

His eyes and that smile—she knew flirting when she saw it. Or maybe it was teasing. Flirting said "I want you." Teasing said "You want me, but you don't have a chance in the world. Ryn had to think on that one."

Celibacy.

Jackson didn't look like a priest, but there really wasn't any other good explanation. He probably played the organ at church. A tattooed organ-playing priest. And his age —*younger*. He had to be in his sexual prime. That explained Jillian's warning. His carnal needs warred with his spiritual calling and his type had been reduced to a simple category: women. When a person suffers from starvation, they're not choosy. They just crave food.

Any woman would be tempting after going so long—or maybe forever—without sex. Was it possible? Was Jackson a virgin?

Ryn tore through her last house on autopilot and dragged her tired, aging ass into the shower. Three weeks separated her from the big four-oh. It wasn't a huge deal, except she would be forty and single with a twenty-one-year-old daughter and an ex-husband with a restraining order against him. She really knew how to pick 'em.

The most important male in her life was Gunner—her ten-year-old German shepherd. She adopted him as a pup and they went through years of training together. The perfect guard dog, obedient to her like a soldier.

"Should we call Maddie?"

Gunner tilted his head to the side. Ryn towel dried her hair while plopping down on the bed and grabbing the phone.

"Not now, Mom."

"Nice to talk to you too, Maddie."

"Well you call me every day. I have a date. Some of us have a life, you know."

Ryn knew. How could she not? Her daughter reminded her of it all the time.

"I thought we could do a spa day for my birthday."

"I have to work on your birthday. Need I remind you why that is?"

No. She didn't need to hear it again. Maddie's father pulled her college funding when Ryn filed the restraining order. Maddie complained that her mother overreacted. She didn't, but Maddie had no way of knowing that because Ryn sheltered her from all the ugly. It was a mother's sacrifice and Ryn never regretted it, even when her daughter treated her with disrespect and contempt.

"Well, if you find someone to work for you—"

"I won't."

The usual sigh escaped Ryn. Someday Maddie would

understand that no amount of money justified selling both of their souls to the Devil. And Preston Iverson was the devil.

"Madison ... I love you." Ryn ended the call before her stubborn daughter had a chance to respond. Of course she loved her only child, but she had too much respect for herself to tolerate any more snide comments. It was like strikes—after three, Ryn ended the conversation.

"That went well."

Gunner did another head tilt. He had her back, licked her tears, and never once complained. Maybe she needed to take Maddie to obedience school too.

CHAPTER THREE

Jɪʟʟɪᴀɴ ᴍᴇᴀɴᴅᴇʀᴇᴅ ʜᴏᴍᴇ after leaving Dodge and Lilith's. She wasn't ready to go inside and deal with Jackson, the second text, and the ramifications of AJ's diagnosis. Choosing the temporary sanctuary of the front porch stoop, she plopped down and watched her neighbors grilling out and tending to their yards and plants. The breeze ebbed and flowed, carrying the smoky aroma of Stan's charcoal grill and the droning screech of cicadas.

A small part of her waited for AJ to come home, which was ridiculous because she had no idea what to say to him. Maybe if she could see him, fall into his arms, the right words would come to her. If only he could feel the conflict that warred inside of her, he'd realize that her past didn't matter. Maybe. If only. But doubtful.

"Hey, kiddo. Did you look over the notes and the profit and loss statement?" Stan asked, hobbling his way up her driveway, shoulders slumped, sweat dripping from his brow, and muddy gardening knee pads still strapped to his legs. The guy never stopped working.

"I did." Briefly.

"Anything we could improve on?"

"You spend too much money on snow removal. Granted, I'm not from around here, but I have a feeling your plow guys show up the second there's a light dusting in the middle of the night. Then there's the insane amount of money going toward insurance. When lightning struck the Dickson's house and caused damage to the roof, that was a legitimate claim for the association's policy. But the most recent claim from the kitchen fire started by the Anderson's college-aged daughter, who doesn't even live there? That should have been a claim for their personal homeowner's insurance."

"Well, we try not to discriminate."

"I think the association needs to worry less about discrimination and more about taking it up the backside. It's okay to be neighborly at picnics, but when you're responsible for people's money, you have to treat it like a business and have guidelines and boundaries in writing."

Stan nodded. "I'll talk to Dodge about it." He seemed a bit disappointed in her opinion.

"Sorry if that's not what you wanted to hear, but you asked my honest opinion."

"No, no ... that's fine. I didn't mean to put you on the spot like that. It's not like this is your area of expertise."

Yes, it was. But he would never know that.

After Stan left, she lay back on the warm concrete stoop, letting the setting sun hit her face. Everything she shared with Lilith replayed like a highlight reel to her favorite movie. Since AJ went AWOL, Luke filled the empty void—which was ironic because up until that point, her entire existence as Jillian Knight felt like one big Luke-shaped void.

Day

JESSICA AWOKE ALONE and naked from what had to be a dream. Restraints. Tears. Love. Sex—the best sex ever. Covering her face with a pillow, she grumbled into it, "Please tell me it wasn't a dream."

"It wasn't a dream."

"Jones!" She bolted up, tossing the pillow to the floor.

"Good morning." The god of all gods stood in the doorway with a towel wrapped around his waist, wet hair, sexy smile.

"Hi," she breathed. "You stayed."

"I stayed ... on the couch."

Her eyes wandered along his body with her breath held captive. The mark on his shoulder wasn't new. It was from Long Beach. "Turn around."

He shook his head. "You didn't make me bleed."

On a slow exhale, she extinguished her nerves. She'd had sex with him, more than once. He'd released her from the restraints, and she didn't. Make. Him. Bleed.

"You're not cured."

She nodded. "But it's a step."

The sexy lips she craved curled into a hint of a smile. "A small step."

"I'm better for you."

"You're better *with* me."

She squinted at him with her brow tensed. "I'm like a dog that's well behaved with its owner."

His teeth peeked through his growing smile as a soft chuckle vibrated from his chest. "I'm not sure you'll ever be 'well behaved.'"

Everything about him captivated her. The vulnerability she felt under *his* control nearly broke her. It wouldn't matter how many blankets covered her body or layers of clothing concealed her nudity, she would forever feel stripped naked in his presence.

"I have to get home and change for work."

The lilac sheet slipped from her breasts. "Could I convince you to stay?"

He looked at her bared chest. No hesitation. No guilt. She was so completely his. He knew it and she knew it.

"Yes, but my patients would be grateful if you didn't."

"How do you do that?"

"Do what?"

"Make me surrender without taking my sense of control."

He dropped his towel and stepped into his jeans. "Surrendering *is* the ultimate control."

"Now you're just messing with me, Jones."

He buttoned his shirt. "Take a shower. Go to work. Be productive today and I'll reward you later."

"So I am your dog. Will we play fetch? I'm pretty good with a Frisbee."

Luke tied his shoes. It thrilled her to see him struggle a little more every day to keep his smile hidden. "I'll pick you up around seven."

"Seven-thirty. I'm teaching class until seven."

"Class?"

"Self-defense."

He nodded, giving her a thoughtful look. "The battered women's shelter?"

"Yep."

"Seven-thirty then."

"Hey!" she called as he began his escape. "That's it?"

She slid out of bed, baring her entire naked body to him. "No kiss goodbye?"

He looked back over his shoulder, puckered his lips, kissed the air then continued to the front door.

"Jones!" She jogged to catch up, stopping him before he opened the front door.

"Do you still love me?"

He sighed as if the sight of her naked body pained him. "I adore you."

"You *adore* me? What? You no longer love me?"

Inspecting the choices on the coat tree, he grabbed a long gray sweater from it then wrapped it around her. She returned a single raised brow.

"People *love* chocolate, surfing, and their gold fish. Adoration is better ... it means to both love and admire."

The tough-as-nails woman melted into a teenaged girl for a bit. "You admire me?" Her voice softened in disbelief.

"I do." He gave her a quick peck on the lips and pulled away as she began to lean in.

She shoved the sweater off her shoulders. "But you don't admire my body?"

He made a swift move out the door. "I do ... way too much," he called as he fled down the stairs.

Her smile beamed with uncontrollable delight from his adoration confession. "He thinks I'm adorable." That smile faded to a frown as she ran to her window and slid it open. "Dammit, Jones!"

He looked up a second before closing the door to his GTO.

"It was another dog reference. Puppies are *adorable*." She scowled.

Luke shook his head, a big grin plastered to his handsome face as he shut the door.

"God, he's adorable." Jessica giggled as she made her way to the shower.

Jessica cursed the traffic and the tourist-filled cable cars that slowed her journey home. By the time she pulled into her single-car garage stall, the GTO that she *adored* sat parked in front of her place.

"Don't mess with my heart, Jones. You'd better let me drive her tonight," she murmured to herself while smiling at him with bared teeth.

"There's my girl." Luke grinned as she approached her front steps.

Did she like being "his girl?" Hell yes!

He grabbed her wrist and pulled her into his body, finding her lips and stealing her breath. She would never get used to Jones, Dr. Luke Jones, looking at her with those seductive blue eyes, pulling her into that sexy body, and kissing her with those lips that she'd coveted for so long.

When her knees gave out, he released her lips but kept her close to the hard planes of his chest.

"Let me run and change. Wait for me in the *passenger* seat."

"Nice try." He followed her up the steps.

After a quick change they were off to Sausalito for dinner. Luke drove.

"This feels like our first official date." Jessica winked, freeing the shiny utensils from the red cloth napkin.

"You're not counting our blind date?" Luke asked.

Jessica smiled at the waiter serving her wine. "No. Although it was our first kiss." She grinned with her teeth clenched together.

The unappreciative victim of that first kiss narrowed his eyes at her.

"Well it was." She laughed. "So ... is this a working dinner?"

"Working dinner?"

"Yes. More unofficial therapy?"

"No. That was yesterday. I can't see you as my unofficial patient tonight."

She sipped her wine. "Why not?"

"Because I have a date."

Everything about the man personified perfection. How was that possible? And why was he with arguably the biggest disaster on the West Coast? "Mmm ... yes, with that nice girl I told you about."

He closed his menu. "You said she was a real catch."

"Do you concur?"

"I do."

"What are you doing this weekend?"

Luke shrugged. "That depends on how much cleaning you get done around my place tomorrow."

"So you don't have any real plans. Great. I want you to meet my family. I'm having tea with my mom at Samovar on Saturday morning, but maybe we could all have dinner or Sunday brunch."

"I'd love to meet your family. How will you introduce me?"

"With my voice. 'Mom and Dad, this is Jones. Jones these are my parents, Grant and Sunny."

"Your mom's name is Sunny Day? Not possible." Luke laughed.

"It's true. Says the firstborn of Tom Jones. Anyway, we kid my dad that she married him just for his name. She lives up to her name too. I think I've heard her swear once, and even then it was when she was quoting someone else. Hands down, I have the most optimistic, laid-back mom in the world. She's walking zen."

"So you didn't get her zen genes?"

Jessica laughed. "Astute observation, Dr. Jones. No, I have my father's personality—a total firecracker. He doesn't do anything in the middle. When he's mad it's a raging inferno and when he's happy it's like glitter exploded everywhere. When we work on cars and motorcycles in his garage he's either singing his favorite song like the next American Idol contestant, or if something's not going right he's slinging wrenches and cussing up a storm. You'll like him, just don't mention that you drink imported beer. He *exclusively* drinks locally brewed beer."

They gave the waiter their orders, including another glass of wine and another *imported* Heineken.

"My roommate in college committed suicide." Luke stared at his beer as he rolled the empty green bottle back and forth in his hands. "He was born in Amsterdam and *he* exclusively drank Heineken, which I'm sure he considered a local beer." Luke's smile looked pained. "Anyway, after he died I started drinking Heineken. It makes me think of him when I drink it, like a silent toast to him wherever he is."

That had to be what Luke's dad started to tell Jessica. She knew it was a small piece and there had to be more to the story. A painful more.

"Well then I toasted your roommate over and over last night before you showed up and tied me to my bed. Of course I navigated to the Heineken because of you."

Luke nodded, taking an extra few seconds to resurface from his past before locking eyes with her again. "So tell me about Jude. Is he a firecracker too?"

Jessica laughed so fast she snorted. "Jetta boy? No. He's

a very unique breed. He's a hair trigger when it comes to self-defense type situations, and he's kinda paranoid—the conspiracy theory type—but he's definitely Sunny's boy too.

She sipped her wine. A smile tugged at her lips. "When he's in his element, aka in front of a computer or preying on every woman in the Bay area, he's Cool Joe, laid back, 'I don't need pot to be this chillin'.' And the women fall at his feet like he's a god. The truth is he's such a man whore, but the weird part is he doesn't have a following of disgruntled women. It's as if they know they're only going to get one night with him, but they still line up to willingly drop their panties and spread their legs. Pathetic."

"Thank God my sisters don't live around here."

"They'd be safe. Jude likes older women—smart, older women. He said it's hard to fuck a woman's brain out if she doesn't actually have a brain."

Luke smirked.

Jessica quirked a brow. "His words not mine."

They enjoyed a sunset dinner by the bay, revealing bits of each other one tragic or funny story at a time. Hand-in-hand they strolled toward the GTO parked in a lot with a backdrop of sailboat masts and the sunlight on the water's surface, reflecting diamond-studded whitecaps. Contentment settled upon them like they'd done it for years.

"I want to take you to my place. I have a surprise for you." Luke leaned over and kissed her as they waited at a stop light.

"What is it?"

"Do I need to define the word surprise?"

"Ugh ... fine, but give me a hint. I like this game."

Luke laughed. "Contumacious."

"I'm not being stubbornly disobedient. Okay, maybe a

little stubborn, but not disobedient. Thank you once again for the dog reference."

"Well there you have it."

Jessica looked at him, eyes narrowed. "Have what?"

"You'll see."

"It's an apron isn't it? I bet you're going to have me dress up in a kinky little French maid's outfit to clean your place tomorrow, aren't you?"

Luke adjusted in his seat a bit. "Um ... no that's not the surprise, but I'm not going to lie, I like your idea."

"I love that, Jones. The hard-ass, no humor doctor role you play has appeared in many of my fantasies, argyle socks and all. But you in this car, getting turned on by the thought of me in a French maid's outfit—reminding me that you are *all* guy—it's the absolute-nothing-else-compares best." She leaned her head back on the head rest, closed her eyes, and smiled in total contentment.

"So now wouldn't be the best time to wake you from your dream state and confess that I'm gay?"

She laughed. "It happens, Jones. I think it's almost impossible to live in San Francisco and not question your sexual orientation. Yet another thing I *love* about this city. It opens its arms to everyone. We're all just ... human."

He pulled into his garage space, killed the engine, and stared at her like he was somehow seeing her for the first time.

"What?" She wrinkled her nose, sliding her tongue along her teeth in case she had a piece of spinach stuck to one.

He rested his arm on the back of her seat and threaded his fingers through her hair, cupping the back of her head. "When we first met, my biggest fear was you would never feel 'normal' again."

"And now?"

"And now I fear you will, and for some reason that feels tragic to me."

She leaned into his touch. "I think we both know that's not possible. Now … about this big surprise—"

"It's not a big surprise … not yet anyway." He climbed out and rushed around to open her door.

"Why thank you, sir." She placed her hand in his and he led her up to his condo.

"Wait out here."

"Sweeping the joint for your Tumblr followers?"

"Funny. But seriously, don't come in until I tell you." He shut the door, leaving her in the hallway.

Her smile grew with each passing second, not from the surprise. The man of her dreams and his adoration for her owned that smile, but … she did love surprises.

"Okay, open the door," he called from the other side.

Her whole body shivered with giddiness. She opened the door. Luke squatted down next to a pudgy little Great Dane puppy—white with irregular black spots.

"Oh my gosh!" She hunched down as the puppy waddled over to her. Jessica picked him up and hugged him to her. "I love it … her … him?"

"Him." Luke stood with a smile that showed his pleasure with her reaction and probably himself as well.

"You got me a puppy? No one has ever done something like this for me before," she spoke with the classic high-pitched puppy/baby voice. Holding the puppy out in front of her, she continued to baby talk it a few inches from its face. "What am I going to name you, huh?"

"He already has a name."

"Oh really?"

Luke moved closer to her and took the puppy, holding it

with one hand and petting it with his other. "Yes, I already named him."

"Please tell me it's not Spot." She leaned in and kissed its head.

"No ... it's Jones."

CHAPTER FOUR
KNIGHT

WITH THE ARRIVAL of Tuesday came an agglomeration of nerves sparked by a lethal mix of hormones and the anticipation of seeing Father Jackson Knight. Ryn's dormant sex life didn't help matters, neither did Jillian saying he would like her. Why would he like her? Perhaps there was a shortage of young perfect-bodied women in Omaha.

She knocked on the door, hoping Jillian would answer. Ryn deemed it best to ease into Jackson's intensity. No such luck. His Holiness appeared before her, inviting her into the gates of Heaven. Granted, she was there to tidy up the grounds of eternity, but hey, it was Heaven and that's all that mattered.

"Ryn Middleton." He made her name sound dirty with a wicked smile on his face while his eyes moved along her body.

It evoked all kinds of feelings: good, bad, and maybe even sinful. What was the punishment for tempting a man of God? The makeup she decided to apply at the last minute may have been a bad idea. She sucked at subtle. Everything about her said lonely, sex-deprived, and easy.

Her shorts felt extra short under his gaze as she flexed the muscles in her legs, hoping it would tighten the appearance of her skin that had lost some of its elasticity. Forty would suck.

"Jackson ... or ... is it okay if I call you that?" Ryn wasn't Catholic. Did he expect her to address him as Father Knight?

He gave her a funny look, his smile still beaming with intensity. "Jackson is fine." He stepped aside and let her in.

"No lesson today?" She headed straight to the first bathroom. Nothing good could come from standing around looking at him.

"No. I rescheduled my Tuesday afternoon students." He followed her.

"Oh, I hope not on my account. I clean quietly with the exception of vacuuming."

"It was no big deal. Now you don't have to worry about being quiet. It's just the two of us."

She pulled on her gloves. "Oh ... okay."

Just the two of them and she didn't have to be quiet. Why was her mind in the gutter?

"Do you want me to turn on some music for you?"

She scrubbed the toilet bowl. "Uh ... sure."

"What type of music do you like?"

She glanced back at him. He leaned against the wall with his arms crossed over his chest. Her gaze stuck to his tattoos. "Whatever. Classical, gospel, piano ... or even organ music if you prefer."

"So, no alternative, rock and roll, or rap?"

She wiped her brow with her arm and continued scrubbing. He brought the room temperature up a good ten degrees with the mix of his presence and the third-degree questioning.

"No, I try to avoid anything that's not ... up lifting. Most songs on the radio these days are all about sex and other, um ... sinful stuff." Her favorite song in high school was George Michael's "I Want Your Sex." If he didn't hurry up and leave, she'd pass out from the heat or confess her sins and beg for forgiveness. Ideally, she just wanted to keep her dignity, clean their house, and get the hell or *heck* out of there.

"So you're religious?"

No. She stopped going to church when she got pregnant out of wedlock. "I'm a believer." It was true, even if she no longer possessed a certainty of those beliefs. Everyone believed in something.

"I have a shitload of scripture in my head that's been drilled into me over the years. Sorry, I meant a lot ... not a shitload. Hope I didn't offend you."

She tipped her chin down to bite back a smile. "No offense taken. I'm sure you're more than covered in the area of forgiveness for that minor sin."

"Are you and your husband originally from Nebraska?"

Her body stiffened. Even then, years later, the word husband made her flinch.

"I'm ... not married." Divorce elicited scowls of disapproval in the religious world, she'd save that topic for later or preferably never. "And I'm originally from Atlanta."

"I see, well ... I'll let you do your thing. Maybe I'll just play the piano. Any requests?"

She shrugged. "Surprise me."

THE WOMAN who could be a game changer wasn't married. That was good, but her anti-sex, gospel-music-playing personality presented a bit more of a challenge than he anticipated. Jackson had committed to not being a man whore, but that didn't mean he'd submitted his application for sainthood.

He played one classical piece after another, tracking her every move as she floated around scrubbing, dusting, mopping, and sweeping. She finished in the main room as if to not disturb him until she had no other choice. They smiled politely at each other as she dusted Black Beauty. God, he loved her eyes and the way she incessantly wet her lips if he stared too long.

She squatted down, disappearing beneath the piano. "I'm just dusting the legs and pedals ... I uh, don't want to you think I'm trying to do anything inappropriate here."

He grinned. "I wouldn't stop you if you were."

"Ouch!" she seethed after a loud thump.

He leaned down to look at her. "Are you okay?"

Balancing on her knees and one hand while her other hand rubbed her head, she squinted her eyes a bit. He tried to focus on her head but the view down her shirt to her pink sports bra and just a tease of cleavage, which also had a smattering of freckles, enticed him in a sex-deprived way. By the time he tore his eyes away from her breasts, she stared at him in shock. Clearly, he'd offended her.

"Do you need an icepack?" He sat up with a guilty grimace. Jillian would kill him if their cleaning lady quit on the first day, claiming sexual harassment.

Ryn crawled out and stood, one hand still on her head, the other pressing the neck of her shirt firm to her chest. "I'll be fine." She focused on the floor, the ceiling, anywhere but him. "I'm going to run the vacuum and then I'll be done."

He relocated to the kitchen while she vacuumed. Time evaporated faster than his mind could conjure a plan. He had to think of something to say before she left and most likely would never come back.

Tick-tock, he grimaced with defeat as she shut off the vacuum and wound up the hose and cord.

"Mother fucking idiots!" Jillian grumbled, opening the front door.

Ryn's eyes popped out of her head. Jackson closed his. He no longer needed to worry about being the responsible party for Ryn quitting. Jillian swooped in just in time to take that honor with her sailor's tongue.

"Oh, hey, Ryn." Jillian stepped inside, holding the screen door open with the backside of her body while she smacked the soles of her shoes together. "I hate it when they spread those stupid fertilizer pellets then takeoff without using a broom or blower on the driveway and sidewalk. Now they're stuck like shit to the bottom of my shoes and if it rains they'll discolor the cement."

"Jill ... not the best word choice." He gave Ryn an apologetic look. She returned one that looked just as pained.

"Sorry, I always say that wrong. They'll discolor the concrete ... I know, cement is the powdered form. It's like the whole itch versus scratch thing." She shut the door and looked up. "So how'd it go today?"

Ryn forced a smile. "Fine. Look around after I leave and let me know if there's something I missed or that you'd like me to do different next time."

Jackson sighed with relief from the promise of next time.

"Thanks, Ryn." Jillian held the door open. "Jesus, Jackson, don't just stand there. Help her take her stuff out."

"Oh yeah." He jumped out of his daze and grabbed the other bucket and vacuum.

"Sorry about your head." He handed her the rest of the

supplies as she loaded everything into the back of her white RAV4.

"It was my fault." She closed the back door and leaned against it with her arms trapped behind her. "You caught me off guard when you said…" she glanced up with a sheepish look "…what you did."

Wearing a guilty half-smile, he shoved his hands into his pockets and shook his head. "Yeah, I was completely out of line."

"It's fine. I applaud you for your commitment. A vow of celibacy at your age must be difficult sometimes."

Jackson bent down, cocking his head to bring his ear closer to her face. "*What* did you just say?"

"I said it must be difficult," she answered with breathy words, eyes on his mouth.

"No, before that." He squinted.

She mirrored his expression. "The part about me commending you for your commitment to God?"

"What commitment to God?"

Her eyes darted to one side and then the other before meeting his again. "Uh … the vow of celibacy."

"Who told you about that?"

Ryn's body sank until the bumper halted her descent. "Jillian," she replied in a small voice.

"She told you I took a vow of celibacy?"

Ryn nodded as her nose scrunched.

"So you thought what? That I'm a priest or something?"

Another uncomfortable nod.

Jackson stepped back, giving her space. The dots connected themselves. "Tell me … did you go to church last weekend?"

Ryn shook her head, eyes wide.

"The weekend before that?"

Another shake.

Jackson chuckled. "Give me your keys." He held out his hand.

"Why?"

"Just give them to me."

She set them in his hand. Fear painted her face in crimson as he slid in the front seat and turned the key. The radio blared with Adam Levine complaining about the summer hurting like a motherfucker.

Ryn covered her face with her hands. Jackson stepped out and peeled them away. She kept her eyes set firm to the driveway.

"Doesn't sound like gospel to me."

She shook her head. "I'm so embarrassed."

He bent down and whispered in her ear. "See you next week, *my child.*"

AFTER A COLD SHOWER TO relieve the flush of embarrassment and to temper her riled up libido, Ryn grabbed an iced tea, a good book, and planted her ass on her front porch swing with Gunner at her feet. The day would go down in history as: Ryn is An Idiot Day. Somewhere between graduating high school, getting pregnant, and marrying Satan, she lost her normalcy gene. Preston physically beat it out of her, leaving a wreckage of insecurity, fear, and social awkwardness like an abused animal whose tail never wagged.

"Hey, Ryn. How was your day?" her neighbor, Drew, asked as he walked up the sidewalk from his mailbox.

"I've had better," she answered on a laugh.

Her handsome forty-something neighbor leaned against the railing to her porch steps. "Sounds like a story."

She teased Gunner's ear with her toes and smiled. "Can I ask you a question?"

"Shoot."

"If not for religious reasons, why would a guy take a vow of celibacy?"

Drew chuckled, scratching his head then leaving his salt and pepper hair a bit ruffled. He was Dermot Mulroney's twin, especially that sexy crooked smile.

"I thought maybe you were going to ask me why the clover seems to be taking over our lawns this year."

"Yeah, that too, but first answer the celibacy question." She grinned.

"Okay, well maybe the guy has STDs or he's afraid of getting them. Maybe he has an unhealthy attachment to sex or ..."

"Or what?"

A sadness stole Drew's handsome features. "Maybe he lost a lover." Cancer stole Drew's wife a year earlier.

"Drew, I didn't mean to—"

He shook his head. "You didn't. It's fine." He shrugged one shoulder. "But it could be the reason."

Ryn nodded. Could Jackson have lost a wife or girlfriend?

"Have a seat." She stood and walked to the front door. "I'll get you a beer." Her lips twisted to the side as she looked at him. "Maybe two."

A few minutes later, she returned with two bottles of beer.

"Thanks."

Gunner waited until she sat down before resuming his spot at her feet.

"So you have a thing for a guy who's taken a vow of celibacy?"

Ryn laughed. "He's younger than me. I'm not sure it's appropriate for me to have a *thing* for him."

"So? My wife was almost ten years younger than me."

"Really?" Ryn looked at him with wide eyes. "I never knew that. Then again when you moved here she was going through chemo and ..."

"And the fucking poison stole her hair and eventually her life."

"Yeah, that." She frowned.

After a long pull of his beer, he sighed. "I was thirty-one when we met. She was my student when I taught an intro to business class at a community college."

"Sounds scandalous."

Drew chuckled. "Her parents were *not* happy. At our wedding when the minister asked who gives this woman, her dad just grunted."

"No!"

"I'm serious. We were married five years before he stopped scowling at me."

"That's just it. I can't imagine dating someone significantly younger than me. Not to be sexist, but I think older women dating younger men get more scowls than the other way around. Obviously your in-laws weren't this way, but most people don't think much of the older-man-younger-woman relationship these days."

"So how young are we talking?" Drew asked.

Ryn smiled while taking a sip of her iced tea. "I don't know. Thirty-ish? But I could be off and I don't think in my direction. With my luck he's in his mid-twenties and the perfect guy for Maddie." She waved a dismissive hand. "It doesn't matter. He's celibate." She laughed. "Of course I have been lately too."

"When I turned forty my wife swore I had a midlife

crisis. *I* swore forty was too young to be considered 'midlife.' We'd been trying to get pregnant but it just never happened. So I told her to quit her job—she was an accountant and hated it anyway—and we traveled the world for two years living like gypsies. We left our naked ass prints on many beaches." Drew wiggled his brows.

Ryn laughed.

"We would have stayed longer, but that's when they discovered her cancer. We were in France. I berated myself for being so reckless. Had we just stayed home, maybe they would have found it sooner. But she refused to regret any of it. She said my midlife crisis was the best two years of her life. She said she'd never felt so alive and we all deserve to feel that way at least once. After all, why the hell else are we here?"

Ryn loved that story. But what she loved the most was how many times Drew had told it to her. Each time it felt like the first, and each time he came up with a new moral.

"So you think I should leave my ass print on the beach." She said that every time too, but it was never the moral.

"Exactly."

Ryn gasped. "Seriously?"

Drew smiled and nodded, looking off into the sunset while sipping his beer. "Rob the cradle, have sex on the beach, and fucking embrace your forties. You're at your prime, Ryn. What do you have to lose at this point?"

A lot, starting with her dignity and her mind. Maybe he made a valid point. There was just one problem. The cradle she wanted to rob had a warning sign that said "celibate."

CHAPTER FIVE

"YOUR FAVORITE NEIGHBOR just pulled in his garage," Jackson announced as he came in the back door, dripping with sweat.

Jillian didn't care, at least that's what she told herself every morning to muster the strength to get out of bed.

"No response?" He plopped down in the chair next to hers. "Good. Let's talk about me then."

His mouth held a pleasant smile, one that said he had a secret ready to burst from his lips. He marked time much better than she did, going through the motion of each day like a good soldier. But it had been a while since she'd seen him look *happy*.

"Let's." She found her own smile. It was his moment.

"I know I was a little pissed about you telling Ryn that I'd taken a vow of celibacy ... which I did not do."

"You had sex."

"I did not." His grin held firm. "But I think I should now. I think I'm ready."

"I agree. You should, but not with Ryn."

"What? Why not?"

"Because she works for us." Jillian drummed her fingers on the table. A tight grin pulled her lips into a firm line.

"She works for you. Technically, I think you hired her."

Jillian shook her head. "She's probably married with kids. Don't be a home wrecker ... that has never been your thing, so don't start now."

"She's not married. I asked."

"Are you going to marry her?"

"What does that matter?"

"Because this house has never looked so clean and unless you marry her it will eventually end with her quitting because of you. *And* ... she'll probably quit working for AJ too, just so she doesn't have to be in the same neighborhood as you."

"You're full of shit. Look at yourself. You're a walking disaster. I had to pick up your room before Ryn came just so she could find the floor to vacuum it. You've been a slob your entire life. And a certain doctor that I shall not name ... he knew it too, and it drove him crazy, and you know I'm right. I know for a fact you thrive in disorder. So either you intended Ryn to be a gift for me or you're using her to worm your way back onto AJ's good side. And just to be clear ... I'm not sure he has one."

She stopped drumming her fingers on the table and rolled her eyes. "Fine, but do me a favor. Choose what it's going to be and make sure she understands."

Jackson shook his head. "I don't understand. What are you talking about?"

"If it's just sex, then make sure she knows up front. Otherwise ..."

"Otherwise what?"

"Marry her."

Jackson laughed. "I'll ask her on Tuesday which she prefers."

Jillian didn't want to laugh. She'd been in the worst mood since she last saw AJ and her depression began to feel like a security blanket—dark but warm.

Unfortunately, she envisioned Jackson asking Ryn if she'd rather have sex with him or marry him and the image brought a huge smile to her face.

"That looks good on you." He smiled back. "Now go."

She narrowed her eyes. "Go where?'

"I know you're dying to go next door."

She wasn't.

"Lay it on the line. Don't take any of his crap and call me if you need backup."

"You don't even like him. Why do you care?"

"True. But I think Jillian needs him."

Loving Jackson came easy, even when he acted the part of a paranoid, overprotective ass. Eventually he came around and supported her with only one goal: for her to find happiness. Was AJ her happiness? Could she be happy watching him die? Did he have to die?

JILLIAN HADN'T PREPARED herself for the defeat in AJ's eyes when he answered the door. She expected grumpiness, and anger, not shoulders curved inward, eyes devoid of life.

"Can I come in?"

The hollow man before her nodded once.

Grabbing two beers, he handed one to her. She shook her head. There was no need for an SOS. He wasn't dying.

He wasn't dying.

"I need you to live." Her voice, barely a whisper, squeezed past the lump in her throat.

AJ leaned against the counter, staring at his feet. "Sorry."

She wanted to tell him everything. He would fight for himself—fight for her—if he knew about her past.

"I know what it feels like to want to give up. I know what it feels like to not feel in control of your body. Living is so much harder than dying."

His cynical laugh sliced through the thick air. "You have experience with dying?"

There existed a headstone with her former name on it. In many ways she was dead. After all, a person couldn't live without a heart, and hers resided in San Francisco.

"I do."

He laughed again. "But let me guess ... you can't tell me about it."

"You know what pisses me off the most? You've had *one* opinion and you're already planning your funeral. Just because some neurologist or oncologist thinks your tumor is inoperable doesn't mean another more experienced or more confident doctor would."

AJ looked up at her. "So that's a no answer yet again to your past."

"We're not talking about my past, we're talking about—"

"Well I think we should. It's a moot point talking about my future that no longer exists. I've told you about my past. I think *all* that's left to talk about is yours."

Anger gripped every nerve as she fisted her hands at her side. It was a low blow. He didn't need to push her away with her own past.

"I love you."

He shook his head. "You're reciprocating. I didn't ask

you to say it back. I said it because I needed to make peace between us. You're saying it because you're scared and pissed."

"I think telling someone you love them after you find out you're 'dying' would be classified as an act of fear or anger, so please don't feed me this line of bullshit that you had some romantic epiphany about us on a whim."

"Are you done?" His face turned to stone, eyes cold.

She stepped closer until they were toe-to-toe. "I'm just getting started."

"I don't want to hear anymore."

"Well. I. Don't. Care." She poked his chest with each word. "You have two parents and a son that will be devastated. You don't enlist in the air force and fight to stay alive to make it home to your family just to turn around and give up. You're not a fucking coward so stop acting like one."

"Six months." He glared at her.

"What ... what are you talking about?"

"I saw the oncologist. It's cancer and he gave me six months to live ... *with* treatment."

She stared at his chest. How did *his* heart feel about that? Hers remained hollow. It had been for many months. Those were crushing words. Luckily, she was safe. No heart. Nothing to crush. But for some reason, his words filled that empty space and formed into something living, beating, and aching so damn bad. How could nothing feel so painfully like something?

"Now that I have your undivided attention let me tell you the rest."

Her head inched side to side. Through a haze of shock her eyes remained fixed to his chest. He had something to live for. You don't stop fighting if there's something worth fighting for. She had Jackson, they kept each other alive.

One ... just one person was enough. How could AJ not see that?

"Sometimes I get blurred vision, but it's been easy to relate it to my headaches because they're so frequent. I don't remember some things, but I'm getting older so I just figured it was age."

The day of his accident he'd forgotten their dinner date. The night he took her for a ride on her Harley he acted confused when she reminded him about his parents and Brooke's family coming for Cage's game. Fucking twenty-twenty hindsight.

He continued. "It's all going to get worse. I'm taking medication for my headaches and seizures, but it's not a cure. If I do nothing I could go blind in less than two months. If I agree to radiation and try to squeeze out six months, I could experience worse headaches, nausea, vomiting, extreme fatigue, hearing loss, difficulty with speech and memory, and more seizures. If I become the exception and make it past the six months, then they tack on stroke-like symptoms and poor brain function. The fatigue and medications could lead to erectile dysfunction. No sex."

He lifted her chin with his finger, but she would not give him her tears.

"Sound like fun to you?"

The strong woman who came in the door vanished, leaving a ghost biting her quivering lip, hating herself for being so weak.

Her pain softened his rigid scowl of determination.

"I. Love. You." His words ripped through the imposter of a heart in her chest. "I'll do this for you, but you have to know it's going to feel like the most painful kind of love ever. You need to *get* that. I would never blame you for turning and walking away. It's your choice. Are you in?"

AJ didn't realize Jillian ... Jessica ... had already experienced the most painful kind of love—letting go. Holding on was so much easier than letting go. It's the reason she held on to Jessica and held on to her memories of Luke.

"I'm in," she whispered.

The pain in his eyes intensified. He cradled her face in his hands, shaking his head. "You're so stubborn."

Contumacious.

The man who'd made claim to her empty chest, kissed her hard but she would not blink. The next day she'd pull it together, make some calls, and find a doctor that showed some optimism. That night, however, she surrendered her emotions and then her body.

"Jillian?" AJ whispered as he held her in his arms.

She fought sleep, wanting to stay with him. The fragility of their time together kept her frozen in place. "Hmm?" She kissed his arm wrapped around her, holding her naked body against his.

"I need you to promise me something."

"What?"

"Don't let me hurt you, physically or emotionally, and don't..." he drew in a long breath "...don't let me suffer. Let me die with some sort of dignity."

"AJ—" She choked on her words, damning the nagging tears.

"Promise me."

"How will I know?" she whispered.

"You'll just ... know." He kissed the back of her head. "I trust you."

She closed her eyes, begging the tears to hold off as she

held her breath and nodded once. Her body shook from the pounding in her chest, an earthquake of pain. Pain that was just too much.

A while later she felt his body relax around hers, so she slipped out of bed, dressed, and went home.

Jackson sat perched on a chair in front of his computer. He looked up.

"Downstairs," she whispered.

He stared at her for a moment. Then he nodded.

After changing her clothes, she wrapped her hands and waited for Jackson. He gave her a sad smile as he reached the bottom of the stairs. He started to wrap his hands.

"I'll fight back, I promise, but I need you to make me feel a different type of pain."

They both slipped in their mouth guards.

He nodded. Before she could meet his eyes, he swung his leg around, knocking her to the floor. Tears flooded her eyes, but not from being knocked down.

"Get up," he growled, his voice devoid of sympathy. Jackson knew what she needed, sometimes more than she did.

"Get the fuck up!"

She crawled to her feet, tears streaming down her face. He hit her again before she had a chance to react. Blood pooled along her lip.

"You feel that?" he asked. His voice grew louder with each word.

"Yes," she gritted, brushing away her tears with her arms as her tongue licked the blood.

"Then show me."

Her ragged breaths came quicker as anger seized her body and she attacked her brother, holding back nothing. She fought her past, beating the shit out of everything that took Luke away from her. She fought the asshole who had been messaging her, making her feel scared and weak, and then she fought the fucking cancer. She fought it through tears and blood. Jillian fought until she collapsed in Jackson's arms. The tears ran dry and the pain numbed. One feeling remained: acceptance.

CHAPTER SIX

Oɴᴄᴇ ᴀɢᴀɪɴ, Jackson witnessed his sister hitting rock bottom and crawling through her blood, sweat, and tears to surface again. After AJ saw the marks on her face the following day, he paid Jackson a visit—with his fist. Jillian broke up the fight before blood stained the carpet. With a scowl and a nod, both men declared a truce, although a silent one, and contingent on the other keeping his hands off her. A promise neither could really guarantee, because they were *all* a bit unpredictable.

Jillian jumped all in and went to AJ's appointments, including getting second and third opinions. Jackson, content that his sister stood on her own feet again, counted down the days until Tuesday—the best day of the week.

"Hey." Ryn smiled as he let her inside.

"AJ home today?" he asked to break the ice before suggesting sex or marriage.

"Yes. I was pretty shocked to hear that he retired from the air force. Honestly, I've worked for him for over five years, but I've rarely seen or talked to him. Yet he seemed ... I don't know, maybe a little depressed today."

"Jillian will cheer him up after she gets home."

"Oh ... are they ..."

"Yes, he's screwing my sister. No, I don't like it."

Ryn looked away with a hint of discomfort in her expression. She took her bucket of supplies to the bathroom. "Is it because of the age difference?"

Jackson followed her. "No. It's because she's my sister and therefore no guy will ever be deserving of her."

"She's lucky. I'd love to have someone feel that protective of me."

"Could you tell her that?"

Ryn laughed. "Yeah, I'm sure she doesn't always think of it as a blessing. So ... how old is she?"

"Thirty."

"And you're older?" Ryn tried to sound indifferent, but he saw through it.

Jackson smiled as she fished for his age. The age thing mattered to her.

"Yes. I'm older."

Her smile grew with a look of relief.

"By seven minutes."

That look of relief quickly faded. "Really, twins?"

"Yes. So how old are you?"

She tapped the toilet brush on the edge and returned it to the bucket. "That's kind of a bold question. You know it's not polite to ask a woman her age."

"You asked Jillian's."

"Let me rephrase, it's not polite for a *man* to ask a woman her age."

"Sounds like a double standard." He chuckled. "Besides, I'm a bold guy, so it's fitting that I ask bold questions."

Ryn cleaned the mirror, occasionally meeting his eyes through the reflection. "How old do you think I am?"

"I'm bold, not stupid, so I'm not answering that."

"I'm in my thirties as well." She rolled her lips between her teeth to contain her smile.

He felt bad for playing her, but he wanted her to think of him as a normal guy. Telling her that he'd already done a full background check on her would not get him past his celibacy phase. Women were sensitive about the whole invasion-of-privacy thing.

"Can I be honest with you?" he asked.

"Honesty's good."

"I told Jillian I'm interested in you."

She gulped—loudly. Then her hands doubled their pace, working at record speed. Her eyes remained focused on her task. He enjoyed seeing her uncomfortable. It meant she was attracted to him.

"She wasn't too pleased because she doesn't want you to quit cleaning our house or AJ's."

Another gulp. She had an excess of saliva.

He continued since she didn't have anything to add yet. "So she said I should make it clear that we're going to just have sex or else I need to marry you."

"Oh my God! What?" She turned, holding the cleaning rag against her chest as if she were standing there topless.

A grin dominated his whole face and nothing had ever felt so good, which was weird because his dick remained in his pants. He worked her for a reaction the same way he had done for years with Jillian.

"I agree. Marriage might be too soon. I wouldn't dream of proposing without asking for your father's blessing."

"I'm almost forty!" she spewed out the words like a last-minute confession with a gun pointed to her head. Even her face scrunched into a frightened grimace.

"Great, so you have a birthday coming up. We should celebrate."

"I have a daughter. She's twenty-one." Another rushed confession.

"I'd love to meet her."

Ryn narrowed her eyes. "As in … you want me to fix the two of you up?"

Jackson chuckled. "I'm keeping you from working. We should have drinks later and discuss what I *want* in further detail."

"I have to take Gunner for a walk…" she hugged the cleaning rag to her chest even tighter "…later."

"Your ferret?"

The hardened statue in front of him relaxed a little. He enjoyed the smile that reacquainted itself with her lips. "No." She laughed. "He's my dog."

"Ohhh … gotcha. So leave me your address and I'll come walk with you." He knew her address, but once again, it didn't seem like a good idea to tell her that.

"You're relentless,"

"You have no idea." He made a point of letting his gaze drag slowly up her body until he could see a small sheen of perspiration on her brow. Mission accomplished.

LEAVING an ass print on the beach carried less intimidation when Jackson Knight seemed unattainable—celibate. Sex or marriage. Who says that? Definitely not a thirty-year-old guy with the most unique eyes Ryn had ever seen, a body sculpted for the front cover of a fitness magazine, and tattoos that were clearly on display for the sole purpose of her enjoyment. And a guy like that definitely did not say that to a nearly forty-year-old woman losing her battle with gravity.

Perhaps she'd hallucinated the whole conversation. It was hard to say for sure. There had been heart palpitations, sweating, and foggy-brained confusion. Had she also imagined the inappropriate way he looked at her? Ryn hoped not. She rather liked how he looked at her. He made her feel a hundred times sexier than she imagined possible.

Clothes were strewn all over her room. It was a walk, not dinner with the president. She didn't need to try on ten different outfits, but she did anyway. After settling on the most boring choice ever—gray yoga capris and a white tank top—she waited on her porch swing with Gunner at her feet.

"You're smiling at no one in particular."

She turned. "Hey, Drew."

"Good day?"

She snorted out a laugh when a wood-paneled PT Cruiser pulled into her driveway, the perfect visual to temper her attraction to Jackson. Then he got out and the PT Cruiser might as well have been a Ferrari. Jackson exuded sexiness. He made ugly beautiful. Could he make her feel half as desirable as he looked?

Drew chuckled. "He's young."

"Yup." Ryn couldn't take her eyes off Jackson as he navigated up her driveway like a catwalk, wearing faded ripped jeans and a fitted black tank top that showed more of his tattoos than she had ever seen.

"Hi." Jackson first acknowledged Drew.

"Hey there. Well, you two have fun at the beach." Drew's steps faded into the distance.

Warmth surged along her skin, overheating her whole body. Someone needed to throw some ice water on her.

"The beach?" Jackson questioned.

"Inside joke." Her eyes took their first blink since he'd pulled into her driveway.

"Hot car." She grinned.

Sex in the flesh shoved his hands deep into his pockets, flexing the muscles along his arms, but her eyes latched onto the wide black waist band of his underwear exposed in the front from his hands pushing down.

"Thank you."

Ryn shook her head with an embarrassingly huge smile plastered to her face. "Are you conducting some sort of experiment?"

"On?"

"What makes a man sexy." She snapped her finger and pointed to the ground beside her. Gunner took his position on command. "Because before you pulled up I would have said no man could look sexy driving a PT Cruiser. I stand corrected."

Jackson cocked his head to the side, watching Gunner. "I'm not part of any experiment." He continued looking at Gunner as if he were talking to him. "But I do know the answer to that question."

"I have no doubt that you do. I'm sure you see it in the mirror every day. Walk." She started toward the sidewalk with Gunner right at her side.

"Nope. But don't stress over it. I'll tell you someday. By the way ... I think I'm in love with your dog."

"You've only just met."

"Well he's beautiful and well behaved. No leash?"

"He doesn't need one."

"What if a rabbit or squirrel runs out in front of him?"

"He doesn't do anything without my command."

"I once knew a Marley reincarnation."

"Yours?" Ryn looked up at Jackson, squinting against the setting sun.

"No. This doctor I knew got it for his girlfriend. He tried to get her to take it to obedience school, but I think they dropped out after the first day. The mutt was a nightmare."

"Gunner was trained to be a guard dog. I don't think I'd be able to sleep at night if I didn't have him."

"Because you're single?"

"Because I'm divorced." Ryn kept her eyes focused ahead. "I left an abusive relationship. He didn't want to accept it even after I filed the restraining order. I don't like guns, but I needed a way to feel safe."

"*Gun-ner.*" Jackson smirked. "Nice."

"So ... I noticed you have some crash-type pads and different equipment in your basement. Are you a boxer?"

"I'm not a boxer, but I can box. Jillian and I like to spar for a good workout."

"Do you know any self-defense moves?"

His lips twisted to the side. "A few."

"Would you be willing to teach me sometime?"

Jackson didn't say anything.

"It's just that Gunner's not always with me and I wonder what would happen if the mace on my keychain didn't work or if I dropped it and was left defenseless. I know I sound paranoid, it's just—"

"I'll teach you."

"You will?"

He nodded.

"I'll even pay you or we could barter for the house cleaning."

His lips curled into the most mischievous grin. "Bartering ... yes, but not for the house cleaning."

"Oh ..." A cold chill inched up her spine. "Do I want to know what you have in mind?"

He looked over at her. "I don't know. Do you?"

She tried to lighten the moment, thick with suggestion. "If you're thinking of trying to take Gunner or Maddie, then the answer is no way."

"Maddie?"

"My daughter."

"I think you already offered me your daughter."

"What? I did not."

"You offered to fix us up."

"I-I-no ... I asked if that's what you were implying."

"And if I would have said yes, you were going to give me her phone number with your blessing."

"I most certainly was not."

"Why?"

It was a good question.

"That's what I thought." His smug smile wasn't sexy. Really it was, but she didn't want it to be.

"For your information, my daughter is too young for you."

Jackson chuckled. "I'm closer to her age than your age."

"So?"

"So, here we are ... on *our* first date. Don't you think I'm too young for you?"

Yes. Of course she did.

"This isn't a date. It's a dog walk."

"It's a date."

Ryn shook her head. "It's not."

"Why?"

"Because you're too young for me. There I said it. Happy now?"

Men like Jackson were put on Earth for one purpose: to rob every ounce of confidence from women like Ryn. They ate it up and saved it for themselves, as if they could possibly need any more. Then they flaunted it to get the attention of the lucky recipients who were Maddie's age. The twenty-somethings thrived on it.

"I know all my ABCs. I'm potty trained. I chew with my mouth closed, and I require limited supervision."

Ryn didn't want to laugh, but she did anyway. "Shut up, now you're just being stupid."

"Oh and I can count to one hundred—forward, backward, and even with my eyes shut."

She sighed. "Have you ever been married?"

"No."

"Kids?"

"No."

"So our total time spent together so far in the past week has been five hours, and we might not have anything in common, which would only be compounded by our age difference, and you expect me to believe you are seriously interested in me?"

"Yes."

"Fine," she huffed, hiding her grin. "I'll marry you."

Jackson laughed. It made her want more.

More laughter.

More resplendent smiles.

He held her gaze, lacing his fingers with hers then gently squeezing her hand. That made her want more too.

More of his touch.

More of the happiness that swelled in her heart.

His touch felt like a spell. For a moment she forgot

about her age, her physical imperfections, and the fear that held her hostage to a past she could never escape.

They finished their walk in silence. It wasn't awkward, it was perfect. The most indelible moments are spent in quietude with a worthy companion. Gunner had been that worthy companion for years.

When they reached her front porch, it felt like waking from a dream. Their age difference returned to her thoughts again as all the insecurities she tried to overcome came rushing back. She attempted to release his hand, but he tightened his grip and pulled her to him. He smelled good, really good. Her eyes closed on their own accord as she took a slow inhale, hoping he didn't notice her trying to smell him.

"Candles," he said.

Ryn opened her eyes.

"I smell like sex candles."

She laughed a little. "Sex candles?" Whatever they were, she needed to buy some.

"Yes. Jillian sells them and until just recently she'd been using Woody to transport them."

Sex candles and then Woody. Maybe she *was* too old. Clearly they didn't speak the same language.

"Well, sex candles smell good on you."

He smiled. It was a hungry smile with his tongue wetting his lips.

"You know what else would smell good on me?" he whispered, ducking his head a breath away from her lips.

The enormity of his dominating presence wrecked her ability to conjure coherent thoughts and formulate words to go with them.

"Um ... what?" She couldn't even remember his question. Why were his lips just lingering over hers? It was torturous.

"You." He touched her lips, just barely.

She felt the very tip of his warm tongue touch her top lip.

"Good night, Ryn." He strode with extra confidence to his car because he stole hers. He stole everything and left her speechless, standing on the porch with her lips slightly parted, making soft panting noises. Pathetic.

"Night," she whispered long after he was gone.

CHAPTER SEVEN

"How's AJ?"

"Still alive." Jillian shrugged.

Lilith gave her a reprimanding look. "Char's a mess. She didn't take it so well."

"I know. That's what he said. How could she? It's messed up. Children aren't supposed to die before their parents."

"Is he?"

"Is he what?"

"Going to die."

Jillian didn't know the answer to that question. She was too close to the situation to even look at the possibilities with any sort of objectivity.

"Surgery seems too risky. I think they've ruled that out. But it's beginning to affect his vision so he's agreed to radiation therapy starting next week after his parents and Brooke leave. They're arriving later today and they go back home on Sunday."

"Yes, Char and I are having coffee. You should join us."

"Hmm ... I'll see. Brooke and her family are staying with

us. Jackson's not too thrilled, so I may need to be there as a buffer."

"He doesn't like Brooke?" Lilith questioned.

"She has kids."

"He doesn't like kids?"

"Just his own."

"He has kids?"

Jillian laughed. "Not yet, but he's working on it."

"Sounds like a story."

"It probably will be, but it's still in the prologue."

"And yours and Luke's?"

"It's just getting good." Jillian grinned.

Day

"How DID KILLING Four make you feel?"

Luke was more determined than ever to work through Jessica's past, lay it to rest, and begin their future. She liked the future part, but lacked motivation to deal with the past since the night they'd had sex. However, he knew it bothered her that they hadn't had it again after that first time with her bound to her bed—that had been a month earlier. Luke found plenty of excuses and ways to distract her, the dog being the biggest one.

"Why can't I move in with you?" She sat on his bed with Jones, who wasn't supposed to be on his bed or any of the furniture.

"Because you're a slob. Down." He snapped his fingers at Jones and pointed to the floor.

Jones rested his head on Jessica's leg in defiance.

"I'm not when I'm at your place."

"You are." He gave up on the stubborn—contumacious —dog and continued with his crossword puzzle, staying in the chair by the window. Luke wouldn't go near her in his bed. It was a bad idea.

"Give me one example."

"One of your shoes is right there on the floor and the other is in the middle of my hallway. You 'clean' my kitchen counter by wiping the crumbs onto the floor. You 'organize' your purse by emptying gum wrappers and toothpicks onto my coffee table and leaving them there. After you wash your hands in the bathroom you flick your fingers before grabbing the towel and leave water spots on my mirror. And you're always taking books from my bookshelf and you never put them back."

Jessica frowned while petting Jones. "Jeez, I just said *one*."

He smirked at her pathetic attempt at pouting. She was the world's worst pouter, and he'd told her as much so many times. Anyone trained to kill could not pout. Period.

"Answer my question."

She flopped back on the bed, staring at the ceiling. "After I killed Four I felt *different*."

"Different how?

"When he killed Claire it hardened me to the world. I had so much hate for the unfairness of it all. But when I killed him it hardened my feelings toward Jessica Day. She was trained in defense, not revenge. I was trained to think of it like that. We were defenders, like soldiers, not killers. We don't call soldiers in the military killers, even if they kill."

"So you were upset with yourself?"

"Disappointed. Separated. In denial. I don't know, I just no longer knew who I was or who I was supposed to be.

Jessica the defender has friends, drinks too much wine, and pursues her career. Jessica the killer just ..."

"Just?"

"Waits."

"Waits for what?"

"Trigger."

"Who's Trigger?"

"The one that got away."

"Matthew Green?"

She nodded.

Luke had to push through his own emotions and leave them behind. Jessica's lover didn't want to know any more. He too wanted it to all just disappear. But Dr. Jones owed it to her and he owed it to Luke. He had to make things right.

"You want Matthew Green dead?"

She shook her head then looked over at him with tears in her eyes. He knew she hated those tears. Maybe someday she'd realize the strength in setting them free. Luke felt privileged that she trusted him with her vulnerability—with her tears. The need to go to her and wrap her in his arms pained him. Why? Why couldn't love heal everything?

"Please don't hate me," she whispered, her face scrunched with pain.

"I'll never hate you."

"I don't just want him dead ... I want to kill him because he didn't save my friend."

Luke couldn't take that away. No one could take that away. Two voices resided inside her, and she needed that separation to keep a small shred of her sanity. He, however, couldn't separate the two. He had to love both of them as one for her to have any chance of offering forgiveness and finding acceptance.

"I can see it..." she blinked, releasing the tears "...in your eyes. You wonder what's wrong with you. You wonder how you could even consider loving someone as awful as me."

Dr. Jones needed to stay focused and not let his emotions override the progress they were making. But that man—the one who loved her more than a clean mirror, or a tidy coffee table, or oxygen for that matter—told the good doctor to fuck off. Then he stood and went to her.

That man, the one who never felt guilty for loving the woman, he sat on the bed and pulled her onto his lap, straddling his legs. She hugged him with a fierce intensity.

"You don't see anything," he whispered. "You're so blind because the only thing in my eyes is adoration. God, I love every part of you so much I can't even think straight. You're my goddamn miracle and there's nothing in life more amazing than a miracle."

Love was not a problem to solve or a choice to make, simply an involuntary feeling that explained human existence. It wasn't contingent on anything, and everyone was capable of giving and receiving it. Words couldn't define feelings. Luke didn't know why he *had* to love her. He just did.

"Show me ..." she sat back, looking so vulnerable with her tear-stained cheeks "...show me how much you adore me, Luke." It wasn't so much a request as a desperate plea.

They held each other's gaze for a few silent moments.

"I won't hurt you," she promised. "You're my everything ... the life that beats inside my chest." She took his hand and placed it over her heart. "Do you feel that? Every. Single. One. Is for you."

He took her hand and placed it on his chest. "Yours," he whispered.

Luke became Jessica's prodigy of love. He accepted her without judgment, held her in reverence, and trusted her *implicitly*. No one loved like Luke loved. For that, she gave him *everything*.

She unbuttoned his shirt and pushed it away from his chest.

Pressing her lips to the scar on his shoulder, she whispered, "I'm sorry."

"Don't—"

She moved her mouth back to his, tasting and savoring him. "Let me ... let me be sorry for what I did to you. Okay?"

He nodded then removed her shirt. "I need to see you ... all of you." He smiled while unfastening her bra.

It was a vulnerable smile. Not like the controlled one he used every day with patients or even his family and friends. There was one very special smile that looked like a child who just had all his dreams come true. That was a very private smile for Jessica.

"What if I want more than your heart?" He cupped her breast and brushed his thumb over her nipple.

She smiled. "Take everything."

He leaned back on the bed, letting her straddle his waist. "You first."

Drifting forward, she kissed his neck, followed by every inch of his chest.

Never. Never again would she hurt him. *He* was the miracle.

She stood and removed the rest of her clothes and then his. That smile, *her smile*, came back to his handsome face.

That smile quickly faded as Luke cleared his throat. "Out."

Jessica frowned at Jones who sat on the floor watching them.

"Sorry, Jones." She ushered him out and shut the door. "Now ... you need to remind me of what this whole adoration thing feels like." She crawled up the bed and laid her naked body on his. There was no room for her past, no room for fear, no room for control.

His hands explored her body, hers explored his. Their lips connected as they shared soft moans. Luke lifted her hips and slid into her. "Luke ..."

"I told you..." he kissed her neck "...if I had you in my bed..." his tongue slid over her nipple "...I'd never want to leave."

"Oh ... my ... God ..." Her eyes closed as she completely surrendered, letting him pull her under to depths of intimacy she never knew existed.

By the time she resurfaced—sated, exhausted, and thoroughly adored—Luke's body was draped *over* hers. She didn't panic and that realization flickered in her watery eyes as she hugged him. Jessica felt certain of very few things in life, but Luke's love had become an indisputable law of nature—of that, she was absolutely certain. His body became her security. He would protect her from her demons ... forever.

"Jess?" he mumbled into her shoulder.

"Hmm?" She teased her hands along his back, tracing each muscle.

"If I wake up tomorrow and live to tell about it ... you should move in with me."

She shoved him off her. Traipsing naked into his great room, she kissed Jones goodnight and put him in his kennel. Returning with two arms full of blankets and pillows, she blew him a kiss while tossing everything on the bed.

Luke turned on his side, resting his head on his hand with amusement tugging at his lips. "What are you doing?"

Jessica ignored him, proceeding to construct a barrier in the middle of the bed, separating the Qin dynasty from the Nomads. "Hurry up and go to sleep. Don't flail, and let *me* wake *you* in the morning."

He chuckled. "I can't even see you."

She peeked through a small hole in the pillow and blanket wall. "Jones is going to be so excited."

"Not if you accidentally snap my neck in the morning."

She blew him another kiss. "I've got you—I'll always have you."

CHAPTER EIGHT

KNIGHT

Jackson scowled at Jillian from his piano as Brooke and her family settled into the lower-level bedrooms for their two-night stay.

"I know your mental state has been the hot topic for years, but this is truly insane."

Jillian pressed her index finger to her lips.

"Don't shush me. Those kids are going to tear this place apart."

"Well, good thing we hired a cleaning lady."

"She has a name you know."

Jillian raised a brow. "Ryn, yes I know. I hired her ... as our *cleaning lady*."

"Well she could be more than that."

"Oh?" A smile crept along Jillian's lips. "Did you propose or offer her your body to help her stave off menopause?"

Jackson narrowed his eyes.

"I'm kidding. Either way she should invite you to stay the weekend so I don't have to deal with your Oscar the

Grouch attitude ... oh wait, that's right, you're Mr. Snuffleupagus."

"Not any more."

"Ryn not into penis role-playing?"

Jackson failed to hide his grin. "Somehow I doubt it."

"Hmm ... that's a shame. I was going to suggest that Lascivio create a line of penis accessories. I think action hero dress-up could be quite fun."

"Would AJ do it?" Jackson raised a questioning brow.

"Would AJ do what?" Brooke asked, rounding the corner from the stairs.

Jillian gave Jackson the hairy eyeball before turning toward Brooke. "Grill out ... even though it looks like it could rain."

"Trust me ... AJ would grill out in the middle of a hurricane." Brooke shook her head.

Jillian smiled. AJ had softened her, exposed her humanity. Maybe it *was* crazy for her to invite her lover's ex-wife to stay with her. Jillian didn't have a boiling pot of jealousy waiting to erupt inside of her, but Brooke proved that with exposed humanity came a little spark of jealousy. It was a miserable emotion. AJ and Brooke had been married and raised a child. Of course Brooke would know him better than Jillian.

"Well, it was nice to meet you." Jackson smiled at Brooke. "I'm going to ... take off."

Jillian nodded. "Good idea." She winked at him as he grabbed his keys and headed out the door.

"Your brother is ..." Brooke stared at the door.

"Yes, he's a freak of nature. But I'd say the same thing about you, knowing you have a twenty-one-year-old son and five-year-old twins." Jillian stopped shy of actually saying the word angel.

"Pfft ... I hired a personal trainer after the girls were born. I've had a tummy tuck and breast implants, but none of it stops me from peeing a little when I jump rope with the girls."

Jillian's jaw dropped.

"TMI?" Brooke scrunched her nose.

Jillian shook her head and maybe fell a little in love with Brooke in that moment. The angel's wings weren't real.

"I wanted to like you and it's official ... now I can."

Brooke laughed. "I wanted to hate you and it's official ... now I can't."

Jillian's eyes narrowed. "Why would you hate me?"

Brooke eased up onto the kitchen barstool and crossed her long thin legs. "Because you found what I lost."

"What's that?"

"His love."

"You didn't lose his love. You lost him. And I don't think I'm with the man you married. I doubt he still exists."

Brooke seemed to think about it as she stared intently at Jillian. "Char told me about..." she paused "...the tumor."

Jillian nodded.

"Do you think that's the real reason for his change in personality?" Brooke's eyes filled with unshed tears.

She had to feel a pang of guilt as if she, too, was responsible for missing something, assuming it was the PTSD.

"It could be, especially now, but even one of his doctors said he probably has PTSD, but sifting through his symptoms to determine which category they belong in is useless at this point. No one is to blame and we can't change what already is."

Jillian said it for Brooke's benefit, but she wanted there to be someone to blame. Having someone to blame made dealing with the pain so much easier.

"You do know that his parents asked him to move back to Portland for treatment so they or *we* can help take care of him while he goes through radiation?"

Jillian did not know that. "I ... what did he tell them?"

"He said he'd think about it."

"When did he say that?" She tried to hide her disappointment, or anger, or whatever feeling triggered some sort of meltdown inside her.

"Yesterday when they talked on the phone."

Jillian had practically been living at his house the previous week to help him out and go with him to his appointments, but somehow that bit of information had not been shared with her.

It DID rain and they still grilled out. Dodge and Lilith came for dinner too, but Cage couldn't make it because he had a late practice to prepare for his first preseason game. The girls played hide-and-seek, then Stan took them out on his paddle boat with their dad.

At one point Brooke and AJ disappeared inside, and when they both returned Jillian could tell Brooke had been crying and maybe AJ too. He wore a baseball hat pulled low on his head, which made it hard to get a good look at his eyes.

Jillian found herself not fitting into Dodge and Lilith's conversation with AJ's parents, and AJ himself seemed to be avoiding her, so after dinner she sneaked out the door and went home. In that moment she regretted shoving Jackson out of the house because she needed a good kick in the ass to push her past the rut she'd fallen into since

Brooke's revelation about the possibility of AJ moving back to Portland.

"Hey, I wondered where you went," AJ said, standing at the bottom of the stairs.

Jillian stilled the punching bag and tugged off her gloves. "I wanted to give you some time with your family."

"That's nice of you, but you didn't have to leave."

She shrugged, wiping the sweat off her brow with her arm. "I needed to work out anyway, and I knew I wouldn't be able to be down here later when Brooke and everyone came back so ..."

"Oh ... well, after you shower come back over for a little bit. Okay?"

She nodded.

AJ started back up the stairs.

"I'm mad," she said. That admission, those two words, ripped through her gut. Jillian didn't want to be mad, and she sure didn't want the insecurity that came with confessing her vulnerability.

He stopped and turned, an uneasy squint tugging at his brow.

The giving-a-shit, channeling her humanity thing, took its toll on her that day.

"I'm mad. Okay? I was mad that time when I took Cage out on a date because you had the balls to go out with Carin after our *moment* in the shower that morning. So, I'm sorry. I should have just told you upfront that I was mad. I didn't, but I am now."

"You're mad at me now?" AJ looked lost. Typical male.

"Yes, and I'm not even going to play the whole mind-fuck guessing game with you." Her voice grew louder with each word. "I'm just going to tell you and then you're going to apologize for even considering leaving me to move back to Portland!"

AJ closed his eyes. "I was going to tell you."

"Tell me what? That they asked you or that you're considering it?"

He looked at her but didn't answer.

"You're leaving." She shook her head.

"I didn't say that." He walked back down the stairs.

She retreated. "Well, you didn't say you're staying."

"I didn't say anything!" An eerie silence followed his echo.

"I can't move to Portland with you," she said, her voice soft—regretful. "But maybe you weren't going to ask me to anyway."

"I don't know what I'm doing." His shoulders slumped. "I haven't even told my son that I'm dying."

"You're not—"

"Don't!" He sighed. "I'll let everyone *but* you think that a miracle is going to happen. My parents believe it, Brooke believes it—hell, even I want to believe it—but you are my real ... my truth. You are the only clarity in this whole fucked-up mess. You don't have to watch me die to accept that it's going to happen. But what if *they* do?"

She couldn't look at him. He'd put her up on a pedestal as if she were invincible, a rock that could not be broken. He was so very wrong.

AJ kissed the top of her head. "I have to go back over there." He turned and walked up the stairs.

"AJ?"

"Yeah?" he answered with his back to her.

"There's no acceptance in watching someone die. There's only a lifetime of regret from knowing you couldn't stop it from happening."

CHAPTER NINE

IT TOOK Ryn several days to recover from a near-kiss, or a half-kiss, or whatever involved Jackson's tongue grazing the top of her lip. Her hormones giving her whiplash didn't help either. Unpredictable periods toyed with her, making it impossible to prepare for them. In the middle of the night she had a hot flash. A. Hot. Flash! What was she, sixty? Then the next minute she thought about sex—nonstop. She imagined having sex with every guy she saw, and it had nothing to do with their looks because she also imagined every couple she saw having sex too.

Sex. Sweat. Sex.

Her body couldn't decide if it wanted to act sixteen or sixty.

Gunner barked while she made a late dinner: an egg salad sandwich. She knew someone had to be at her house because it's the only time he barked when she was home.

"Who's here, baby?" She looked out the front window and jumped, pressing her back against the wall next to the window, trying to hide.

"Oh God." Ryn closed her eyes. Her khaki shorts had

permanent oil stains from lemon wood polish and her large T-shirt looked even more grotesque and two sizes too big, resembling a night shirt. She couldn't bear to think about her bra: a compression sports bra that made her chest one small speed bump. Maybe the large shirt was a blessing.

The door bell rang. "Just a minute." She grimaced. He could probably tell from the nearness of her voice that she was two feet from the door. There was never an extra dose of confidence around when she needed it.

"Hi ... what are you doing here?" She tried to keep most of her body hidden behind the door.

"I've been displaced from my house by twins."

"Twins?"

"Five-year-old girls."

"Oh ... cute."

"Not cute."

"You don't like kids?"

"Just my own."

"Oh, wow ... you have kids?"

Ryn didn't realize she was just one of many victims that fell for that line.

"Not yet, but mine *will be* awesome."

She nodded slowly. "I see ... sort of. Well, I'd invite you in but—"

"Great. I'd love to." He squeezed through the small opening. "Nice place."

There was nowhere to hide.

"Thanks. I'm kind of in need of a shower and clean clothes, and I was just getting ready to eat—"

"Great. I'm starving." He slid his hands in his back pockets and grinned.

Jackson looked much more edible than anything she had in her kitchen.

"O-kay, we're having dinner together now?"

"Of course. I need to know if my future wife can cook?"

Ryn laughed. It was a nervous laugh, a so-we're-still-playing-this-game laugh. "It's egg salad."

"Minus the egg shells?"

She gave him a crazy look. "Yes."

"Great."

"Great," she replied, amused at how many times he had said 'great.' Jackson Knight was easy to please. She hoped that would work in her favor.

The exotic, inked human specimen looked out of place sitting at her kitchen table. It had two chairs on one side and a bench seat on the other. Jackson took the bench, propping his legs on it, crossed at the ankles.

"So I don't have a lot of money..." she handed him a plate with the sandwich and small wedge of watermelon "... and my first wedding was in my parents' backyard where I wore a hundred dollar dress from JC Penny. I want the fairytale wedding with a one-of-a-kind Vera Wang dress, six bridesmaids, and Ed Sheeran singing at my reception. Is my future husband willing to give me that?" Ryn sat across from Jackson, taking a bite of her sandwich to mask her grin.

"That depends. At what frequency do you see you and your future husband having sex?"

She covered her mouth with a napkin to keep from spitting her partially-chewed bite across the table. "Um ..." she cleared her throat. "Three? Four times? I think that's pretty average."

"Clearly my future wife doesn't understand we will be anything but average, but I will agree with her for now to four times a day as long as it's open to negotiation for more in the future."

"Day?" She choked.

"Yes, day," he confirmed, biting into the wedge of watermelon. "Surely with the one-of-a-kind dress *and* Ed Sheeran, you weren't implying per week … were you?"

She gulped down some water, shaking her head. "No … no of course not."

Jackson took a mammoth bite of his sandwich and smirked. "I didn't think so," he mumbled.

The conversation crossed the line from fun to really uncomfortable.

"Who's twins are at your house?"

"AJ's ex-wife's."

"Oh, isn't it a little odd that his ex-wife and her family are staying at your house?"

"So you get it too? Good, it's not just me." Jackson nodded. "His son has his first game tomorrow so the whole damn family flew to Omaha and my sister, who lives off instinct and usually bad instinct at that, said they could stay with us since AJ doesn't have room for everyone at his house."

"Well she's a better woman than I am. That would be too weird and uncomfortable for me."

"Jillian makes her own rules as she goes and nobody understands them but her."

They finished eating, with Ryn giving him a look of incredulity as Jackson returned his usual cocky smirk. She put their plates in the dishwasher, feeling rather awkward about their odd dinner. "Well, I uh … need a shower."

Jackson stood. "I like showers."

She coughed out a laugh. The problem was, he wasn't laughing. Her heart raced, making it impossible to calm her breathing and hide her nerves. "Yeah, sure. We've known each other for what? Not even three weeks?"

"Three and a half and so what?"

He possessed an over-the-top confidence. That wasn't good because her you're-ten-years-younger-than-me insecurities seemed to match his level of confidence.

"*So* we're not taking a shower together."

"Why?" He took one step toward her.

Her heart felt like a humming bird in her chest. "Because that would mean you'd see me naked."

"So?"

"So that's just not going to happen."

"How are we going to have sex four times a day if I can't see you naked?"

"In the dark. We would only have it in the dark." The absurdity of their roleplaying both baffled and thrilled Ryn.

"Why the modesty? You're ten times sexier than you think you are, and once you realize that, it's going to double."

"Agreed. You want to see me *feel* sexy? Then you have to let me *look* sexy first. And that will require some preparation."

"Preparation?"

His interest in her should have been flattering, but it wasn't because he was ten years younger and he was a guy. He could never understand the emotional barricades she had to overcome with her own insecurities ... insecurities brought to the surface *because* he was ten years younger and looked like sex personified. Even if she were his age, his interest in her would be hard to believe and still unnerving.

"Yes, my body requires more maintenance than yours for it to look and run right." Her breasts had been held hostage in a compression sports bra all day and they were going to look like roadkill when she removed it. Every woman who has worn one knows about this horrific side effect. They would require a very cold shower to perk up a little and convince her nipples it was safe to come out. Then there was the small issue of grooming. She had pubic hair—not too common anymore. There stood a good chance that Jackson had never actually seen pubic hair on a woman. It was bushy ... very bushy.

"I'll wait."

"Wait, what do you mean wait?"

He made a shooing motion with his hand. "Go *prepare*, come back downstairs, then we'll go back upstairs and shower together."

"That makes no sense. I'll have already showered."

"Well then when do men shower with you? Apparently not when you need a shower nor when you've just had a shower."

Most. Bizarre. Conversation. Ever ... times one hundred.

"Men *don't* shower with me."

"Ever? You've never showered with a man?"

Was that so strange?

"No. Why are we having this conversation?"

"You started it."

"Wh—I did not!"

"Fine." He took two long strides. Palming the back of her head, he kissed her.

It wasn't a peck or a partial kiss like before, it was the full kiss—the kind meant for tasting, not just feeling. The kind where his tongue couldn't get enough of her. She could have faded into the moment had she not thought about the egg salad she just ate, her breasts trapped beneath a heavy layer of cotton and spandex, and the bush overgrowth—a visual chastity belt.

"No!" She wriggled from his embrace as his hand went for her breast—her squashed, speed bump uniboob.

"Sorry." He held his hands up while pulling his brows together as if he'd stepped on her toe. "Too fast. I-I'm sorry."

"No, not too fast ..." She put her hands over her face, shaking her head. "God, does that make me sound easy or what? Sorry, I'm really not good at this." On a deep sigh, her hands fell from her face. "If you let me shower, *alone*, I promise to return as the much more put-together version of myself. Deal?"

The smile on his face held so much promise, but his eyes filled with expectation. Expectation that on her best day after hours of cosmetic surgery, and a lobotomy to erase the memories of her past, she could never live up to.

GUNNER WASTED no time earning Jackson's respect. While Ryn threw together the best version of herself, which he deemed ridiculous because it was impossible to improve on stunning, Gunner stood guard at the bottom of the stairs looking at Jackson with an I'll-tear-you-apart look on his face.

The second Jackson started to move, either toward the window or the kitchen, Gunner gave him a warning growl. There would be no snooping through Ryn's things on Gunner's watch.

"Better?" Ryn smiled as she came down the stairs wearing a long black and gray striped skirt with a red sleeve-less top.

"Clearly you don't understand what draws me to you, but I can see you feel more confident in that."

She frowned.

The guy who never slept with the same person twice wasn't good at the emotional side of relationships. For years it had been his opinion that women's clothes were nothing more than expensive wrapping paper.

New guy.

New opinions. What opinions? He wasn't sure yet, but something told him women like Ryn didn't have sex in alleys, and they needed constant reinforcement in the form of compliments—compliments beyond "I want to stick my dick in you." So he reached into his magic hat and pulled out something that had nothing to do with sex.

"I'll start with your lips. Even now when you tried to frown, one side stayed curled into a smile. It's like your body rejects sadness."

She stopped at the bottom step, paralyzed by his words.

"Then there are your freckles that give your face this rare innocence. And I would stare at them all day if your eyes weren't so greedy. They demand my attention all the time."

Ryn rubbed her lips together. "My eyes are greedy?"

"Yes, you should really be ashamed of them. Total attention hogs. But my point is really that I don't care what you're wearing. It doesn't change what I'm looking at."

"Oh ..." she released a long breath "...wow, that's ... we should go for drinks. I think I need some liquid courage to respond to your comments that really leave me ... speechless."

"So speechless is good?"

Taking the last step with a bit of blush pinking her skin, chin down, she grinned. "Yeah, speechless is good."

"You have a favorite bar?"

"I do." Ryn grabbed her purse.

"After you." He held the door open.

CHAPTER TEN

THE ALMOST FORTY-YEAR-OLD who had to pinch herself at least a dozen times in the car, received the ten minute summary of the sexiest and quirkiest guy alive. New York, parents died, and a string of temporary jobs was not what she imagined, but her history didn't fit her either. At least she hoped it didn't.

"What are you drinking tonight?" Jackson asked as she slid into a small dimly lit booth in the corner.

"Bloody Mary. That's why I come here." She pulled out her wallet.

"Don't even." He shook his head, walking to the bar.

After a few minutes of staring at his backside, she smiled to herself. He was right, her eyes were greedy. They wanted to be on him all the time. She looked away from him long enough to notice how many other sets of greedy eyes clung to his body. Then, as if her observation brought it on, several *younger* women moved in as though they were trapping him in their circle. One of them teased her finger over the cross tattooed on his arm. The twenty-something looked about Maddie's age.

After breaking from the pack, the most sought after man in the bar found his way back to the booth.

"How great is it being you?"

He set her Bloody Mary down next to his beer then looked behind him at the predatory eyes still glued to him.

"Apparently not as great as being you."

Ryn scooted over as he slid in next to her. Never before had a guy sat next to her in a booth when it was just the two of them. She glanced over at his growing fan club. They were all young, thin, and scantily dressed, which made Ryn feel every inch of her long, conservative skirt.

"I don't think they're jealous ... I think they want to claw my eyes out, or maybe yours for being so blind."

"Does my future wife need reminding that she's the sexiest person in this place?"

An unavoidable laugh escaped. "Now you're just being ridiculous. I'm not a self-professed wallflower, but *come on* ... I'm not them."

"Thank God for that." He slid his hand through her hair and brought her mouth to his.

Another all-in kiss. The demanding stroke of his warm tongue temporarily dissolved all thoughts of the women watching them. The way he held her mouth to his, not giving a damn what anyone else thought, told all those wanton eyes that he was not available ... at least not that night.

The hand that wasn't holding her head rested high on her leg then eased up until just his thumb brushed her bare skin where her skirt met her shirt. Ryn's hands stayed clenched at her sides. They yearned to touch him, grab him, possibly attack him. Therefore, she deduced it best to hold still and let him lead the way.

Jackson released her lips, leaving her waiting for the

next breath. An eternity later it reappeared, and she went straight for her drink, guzzling it down to the very last drop. A stalk of celery, a straw, and a spear through an olive and baby pickle mingled with the ice in the bottom.

He stared at her with a shit-eating grin. "So you like the Bloody Mary here, huh?"

Taking a bite of the celery, she nodded. "Uh huh, it's an in-house mix, the best tomato juice, fresh lemon, and a dash of bitters. And I'm going to need another pretty quick before we can talk about that kiss."

He nodded to the waitress a few tables down. Her unapologetic gawking made it easy to get her attention. Miss Flirty Smile winked as he pointed to Ryn's empty glass.

"I like kissing you. I think it's fair to say it's the highlight of my day."

The pinch-me moments crashed into the shore again and again. Ryn could see them coming, but each time they knocked her down, pulling her under. "I'm not sure what that says about either one of us." She took another bite of celery, wishing the bartender would hurry up with her drink. "Maybe we should talk about something else."

He angled his body toward hers, resting his arm behind her while taking a long pull of his beer. "Okay then ... tell me about your daughter."

Maddie was a tricky subject, however, unavoidable.

"She's studying law at Creighton. I can't even begin to tell you how smart she is, too smart really, but our relationship has been strained over the past few years."

"How so?"

The waitress brought Ryn's Bloody Mary. It was a miracle that she didn't spill it, with her eyes on Jackson and his tatted arms. "Anything else I can get you?"

He kept his gaze on Ryn. "No, thank you."

Shaking her head she chuckled. "Our waitress is quite attractive."

"Is she?" He still didn't turn.

"I've never been with a guy that wouldn't have checked out that waitress at least once. I don't mind, you're—"

"Well you should. Any guy that takes his eyes off you is a fucking idiot. Excuse my language."

Her drink called to her again. This time she stopped gulping at half the glass. It was progress.

"Okay, I'm ready to talk," her buzz declared as she licked her lips. "Let's start with your vow of celibacy. If not a priest then why? And if it's because some love of your life died, then just nod once and don't say anything. I'm not in my right mind and even then I'm not sure what I would say back to you."

Jackson studied her through slightly squinted eyes. "First, it really wasn't a 'vow of celibacy.' Jillian takes too many liberties with things I say. Moving felt like a fresh start, a chance to be someone different. So I decided to seize the opportunity."

"So if being celibate is different, then ..." Even with that warm buzz, Ryn managed to add everything together. "You must not have been celibate in New York."

Jackson frowned. "I was the opposite of celibate, as in very much not celibate. Like *every day* I practiced not being celibate."

"So you had a girlfriend."

"No ... no girlfriends."

"Oh ..." Yes, two plus two equaled four. No girlfriends and not being celibate every day equaled a really bad answer. "You're a playboy."

"*Was* and I didn't actually call myself that."

Six gulps later the second Bloody Mary vanished. This time Ryn signaled the waitress for another, although it took a little more waving to get her eyes drawn away from Jackson. Ryn stopped shy of jumping up and down on the table.

"I take it something happened. Did you get someone pregnant?" *That* Ryn could relate to. "Or did you catch some nasty STD?" Bloody Mary asked that question. There wasn't even a flinch like she shouldn't have asked it or that she needed to take it back. Maybe she didn't need another drink after all.

His brows drew tight. "No kids or STDs. I just liked sex but not relationships. My uncomplicated lifestyle suited me at the time."

"But now?"

"Now I'm different."

"Why?"

"Because I choose to be."

The vodka seeped into her brain. They were the best Bloody Marys and never stingy on the alcohol. "You should *choose* to show me all your tattoos." She slapped her hand over her mouth. "Oh God, I just said that out loud."

Jackson's eyes widened and it's possible his ears perked up a bit too. "You did. Keep going. I think I like you uncensored."

The impish twist of his lips had her grabbing for more of her drink, but her hands were greeted by an empty glass. That made his eyes glimmer with even more delight. "I'd love to show you my tattoos, but not here." He ducked his head to her ear. "I'd have to remove *all* my clothes for you to see *all* my tattoos."

"We can't have sex!" she blurted so fast it sounded like one long—loud—word.

Jackson looked around at a few of his adoring fans while

wiping his hand over his mouth as if he could hide or remove the smirk on his face.

"Oh bloody, Bloody Mary ... cut me off right now. What I mean—"

Her most wildly entertained date held his index finger to his lips over his permanent smile.

Taking the hint, she lowered her voice, not realizing how loud she had been. "What I mean is I have some things to attend to in the sex department."

Biting his lips together, he nodded. "More *preparation?*"

With inebriated confidence she sat up ramrod straight and nodded. "Exactly."

"Mmm ... I see, well you didn't finish telling me about Maddie."

Her posture sank again. "Oh Maddie, Maddie, Maddie. She's so aanng-ger-ee with me all the time. I'm trying to protect her from *him,* but she just doesn't see the whole picture."

"Him?"

"The ex. He's not a nice man." She slid her celery in and out of her mouth, running her tongue down the center groove.

Jackson cleared his throat. "You're not eating that celery like we can't have sex. You need to take a bite or put it back in your glass ... now."

Ryn bit into it, eyes wide, then she chewed it slowly, keeping her gaze locked to his.

"That's better. Now ... the ex, why is he not a nice man?"

"He has too much money and anger management issues."

"Anger management issues?"

Ryn tapped her fingernail against the side of her glass,

exhaling a breathy laugh. "I'm a little inebriated. A couple swigs past tipsy, but not officially drunk. Talking about the ex is not a good idea right now. He probably has someone following me and listening in on our conversation."

Jackson took a slow glance over his shoulder. "Why would he have someone follow you?"

"Because he's a psycho," she whispered in his ear then chuckled. "If he gets within a football field of me, he'll be arrested. Sometimes I feel like someone is following me, but I can never detect who. It's just an unsettling feeling."

"So it was physical abuse?"

Ryn twisted her lips. "Hmm ... yeah, I'd say seven trips to various hospitals in less than a year would qualify as physical abuse."

Jackson didn't flinch or even blink. Most people had some sort of involuntary reaction if she confessed her past.

"It started years ago when Maddie was a baby." Ryn rested her elbow on the table then her chin on her hand. "I think you should take me home." She yawned. "We've been here less than an hour, and I've consumed way too much alcohol in that short amount of time. I'm off kilter around you."

He grinned behind the mouth of his beer bottle as he took the last swig. "Why is that?"

There was the lack of sex with something or someone other than an inanimate vibrating object, the age differ-ence flashing in neon, and the nervous vibe that someone set everything up as a joke. At any given moment it seemed possible that her friends and family could jump out and yell *surprise* or *gotcha*—a fortieth birthday prank of sorts. Ha ha. Ryn actually thought this guy was inter-ested in her.

"Why is that ... good question. Let me see, you kinda

came out of nowhere. You have this Magic Mike stripper's body—"

"Who's Magic Mike?"

Her laugh came out as a cough. "It doesn't matter. My point is you're unexpected ... too unexpected. I'm trying to make sense of this little game we're playing. I'm on the cusp of losing my youth, truthfully I've already lost it, but I enjoy the warm comfort of denial. Then you swoop in just before I turn forty and kiss me like we're teenagers, joke about marrying me, and the way you look at me ... well, there are no words." Closing her eyes she shook her head. The alcohol was no match for how dizzy she felt under the intensity of his gaze.

"These little muscles in your jaw twitch when I look at you. I like to imagine they're the gatekeepers to the words you're dying to say ... the ones that I'm certain will land you naked in my bed." Jackson rolled his lips between his teeth and studied her, always with a look of intrigue. "Then you swallow hard about every ten seconds. Need I tell you what image *that* conjures in my head? But then I feel your heavy breaths, even though I know you're trying to control them, and swear I can actually hear your heart beating in your chest. I know you say we can't have sex, but I say it's too late. These little things you do fuck me in ways I never imagined possible. No matter what I say, you never look away. Your eyes can't hide what your body tries to deny."

Pantyliner. Ryn needed a pantyliner to absorb whatever trickled down her sex. In a desperate prayer she hoped it was her melting libido and not the untimely arrival of her unpredictable "friend." Did he see *that* in her eyes? Fear. Embarrassment. Anguish.

"You should go pull the car up front."

He narrowed his eyes, but only for a second. "Okay."

Her living dream disappeared out the door. His car was twenty yards from the entrance to the bar. It wasn't raining, and she gave no explanation for her odd request. Yet, he did it—no questions asked. The undefinable connection between them began taking on a life of its own. It was a lucid dream, and anyone who tried to wake her would be murdered—unless she herself died of embarrassment first.

"Please don't let Bloody Mary be the theme for the night," she whispered to herself, making a quick dash to the restroom.

No blood.

Ryn sighed as she dealt with the juice fest in her nether region with the most unpredictable terrain. One day sex felt like trying to start a fire with flint and metal, the next day just the thought of sex brought on a tsunami of secretions. Jackson was the earthquake that triggered that tsunami. Her cotton panties were drenched and sadly, she had a wet spot on the backside of her skirt to prove it.

"Lovely," she murmured, looking over her shoulder with her back to the mirror.

A quick air-dry later, she wormed her way through the growing bar crowd to the wood-paneled chariot.

"Ryn?"

She turned before opening the car door.

"I thought that was you."

Eyes wide like the dots to two big question marks, she smiled. "Hi ... uh..."

"Brad. We had coffee about a year ago."

Ryn nodded but her brain shook its head at the complete lack of recognition.

"My daughter, Nora, went on a spring break trip with Maddie. We had coffee at the airport waiting for their flight to arrive."

"Yes, I remember." She finally did. Brad was in his fifties, but his loss of hair since she last saw him added another decade to his physical appearance, especially since he refused to just shave it all. The wispy combed-over strands were not attractive.

"You look amazing."

"Oh, well, thank you."

His inspection of her amazingness gave her a bad case of the creeps. "My divorce is final now. We should go out sometime for more than just coffee."

"That's a nice offer, but I ..."

"You?" He inched closer.

"She's taken."

Ryn jumped.

Jackson stepped out of the vehicle, resting his arms on the roof.

"Oh, hi." Brad smiled. "I didn't realize Maddie had a brother."

Ryn closed her eyes. There wasn't a depth of hell deep enough to escape the humiliation.

"Funny guy. If you're lucky, Ryn will get in the car before I have a chance to teach you a little lesson in manners."

Brad held up his hands. "Sorry, man. Honest mistake." He tipped up his chin. "See you around, Ryn."

"Oh my God." She sank into the seat and yanked at the seat belt, fumbling to fasten it. "That was the worst reality check ever."

Jackson pulled away from the curb. "That you're taken?"

"What? Taken? Are you serious? I'm taken alright. Taken for a fool. Who am I kidding? I'm not old enough to be your mother, but he thought so. What does that say about me?"

"He's an idiot."

"He wasn't trying to be mean. It was an observation."

Jackson shrugged. "You don't look old. I look young. It's this new moisturizer I've been using. I think it's cut my wrinkles in half."

The tight purse of her lips could not deter her smile. "Shut up. You're so full of shit."

"I'm not. It has this coconut oil base, and I dab just a little around my eyes at night before bed."

"Enough. Just ... don't speak." She laughed. "My ego needs a few moments of silence to grieve."

All talk ceased as his hand took hers. She looked at their interlaced fingers and then at him. He could take her absolutely *anywhere*.

CHAPTER ELEVEN

A CRISP, cool morning breeze crept though the western-facing window. The bed creaked with distress as Jillian flailed, tangling the sheet around her body and burying her head under the pillows.

"Jesus! What's that sound?" Tearing the pillow from her face and flinging it across the room, she opened her eyes.

"Morning." Jackson smiled around the tiny straw in his mouth and continued slurping the nearly empty contents of a juice box. "These are good. You should get them more often."

Stretching on a big yawn, she rolled her head side to side. "Those are for the five-year-old twins staying with us. But I guess you're not too far off, so ..."

"You look like crap." He shot the empty juice box across her room to the trash and of course he made it.

"Thank you. I love you too."

"I told you inviting the ex-wife and her family to stay with us was monumentally stupid."

Sitting up, she crossed her legs, resting her elbows on

her knees. "Nice try, but that's not it. AJ's parents want him to move back to Portland for his treatment."

"But he said no?"

"He hasn't decided."

"I'll be back." Jackson turned and Jillian leaped out of bed to chase after him, stopping him at the front door.

"Don't you dare. You'll have to go through me to get to him." She stood tall, which was still short, and fisted her hands on her hips.

Jackson raised a single brow. "You do realize our sparring is for practice and exercise, but in a no-holds-barred situation I would take you down because I'm just physically that much stronger than you, right?"

"Maybe, but if I have to defend AJ from you, I won't fight fair."

"Which brings me to my next point." With a wide stance, he crossed his arms over his chest. "I'm doing this for you."

"On our way back from Portland AJ hit me so you hit him back. I get it, even if I let him do it. But this isn't about me and that's what hurts the most. I have to let him make his own decisions and in the end he might not choose me. Hell ... he might not even choose himself. The love he has for his family is admirable, it's *us*, Jackson."

The growing lump in her throat made it difficult to breathe, let alone speak. "If I were dying would you let me go ... would you let me die in the arms of anyone else?"

Jackson flinched. "That's not fair."

"Agreed. Life is not fair, but it's all we have. I'll let him go and so will you." She pushed his arms away from his chest and hugged him.

"You want to go with him."

She nodded. "But I'm not." A painful laugh broke from her chest. "He didn't ask me ... and I don't think he will."

Jackson kissed the top of her head. "He's a fool."

Resting her forehead on his sternum, she nodded. "Tell me a story, like a Sesame Street story."

"Pfft ... none of that." He retreated to the kitchen, stealing another juice box from the refrigerator. "Ryn agreed to marry me."

"Peachy." Jillian hopped up on the counter and took the juice box Jackson offered. "When's the big day?"

"We haven't set a date yet. I think I should ask her father first."

"Good call. She give you her virginity yet?"

A small smirk grew around his straw. "She has a daughter—twenty-one."

"You should ask for her permission as well. I'm guessing it's proper etiquette. Though she won't give it to you."

"Why?"

"Because she's going to be pissed that her 'old' mom is marrying a guy that she wants to nail."

Jackson tossed the box in the trash and grabbed a Red Bull to wash down the juice. "I'm pretty sure a woman can't actually 'nail' a guy—not the right equipment. I can't believe you sold enough Lascivio crap to win a car. You're clearly not the sexpert everyone thinks you are."

"Whatever. So how did it happen?"

"The proposal?"

"Yes. Did you get down on one knee and all that jazz?"

"Nope. I gave her the option of marriage or meaningless sex. She thought about it for a while and chose marriage. I think it was a good choice. But I also think it's going to be a while before we have sex. For some reason she feels the need to 'prepare' herself. What do you think that means?"

Jillian giggled. "I'm not sure. She's pushed a baby out of her vagina so accommodating your wee little penis shouldn't be the issue."

That earned her an exaggerated eye roll.

"Maybe..." she held up her index finger "...she doesn't think that's the hole you're going to use."

"Really? You think she's preparing herself for anal sex with me?"

"No, not really." She returned the same eye roll. "I think you make her completely self-conscious. She probably has a bit of overgrowth."

"Pubic hair?"

"Maybe."

"Huh ... maybe I should tell her I've had sex with women who have pubic hair and it's no big deal."

They both laughed.

"Yes, there might even be an e-card that says that. No sense in beating around the *bush*."

"Good morning."

Jillian hopped off the counter.

"Hey, Brooke."

Jackson gave her a half-smile and went to his room.

"He didn't have to leave ... unless you two were talking about me?"

"No." Jillian laughed. "Unless you have pubic hair."

An uneasy smile tugged at Brooke's mouth. "I ... I have some."

Jillian's smile doubled. It wasn't a question and the fact that Brooke shared that personal bit of information with her was too hard to take seriously. "A landing strip?"

"Huh?"

Jillian shook her head. "Never mind. So how'd you sleep?"

Brooke shrugged, taking a seat at the table. "Honestly, not so good. I can't stop thinking about Cage. He's not going to take the news about AJ very well. He idolizes his dad. That's why he's here. Cage couldn't wait to graduate high school so he could move closer to AJ."

"Then I'm even more surprised AJ's parents want him to move to Portland and leave Cage behind."

Brooke gave Jillian an uneasy look. "Cage is one of the reasons they want him to come to Portland. They don't want him feeling the burden of being pulled between football, school, and AJ's treatment. And ..."

"And?"

Brooke released a heavy breath. "Jim's worried that AJ could do something."

"Something?"

A single nod. "He thinks AJ could become suicidal if or when things get bad."

Every ounce of her wanted to refute what Brooke said, but she couldn't. Of course AJ would rather die than live in misery or be a burden to anyone around him. Jillian would have been the same way.

The dense silence weighed heavily in the room.

"So, anyway, are you joining us at Lilith's for tea and coffee in a little bit?"

"I have something I need to do before we leave for the game later."

Brooke nodded. "Okay, well I'll see you a little later then."

Jillian's mouth pulled into a tight smile.

———

Dark, full clouds stretched for miles. Mother Nature painted the sky to match the mood. Perhaps it was to give the Monaghan family permission to feel sad. So much sadness.

"Jillian." Jim answered the door. "I assumed you'd be having coffee with the ladies."

"Not this morning. Is AJ here?"

"He's still asleep. I didn't want to wake him. Char said he was awake most of the night. Migraine."

She frowned. Guilt for not being there seeped into her conscience.

"I'll tell him you stopped by when he wakes."

There was no need. Jim didn't know Jillian and since he said she should leave, then he most certainly didn't understand her relationship with his son.

"Actually, I'm going to peek in on him." She stepped past him, not waiting for his approval.

"I'm not sure that's the best id—"

"It's fine. You should go see if Dodge needs an excuse to leave the hen house."

"Well, okay ... I guess."

"Bye, Jim." She waved without another look back.

The room was black, trapped in silence until Jillian gently shut the bedroom door behind her. Breathing in a shaky breath, she slipped off her boots and clothes, then slid under the sheet.

AJ didn't move. Pressing her lips to his shoulder, she waited to feel his heart ... waited to feel his next breath. His chest rose and fell in a long, relaxed breath, and she sighed.

"I'd take it from you if I could. You have so much more to live for than I do," she whispered, resting her hand against the side of his head as he continued to sleep. "I forgive you." Uninvited tears stung her eyes. "I know you're going to leave me." She bit her upper lip, hard. "It's okay to go. They need you more."

Maybe someday it would be okay for her to need someone more than anyone else. Then again, maybe she *was* the ultimate survivor and needed no one. Who could live like that?

"What if I need *you* more?" AJ whispered, startling Jillian.

Resting her cheek on his back, she snaked her arms around his waist. He grabbed her hands and squeezed them, wringing the tears from her eyes—the life from her soul.

"Then I'm the luckiest woman alive. And I know I am ... but not because you're going to stay. It's because I've had the privilege of loving a man that's going to be completely selfless and go home for all the right reasons."

"I have season tickets to Cage's games. I want you to go to them ... all of them."

She squeezed his hands back. So. Very. Tight. "K."

"And I want you to make sure he stays out of trouble. I know that's a tall order for you."

Jillian smiled.

"When?"

"When?" he questioned.

"When are you leaving?"

His chest expanded slowly. He inhaled a deep breath, the kind that gave one courage. "I'm going back with them tomorrow."

She held her breath. She held everything completely together—absolutely still.

"Jillian?"

"Hmm?"

He rolled over and pulled her into his arms. The

desperation in their embrace crushed something inside her. Something that could never be repaired.

"I need you to be okay with this. You are the strongest person I have ever met, and I've met some really strong people. If you can't do this, I won't be able to either."

That strength he referred to had become her greatest weakness. A burden—a curse.

"Tell me you'll be okay."

A little girl's voice—the one she heard when Claire died, the one that wept for her parents, and the one that whispered goodbye to her heart in argyle socks—it screamed so loud.

I'm not okay. I'm not strong. I'm not anything you think I am!

"I'll be okay," she whispered.

***

CAGE JAMES MONAGHAN came into the world at six fifty-five in the evening on August third. It was the only time Brooke had seen AJ cry. He held his son in his arms and promised to give him everything.

AJ added father to his list of failures in life, but Cage never did. While he loved his mother, he wanted to be with his father the hero. It was bittersweet trying to live up to the rock star status Cage had bestowed upon him. The gifted son of the fucked-up war veteran grew up to be a good man, a hard working student, and an amazing quarterback. All despite AJ's influence.

The packed stadium roared to life as the sun made a brief appearance to say everything would be okay. Cage would be okay.

AJ didn't keep track of the score. He watched his boy

light up the field, his ex-wife cheer on their son, his parents beam with pride every time Cage completed a pass, and the deflated woman who took so much more than he ever imagined he had to give.

Jillian clapped when the crowd clapped and stared at the field the entire time. He heard her every word that morning. Felt the depths of her grief—saw the vacant look in her eyes. Every day he saw deeper into her heart ... into her past. In such a short amount of time the things he hated most about her turned into the things he couldn't imagine living without.

If she ever stopped getting the mail in her boots and panties, it would be the greatest crime ever at Peaceful Woods. The sex toy consultant with a Harley—that was Jillian. That was the woman he loved. That was the woman he fucked like his life depended on it. Somehow he knew the last image he would ever have would be of her.

"Good game, huh?" His dad rested a firm hand on AJ's shoulder as the team walked off the field, celebrating their first victory.

AJ nodded. The time came for him to rob all of that happiness from Cage, tearing his world apart before saying goodbye, forever.

Everyone met up for dinner. The bar and grill bulged to capacity with rowdy victory partying. AJ didn't rush anything. He gave his family time to share a meal, laugh, and celebrate. After the last bite, final beer, and check paid, his parents went home with Brooke's husband, their girls, and Jillian. AJ and Brooke drove back to Cage's place, and they ended his world as he knew it. Their two-hundred pound grown son sobbed like a little boy in his daddy's arms. A Band-Aid, kiss, and sucker couldn't fix it. Nothing could fix the ugliest part of life that knocked on AJ's door.

Cage promised to come visit the first weekend he had off. He also promised AJ that he wasn't dying. His son held the same optimism Char and Brooke clung to. *That* he could have. AJ wouldn't take that from any of them. After all, what's left when all hope is gone?

Jillian. That's who remained when all hope faded into darkness. After the drive home with Brooke, he took a long shower. He closed his eyes and let his tears mix with the water and soap that he massaged through his hair. He cried for the boy who loved him so unconditionally, the father to the grandchildren he would never meet, the man who would do things so much bigger, so much better than AJ ever could.

"I'm so ... very ... sorry."

He knew she'd come. She was his real. The keeper of his past. The defender of his honor. The breath he needed to get to the next one.

"Why?" His voice broke as he turned and fell to his knees at her feet.

She ran her hands through his hair as he hugged her waist. "I've had too many opportunities to contemplate death. I think it's different for everyone, but for me ... when my time comes, I won't ask any questions. I'll simply say *thank you*." Her words fell upon him, soft and steady.

He looked up at her and after a long moment, he nodded. Then he dried them off and led her to his bedroom.

"Jill—"

She pressed her finger to his lips as he sat on the bed before her. "Show me."

He nodded again and then he showed her. When he

filled her, he rushed nothing. There was no hurry. All they had was now. Their hands caressed for a final lasting memory. Their lips said goodbye over and over. Their tears released the anger ... the unfairness of it all. Then with a final thrust, he spilled into her with an angry grunt. The kind that said fuck you world. Fuck you cancer. Fuck you PTSD.

He fell asleep in her arms and woke beside a note.

Thank you. ~J

"Good bye, Jillian Knight," he whispered, folding the note.

CHAPTER TWELVE

IT RAINED for almost forty-eight hours straight, a few weeks too late for the brown lawns and cracked fields to make a comeback with fall just over the horizon. Even the residents of Peaceful Woods agreed to stop watering the lawns and simply succumb to the inevitable.

Ryn received a message from AJ that he no longer needed her services. He thanked her for all the years she worked for him and promised to write her a glowing recommendation to keep on file for future clients. She didn't call him back. The message was brief, melancholy, and a little haunting. The For Sale sign in his yard explained the termination of services, but it took her by surprise, given his relationship with Jillian.

After a mad dash in the rain to the Knight's front door, she paused to take a few deep breaths. She hadn't seen or talked to Jackson since he took her home Friday night. She invited him in, but he insisted it wasn't a good idea until she took care of the needed "preparations." Her face flushed every possible shade of red, and that's when he kissed her— the complete opposite of a chaste kiss. It held so much promise, leaving no confusion as to his intentions ... his plans for her.

It took a full twenty-four hours to wipe the smile off her face. In a moment of insanity, she trimmed her girly parts then shaved them bare for the first time ever. It certainly made her look younger—like ten—at least in the pubic region. Sadly, she failed to consider the side effects. The worst being red bumps and itching. Dogs with fleas didn't scratch as much as she had been scratching down below. Lotion and body oil failed to provide relief. As long as she didn't touch the area or rub against anything she was fine.

"Ryn." Jackson dragged her name into two long syllables, like a jungle cat purring it.

"Mr. Knight." She squeezed past him, making sure their bodies didn't touch.

"Mr. Knight, huh?"

"Yes. I'm working ... for you. It might be a good idea to keep things professional while I'm here."

"That sounds like a terrible idea." He towered behind her, bending down to kiss the back of her neck.

A flush of heat spread along her skin in spite of the shiver his touch evoked. "So ... why is AJ selling his place?"

"Because he's dying."

Ryn turned toward the scratchy voice. Jillian emerged from her bedroom resembling something like roadkill.

"Welcome back, Sis."

She brushed past him, wearing her panties and a shrunken red tank top, hair matted to her blotchy face. Although they were siblings, it was still a little awkward for Ryn.

"What do you mean he's dying?" she asked in a small voice.

Jillian opened the refrigerator door. Jackson looked at her with a mild frown before moving his focus back to Ryn.

"He has a cancerous tumor in his brain, so he's moving back to Portland with his parents. Treatment doesn't look promising."

A sting of emotion pricked the corners of her eyes. Ryn rarely saw AJ, but there was something about being in his home around his personal belongings that lent a sense of familiarity, a feeling that she knew him better than she really did.

"Jillian ... I'm so sorry." Ryn rested her hand on her chest, maybe to comfort her own heart, maybe because she felt the pain in Jillian's.

Grabbing two things from the refrigerator Jillian placed them on the counter and stared at them: a bottle of Heineken and a juice box. Jackson opened the beer and dumped its contents down the drain. Jillian had no reaction. He inserted the bendy straw into the juice box and placed it in her hands.

"You've got this," he said to her with a whisper of sympathy as he kissed the top of her head.

Ryn fell hard for Jackson, the way someone slips at the top of a steep hill and tumbles to the bottom, gaining speed and momentum the whole way down. She tried to stop it, but the force—his gravitational pull—was too strong. With each passing second her heart fell for that man ... the one who loved his sister so completely.

Jillian looked at Ryn. A sad smile worked its way to her lips. "I'm going to pull it together soon, and then we'll start planning the wedding." She brushed past her with a zombie's gait, straight to the bedroom and shut the door.

With wide eyes, she looked at Jackson.

"What?" He shrugged while biting back his shit-eating grin.

"You told her we're getting married?"

"I may have mentioned it."

"It's a game, a-a ridiculous joke ... some sort of twisted improv." Her hands flailed in the air.

The dramatic emphasis to her point didn't faze him. Narrowing his eyes, he rubbed his chin. "I'm sensing some sort of apprehension from you."

"Apprehension? We've known each other for two seconds!"

"True." He nodded. "But they've been the best two seconds of my life. I want more ... more seconds with you."

Flip flop. Head-over-heels. Tumbling down.

"I need to get to work, Mr. Knight."

He killed her every time with his sexy grin. Backing her against the wall, he cradled her face and kissed her unconscious. Every time—a total blackout.

The white tape on the bridge of his black glasses came into focus first when she opened her eyes. "I've been meaning to ask ... Why are your glasses taped together?"

He released her face, straightening to his full height. "Because Jillian busted them."

"Why don't you get a new pair?"

"Because Jillian would stop rolling her eyes every time she saw me."

"And that's a bad thing?"

"Yes." His gaze melted over her body. Then he traced her lips with the pad of his index finger, trailing it slowly over her chin, down her neck, making a straight line to her breast. Stopping on her nipple, he circled once, bringing it to an embarrassingly hard peak before he grinned.

Smug bastard.

"Get to work, Miss Middleton."

With an overload of confidence, he strode away. A few seconds later she heard the back door to the garage shut. Finally, she could breathe again. His inappropriate touch matched his look. Everything about Jackson screamed inappropriate, dirty, and sinful. Two questions bubbled in her mind: why did she let him touch her like that, and why did he stop?

"I'm going to Lilith's."

Ryn jumped at the sound of Jillian's voice. "Sorry, you startled me." She hoped it would explain her red face and the light beading of sweat along her brow.

"Where's Jackson?" Jillian asked, pulling her wet blond hair into a pony tail as she slipped on her red rain boots.

Ryn took a deep swallow, gathering her senses. "Uh ... the garage, I think."

Jillian nodded. Opening the front door, she stopped and looked back at Ryn. "He likes you."

She rolled her eyes. "I'm sure he's liked a lot of women."

Jillian shook her head. "Truth?"

Ryn squinted a bit. Did she want the truth? After a few seconds, she nodded.

"My brother has fucked a lot of women, but I don't think he liked any of them. He liked sex. Period."

The door closed behind her leaving Ryn with *a lot* to think about.

As EXPECTED, Lilith waited for Jillian with a patient smile and eager ears. Dodge didn't say a word when she walked through the door. He just gave her a hug and a sad smile before leaving.

"He's not good with emotions."

Jillian nodded at Lilith. "There's really nothing to say."

"There's everything to say, dear. You let him go."

Jillian plopped down on the couch. "I did," she replied with a deep sigh. "It was never going to work out anyway. The guy refused to take me on a real date ... one with cloth napkins."

Lilith smiled. "You're an amazing woman."

"Well I don't feel so amazing right now."

"Is there anything I can do?"

Jillian closed her eyes. "Yes, you can just listen."

Day

"Dammit, Jones!"

Jessica jumped out of bed, leaving a mattress covered in tangled sheets and a collapsed wall of pillows, but no Luke. Then it registered, the angry voice came from the other room.

"What's going on?" she asked as Jones ran to her. Picking him up, she kissed his head.

Luke had a murderous look on his face as he scrubbed the floor on all fours, wearing a T-shirt and pajama bottoms. "I took *your* dog outside, but he refused to do his business, instead deciding to hold it until we came back up here."

She giggled, setting Jones down. He ran into his kennel as if he'd been sent to jail. Luke put the soiled paper towels in a plastic bag and washed his hands.

"Are you laughing at this situation?" The look he shot her over his shoulder would have killed a lesser woman.

"I can't even count how many times I've yelled 'Dammit, Jones,' but never at the dog."

Luke dried his hands. "I'm not laughing."

"Of course you're not." She bit her lips together.

He grabbed her arm and yanked her into his chest, stealing her breath. Then he turned them around and lifted her onto the counter. She ran her hands through the sexiest unkept hair ever.

"You woke up alive," she reminded him with a beaming smile.

Burying his face in the crook of her neck, he mumbled, "Indeed, I did." With a smooth, swift stroke he pulled her tank top off, returning his mouth to the sensitive skin of her neck. His hands cupped her breasts with firm pressure. "In fact..." his hands slid down and he curled his fingers around her panties, working them under her backside and down her legs "...I've never felt so alive."

"Luke," she whispered with an impatient need, grabbing the hem of his shirt.

He helped her by pulling it off and sliding down his pants. No underwear. She smiled. He smirked and it was so damn sexy.

The hiss of his breath filled the room as she stroked him. He rested his hands on her legs and closed his eyes, letting his chin drop to his chest.

"So I'm moving in?" He was steel in her hand, a pinch-me moment to think that she, fucked-up-in-the-head Jessica, had such a visceral effect on him.

Gripping her ass, he tugged her to the edge of the counter then pushed her legs apart. Looking into her eyes he promised her forever before his lips spoke the actual words. "I'm never letting you go."

She shivered as he slid inside her, claiming her lips with

his, her hair with his hands, and her soul with every beat of his heart.

"I'M DRIVING." Jessica punched as much confidence into her demand as possible when Luke picked her up to meet her family for dinner. They decided to wait until he met her parents before they jumped into cohabitation.

"Get in, babe." He shook his head as she went to open his door, but not before he slammed down the lock.

The scowl on her face held great promise of a beating later that night. She reined in her stubbornness and got in the passenger side, but only because they were going to dinner with her parents.

"If I didn't love you so damn much, I'd hate you for being so possessive and selfish. You have four siblings. How is it you don't know how to share?"

Luke smiled as he pulled away from the curb.

They were the last to arrive, only because her parents and Jude arrived early. It was no surprise they wanted to interrogate her brother to see what he knew about the man she deemed worthy of meeting her parents. Jessica's secret was safe, although Jude was not happy that her brilliant therapist had crossed all ethical lines with her.

"Hey!" She released Luke's hand to hug her parents as all three stood to greet them.

"This is a mistake," Jude warned in her ear when she hugged him.

"Shut it." She batted her eyes at him, feigning innocence. "Mom and Dad..." she gave Jude a barely-detectable scowl "...*and Jude,* this is Luke Jones, my ... boyfriend." She said it like a question as she looked up at Luke with a bit of apprehension. Boyfriend seemed so childish for a distinguished psychiatrist.

He kept his eyes and friendly smile focused on her family, so she assumed the label was okay.

"Luke, these are my parents, Grant and Sunny, and my brother, Jude."

"It's a pleasure to meet you." He shook their hands, then they all sat down at the table two seconds before the waiter rushed over to get their drink order.

Jessica ordered wine. Luke ordered beer—a local brew. Grant nodded in approval. Jessica rested her hand on Luke's leg. A silent thank you.

"So Jessica told us you're a doctor." Sunny smiled.

Yes, she had told them that, but they already knew. They knew more about Luke than she did. Since Claire's death, her father made every move Jessica made his highest priority. He and Jude had both offered to fill her in on all the details, but she didn't want to know, at least not that way. Luke would share his past on his own time.

"Yes. I'm a psychiatrist."

They nodded.

"Our daughter's psychiatrist?" Grant questioned.

That ... that was the one piece of information they didn't know. She begged Jude to keep it a secret, to make sure their father never found out.

"I was."

Jessica turned toward Luke. Stunned. There was no other word. Not in her wildest dreams did she imagine him telling them that, not with his professional career at stake. A bubble of silence enveloped their table.

Grant looked at Jude. Of course he wondered how that bit of information failed to make it to him. Jude glared at Jessica with apparent anger over the secrecy that was blown with two simple words from the good doctor himself.

Grant cleared his throat. He was a dark-haired, burly man with a Tom Selleck mustache. Most people found him intimidating. Jessica, however, was a daddy's girl and knew his softest side. That side wasn't on display during dinner. "And now you're romantically involved?"

"I'm in love with your daughter."

"Enough to risk ending your career?" her father continued as Jude and Sunny watched like spectators at a Wimbledon match.

Jessica feared the answer. The question weighed heavily on her own mind. Truthfully, she didn't know what she wanted his answer to be. Thinking of herself as a monster for so long made it easy to feel unworthy of Luke's love, and even more unworthy of him taking such a life-changing risk for her.

"Yes."

Sunny looked at Jessica, both of them teary eyed.

Grant nodded. "And dealing with her past?"

"It's my number one priority."

Another nod. "If you hurt her—"

"I'm certain I won't live to tell about it, sir." Luke smiled and finally, so did her father.

It seemed Luke had passed her father's test and everyone relaxed, except Jude. The thing she loved most about him was also the thing she hated the most. He believed no man would ever be worthy of his "little" sister. There was a better chance of San Andreas making Vegas a beach town than Jude accepting Luke as a worthy man.

"So ... we have a bit of news." Taking a breath of courage, she forced an uneasy smile.

"You're getting married?" Sunny jumped in with a

hopeful guess. Jessica inherited her mother's beaming smile, but not her curly auburn hair that she wore long and wild like the seventies hippy her name implied.

"Uh ... no." Jessica gave Luke an apologetic look. They had never discussed marriage. He almost went down that road, and perhaps he didn't care to do it again. It didn't matter to Jessica. She would take him however she could get him. Everything else was inconsequential details.

"You're pregnant?" Jude crossed his arms over his chest, a devilish grin on his face. The smug pot-stirrer knew better. He just liked fishing for a reaction. Some things never changed between them.

Sunny went from hopeful to terrified and Grant looked ready to kill.

"No! Jesus, Jude. Stop being such an ass."

The urge to stick her tongue out at him overwhelmed her. Another habit that felt impossible to break. However, the one thing she wanted more than to be that childish twin was to make Luke proud, so she pulled on her big girl pants to regain her composure.

"Luke got me a dog, Jones. He's amazing."

The frown on Luke's face showed his objection to that statement, but he didn't say anything so she continued.

"He asked us to move in with him and I said yes."

"You live in a safe part of town?" Grant asked.

Jessica rolled her eyes. It was a ridiculous question. In all his background checks, Luke's address had to be at the top of the list. It was possible he had a satellite put in space just to follow his daughter.

"Yes. It's a newer building with underground parking and video surveillance."

Jessica opened her mouth to speak, then closed it before the words came out. She wanted to remind her father that she had the skills to take care of herself, but once Claire died her father trusted no one, not even his own daughter.

"Well, I hope you two are happy and maybe someday you'll make a real commitment beyond just playing house." Grant tipped back his tall glass of beer, keeping his eyes on Luke.

"So ... shall we get the waiter back over here to take our order?" Sunny, God bless her, she knew how to save the day, even if she was the one to first mention marriage.

THEY SURVIVED DINNER, just barely. There wasn't much to say on the drive back to Jessica's. Luke shut off the engine and they both sat in more silence.

"I'm going to marry you." Luke kept his eyes trained on the parked car in front of them.

"You don't have to say that. It doesn't matter what they think. I'm not waiting for you to get down on one knee."

He climbed out of the car and opened her door, offering his hand. She took it and let him lead her up the stairs. Before she could fish out her keys, he kissed her. His touch healed her more than anything. Luke gave her strength, he gave her hope, he gave her life.

"I won't get down on one knee," he whispered over her lips. "I'll get down on both knees because I won't ask you to marry me, I'll beg you to marry me." Feathering his lips down her neck, he continued to whisper, "But for now, I need to give you back the life you lost. I want you whole ... complete. When I marry you, I don't want to share you with your past. I want it to only be us and our future."

She wrapped her arms around his neck and held onto him like her life depended on it, and maybe it did. "I love you ... I love you ... oh my God I love you so much." She hung from his neck and wrapped her legs around his waist.

He chuckled and kissed her on the lips at the same time. "Pack an overnight bag and we'll get the rest tomorrow. We need to get home and let your mutt out of his kennel."

Home.

They were going *home*. Really, Jessica was already there. Luke was her home. He would *forever* be her home.

CHAPTER THIRTEEN
KNIGHT

FORTY.

Over the hill.

The view was good from the other side. The forty-something had a birthday date with her twenty-something daughter and thirty-something boyfriend. Boyfriend? While the term implied something more than friends, "boy" screamed cradle-robbing cougar.

Jackson Knight had become more than a fun-banter-role-playing fantasy. She fell for him for one reason: he loved his sister. Who falls for a guy because he loves his sister? Someone who lived her entire adult life wishing a man would wrap her in his protective arms, kiss her on the head and say, "You've got this," in her darkest hour.

That man deserved to see Ryn in a new dress, one that said, "This is how sexy you make me feel." As an unexpected gift, Maddie rearranged her work schedule to spend the day with her. Though instead of a spa day, they decided on shopping, but only after Ryn agreed to buy Maddie a new dress as well.

The new adult age was a difficult time. She remembered it all too well. The early twenties felt like legal freedom without the maturity to go with it. Too old to justify holding onto the selfishness of adolescence, too young to really let it go. At least that's how Ryn saw it from the outside. She went from child to mother and skipped the wild freedom of her twenties.

"So tell me about this Jackson guy," Maddie asked as Ryn slipped into her black strapless dress that showed a lot of leg and too much cleavage that was not perky enough to hold it in place well. Maddie assured her she looked hot "for a mom."

As expected, she regretted caving to Maddie insisting she buy that dress. It didn't make her feel young, it made her feel like a forty-year-old woman trying and failing to hold onto her youth. But once she saw past her insecurities to the woman in the mirror, she had to admit the reflection had a little sex appeal going on in that dress.

Ryn turned, letting Maddie zip it for her. "He's from New York and he teaches piano lessons."

"Piano lessons? Really?" Maddie wrinkled her nose. "What is he like ... eighty?"

Nerves hijacked her body, starting with her heart pounding in her chest. They'd had dinner several times since she last cleaned his house, and each night ended with kissing that felt more like mouth fucking and Jackson's hands making bolder moves exploring her body, but always on the outside of her clothes. Wound tight and ready to self-combust was an accurate assessment by that point.

"Actually, he's a little younger than I am."

Maddie applied a thick coat of dark purple lipstick that looked quite hideous, but Ryn didn't dare say anything.

"Is he weird?"

Ryn laughed. "I don't know how to answer that. I'm not sure how your generation defines 'weird.'"

"Well, what kind of car does he drive?"

"A PT Cruiser." Ryn's voice bubbled with amusement.

Maddie paused mid stroke, wide eyes looking at Ryn's reflection in the mirror. "You're kidding."

Ryn shook her head.

"Oh my God, only old people drive those things. Is he short and suffering from male-pattern baldness? He wears plaid pants pulled up to his armpits with a bowtie and a fedora, doesn't he? Oh, Mom, you can do better than that."

"He's good looking. Just keep an open mind, okay?" She slipped into her black heels.

"Have grandma and grandpa met him?"

"No. This will be their first time meeting him as well."

"I'm sure they'll love him because he sounds nothing like Dad, which is unfortunate because all my friends think he's hot. It's pretty weird hearing that because he's my dad, but it's kind of cool too."

Ryn bit her tongue, she always did—but she wouldn't forever. Maddie's days of believing her father walked on water were numbered.

"So where is he taking us for dinner?"

"I don't know. Some place fancy I assume since he insisted we dress to the nines tonight."

"He's paying?"

Ryn nodded as they walked down the stairs with Gunner in tow.

"Is he rich?"

"I don't know anything about his bank account."

"Well he teaches piano lessons for God's sake, he can't be that rich."

"Money isn't everything, my dear child."

"Clearly it isn't to you, or you wouldn't have left Dad."

Another dig that kept getting harder to ignore.

"Oh my God, Mom!" Maddie called looking out the front window. "It's not just a PT Cruiser ... it's a purple PT cruiser with wood panels. It's totally like Barney meets National Lampoon's Vacation."

"Be nice, *please*." Ryn grabbed her purse and kissed Gunner on the head.

"Oh. Fuck ..."

"Madison!" Ryn scolded.

"Sorry but ... he ... he just got out. No way ... no freaking way." Maddie plastered her face and both hands to the window.

Ryn opened the door and stepped out onto the porch. Jackson grinned as he met her with a dozen red roses.

"Happy birthday, beautiful." He bent down and kissed her, keeping it PG ... maybe PG-13.

"Thank you." She smiled back, reaching up to rub the pad of her thumb along his lips to wipe off the transfer of lip gloss. "Let me just put these in water. Maddie!" She jerked her head toward the door when she saw her daughter still gawking in disbelief out the window.

Maddie peeked around the door.

"Maddie, this is Jackson Knight. Go say hi and *be nice* while I put these in a vase."

"Nice to meet you, Maddie." Jackson offered his hand.

Maddie took it and whimpered a little when the arm of his suit coat rode up enough to share a glimpse of a tattoo. "H-hi," she stuttered.

He released her hand, but hers stayed frozen in midair for a few seconds.

"You look beautiful in your dress as well, and you have your mom's eyes."

She nodded. It seemed as if that's all she could do. Maddie looked like a younger version of Ryn except with her dad's dimples. Maddie's pin-straight blond hair cascaded to her butt. She looked and carried herself with a model's posture, yet Jackson's eyes stayed on Ryn. Falling never felt so good.

"Ready?" Ryn asked, shutting the door.

Jackson offered one arm to Ryn and the other to Maddie, escorting them both to the car.

"Maddie's disappointed you're not balding or wearing a bowtie and fedora."

"Mom!" Maddie shrieked as Jackson opened the back door for her.

He chuckled. "At one time I had my head shaved. I considered getting a tattoo on the back of it, but it never happened."

Ryn had never seen her daughter stunned into complete silence. It was kind of nice for a change. Jackson shut Maddie's door and walked Ryn to the other side.

"Your dress is going to put an end to my celibacy," he whispered in her ear before opening her door.

She gulped, thankful for the pantyliner she decided to wear because only the hottest women wore them on dates.

"So be *prepared*." He pecked her cheek.

"O-kay."

That one word stutter of a response brought a seductive grin to his face as he opened her door. She couldn't stop thinking about that promise—a promise of sex—her age, her body, his past, his expectations, her minimal experience, his expertise. It overwhelmed her.

"So, Maddie, what made you want to become a lawyer?" Jackson asked.

After a few seconds of silence Ryn looked over her

shoulder at Maddie in the backseat. "Maddie, he asked you a question."

She closed her unhinged jaw and swallowed, eyes still glassy. "Uh ... money. And I like to argue."

Her mother smirked. "She won quite a few awards on the debate team in high school."

"I thought about law school at one point," he said.

"And you chose piano instead?" Maddie asked with a condescending edge.

"In college it's called music, but I didn't get a degree in music. It's just a hobby. If you don't have passion about your pursuit in life, it will never take you where you want to go."

"Pfft ... if I followed my true passion I would be in medical school at Harvard."

"Why aren't you?" Jackson looked at her in the rearview mirror.

"My dad won't pay for my college because *somebody* pissed him off. But I'm not mad at *him* ... my dad's the best and he still sends me a nice allowance for other things."

Another dig at Ryn. Jackson rested his hand on her leg, she returned a weak smile. Just because she'd learned to tolerate it, even expect it, didn't make it hurt any less.

Seeing the restaurant parking lot filled to capacity, Jackson let the ladies off at the front door and searched for a parking spot down the street.

Ryn's parents were already seated.

"Happy birthday, baby girl!" Her mom hugged her and so did her dad.

"Thank you."

"Where's this mysterious guy?" her dad asked.

"Oh my God." Maddie plunked down in her chair and rolled her eyes. "Wait until you meet him. He's so out of her league. No offense, Mom. But seriously, guys like him don't date women in menopause. There must be something wrong with him ... like maybe he just got out of prison and he has mommy issues or—"

"Madison!" Ryn warned and Maddie jumped. "That's. Enough."

She wasn't in menopause yet, even if her hormones hadn't received that memo.

Maddie sank in her chair while messing with her phone. "Christ, Mom, you don't have to reprimand me like a child."

"Then stop acting like one."

"Okay, this is supposed to be a celebration. Let's all calm down a bit." Ryn's mom smiled as Jackson approached the table.

The birthday girl staving off anger to the point of near tears, forced a smile. The knowing look on Jackson's face confirmed she wasn't hiding it well.

"Jackson, these are my parents, Ryan and Lynn."

"Bet you can guess how my mom got her name," Maddie mumbled, still staring at her phone.

"Nice to meet you." Jackson offered his hand as both of her parents stared.

"Mom, Dad!"

They shook their heads. "Sorry, uh ... nice to meet you too. Thank you for inviting us to dinner," Lynn said as they took their seats.

"My pleasure. I'm quite fond of your daughter."

They nodded. Of course they wouldn't be as bold and inconsiderate to ask why, but Ryn could still see that question on their faces. In all fairness, she still pondered it too.

"We just want her to be happy."

"Done." Ryn smiled, looking over her menu. "Maddie, your friends can wait. Please put your phone away."

Maddie rolled her eyes again. The waitress took their drink orders, ending with Maddie.

"I'll have your most expensive scotch."

"Madison—"

"What? I'm twenty-one and Jackson is paying so ..."

Jackson grinned. "Absolutely. As long as you drink every last drop."

Maddie smiled, batting her eyelashes. "Of course."

The waitress brought their drinks and took their dinner orders. Maddie grimaced, taking a small sip of her Scotch. She might as well have ordered a glass of gasoline.

"I'm impressed a young girl like you enjoys Scotch. It's usually an acquired taste."

She took several big gulps of her water then cleared her throat. "Well I'm a lot more mature than what I'm sure my mother has led you to believe."

"Clearly." Jackson took a long pull of his beer then smiled at Ryn's parents. "Are you both retired?"

"Ryan is, he retired from Kiewit as a civil engineer. He worked there in Atlanta then transferred to Omaha when Ryn..." Lynn's eyes shifted to her daughter's "...needed us. I still work twenty hours a week as a pediatric nurse."

Ryn needed her parents when she decided to leave her abusive husband. It took an army of support to find the courage to leave the man who threatened to kill her.

"Look, it's Dad!" Maddie jumped out of her chair.

Ryn looked over her shoulder and froze. Jackson turned to watch Maddie run into the arms of a tall man with copper-blond and gray hair, a custom-tailored suit, and a gold Rolex.

"He can't be here," Lynn whispered to Ryan.

"I see my lovely wife is celebrating her fortieth birthday."

The hair on the back of her neck stood erect. Would she ever hear his voice and not tremble?

"You look amazing, Ryn ... you always did," he whispered in her ear.

"Can he join us?" Maddie beamed, but Ryn knew his being there was not a coincidence.

"No. He can't and I have a restraining order to prove it."

"Jesus, Mom, it's dinner. Not a reconciliation."

"Yeah, Ryn ... we both know the restraining order is because you can't control yourself around me. After all, that's why Maddie was conceived."

"TMI, Dad." Maddie rolled her eyes.

Jackson stood and offered his hand. "Jackson Knight."

"Preston Iverson." He sized Jackson up before accepting his hand.

"You should absolutely join us." Jackson signaled to the waitress, and she brought over another chair. "Here, you can sit by me."

"Perfect, Mr. Knight. I don't really like you sitting by my wife anyway."

"I'm not your wife." Ryn glared at Preston and then at Jackson for encouraging him to stay.

Jackson gave her a playful wink which only infuriated her more.

"Try some of this scotch, Daddy." Maddie slid over her glass while giving Jackson a challenging look.

Preston rested his hand on Ryn's leg. Her heart exploded as fear coursed through her veins. "My, my, when did you start letting our daughter drink scotch?"

She couldn't speak as tears stung her eyes.

Preston brought the glass to his mouth as Jackson rested a hand on the back of Preston's neck, his fingers on one side and thumb on the other.

"How's the scotch, Mr. Iverson?" Jackson asked.

Preston swallowed then coughed once before his eyes rolled back in his head. His limp hand slipped from her leg as the glass of scotch landed in his lap before his body collapsed to the side toward Jackson.

"Whoa!" Jackson kept him from falling to the floor.

"Daddy?" Maddie jumped up.

Jackson shrugged while gently easing him to the ground.

"Mom! Call 9-1-1."

Ryn couldn't move, let alone call for help, but a few seconds later one of the wait staff came over and let them know an ambulance was on the way.

"Is he breathing?" Ryn asked, not that she really cared. Preston Iverson had worked hard to earn her hatred to the point of wishing he were dead.

Jackson nodded. "I think he just fainted. Maybe he's diabetic."

Maddie hovered over him trying to wake him up as a path was cleared for the paramedics.

Preston came to as they loaded him on the gurney. Maddie insisted she follow the ambulance in her dad's car. No one objected.

"I want to go home." Ryn couldn't stop shaking.

"Sweetie." Her mom hugged her. "Don't let him ruin your day. Stay and eat."

"I can't." She shook her head.

"Maybe it is best to reschedule the party," Jackson suggested.

Her parents nodded with a mix of concern and anger on their faces. "Okay, we'll call you tomorrow, darling." Her dad hugged her. "Nice to meet you, Jackson."

He smiled, tossing a wad of cash on the table before

taking Ryn's hand and leading her from the restaurant. "Wait here while I get the car."

"No!" She grabbed his arm and bit her quivering lip. "Don't leave me."

His brows knitted together. "Okay, I've got you." Wrapping his arm around her waist, he led her to the car.

After they drove a few blocks from the restaurant, Ryn broke the silence. "Why did you invite the man who used to abuse me to eat with us? I still can't hear his voice without feeling his fist. Why would you do that?"

Jackson sighed. "I hate how you let your daughter treat you. You know damn well she's the reason he was there."

"She just doesn't understand."

"Well maybe it's time you explain it to her."

"What I tell my daughter and when I tell her is none of your business. And Preston ... you did something to him. I saw you with your hand behind his head. Did you inject something into him? God ... you're so stupid. Do you have any idea how much money that man has? He could destroy you."

He smirked. "I didn't inject him with anything. I simply applied a little pressure to his carotid arteries, causing him to take a little nap. The fact that Maddie chose to leave as well was just a bonus."

"That's my daughter you're talking about! You have no right to judge her. I can't be with someone who ... who ..." She searched for the right word as fire welled in her gut. Anger stole her voice, just as it always had with Preston. He beat her down, physically and emotionally, leaving her broken and mute.

"Don't get out," she warned, throwing open the door before the car came to a complete stop.

"Ryn—"

"I mean it." She hopped on one foot and then the other, removing her heels on the way to her porch.

Jackson jumped out. A few steps later Gunner greeted him with no intention of letting him go any farther.

"Can we talk about this?"

She turned. "Talk."

"Can you call him off?"

"Nope. Talk." She crossed her arms over her chest.

An older couple walking by on the sidewalk stopped.

"Is everything okay, miss?"

Jackson gave Ryn a pleading look.

"Yes, I've got it, but thank you." It pleased her that they stopped. Where were couples like them when Preston dragged her back into their house by her hair after she tried to flee?

"Well?"

He tipped his chin down but only for a moment before looking at her again. "I don't sugarcoat things. It's not my style, and it's not how I was raised. So here's the deal: I love being with you and it may sound crazy because we've known each other two seconds. But you're the last person I think about before I close my eyes and the first when I open them. Every day I don't see you feels like wasted time. But the look in your eyes when Maddie put you down and then again when Preston arrived at the restaurant ... it's like the light ... the *life* inside you just vanished. They've been this one-two emotional punch of physical and verbal abuse."

His brows pulled tight as if he felt the pain in his own words.

"The truth is not protecting Maddie, it's only hurting you. So it's up to you, Ryn. Coddle your grown child and just keep turning the other cheek until she breaks you ... because she will. But I can't stand idle and watch."

Until he turned to walk back to his car, she didn't notice the flood of tears streaming down her face. Jackson's words hurt, they even cut a little deep in parts of her heart. However, they felt real and completely different than anything Preston had ever done or Maddie had ever said. Perhaps, for the first time, it was the truth.

"Happy birthday, Ryn." His sad smile clenched her heart as he got in his car and backed out.

Forty sucked.

CHAPTER FOURTEEN

WITHIN ONE WEEK, fall graced Omaha with dropping temperatures, a sweet relief from the humidity. Nights were spent with windows cracked and a welcome break from the constant droning of air conditioners.

Jackson made a point of not being home when Ryn came to clean. The need to see her began to feel like toxic desperation. The need to let her figure out her own self-worth was greater.

Jillian refused to talk about AJ, and she refused to call him. She insisted he had her number and if he needed her he'd call. If not, she claimed to have made her peace with him and his situation. Jackson knew she'd put AJ on a shelf in her head, or maybe even her heart, close to Luke, and that's where he would stay—tucked away and separated from everything else in her life. It was the only way she could keep going.

"Ryn call?"

"Nope. AJ call?"

"Nope." Jillian poured a cup of coffee. "She's not dying so you actually have a case to plead."

"I already did."

"You insulted her daughter, and then you insulted her by implying her unconditional love somehow made her a doormat."

Jackson popped the top to a Red Bull. "That's what you got out of my explanation?"

"Yep and I'm a woman."

"So?"

"So she is too and if your sister, who lacks the female drama gene, thinks you were a bit harsh, then you were a bit harsh. Her daughter is an extension of herself, so basically you slapped her across the face and then punched her in the gut. Even if every word was true, and from what you've said I think it is, it doesn't make it any less insensitive."

"This ... this is the reason I used to get laid and then moved on. I don't speak 'woman.' Clearly I'm too much of a man to make a relationship work."

Jillian laughed. "So guys in relationships are not true men?"

"They probably were at some point, but I believe they had to remove one testicle to make the relationship work."

"Luke had two."

"Bullshit. You completely castrated him and just when he started to grow a new pair, you did it again."

"Wrong ... you're so very wrong. It was just the opposite. A guy has to have two huge balls of steel to be with me and you know it."

Jackson grinned. "It doesn't matter. Ryn never saw my balls anyway."

"Just as well. They really are the most unmanly part of the male body. I mean ... they're sensitive as hell and ugly, man are they ever ugly. Like twin turkey wattles. The penis is the only thing that saves you, and men with ED might as well trade it all in for a vagina because at that point it's nothing more than dead flesh that leaks like a hose."

He chuckled, rubbing his hands over his face. "See you just proved my point. You verbally attempt to castrate men all the time."

"You think?"

"I know. Lucky for me, I knew you before you had boobs and such a smart mouth. Remember those days? You know I caught you kissing one pillow and dry humping another while listening to "Baby One More Time."

The laughter that erupted from Jillian brought tears to her eyes and an even bigger smile to Jackson's face. "Oh my God! I was so embarrassed ... I still am."

"Well, put yourself in my shoes. Every time that song came on the radio I had the most awkward image of you and those poor pillows."

"Sorry, I didn't have a lock on my door like you. But don't think I didn't notice how many times mom asked you why there was always an odd number of dirty socks in your hamper when she gathered the laundry."

"That didn't last long. I eventually threw in an extra clean one to keep the number even." Jackson tossed his can into the recycle bin by the sink.

Jillian sighed. "It's crazy, but that was us when we were normal ... innocent. I miss those kids."

"We're still pretty awesome."

"Yeah..." she raised on to her toes and pulled him down to kiss his cheek with exaggerated smack "...at least to each other. Now ..." she headed toward her bedroom "...give up a testicle and call the girl."

Apologizing for whatever Jackson did wrong in the very complicated female brain required a grand gesture. There was no need to remove a testicle, even though they both retreated closer to his body reminiscent of a cold shower— just in case. It's as if they anticipated what was about to happen the closer he got to her house.

The sexiest ass in tight cut-off jeans greeted him as he pulled into her drive way. On all fours pulling weeds by the porch, she looked over her shoulder and wiped her brow. He liked her in that position—a little too much.

"Focus," he whispered to himself just before getting out of Woody.

Gunner charged him, halting Jackson's movements until Ryn showed enough mercy to call him back to the porch. It was progress.

"Hi." She stood and brushed the dirt from her legs then tugged off her gloves.

"Hi. I came to apologize."

"For what?"

That wasn't the response he expected. It was a test. It had to be a test. Women loved playing mind games. The probability of him passing it was not good.

"For last week."

"You're going to have to be more specific."

"For what I said on your birthday." His comfort zone retreated a good ten miles away.

"Which part?"

"The part about Maddie."

"You didn't mean it?" She stared at her fingernails, picking the dirt out from under them.

Of course he meant it. He wouldn't have said it if he didn't mean it. His poor testicles.

"I shouldn't have said it." Seemed like a safe answer.

"So you meant it, you just regret saying it to my face?"

The slit-eyed look she gave him said there would be no bonus points for honesty. He wasn't even in the same realm as his comfort zone anymore. Casual dating and random sex never required much thought or carefully plotted script. No wonder he'd been so good at it.

"I'm going to go with ... yeahhh—no?

"Yeahhh—no?"

A single slow nod. It was best to just stop talking.

Tilting her head to the side, she twisted her lips, eyes still narrowed. She was good—Jillian good—at ball busting.

"How am I doing?" she asked.

Gunner mimicked her head tilt as Jackson's eyes flitted between her and the dog.

"Uh ..." On the ride there he convinced himself she was worth it. Testicle-sacrificing worth it. At that exact moment he wasn't sure anyone was worth it.

"You have any balls left?" she grinned.

Jutting his head forward, his eyes widened for a second before narrowing into a scowl.

Her nose wrinkled. "Don't hate me. I decided everything you said was right, even if it did hurt. I'm going to have a talk with Maddie. She's just been too busy to make time. I tried calling you about twenty minutes ago. Jillian answered, you must have left your cell phone."

Jackson patted his hands over his pockets, she was correct.

"I called to apologize, hoping that it wasn't too late. You broke my heart a little when I cleaned your house and you weren't there. I thought you were really mad at me and didn't want to see me. But then Jillian explained the situation and..." she bit her lips together for a moment "...don't hate me, but she said I should make you sweat a little."

It was clear that Jillian craved the taste of her own blood. Jackson would happily oblige her as soon as he got home.

"Thanks for reminding me why I have meaningless, sex-only relationships." Turning, he walked back to his car.

SOMETHING WENT HORRIBLY WRONG. Ryn watched in shock as he returned to his car. The only part of a man more sensitive than the aforementioned testicles was the male ego —like a Georgia peach.

"Well ... wait! Oh my god! You're really mad. It was a joke. I'm sorry." She chased after him.

When she grabbed his arm, he turned, wearing the biggest shit-eating grin ever. He looked like a joker.

"You! Not. Funny." Pointing her finger at him, she gave him a cold glare. There were two possibilities: kill him or attack him. A week and a half earlier, after Jackson took her home on her birthday, she swore things couldn't get worse. They did. She started her period.

Hello ovulation.

Ryn thought about sex all the time. Not normal fleeting thoughts of sex. Forty-year-old-whacked-out-hormones type thinking about sex. Woman-who-hadn't-had-sex-in-a-very-long-time type of thoughts. When images of having sex with Humpty Dumpty—the mailman with a combover—in his white box on wheels crossed the conscious part of the brain, it was time for therapy.

"I'm extremely funny. What are you talking about?"

"I..." she shook her head with a soft chuckle "...I don't know how to navigate this. Maddie came along before I had a chance to experience my young, vibrant, and wild years. The longest relationship I've had, outside of my debacle of a marriage, lasted two months and that was five years ago."

"So?"

"So..." she shrugged "...what is this with us? If not random sex, what's in it for you?"

Drawing in a long breath, he wet his lips. "I'm not sure how to answer that."

"Because you don't know?"

With a slow head shake, he bit the corner of his lip. "No. I know. I'm just unsure if you want the truth or if you want me to say what you want to hear ... which might not be the truth."

In all honesty, she didn't know either. Maybe it was too soon to even worry about defining their relationship or think very far into the future. Time wouldn't make the conversation easier, so she chose to hear the truth.

"I want the truth."

There wasn't a second of hesitation before he answered with steadfast resolution.

"I want a wife. I want kids. I want home to mean something so much greater than an address. I want sex, lots of sex, with the same person for the rest of my life."

Once again, that decade between them spanned the distance of eternity.

He shrugged as she gave him a blank look. "You wanted the truth."

"I did." Ryn nodded slowly.

"So ... it's your turn. What do you want?" He leaned back against his car, hands shoved into his front pockets.

"Wow," she breathed. "I haven't given it much thought. My mind is always in the past, reliving that whole nightmare. I guess I'm just so grateful to be alive and out of that situation that I've never allowed myself to think very far into the future."

"Except for our wedding. You *did* agree to marry me."

"Except for that." She winked, giving him a big smile. Talking about their imaginary wedding shot to the top of her favorite pastime list.

"Today. If you could do absolutely *anything* right now, what would it be?"

Keeping her gaze locked to his, she stared and then stared some more. The smile on her face grew with each passing second.

"Truth?" she asked.

"Always."

"I want to see your tattoos ... *all* of them."

———

TRUTH OR DARE TURNED into a bad idea, times ten. Sex. Would it have really been so hard to just ask Jackson for sex? Instead, they were engaged in the most awkward game of show and tell ever. Times ten.

"I was kidding." She wasn't.

Ryn chewed her lip like rawhide as she sat on her bed— nerves of a virgin or sacrificial lamb. The exact second after her wish tumbled from her lips, Jackson grabbed her hand, dragging her inside the house and straight to her bedroom.

He shrugged off his shirt. She gulped.

"Uh ... the blinds are open."

He unbuttoned his jeans. She gulped again.

"Maybe ... um, maybe that's enough. My God, you look like a human canvas. It's uh ... a lot to take in all at once. We should maybe do this in phases."

He smirked. Confidence bled from every inch of him.

Where to begin? The man was born to be inked. A few bold black words interspersed with intense colors: roses, hearts, branches, a dragon, numbers aligned in dates, musical notes.

"Are you hungry?" Ryn squeaked. "It's getting late. You know what they say about eating after eight at night. It ... it all goes to your ass."

He turned his back to her and slowly slid down his pants and briefs at the same time. She no longer could swallow. Her mouth fell open. Drooling came next.

"Oh ... okay, I see that's not an issue for you."

He stepped out of his jeans, completely naked before her. "Do I meet your expectations?"

The room felt smaller, too much light, not enough air.

"Exceeded," she whispered with a breathy voice.

Jackson turned around. He deserved a medal or at least a high five or fist bump. Touching him, however, was *not* a good idea.

"Take your time. My eyes will wait for yours."

Ryn nodded once. Yes, she stared at his junk which was far from junky looking. Everything was grand and perfectly structured. It all hung quite well. It was definitely more of a package. A very impressive package. UPS had nothing on him.

What seemed like a week later, she blinked and met his patiently waiting eyes. "Kudos to your parents. Really just..." she popped her lips "...yup."

"Do you have any tattoos to show me?"

"No ... nothing, nada, zip, zero, zilch." Long after zilch she continued to shake her head. Of course her eyes had slipped a bit south again. "Stretch marks. I have a few 'pregnancy tattoos.' And I have a nice C-section scar."

The giggles came out of nowhere. Ryn covered her face

and laughed. "What are we doing? Put your clothes back on ... this is too weird."

A minute or so later, she felt his hands wrap around her wrists, uncovering her face. Taking a tiny peek with one eye first she opened her eyes. The details of his body could never be erased. Panning her gaze around the room, she looked at everything but him. The moss green walls adorned with pewter-framed photos of Maddie served as a nice distraction, so did the sheer white curtains dancing in the breeze of the open window. Shifting her eyes to the floor around her, she frowned at the dull, scratched wood that needed to be refinished. Finally, she elevated her eyes to meet Jackson's, which were level with hers as he waited on his knees before her.

"Hi." He smiled, fully clothed again.

"Hi." It was impossible to not smile back.

"Were you laughing at me?"

"No." She laughed again, but not at him. "It's just ... it felt like we were two young kids sneaking into the bedroom to show each other our private parts. When I was seven, I remember my mom walking in on me and my cousin. It wasn't sexual or anything like that. It was just a show-me-yours-and-I'll-show-you-mine moment of sheer curiosity."

"What did your mom do?"

Ryn shrugged. "Well, you know, she's a nurse so she asked us if we'd had enough time to check everything out. Then she asked us if we had any questions. We honestly didn't know if what we'd done was wrong. Remember, we were seven. We both shook our heads. Then she whispered that once you're seven, little girls are not allowed to see naked boys and little boys are not allowed to see naked girls. Then she said she'd let it slide since we'd both recently turned seven, as long as we promised to never do it again."

Jackson chuckled. "Your mom was pretty cool."

"Yes, she still is."

"There's only one minor flaw in your story."

Ryn narrowed her eyes. "What's that?"

"Today ... I showed you mine, but you didn't show me yours." Strong hands gripped her legs as long fingers slid higher, stopping just under the frayed edge of her very short cutoffs.

A nervous chuckle rattled in her chest. "Yeah, about that ..."

Jackson dropped his head in defeat.

"I fear you have these expectations, given your past and all, so ..."

Two perfectly-arched brows looked up at her. "Expectations?"

"Yes, like um..." she rolled her eyes to the ceiling "...say you lived by the ocean and then someone showed you their pond. You wouldn't be impressed."

He shrugged a single shoulder. "I might be."

Ryn shook her head in defiance. "No. There's just no way you could be."

"The ocean is big, but it's also very dangerous—sharks, jellyfish, tsunamis, pirates. Maybe I don't want the massive crashing waves and the fear of being pulled under by the tide, feeling lost at sea. Maybe I want the serenity of a pond and the way it reflects the beauty of everything around it."

"Maybe you're crazy." Pressing her palms to his cheeks, she grinned.

His eyes homed in on her lips, sending her heart into a frenzy, waking all the butterflies in her tummy. She felt so alive.

"Ryn," he whispered a second before his lips brushed hers. "Let me swim in your pond."

She laughed. It didn't matter that his thumbs were half an inch from her wet panties. It didn't matter that his lips were sealed to hers. It didn't even matter that his tongue teased the tip of hers. She laughed.

Jackson sighed while sitting back on his heels, head bowed again.

With a quick hand she covered her mouth, hiding her smile and stifling her giggles. "I'm so sorry." The sound of her laughter abated though it still shook her whole body. "But you did not just ask to 'swim in my pond.' Did you?"

Scrubbing his hands over his face, he grumbled something indecipherable. Standing with one swift motion, he walked toward her door.

"Don't leave! I'm sorry. I couldn't help it. Give me another chance." Once again she chased after him.

His long legs made quick strides to his car.

"Where are you going?" she called, throwing open the screen door.

"I'm going to figure out a way to be with you *and* keep my testicles."

CHAPTER FIFTEEN

A CHILLY BURST of air breezed past Jackson when he opened the back door to their townhouse. The smell of burnt popcorn hung like fog as he pulled his T-shirt up to cover his nose. Every window in the place was open to its max. It felt like an arctic gust whipping through their house.

Jillian sat perched on the counter, legs criss-crossed, with a heavy red hoodie shielding her from the temperature that read fifty-five degrees on the thermostat. She poked around her bowl of popcorn, tossing five black kernels in the sink for every one brown piece she deemed edible.

He needed some guy friends. Stat. The women in his life were hell-bent on testing his last bit of patience.

"Want some?" Jillian looked up from the bowl.

"What do you think?"

She shrugged. "Damn bag got away from me. I set it to five minutes, but I go by the time between pops and—"

"I don't care." He grabbed a beer from the refrigerator.

Sliding her fingernail between her teeth to free a hull, she watched him guzzle the contents all at once. After tossing it in the recycle bin, he fetched another one.

"Someone's grumpy. I am too, but you go first."

Catching his breath after the marathon beer chug, he glared at her. "New rule. If I leave my phone behind you don't answer it. And if you ever discuss my *testicles* with someone again, I will make your life a living hell. Got it?"

Wrinkling her nose, she lifted her shoulders. "Sorry. I was just trying to help. I take it, it didn't go so well?"

Finishing his second bottle, he tossed it then rested his hands on his hips. "Let's see ... after I called her bluff on the devious little ruse you plotted, things went good ... really good. Then they went not so good, then really good again ... then bad ... really, really bad."

Dumping the remaining charred pieces of popcorn into the trash, she brushed off her hands. "Lucky for you, I have the patience to deal with your code talk. The first good?"

"She asked to see my tattoos. *All* of them."

"Sex?" Jillian perked up.

"Not even close."

"You completely stripped for her and it didn't end in sex?" Jillian's jaw dropped. "Has that ever happened to you before?"

"*Never.*"

"ED?"

"Fuck you."

She chuckled. "The not so good?"

"She laughed. Apparently it brought back some childhood memory for her."

"That's odd. So what was the really good again?"

He smirked. "She got all insecure on me, comparing other women I've been with to the ocean and herself to a pond. I told her I prefer ponds. There was some kissing that felt like it was going somewhere then ..."

"Then?"

"Then she laughed again, really hard."

"Why?"

"Because of something I said. God!" He pressed the heels of his hands to his eyes and shook his head. "I know better than to chat it up, but she's different, so I thought I needed to say something. Something romantic. Something profound."

"*Aaand?*"

With a grimace, he looked at Jillian. "I asked her to ... let me swim in her pond."

Sister dearest bit back her laughter and just nodded, but tears welled in her eyes. "Well ... I'm not sure how romantic or profound it was." She snorted a little laugh that had to escape. "But, you could have said worse things. You could have asked to dock your vessel in her canal. That is ... if you wanted to stay with the nautical theme of the evening."

Another snort of laughter.

"Downstairs. It's cold as fuck in here and I need to warm up. Kicking your ass should light a nice fire in my belly."

"Wait." The laughter evaporated and what she had to say dissolved her smile. "I need to show you something." Retrieving her phone from the pocket of her hoodie, she held it up.

Colossians 3:5-6

Jackson read it then inspected the phone. "This is your new phone?"

A nod.

He Googled it because he wasn't sure of the exact verses, but he knew it had something to do with sin.

"Mortify therefore your members which upon the earth;

fornication, uncleanness, inordinate affection, evil concupiscence, and covetousness, which is idolatry.

For which things' sake the wrath of God cometh on the children of disobedience:"

Jillian snatched her phone back. "You and your King James Version." She did her own Google search. "Put to death therefore what is earthly to you: sexual immorality, impurity, passion, evil desire, and covetousness, which is idolatry. On account of these the wrath of God is coming."

"Yeah, that's what I said." Jackson grabbed her phone away.

"Maybe ... maybe we should go in."

Jackson's focus shifted from the phone to his sister. "Go in?"

"Back to G.A.I.L until this gets figured out. Or maybe we should request a new location, new identities. Omaha isn't exactly some small town. Obviously our identities have been compromised. Now we're just being taunted."

"First, *we* are not being taunted. You are. Second, why were you not suggesting relocation and all this after the first two messages? Could it have had anything to do with *you* having a reason to stay? But now AJ's gone so you want to just up and leave?"

"I'm just saying ... it's a new phone and I'm still getting these cryptic messages."

"Who have you given your new number to?"

Jillian shrugged. "I don't know ... AJ, Dodge and Lilith, Cage, a few people with Lascivio, mowing man Bill."

"AJ—"

"Oh for the love of Pete! Stop it. AJ. Loves. Me. He's not stalking me. Why would he move back to Portland? Isn't it a little hard to stalk someone from halfway across the country?"

"Then it's Lilith. She lied to you about being deaf. I'm sure she's lying to you about keeping your past a secret. I should have removed her. Listening to your womanly intuition about her was a big mistake. It's clear after today that all women are fucking head cases."

Jillian gave her customary eye roll. "You're so delusional. I think your case of blue balls has affected your brain."

He tossed her phone to her. "I'm not leaving. Now *I* have a reason to stay."

"You're staying for a woman who can't stop laughing at you long enough to have sex with you?"

Someone begged for a beating. "If I wanted to have sex with her ... we would have sex." He held his scowl even though what he'd just said registered a second too late. Of course Jillian didn't waste a single moment before jumping all over it.

"So ... even today, when you were standing in front of her *naked*, you didn't *really* want to have sex with her?"

"That's not how I meant it. I don't want just sex with her. I want more. The more is getting in the way. It's turned sex into a delicate situation."

"It's turned you into a pussy."

"Fu—"

"I know ... fuck me. But seriously. She's forty. I bet she's dying to have a shit load of meaningless sex with a hot guy while her hips can still thrust without fracturing. You're trying to court her. You know what happens in those old movies where the well-mannered, high-society guy tries to be a gentleman and court the lady?"

Jackson rolled his eyes to the ceiling and shook his head.

"The sweaty stable boy with bulging muscles, ripped pants, and old leather boots swoops in and fucks her like a wild animal in the tall grass near the river. And *that's* who she ends up with at the end of the story, because no matter what women say about chivalry ... they don't really want a guy who's going to spread a blanket out under a tree and feed them grapes and cheese cubes. They want a guy who's going to spread their legs, bury his face, and feed himself without first asking permission to 'swim in her pond.'"

"Damn..." he exhaled a heavy breath "...I've lost my sex mojo."

CRICKETS CHIRPING.

The pitter patter of the pond fountain.

The occasional popping of a motorcycle on the main road.

The windows were closed, yet Jackson heard every little sound as red numbers on his digital night clock flicked to midnight.

Two beers and clumsy sparring with Jillian should have slam dunked his brain into a deep coma. It didn't. All he could think about was Ryn. She didn't wear an anorexic body or grin like a clown from Botox. Her breasts were real and they didn't stand out. If he looked closely, a few fine lines around her eyes were visible. He hadn't seen her stretch marks or her scar from childbirth, but she confessed it. They didn't meet at a bar and fuck in the bathroom or alley ... most of his conquests never even made it to his car, let alone his house.

Truth? What he'd done with women in the past could hardly be considered dating. It was more fucking about. Two people using bodies for pleasure. There were never emotions, at least not for him. Any girl pathetic enough to mistake a quick fuck for something more, especially when names were rarely exchanged, had bigger issues than Jackson.

What makes a man so callus, so immune to emotions, so obsessed with instant gratification? A secret. The kind of secret that one person alone has to keep to himself for eternity. The kind of secret that shatters lives, destroys families, and ends in blood.

Jude Day had a secret. A secret that annihilated everything he believed to be true and forever changed his perception of his parents. Jackson Knight needed to believe that secret would remain buried in San Francisco. His entire existence clung to the hope of new beginnings.

The night stretched on, dragging him in and out of restless sleep. He didn't wait for the sunrise. It never waited for him. Rubbing his face like he could erase the previous day, he lumbered from his bed straight into his running attire. Five miles later, he returned for a shower, Red Bull, and protein drink. The day required an extra boost of ... everything.

After a string of agonizing piano lessons with women who were not serious about playing the piano, he texted Ryn, saying he had something to show her. It was the truth, of sorts.

"Jackson?" Greta called before he could shut the car door.

He shut it anyway then rolled down the window.

"You on your way out?" she asked with a labored breath from crossing the street.

He made a mental note to not get old. "Nope. Just keeping Woody company."

Her brows pulled together.

"Yes." He chuckled. "I'm on my way out."

"Oh." She nodded, maintaining her confused look. "You're a funny guy."

"I try. What's up?"

"I'm having a party at my house next week, and Jillian said you have a lady friend now. Guess you couldn't wait forever for Marvin to die." She winked, but it resembled more of an out-of-control eye spasm or an eyelash in her eye. "Here's an invitation for you to give her. We'd all love to meet her."

"Oh." Jackson took the shiny black envelope, inspecting both sides. It looked familiar. "What kind of party is it?"

"Well, a Lascivo party of course."

"W-what? Are you serious?"

"Yes. After the ValuPak incident, it's time to show Marvin that I'm not all dry and shriveled up. I'm still a vivacious woman at heart, even if my body is a little slower and not as flexible. Jillian said you're never too old to nurture your sexuality."

Jackson rubbed his chin, nose wrinkled a bit. "She did, did she?"

"She sure did. Marvin can ValuPak it all he wants, because after my party I'll no longer be requiring his *services*, if you know what I mean."

He didn't or at least he sure as hell didn't want to, but on a sigh he asked the obvious question anyway. "What was the ValuPak incident?"

"Jillian didn't tell you?"

Head shake.

Making her usual quick scan as if anyone in the hearing-aid community could really hear her, she leaned in closer to the window. "You know that ValuPak envelope of coupons everyone gets in the mail?"

A nod.

"Well, sometimes there are coupons for bras and other feminine things. So last week I stepped out into the garage to get my flyswatter that hangs by the door, and you wanna know what I saw?"

He didn't. He really didn't.

"Marvin sitting in a lawn chair by his work bench *playing* with himself while he had three of the coupons from the ValuPak stuck to the side of the bench with magnets. One was for a bra sale at Penny's, one was for a thirty-day trial at a fitness studio, and the other was for Hardee's. Everyone knows the hot women on those commercials don't really eat that stuff."

Jackson would not be eating anything for a good long time.

"So..." he held up the envelope "...I'll give this to Ryn."

"Ryn! That's her name. Jillian told me but I forget. I knew it was a songbird, but all I could think of was Robin. Well, toodaloo ... tell her I'm giddy with excitement to meet her." Greta waved as Jackson backed out of the garage.

THE NIKE SLOGAN played on repeat in Jackson's mind as he made the two right and one left turn that separated the five miles from his house to Ryn's. The gusty winds that had ripped the amber leaves from the trees earlier in the day had died down. The blinding angle of the setting sun made it difficult to see pedestrians in the crosswalks as the bars and restaurants bulged with the Friday night crowd. Even Ryn's street had cars lined on both sides, walking distance from the entertainment district.

Just Do It.

The line between psyching himself up and psyching

himself out disappeared, leaving him lost in the blurry middle. Before his brain shifted into overdrive, he hopped out and strode toward her door with the confidence of this guy from San Francisco he used to know.

One lock clicked and then another. Even with Gunner, Ryn kept her doors locked at all times.

"Hi." She smiled with a bit of hesitation. Her look said "are you still mad at me for laughing at your pathetic advances?"

He grinned. The less he said the better.

"Come in. I ran late at my last job so I need to shower. Dinner is in the oven." She walked toward the kitchen.

The view of her ass shifting slightly side to side in her yoga pants fed his intentions.

Just Do It.

"Smells good. What is it?"

"Lasagna, but it has about thirty minutes, so maybe I should run and take a quick shower." She slipped off her oven mitts after pulling the foil from the top of the casserole dish.

"No."

She froze. Only her eyes flitted from one side of the room to the other, trying to solve his mysterious response. "No ... what?"

Just. Do. It.

"One question." He pulled off his shirt, needing all the persuasive ammunition he could get.

Ryn's eyes widened.

"And it's a yes or no answer." He stepped closer, backing her into the refrigerator. "Do you want me?"

"I-I need a shower."

He shook his head, inching closer yet. "Try again."

"I've been cleaning houses—"

Another head shake that silenced her. She. Was. His. Once a woman responded to his non-verbal commands, it was equivalent to folding in a poker game.

"Yes ... or no?" he whispered in her ear.

Backed into a hard surface with no place to go, breathless, and stumbling for words ... that's what he knew. There was only one word he needed.

"Say it."

"I probably smell like—"

"Say. It."

Sliding his hands along the outside of her T-shirt, he stopped and kneaded her breasts with a firm pressure that made her hiss.

"I'm too—"

"Say it!" he growled, pinching her nipples so hard she jumped.

"Yes!" she yelled. "Yes, I want you to fuck me!'

Stilling his hands, he raised his face from her neck and just stared at her for a moment. Her breaths came so fast she could hardly catch them. Ryn looked shocked as if she, too, couldn't believe those words came from her mouth. He didn't say it, but he sure did think it: *Holy shit! Jillian was right. Ryn wants me to fuck her like the stable boy.*

If he didn't snap out of it, she could change her mind. They both could overthink everything.

Just Do It.

CHAPTER SIXTEEN

THE OVEN HEATED to 375 degrees. Ryn did too. Tomato, oregano, and basil filled the air. A bag of Romaine lettuce waited by the sink to be cleaned and chopped into a salad. The cracked window welcomed the soothing yet dramatic tones of the Japanese wind chime on her back deck, dancing in the breeze. There was the compression bra issue again, but his magic touch managed to draw them out of hiding. The dirt and grime from a long day of cleaning clung to her body, and the shivering fear of *everything* left her trembling. If she'd had a tail it would have been between her legs.

The problem? He turned her on. Her thoughts couldn't stop her body from feeling so reckless. Resisting was far more painful—impossible—than submitting.

"My boobs look like pancakes and I'm not well groomed in certain *places*." The words were out. It was as much a relief as an embarrassment. The truth felt like a baby in the womb: innocent and destined to come out.

Jackson smirked and she pressed her lips together, hiding her grin. She loved the invisible string between his smile and hers and how they played off each other.

"This is going to be fun ... so much fun."

"Sex?"

"Making it my mission to show you how sexy you are." He kissed her before she had a chance to argue. Each stroke of his tongue controlling and demanding as his hands curled around the waist of her yoga pants.

She tugged the button and zipper to his jeans. He pulled away, leaving her mouth begging for more as he peeled down her pants until she stepped out of them. The flush of her cheeks intensified at the realization that her panties could not have been any less sexy. They looked like hand-me-downs from her grandma. It had been a busy week and the laundry fell behind. Before he could make a good inspection, she slid them down and wadded them in her hand.

He grinned, looking down at the bunched nude cotton she fisted. When his eyes shifted to hers, she maintained a neutral look as if to say, "There's nothing to see here." There was no way to hide the fact that she removed her underwear in one quick, desperate move. It had been far from graceful or indiscrete. Jackson just stood there waiting for her to do something with them.

Leaning toward him, eyes locked to his, she reached behind her and cracked open the refrigerator door just enough to toss her panties inside before leaning back against it like it never happened. She made a mental note to burn all her undergarments and replace them with rigid under-wires and ass-floss panties.

"I need you to hurry up." She grimaced, locking her knees to keep her legs from shaking. "I'm naked from the waist down and completely coming apart inside."

Their mouths crashed. He didn't give her another chance to speak or even form a coherent thought. Moisture pooled between her legs until she felt it drip like lava down her thigh. Her legs pressed together in mortification.

He slid two fingers between her wet folds, stopping her motion. She moaned while he pressed his body firm to hers, as if he wanted to feel her sounds vibrate between them. The only thing sexier than him—which was basically *everything* that could possibly be sexy—was his physical desire for her.

He. Wanted. Her.

It took a moment in the heat of distraction for that to sink into her brain. When it did, all dignity evaporated and she widened her stance. Yes, she widened her stance. It may not have seemed like much to him, but for her it represented a brazen move. It said, "I need as much of you as I can possibly fit inside me, NOW!"

Three. Three fingers fit nice and snug. His tongue made languid strokes up her neck with his teeth teasing her skin. When his hand stopped moving, she raised onto her toes and lowered back down. For a fleeting moment she felt embarrassed by the desperateness of riding his hand, but when his palm grazed her sensitive clitoris it no longer mattered. As long as he didn't stop kissing her, touching, needing her.

"Oh ... God ..." Her eyes rolled back in her head. An orgasm approached the precipice. "Wait!"

As he pulled his hand away, her eyes flew open. Did she dare tell him she hadn't finished? Half the blood in her body had converged between her legs, like water against a damn. A painful case of pink balls.

Pulling a condom out of his pocket, he grinned. The words teetered on the tip of her tongue. Jackson Knight embodied a godly specimen. However, she'd never reached an orgasm from penetration. That confident grin said he'd be the first, but Ryn had her doubts.

Her teeth made a death grip to her lower lip as he pushed his jeans and briefs down. Steadying herself with one hand on his bare chest, her other hand rested over her heart. She didn't feel it there until he rolled on the condom and shifted his eyes to her.

His signature take-charge demeanor paused for a moment. He peeled her hand from her chest, inching it towards his face. She looked up as he pressed his lips against her palm, closing his eyes for an eternal second that stopped the progression of time ... and her heart.

When he opened his eyes, she felt the pull of a black hole sucking her into something so unknown it sent chills racing along her skin. He guided both of her hands to his neck then slid his beneath her butt and lifted her up. Within a breath he impaled himself inside her ... all the way.

She gripped his thick, dark hair and screamed into his neck, muffling her string of curse words. He paused, but only until she silenced long enough to draw in a quick breath. Then he reared back and plunged in again.

Another cry.

Again and again, he repeated the slow rhythm until her cries morphed into moans. Then he picked up the pace —*really* picked up the pace. Her back threatened to break against the refrigerator door as glass on the inside rattled along with the ceramic jars on top.

After a few minutes the most unexpected thing happened. That abandoned orgasm? It came back to life, building to a mind-numbing intensity with each thrust.

"Harder!" That came from the woman who possessed

Ryn's body because she had never said that during sex, even when that's what she wanted.

Jackson's mouth found hers again, and every inch of his body brought unexpected pleasure to hers. The pain in her back vanished as all feeling gathered in one single spot. The spot he'd angled his pelvis to hit every. Single. Time.

"Yes ... yes, there ... there ... there!" she yelled through a never-ending orgasm, the first with a man inside her.

The drain of energy made it hard not to collapse until he finished. They raced in tandem and she just wanted to stop peddling. Instead she held him tight, contracting all her muscles until he groaned on a final thrust, stilling for a few seconds before his body completely relaxed against hers, keeping her pinned to the refrigerator.

His sultry breaths blanketed the skin along her neck in ragged succession. If he'd wanted to stay inside her forever, that would have been fine by her. Once he completely shattered her vagina, which happened in the first three thrusts, they fit together quite nicely.

Jackson lifted his head just enough to move it from her shoulder to her forehead. Rolling it slightly side to side against hers, he grinned. "I'm out of practice."

That made front page news because if what just happened was a result of him being out of practice, then she was in trouble. Epically huge trouble.

"Can you stand?" He kept his forehead against hers.

She nodded as he kissed her softly on the lips and eased her to her feet. Being fucked against the refrigerator left no room for modesty, but she still crossed her legs and rested her hands over her exposed area as he removed the condom and pulled up his pants.

He grinned, nodding behind him. "I'm going to run to

the restroom while you see if your panties have cooled down. Okay, hot pants?"

Rolling her lips between her teeth and closing her eyes, she nodded. When the door to the bathroom clicked shut, she whipped around and retrieved her panties from the refrigerator. She stepped into them and yanked on her yoga pants at lightning speed. The sex and panty retrieval warranted a hand washing before she proceeded to prepare the salad. Gunner sat by the back door looking at her.

"What?" She shrugged, daring him to make her feel guilty. The dog possessed an eerily accurate perception.

"Can I do anything to help?"

"You could open that bottle of wine." Playing he-didn't-just-fuck-her-brains-out-against-the-refrigerator cool required effort, but she did her best.

He poured them each a glass. "You're quirky ... I like you."

She laughed, keeping her head bowed, eyes trained to the cutting board. "Really? I think the fact that you asked to 'swim in my pond' and then your response after what just happened is to tell me that I'm 'quirky' makes *you* the quirky one."

"You could be right. I think introverted people can be quirky."

"*You* are not introverted." She slid on the oven mitts and pulled the lasagna out of the oven.

"I am, actually."

"Both you and Jillian have made reference to your habits with women before you moved here."

He carried their wine glasses to the table. "I've always spent a lot of time on the computer or playing the piano, only recently did I start teaching lessons. Most of my social interaction over the years has been via the internet or quick lays."

"Quick lays? Wow ... that's ..."

"Honest. I told you I'm not good at sugarcoating." He smirked. "Well, actually I'm pretty good with the women in my neighborhood."

Ryn dished out lasagna and salad for both of them then sat across from him. "The quirkiness you're referring to is just my nerves around you. I'm not really an introvert. At least, not by nature. I was very outgoing in my day."

Shaking his head, he blotted his mouth with a napkin. "Don't say 'in my day.' It makes you sound eighty."

"Fine, pre-Preston I was outgoing. So basically as a teenager. I was in the drama club and got the role as Dorothy in *The Wizard of Oz*. I worked at a daycare part-time after school and on the weekends, and I was an ambassador for Students Against Drunk Driving."

"SADD, huh? For personal reasons or just because it's a good cause?"

Ryn stared at her plate for a minute before shifting her eyes to him. "My older brother was killed by a seventeen-year-old girl who chose to get behind the wheel."

"Ryn, I'm—"

She shook her head. "I don't talk about it much. The driver was my best friend's sister. We were thirteen when it happened, my brother was fifteen. He rode his bike home from a Friday night baseball game. We lived just two miles from the school. I was at their house that night. Her parents got a call from the hospital. She wasn't injured it was more of a panic attack. Just as they were getting ready to pull out of the driveway to head to the hospital, my parents pulled in to get me because the sheriff had already delivered the news of my brother. In a matter of seconds everyone made the connection."

"Jesus ..."

"Yeah. I haven't spoken to Heather since that night. We saw each other at school and she wrote me a few letters, but it was just too much." She gave him a sad smile. "I've never gone to my class reunions in fear that she'd be there. Isn't that ridiculous? I know ... I've always known it wasn't her fault, her sister's the one who killed him, but it just hurts to be around her."

Jackson moved his leg so it touched hers—intimate and kind.

"I'm sure she knows you don't blame her."

She nodded. "Anyway ..." taking a deep breath then releasing it, she tried to smile "...sorry for the detour from my point, which is I'm not a born introvert so you cannot label me as quirky. Especially since I'm not the one who wears taped glasses. Which by the way I notice you don't wear them all the time. Are you farsighted?"

Jackson looked down at his plate as he stabbed his fork into the lettuce. "Something like that."

"I never asked. When you called, what did you want to show me?"

<hr>

THE SELF-PROFESSED introvert who occasionally wore glamour glasses, stared at the woman trying to hide her desolate expression. The subtleties in her appearance drew his attention: the way her hair looked messy and sexy at the same time and the way her brows peaked when she gave him a wide-eyed look every time she asked him a question. The tragic story still suffocated the air. Her question evaporated what little oxygen remained in the room. Was she not paying attention to the event that took place against her refrigerator?

That voice in his head, the one that guarded his testicles, yelled, "Man-up or maybe give her a little reminder of what you came to show her." Sometimes it felt impossible to rehabilitate from the man he used to be. Perhaps a man who never entertained the company of a woman beyond sex could not be rehabilitated or domesticated.

"I washed Woody." But he tried anyway.

"Oh ..."

"Woody is my car." Jillian would have been laughing her ass off.

Ryn nodded. "Well, I'll have to take a look at *Woody*."

Planting his elbows on the table, he dropped his head into his hands. "Jesus ... why is this so hard?" He lifted his head. "I didn't wash my car. That..." he gestured to the refrigerator "...that's what I came over to show you."

The unfamiliarity of giving a damn about what a woman thought, left him blind to the truth. Falling for her didn't happen all at once. It took him without warning—an unsuspecting culmination of a hundred tiny things. In that moment it was the way her smile grew in minuscule increments until her whole face beamed with sheer happiness.

"I liked *that*. A lot." She blushed but never took her eyes from his. "In fact, I'm okay with you coming over anytime to show me *that*."

The same woman twice. That would be a first—a good first.

"Oh, here I have something for you." Leaning to one side, he grabbed the black envelope from his back pocket and handed it to her.

"Black huh? This must be my belated birthday card." She opened it.

"Shit. Your birthday. Well ... no that's not it. I brought flowers, remember? And then dinner—"

With a slight head shake, she tracked the words on the invitation. "You want me to buy sex toys?"

"What? No."

Tilting her head, she pursed her lips. "That's fine. You're right. I probably could use some practice."

"God ... no, that's ... it's ... my neighbor invited you because she wants to meet you. Lascivio is the company Jillian works for."

"Oh, okay."

"So you'll go?"

"Yeah, sure."

"You don't have to buy anything."

"I'm not going to show up and then not buy anything. I'll get something."

"Like what?"

Ryn smirked. "I don't know. Do you have any suggestions?"

He raised a single brow. "Maybe a candle?"

Gathering their plates, she took them to the sink. "I'm not going to just buy a candle at a Lascivo party."

Jackson carried the rest of the dishes over to her. The fact that she gave careful consideration to purchasing sex toys confirmed he'd been off his game earlier.

A do-over. That's what he needed to prove that nothing Lascivo sold would compare to him.

"Tell me what you think you want and I'll prove you don't need it."

She closed the dishwasher and leaned against the

counter with her arms crossed over her chest. "And how exactly are you going to prove it?"

Holding up both hands, he spread his fingers wide. "Sharp teeth, one tongue, two lips, ten fingers, and a very large cock. Take your pick."

A blush crawled up her neck, slack jaw, lips parted.

Jackson smirked. Yeah ... he still had it.

CHAPTER SEVENTEEN

DAY

Samovar defined tea at its best. Jessica loved stealing the occasional evening with her dad working in his garage, but she also cherished Saturday morning tea with her mom.

"How's my girl?"

A smile overtook her face as she poured her favorite Golden Phoenix Oolong tea. "In love, Mom. But you already know that."

Sunny winked. "Yes. I do. Have you been making any *other* progress?"

The *other* progress always referred to her past.

"I think so. He still devotes several hours three times a week to *listening* to me. Sometimes it's just going over what we've already talked about and other times he asks me the harder questions."

"Like what?" Sunny bit into her scone.

"Like things that involve G.A.I.L."

"If you two get married—"

"I know." Blowing on her tea, she took a cautious sip. "And we will someday because he is ... *everything*. With each passing day he becomes my new past, and I feel like eventually he'll be the only past I need. It's ridiculous, I'm sure, but I wonder if our life together can erase those memories. You know what I mean?"

"I think so. I hope so because I love who you've become with Luke. Each week, more and more, the woman before me resembles the girl I used to know: that innocent smile, the renewed sparkle in your eyes—amber like the desert sun."

"It's my boys. It's all my boys."

Sunny grinned. "How does Luke feel about being referred to in the same company as the dog?"

"*The dog?* You know Jones is our baby. In fact, *my boys* are meeting me here in a little while for a jog."

"Jude said you wouldn't take him to obedience school."

"I see Luke's been running his mouth." Jessica rolled her eyes. "I *did* take him. He just didn't fit in."

"I heard it's because you gave him a treat even when he didn't do what he was supposed to be doing."

"Mom, the other dogs were being rewarded and he saw it. I didn't want him to feel like he was being punished."

"Well, if he wasn't following directions like the other dogs then maybe he really didn't deserve a treat. If you don't make him work for the reward, then the reward system won't work."

"Now you sound like the instructor. It doesn't matter. We didn't return after the first day because all the other dogs were giving Jones a complex."

Sunny held her tea cup, letting the steam rise near her face while she studied Jessica. "How's the *sleeping* going?"

"You mean have I put him in the hospital?" It felt impossible to look her mom in the eye.

"I've never blamed you for what happened to me."

"*What happened?* Are you serious? I happened to you,

that's what happened. Don't make it sound like you fell down the stairs."

"It was an accident."

Pain gripped Jessica's heart as her mom's hand rested on hers.

"Luke's fine. We've sort of figured it out."

"I'm glad."

She nodded.

"Your father will be flying out to D.C. for the week so I'm going to visit Cathy while he's gone."

"I can't believe you're still friends with her."

"We're *still* friends because she has been my friend since first grade. It's not fair to judge her."

Jessica guffawed. "She cheated on Daniel with. His. Brother."

Sunny stared at her tea. "Yes, but it's not that black and white. You don't know all the details."

"You're right. It probably isn't, but I don't want to know the details. Cheating is cheating, period."

"Love is reckless because true emotions are immune to logic. The most beautiful love stories are often the most tragic."

"God, I hope not. I want my love story with Luke to be beautiful, but not tragic."

Sunny's lips pressed into a smile that failed to disguise her concern.

"What is it?" Jessica asked.

Her mom shook her head. "Nothing, dear."

"You sure?"

"Positive." She looked out the window. "There they are."

Jessica waved at Luke then stood. "Safe travels. Call me

when you get to Cathy's." She bent down and kissed her mom on the cheek.

"I will. Love you, Jess ... and hey..." she grabbed her hand "...I hope you know, I guess I hope you've always known. What happened after you came home from the hospital ... I forgave you the moment it happened. I've always forgiven you. Okay?"

Tears stung her eyes as she looked to the ceiling, blinking them away. "Thank you. I love you too."

"HEY, BOYS!" Jessica beamed as she began to squat down.

"If you kiss the mutt first, you can forget about kissing me."

Wetting her lips, she stood back up and wrapped her arms around Luke's neck, holding on tight as he lifted her up. Luke kissed her whenever, however, and wherever he wanted—except his office. They'd had more than one argument about that.

"How's our girl?" He nipped at her neck before sliding her back down his body.

"I'm good. You could say I threw another shovel of dirt onto my past."

They held hands and walked toward Yerba Buena Gardens. "How so?"

"My mom forgave me for the attack that put her in the hospital."

Luke squeezed her hand. "She hadn't before now?"

"She did right after it happened and many times since."

"Today you forgave yourself." His words stopped her. Jones tugged at the leash while Luke bent down, level with her face.

"How did you know?" she whispered.

Cupping the back of her head, he pressed his lips to her ear. "I have a degree in psychiatry."

"That makes sense." She smirked.

"Luke? Is that you?"

He turned toward the woman's voice as Jessica stepped to the side to see past him.

"Jones!" Jessica chased her disobedient dog after Luke dropped his leash. He just ... let go of it. "Dammit, Jones, come back." Thankfully, another dog captured his attention allowing her to grab the leash. After giving the other dog's owner an apologetic smile, she tugged Jones toward Luke and the tall blonde in a black, short-skirt business suit, with a good mile of legs and stupidly high heels, who happened to be embracing him.

"Excuse me, sir, I think you lost your dog." Jessica grinned with bared teeth as the blonde pulled away and adjusted her messy bun of hair while giving Jessica a coy smile.

Luke grimaced, taking the leash in one hand and Jessica's hand in his other. "My apologies. Jessica this is Dr. Eva Lorenzo. Eva this is my girlfriend, Jessica Day."

His girlfriend. With a quick look up at him and the hint of a smile, she forgave him for the dog-chasing incident.

"It's a pleasure to meet you." Eva extended her hand and Jessica released Luke's to accept it.

"You too. Are you in town for the medical conference at the Moscone Center?"

"How did you know about that?" Luke asked.

"While I waited for my mom at Samovar, the waiter said they'd been pretty busy because of it."

"Yes, I am in town for it." Eva said to Jessica while looking at Luke.

An awkward silence followed.

"Did you go to medical school together?"

"We did." The grip Luke had on her hand tightened with his answer.

The conversation, if it could really be considered that, felt strained and odd.

"Eva was Fran's roommate in college."

Another awkward silence while the two much taller people stared at each other.

"Well, that makes sense. I don't know who Fran is, but—"

"She was my fiancée."

Eva nodded, casting her eyes downward for a moment. Maybe it wasn't such a relief that she caught Jones so fast. Missing the most uncomfortable conversation ever would not have been a bad thing.

"I can take Jones and head home if you two need a few minutes alone to talk behind my back or reminisce about your engagement with Fran."

Eva's eyes widened as her lips parted. Not so much as a flinch came from Luke. He knew Jessica's inappropriate humor and he'd perfected ignoring it.

"It was good to see you, Eva." Luke gave into Jones's incessant tugging and pulled Jessica with them.

"I'll give Francesca your best."

Luke kept walking, failing to acknowledge Eva's parting comment.

"I'm sorry."

Jessica's legs sped to a jogging pace to keep up with Luke's long strides. "Why are you sorry?"

"I've not told you anything about Fran, including her name. I put you in an uncomfortable situation back there and I should not have."

"Luke, I'm fine. It's not like I didn't know you were engaged. I just don't understand the weird looks you two were sharing."

"While you were chasing Jones she told me something and I had trouble processing it."

"Can I ask what she told you?"

Luke stopped so abruptly Jones's momentum jerked his arm, causing him to flinch. "You can ask me anything. You know that, right?"

That was a good question. Jessica couldn't say for sure why she'd never pressed Luke for information about his ex-fiancée. Had she been so self-absorbed with her own past that she didn't think Luke might have needed to discuss his?

"I think so." She nodded, narrowing her eyes a bit.

They continued toward his condo.

"Fran is on the heart transplant list," Luke said in a Dr. Jones matter-of-fact way.

"Why?"

"She has congenital heart disease. I think she had two, maybe three surgeries as a child. For years she was fine."

"So what happened?"

He shrugged. "Eva didn't go into detail other than to say Fran needed a transplant because the medications are no longer working. Sometimes there can be scar tissue from childhood surgeries that can cause problems later in life."

"Where does she live now?"

"Scottsdale with her parents."

"Maybe you should go see her. Do you want to go see her?"

They stepped into the elevator. "Why would you ask me that?"

"Because you said I could ask you anything."

Easing his head back against the elevator wall, he closed his eyes on a heavy sigh. "I don't know."

Jones looked up, cocking his head.

"Why did you get Jones for me?"

Luke's brow furrowed then he opened his eyes.

"I thought you'd like him."

Jones shifted his head tilt to the opposite side. Jessica puckered her lips and blew him a kiss. "Don't worry, Jonesy, I love you."

The elevator door opened. Jessica and Jones followed Luke into the condo.

"So you, who thrives on order and cleanliness, just thought, 'Hey, I think I'll get Jessica a puppy,' for no particular reason?"

"Why are you asking me this a month later?" He grabbed a Heineken from the refrigerator.

Luke drinking before noon gave her an uneasy feeling. "It's crossed my mind quite a bit, especially since you call him 'mutt' and I think he's given you a few gray hairs."

"Maybe I wanted you to stop calling me Jones."

She hopped up on the counter. "I don't buy that."

A long pull of beer bought him time to reply. "Dogs can be therapeutic."

"Jones is part of my therapy?"

"Yes."

"How so?"

"You've referred to yourself as a monster. Jones brings out your nurturing side. Monsters don't nurture."

"So it was a test to see if I'm truly a monster?"

Luke shook his head. "Yes," he answered, thick with sarcasm.

"Tell me about Francesca."

Chuckling, he set his beer onto the counter and crossed

his arms over his chest. "You're asking a lot of random questions today."

"I'm not. They're all about you. I'm just trying to figure out how you tick. It's my turn to 'study' you. That's not random. Besides, 'Tell me about Francesca,' is not a question."

"What do you want to know?"

"My God, Dr. Jones ... you'd make a terrible patient."

Talking about Francesca evidently required a second beer. Jessica frowned while he retrieved another one from the refrigerator.

"I saved Fran from a burning building."

The pads of her fingers drummed her lower lip, eyes wide. She laughed but it came out as a cough. "You're joking."

"It was my sophomore year of undergrad while I was still a volunteer firefighter. She lived with three other girls in a rundown apartment building. There had been a party in the apartment below them. Someone fell asleep or passed out before putting out their cigarette. Her friends were all out of the building by the time we arrived, but Fran went back for her fish." He shook his head. "A fucking gold fish in a bowl of water."

"And you saved her?"

"And the fish from the third floor window. The next week she dropped off a cookie bouquet at the fire station to 'her hero.'"

"So you ended up dating." Hearing every little detail felt unnecessary and a bit more nauseating than she anticipated.

"For a year before I proposed."

Of course she wanted to know how he proposed. Did he get down on one knee or two?

"What did she do?"

"She said yes."

"No. Her profession."

"Oh, she was in school, too, at the time. She became a court interpreter."

"Long hours. Stressful job."

Staring at the label of his beer, he nodded.

"Who broke off the engagement?"

The muscle in his jaw twitched. "I'm not sure."

That answer fizzled her desire to know anymore at that point.

"We didn't get our run in, so I might go for a bike ride. You want to come?"

"No more questions?" He finished the second bottle of beer.

The beer chugger before her looked like Luke, but his actions were that of someone much different—someone teetering on the edge of control. But why?

"No. But if you need to talk I'm always ready to listen."

Beer number three. Jessica declared it an official what-the-fuck moment.

"How emasculating of you to my manhood and my profession."

"How sexist of you to assume only men can listen when by nature your gender practices selective hearing ninety percent of the time. And if you're wanting to flash your doctor badge, I suggest you first do some inner reflection as to why you're on your third beer before noon in less than an hour after finding out your ex-fiancée needs a heart transplant."

The impromptu speech filled with valid points did not deter Luke as he popped the top to another beer.

"Take care of my puppy. I'm going for a ride."

CHAPTER EIGHTEEN

KNIGHT

THE LIST of things that could top being fucked by Jackson Knight against a refrigerator was short. The birth of Maddie held the number one spot, refrigerator sex sat at number two. The fact that there were only two events on Ryn's Life's Best Moment's List seemed pathetic. Dwelling over the sleepy details of her life was a waste of time. As she sat in her car, checking her makeup one last time, the past didn't matter. It only took forty years to be *that* girl—the one who got the guy that everyone else wanted.

Maddie needed help moving to her new apartment, closer to campus. Ryn had not seen Jackson since the infamous sex night. He wanted to stay for a do-over, which was ridiculous because perfection was perfection. Period. More than that, she *needed* a shower and time to think about his lips, tongue, teeth, ten skilled fingers, and one gifted cock.

With twenty minutes before Greta's party, Ryn couldn't keep herself from saying hi to Jackson before heading across the street. She knocked on the door anticipating his sexy smile and a mind-numbing kiss to get her in the mood for the party. Instead, Jackson greeted her with rivulets of water racing down his body and a white towel tied low on his waist.

"Jillian is already over there."

Sexy smile. Check.

"You look amazing, by the way."

Twenty six letters and infinite ways to assemble them into words, yet she couldn't conjure a single one let alone remember what she had on that looked so amazing. A short wrap skirt and a sleeveless blouse felt about right, but really she couldn't remember.

"If you keep looking at me like that you're going to be late to the party."

With wide eyes, she nodded yes to ... something. Yes to being on time or yes to being late ... or just simply yes to him.

"Do you want to step inside for a few minutes?" He chuckled, which brought her attention back to his face after her ogling started to feel like a hallucination.

"Maybe for a minute..." she stepped inside coming to an abrupt halt as she closed her eyes "...or two."

Another chuckle. "Are you okay?"

"You smell like sandalwood and ... patchouli." Her eyes opened with her head still spinning from the intoxicating fragrance.

"I call it bar soap and shampoo, but I'm glad you like it."

His eyes were unquestionably beautiful, even mesmerizing, but they didn't demand her attention like his bare, tatted chest or the towel that looked like it could come loose at any moment.

"You seem distracted."

She nodded.

"Maybe I should put on some clothes."

Worst idea ever, in Ryn's honest opinion.

Pressing his hands against the wall above her head, trapping her under a bridge of muscled flesh, he leaned forward until his lips grazed her ear. "Is that what you want?"

The question was absurd. Barely worthy of an answer. "No." She swallowed.

He sucked her earlobe, teasing it with his teeth. "Remove the towel, Ryn."

The strain of her nipples against the lace of her bra and the slide of her new thong between her legs when she shifted her weight had her ready to orgasm from just the words: *remove the towel, Ryn.*

Jackson moaned with his lips pressed to her neck as she feathered her fingers over the peaks and valleys of his abs, down to the towel. His dizzying scent intensified with each ragged breath she drew into her lungs. She wanted to taste him ... devour him.

"Stop!"

Ryn jumped, pressing her palms to the wall behind her as Jillian flew through the front door. Jackson grumbled a few expletives while keeping Ryn caged beneath his arms.

"Back away from the girl and go put some clothes on."

"This coming from my sister who is basically a nudist?"

"I told you to send her *straight over* if she knocked on the door."

Ryn felt like a teenager getting caught with a guy. Ten years their senior, yet she shrank beneath the awkwardness of the Knight twins' arguing over her.

"Come on, Ryn. Chicks before dicks."

Of course Ryn had no idea what that meant, but she let Jillian pull her toward the door anyway.

"She still has a few minutes before the party starts. I'll send her right over."

It was impossible to look at Jackson after that comment. Ryn's whole body flushed with embarrassment.

Jillian pointed a finger at him. "Knock that shit off. This is Greta's night. Do you remember when Mom used to go grocery shopping after dinner and she'd come home with twenty dollars' worth of groceries because after eating nothing tempted her?"

Jackson rolled his eyes to the ceiling.

"Well Ryn needs to show up to Greta's hungry. Got it?"

Before the door shut, Jackson yelled, "Then you're welcome. I think she's starving right now."

Ryn whipped her head back, mouth agape, as Jillian dragged her toward the street. Jackson winked through the glass storm door with a cocky-bastard smirk. Then he removed his towel, turned, and sauntered away from the door.

"He just flashed you, didn't he?" Jillian asked without ever turning back.

"Um ..."

She laughed. "I apologize on behalf of the Knight family. We have no self-control."

<hr>

"Oh my goodness! You are just adorable," Greta said as she gently touched the ends of Ryn's hair before resting her palms on her cheeks. "Oh ... and your eyes, and these freckles, and you have the cutest little button nose."

Ryn felt ten years old under Greta's exaggerated, yet flattering assessment. "Thank you. So nice to meet you."

"Well..." Greta motioned for Ryn to follow her to the great room "...you're just lucky Marvin is still breathing, otherwise I would have already snatched Jackson up."

Ryn equated Greta to warm chocolate cake: sweet, addictive, and sure to evoke a smile.

After handing Ryn a glass of sangria, Greta brought two fingers to her mouth and catcall whistled. "Settle down, ladies, so Jillian can get started."

The small group of fifteen women, all over sixty years, turned the volume down to a few soft whispers as their eyes bugged out with each new item Jillian placed on the coffee table. Ryn bit back a smile. It was the most unusual group for a Lascivio party. Their fearless leader took them through everything, explaining how each personal pleasure device was to be used before passing it around for everyone to inspect up close.

When the nipple clamps came around, Ryn took a quick picture and sent it to Jackson.

Ryn: *What do you think?*
Jackson: *I think these work better.*

He attached a photo of his teeth biting the tip of his thumb. She giggled.

Next she sent a photo of the edible lubricant.

Ryn: *?*
Jackson: *Let me save you some money.*

The photo attached showed him licking his lips. She squeezed her legs together.

Ryn: *Jillian said 'nothing' is better than this one.*

She sent a photo of a "top of the line" vibrator.

Jackson: *Your choice.*

Greta passed her a textured cock ring as Ryn looked at his text.

"I've got it, sweetie." Greta grabbed Ryn's phone that fell in the crack between the cushions when she went to pass the vibrator to the next person.

"No I've—"

Greta looked at the screen. "Oh my ... what or who ..." Her other hand covered her mouth.

"What is it?" Lynette asked looking over Greta's shoulder. "Oh my goodness!"

"He's just being—" Ryn grabbed her phone back, not realizing he sent a photo after his last remark. "Oh shit."

"Is that Jackson?" Every eye in the room landed on Ryn.

She flipped the phone so the screen pressed against her leg. "N-no, it's not what you think. It's ... just a friend playing a prank." It was exactly what they thought: Jackson's big, very erect cock.

Jillian narrowed her eyes then stepped closer to Ryn. "Is what Jackson?"

Ryn shook her head like an errant child in school. "Nothing."

Jillian snatched her phone. Ryn squeezed her eyes shut.

"Eww ... not cool, Bro ... not cool," Jillian whispered to herself.

Ryn peeked open one eye. Jillian wore a wicked smile. "Get some more to eat and drink, ladies, then feel free to play with the toys and browse through the catalog."

Once everyone focused their attention back on all the other embarrassing things in the room, Jillian grabbed the strap-on penis from the coffee table and took a picture of it with Ryn's phone.

"What are you doing?"

"Reciprocating." Jillian smirked as she moved her thumbs across the screen.

Ryn: How do you feel about anal play? I've always had a thing for m/m porn. Is your sexy ass as tight as the rest of your body?

Jillian tossed Ryn's phone to her. "No matter what, don't text him again or answer any of his texts.

Ryn stared at the message—horrified. "What if he takes it seriously?"

"Oh ... he'll take it seriously."

"What if he's..." she grimaced "...okay with the idea."

Jillian giggled. "Then I guess you'd better add a strap-on and a bottle of lube to your order tonight."

Ryn's eyes remained glued to her phone. "He's not responding."

"Ah ... excellent. Just as I suspected, he thinks you're serious. God, I'm good."

"Jillian?" Greta called. "Are butt plugs contraindicated if I have hemorrhoids?"

"Oh my God," Ryn mouthed. Jillian winked before excusing herself to help Greta.

She stared at her phone, willing Jackson to reply, but he didn't.

An hour and three glasses of Sangria later, she placed her order and walked back across the street while Jillian and Greta finished up with the rest of the ladies and their orders.

The alcohol almost erased the memory of Jillian's prank —almost. Jackson opened the door with his body covered by a pair of jeans and an Eat Local T-Shirt.

THE QUIET ONES were always the kinky ones. Jackson assumed with a fair amount of confidence that Ryn was the exception. Her skittish reactions to his sexual advances pointed in the opposite direction of kinky. The text, however, surprised him, and he wasn't easily surprised. The tipsy, sexy, cock-hardening woman at his door was a partial explanation for the bold message. The still slightly disturbing part was drunk people didn't get new ideas from alcohol. The alcohol just brought out thoughts that were already in their brain.

Her eyes perused his body then a giggle escaped as she homed in on his shirt. "Eat Local." She bit her lip, glassy eyes meeting his gaze. "I'm local."

Jackson found the deep, uninhibited tone of her voice to be quite sexy.

"Miss Middleton, are you drunk?"

Twisting her lips, she shook her head twice. After a few seconds she narrowed her eyes and nodded as if her thoughts couldn't keep up with her body. "A bit, I'd say."

"Keys." He held out his hand.

"I love that you're younger than me, yet more responsible." She handed him her keys.

Ryn lost her brother in a drunk driving accident. He knew she'd give him the keys without question. "Come on. I'll drive you home." He took her hand and led her to her car.

"I love it when you hold my hand. People don't do that much these days. Everyone's too busy texting or holding their phones to their ears to pay attention to the people around them."

He helped her in then got in the driver's side. "I agree," he said.

"You do? Aww ... see you're not too young for me after all. If I said the same thing to Maddie she'd tell me something like 'holding hands is for old people.' It seems like kids these days are either texting each other from across the table or practically screwing each other on the dance floor of some club."

Jackson chuckled as they pulled out of the development. He'd been on those dance floors many times, and they usually led to a bathroom, back alley, or backseat fuck before he went home alone. But Ryn was different, he was different. That Jude guy died and there was no reason to wake the dead.

"Greta is hilarious and she has a huge crush on you. God, I hope I have half her spunkiness when I'm her age. She must have ordered one of everything from that catalog. I think she's secretly trying to kill her husband so she can ride off into the sunset with you and your Woody." Ryn giggled. "Did I mention that was the best Sangria I've ever had?"

Jackson smiled. Ryn's random chattiness made her a fun drunk, although she seemed just a bit tipsy as her words were not slurred enough for it to be considered drunken babble.

"Did *you* buy anything?" Jackson asked as he pulled into her driveway.

She turned, wearing a tightlipped grin and a playful sparkle in her eyes. "I did." Her brow furrowed. "Hmm ... the funny thing is I can't remember for sure what I did get." She shrugged then eased out of the car.

Since she'd left him painfully turned-on after his shower earlier that night, his need to be with her felt urgent.

However, her butt-clenching text had him second guessing where their relationship was headed.

"I really appreciate you going to Greta's party tonight." He stopped at her door, hands in his back pockets as she stepped inside.

Her eyes were all over him as she wet her lips. "Aren't you coming inside?"

A great question.

A sly sexy grin pulled at her lips. "Are you still standing on my porch because of the text?"

The confirmation that it wasn't a drunken text didn't help ease his apprehension.

"I ... I have an early lesson in the morning and I didn't run today so I need to get that done first thing tomorrow."

She raised a single brow. "You drove my car. How are you going to get home?"

Another great question.

"Do you have to work in the morning?"

She nodded.

"I'll walk. It's not really that far."

Ryn sighed. "If I were like ... twenty minutes more sober, I don't think I'd say this, but I'm not there yet so I'm going to tell you. I bought new lingerie: a black lacy bra and a matching thong—the kind I don't have to hide in my refrigerator."

A confident Ryn in black lingerie had a good chance of blocking out the vision of her kinky alter ego in a strap-on penis acting out some fucked-up m/m fantasy. He stepped inside and shut the door behind him.

CHAPTER NINETEEN

Even under the lightly numbing veil of Sangria, Ryn felt something so different about the way Jackson looked at her. His eyes filled with desire and something else. That something else happened in the extra few seconds his gaze lingered before he touched her. It felt as though he disappeared and in the next breath when he returned, his face lit up with an emotion that looked like gratitude. But for what?

Her nerves were a ticking clock so she took his hand and led him upstairs, commanding Gunner to stay downstairs. When she released his hand and turned, he leaned against the shut door, arms crossed over his chest. The heat in his eyes lit a fire in her belly and a bit lower too.

"Let me see everywhere you don't have a tattoo."

His words could not have been more sobering, evaporating any residual alcohol from her bloodstream.

"I-I don't have any tattoos."

"Show me."

Her shirt had stayed on when he fucked her against the refrigerator. Maybe the lingerie statement had been misleading. She imagined them in her bed, under the covers, lights off.

Motioning to the wall next to him, she nodded. "Shut the light off."

A clenching, nauseating feeling knotted in her stomach as he shook his head.

"I'm ... well ... I'm ten years older than you and my body shows it. And you ..." She wrung her hands together feeling an inch tall for being so self-conscious. Jackson Knight wasn't just ten years younger, he represented the pinnacle of physical perfection at any age.

"On our first date I told you someday I'd tell you what makes a man sexy. Remember?"

She nodded. Her reference that day was to *him*. The point being that nothing made him that way ... he just simply *was* sexy.

"Take your clothes off and I'll show you that what makes me sexy in your eyes is the desire you see in mine."

After a deep breath, she fought through her insecurities and unbuttoned her blouse with shaky hands. He just stood there, watching her undress, watching her fall apart from the inside out. One man made her feel like a hundred sets of eyes seeing her in her most vulnerable state.

Shirt. Skirt. Borderline tears.

But tears weren't sexy. Never had a guy asked her to strip for him. She wanted to be sexy, confident, and worthy of that look in his eyes.

"Keep going."

Even her lips quivered as she bit them together and nodded once.

Thong. Knees ready to give out.

Bra. Eyes cast downward, blinking back tears of fear.

His feet came into view as she held her breath.

"Look at me."

One agonizing inch at a time she lifted her chin. That look, that *something*, met her gaze.

"That desire in my eyes ... it's you."

It was a dream. One she hoped to believe someday.

"Now take off my clothes."

Standing, even just breathing, proved to be difficult. Undressing him felt impossible.

"Why me?" she whispered with raw honesty.

He tipped her chin up with his finger then brushed his thumb along her lower lip. "Because you matter."

What did that mean? Had no one mattered before her? Impossible.

His hand dropped back to his side and he waited.

Her.

He wanted *her* to undress him. He wanted to be with her ... inside her. Only in a dream. It had to be a dream. She wanted to close her eyes and not wake up.

He helped her remove his shirt. She took a moment to stare then her shaky hands unfastened his jeans. His erection strained against his briefs.

Ryn swallowed hard before easing down his pants. He toed off his shoes and stepped out of his jeans. Kneeling at his feet, she stole another breath of courage and reached up to remove his briefs. He threaded his fingers through her hair. It was a simple yet sensual gesture that sent a heavy pulsing sensation to settle between her legs.

Resting her palms on his hard quad muscles, she rose up on her knees. His grip on her hair tightened. It had been a long time since she'd trusted a man with every piece of her vulnerability.

"Open." He let go of her hair with one hand while gently tugging her head back with the other.

She opened, but only from the shock that he said that to her. It wasn't a question or even request. It was a demand. He looked down at her with dark, hooded eyes as he fisted the base of his cock, guiding it into her mouth. He teased it against her tongue until she took over. Bringing both hands back into her hair, he held it back to see her face as he made gentle thrusts.

"Touch yourself."

It was official. She was in over her head and sinking deeper with every word that fell from his lips. Kneeling in front of him with his cock in her mouth, it was a little late to turn back. The most surprising part: she didn't want to stop.

"Ryn." It came out with an edge of warning, a side to Jackson she hadn't seen. She liked it. A lot.

The uncontrolled moan she released while sliding two fingers over her clitoris, drew a painful "fuck" from him. With a groan, he pushed a little deeper toward her throat. The tightening grip on her hair revealed his teetering control. He grabbed her arms and pulled her up. The wild look in his eyes showed more than a slip of control.

He shoved her down onto the bed, plunging her heart into her throat. Who was this guy and why was she so turned on by his Jekyll and Hyde transformation?

"Spread your legs."

Please didn't seem to be in his vocabulary and *no* wasn't in hers. After retrieving a condom from his pants, he rolled it on, his eyes giving her a challenging look that dared her to do anything but what he asked.

Pushing her knees back until they nearly touched her ears, he buried his face between her legs, eliciting a scream from someone. It couldn't have been her. Ryn Middleton did not scream during sex ... not ever.

Jackson became the ultimate sex toy, crawling up her

body, sinking into her, and taking her to a whole new world. The woman beneath him, moaning, begging, and digging her nails into the flesh of his toned ass, was one lucky, *lucky* girl. After seeing stars, she sucked her lower lip into her mouth as he collapsed on top of her.

Breathing was overrated.

"Fuck forty." He teased his teeth along her shoulder.

She chuckled between labored breaths. "I think you just did."

JUDE DAY WASN'T USED to fucking women in a bed. He wasn't familiar with words beyond "goodnight" after zipping his fly and walking away from a random act of selfish pleasure. Taking Ryn against her refrigerator felt familiar to Jackson. It had a spontaneous feel to it, even though he stayed for dinner and he did see her again—very un-Jude. However, lying next to Ryn in her bed with the entire night ahead of them left Jackson in uncharted territory.

"I should go." He kissed his way down her neck, palming her ass with one hand and squeezing her breast with his other.

"Okay," she answered in a breathy voice.

An out. She gave him an easy out.

No begging. No pouting. No clinging.

The woman proved to be nothing short of a dream. The perfect mixture of maturity and vulnerability. She gave him the option to leave without a guilt trip, and the sultry way her eyes moved over his body felt like an open invitation to come back and do it again and again. The perfect situation.

So why didn't he want to leave? What the hell was wrong with him?

"Or ... I could stay." Sucking her nipple into his mouth, he tugged at it with his teeth until her back arched off the bed.

"Oh God ..."

Ryn's soft moan had him hard again. His bout of celibacy left him uncharacteristically needy for sex, or maybe it was her. No woman had ever made him feel so insatiable. Every inch of her tasted divine. He couldn't stop sucking and lapping his tongue over her breasts as two of his fingers slid between her slick folds.

A distant voice from his past reprimanded him for being such a pussy as he fingered her to another orgasm, aiming only to pleasure her. She clawed at his back then tugged his hair, another foreign sensation. Jude sported a shaved head. He never knew a woman's death grip on his hair could make his dick pulse. Jackson would keep his pain-in-the-ass hair because his dick rather liked the connection.

Ryn's body writhed beneath his. "Jackson!"

After he removed his fingers, her eyes fluttered open and he released her nipple. She looked down at the teeth marks he left as a souvenir. "That's a first."

"Yeah?" He kissed the bite marks and grinned. "Well it won't be the last."

Ryn pulled the sheet up over her chest and bit her lips together. "So ... I'll see you Tuesday?"

That old voice told him to get his pathetic ass up and say something to ensure he'd leave with both balls intact.

"Tuesday." He nodded then rolled out of bed and dressed without making eye contact. Tuesday, next week, next month ... it should not have mattered. Yet, it did matter. It mattered like a sucker punch to his junk.

RYN MADE it to her 6:00 a.m. barre class the next morning. The sexiest man alive groping her body—her soft parts that needed to be firmed up—served as the greatest incentive ever to feel the burn. Being with Jackson flooded her brain with a mind-fuck of emotions. Every time he touched her it brought on a war between unfathomable desire—the incredible feeling of *being* desired—and the insecurities that had been ingrained in her about her body, her age, her ability to please a man. Did he think she needed to lose weight, exercise more, get that boob job she'd thought about for years?

After class she went for coffee with her instructor, Val. She was a year older than Ryn, recently divorced. Val was the closest thing Ryn had to a female friend, who also qualified as a confidant.

"You seemed possessed during class today." Val gave her a Cheshire cat grin over the rim of her coffee cup.

Ryn couldn't hide her guilty smile. "I've been seeing a guy."

"Go on." Val rested her arms on the table and leaned in giving Ryn her full attention.

"He's ten years younger than me."

Val's eyes bugged out. "Ryn! Oh my God. Do tell. Who? What? Where? When?"

"I work for him. I'm sure I should have some rule against that, huh? But I'm self-employed and it's never been an issue or even a possibility before now. He's kind, and funny, and he plays the piano ... like he can *seriously* play the piano. But he's also a god, Val. I'm talking celebrity-sports star-fitness model god. It's not that I have some awful self-esteem, but if you saw this guy you'd understand. I have no idea why he's interested in me ... in *that* way. I feel like

I'm having my own Shallow Hal moment. You know, like he's looking at me but seeing what he wants to see and it's just an illusion."

"Ryn—"

"Don't." She shook her head. "I need you to be my forty-something friend. I don't need you to give me a self-esteem boost. I'm not saying I think I'm ugly or lacking in all sex appeal. I'm just being realistic. I love ice skating and I'm pretty good at it, but I'm never going to make the Olympic team. Do you get what I'm saying?"

Val squinted a bit. "This guy is the gold medal of guys?"

"Exactly."

"Have you had ..." Val wiggled her brows.

Ryn blushed. "Yes. Oh. My. God. Yes."

"And?"

Ryn laughed. "Back to the Olympic scenario ... if sex were an event. He'd take the gold."

"I hate you." Val shook her head.

"You should." Ryn sighed. "I think there is a long line of women who hate me. Hell, I'm jealous of myself. I just know someone is going to shake me, and when I wake I'm going to be so pissed it was all just a dream."

"So he's a god. The sex is award-winning. Yet I get this vibe that something's wrong."

She chewed the corner of her lower lip and nodded. "It's the age thing, but not like I'm going to break a hip during sex. Although his stamina is—"

"Yada yada ... he's a fucking stallion. I get it." Val rolled her eyes.

Ryn chuckled. "Anyway, he lived a cavalier life before he moved to Omaha, but now he's looking for something different."

"A mature woman?"

With a twist of her lips, she shook her head. "A wife—a child-bearing wife."

Val's eyes grew wide as she mouthed *Oh.*

"Yeah. This is so messed up. When we're together I can't stop wondering if he's attracted to me or my maturity and child-bearing hips."

"I thought you had a C-section with Maddie."

"You know what I mean."

Val laughed for a moment then it fizzled when she looked at the true concern on Ryn's face. "Is it really about believing he could be genuinely attracted to you, or are you not wanting the same thing? I have two teenagers and I can't imagine starting that all over again—nursing, diapers, sleep deprivation."

Ryn rested her chin in her fist and nodded slowly. "It's everything. My hormones are all over the place. I don't even know if I could get pregnant. And if I did, can you imagine what a monster I'd be with even more hormones coursing through my veins? And you're right, there's the new-mom thing. At one point I dreamed of more children with a man who loved me, but I think over the past few years that dream disappeared, and now I don't know if it still exists." She laughed. "But really ... it's all so insane because I've known him for less than two months. He's mysterious, unpredictable, and I'm so far out of my comfort zone I can't think straight when we're together."

Val shrugged. "You're in your sexual prime. Go for it."

"In less than ten years he'll leave me because my female parts will be all dry and shriveled up. And the crazy part is I wouldn't blame him because the guy was made to ..."

Val perked a single brow. "Made to ... fuck?"

Ryn smiled. "I think so. I'm not even sure he's wired for

monogamy. It would be like Secretariat being a circus pony —all that wasted potential."

They both laughed.

"I'm scared, Val."

She grabbed Ryn's hand. "He's not Preston and you're no longer that woman."

"I know, but he's still alive and in my life because of Maddie. Even after all these years I swear he's still messing with my mind. I second-guess everything, including what I want. I'm forty, for God's sake. I should know what I want by now, but I don't because somewhere along the way I lost a piece of myself. And because of Maddie I feel this incredible guilt like regretting Preston means I regret Maddie."

"Ryn?"

She took a cleansing breath, ashamed those words even came out of her mouth. "What?"

"If being somebody's wife again or having another baby is even a one percent chance in your mind, then get the guy. Suck him—pun totally intended—for all he's willing to give you and then..." Val winked "...give him to me."

CHAPTER TWENTY
DAY

Jones looked at Luke. Luke looked at Jones. Neither would concede that the other deserved to be in the dog house. As Luke's gaze drifted to the fourth empty Heineken bottle hanging from his loose grip, he felt fairly certain the mutt would be sleeping in his spot that night.

Francesca needed a heart transplant or she would die. He remembered the days when he would have given her the heart from his own chest. Those days were gone and his heart left a few hours earlier to go for a bike ride. Even four beers in before one o'clock on a Saturday, Luke knew with every bit of his existence that Jessica Day was meant to be with him.

Somewhere along the way he unintentionally convinced her she needed him. Every day he wondered what would happen to them if she realized he needed her more. Beneath all the pain, the regret, the blood, the deaths ... Jessica Day was a survivor. It's not what she did, it's who she was, and nobody could touch that part of her: not Four, not Matthew Green, and not Dr. Jones.

He closed his eyes and an hour later, which felt like two

seconds, the door opened. The sweat-soaked body of the woman who carried his heart like a torch walked to the kitchen and filled a large glass with icy water from the refrigerator door. She didn't acknowledge him. He couldn't blame her. Some strange and completely irrational part of his mind wanted her to be pissed at him. Jessica could never be ordinary and he accepted that—a sick part of him even loved that about her—but just for one moment he wanted the Jessica that showed she had a jealous side.

"I don't want you to be a martyr."

She turned with narrowed eyes, wiping her mouth along the back of her hand. "You assume I'm suffering somehow?"

Moving his empty bottle like a pendulum, he clenched his teeth but the words still came out. "My ex-fiancée is dying and you tell me to go see her."

Jessica set her empty glass on the counter. "She's not necessarily dying."

"It doesn't matter. That's not the point."

"O-kay ... so tell me what *is* the point?"

Luke slammed the bottle onto the coffee table then tugged at his hair. "The point is you should be concerned that my going to see Fran could stir up emotions from my past. That ... that seeing her in such a helpless state could cause me to leave you to be by her side because I might think she needs me more than you do."

"Whoa ... how many beers have you had?"

He didn't answer, choosing instead to stare at the floor, breathless with anger. Anger about what? He wasn't sure.

"Jesus, Luke. I was jealous of slutty Lickey, and then your lunch date in Tahoe before I knew it was with your sister. But that was when I didn't know how you felt about me. That was before you promised that someday you'd beg me to marry you. That was before you asked me and Jones to move in with you. If something has changed, then now would be a good time to confess. Otherwise, I'm not going to be jealous of your ex-fiancée, who may or may not be dying, unless you keep saying shit about seeing her and it stirring up emotions that would make you leave me."

"I'm not leaving you." It was the truth, but he still couldn't look at her. Jessica's sharp perception would've seeped through his vulnerability until everything came crashing down.

"Go see her, Luke."

AFTER SOBERING UP, Luke apologized to Jessica for his reaction to the morning's events. It came as no surprise that she forgave him. In spite of her past, which included killing someone with a knife, Luke knew she was the better person. If she were him, she would have already packed her bags and been on a plane to Scottsdale.

Instead, after a week of an awkward existence as room-mates, the kind that didn't have sex and gave each other polite smiles in passing, they packed up the essentials and Jones, then drove to Tahoe to spend the weekend with Luke's family. It may have been a cowardly move, but he decided they needed a change in scenery to bring Jessica out of her withdrawn state. Of course he didn't let her drive, but she didn't ask either. However, the death-look, that he'd come to know all too well, stuck to her face the entire way there. At one point when they stopped to let Jones do his thing, he almost handed her the keys. *Almost.*

"Tell me why you're mad."

Jessica coughed a throaty chuckle. "We're twenty

minutes from your parents' place and you want to have a conversation based on your assumption that I'm mad?"

"Are you not?"

"No. I'm not mad."

An interesting thing about medical school and specializing in psychiatry was the lack of information about the intricate workings of the female mind. Unfortunately, he proved to be his biggest obstacle. The change in their relationship stemmed from the Fran revelation. It made no sense why she would really want him to go visit Fran, but with each passing day filled with her withdrawn attitude and kissing Jones more than him, it became quite clear that's exactly what she expected him to do.

"Then why haven't we ..." Sex. He wanted to know why they hadn't had sex. No amount of education, plaques on the wall, or professional accolades could completely hide the man behind the doctor.

"Why haven't we ...?"

"Exercised."

Dr. Jones went MIA whenever Luke tried to have a conversation that involved their relationship.

"Exercised? Well, I don't know why *we* haven't exercised, but *I've* been doing it every day while you've been stuck at your office 'catching up on dictation' until after dinner most nights. Jude's been quite happy that I've been available to spar almost every night."

Luke *had* been at his office with legitimate work to do, but nothing that he couldn't have done at home. Dr. Jones would have made the brilliant assessment that Luke had been avoiding not only Jessica but Fran and his past too. The woman beside him possessed too much intelligence to dismiss the reaction he had to the news of Fran.

Since she and Jones moved in with him, Jessica had

adopted Luke's healthy way of sleeping in the nude. He'd been living with live porn. There wasn't a guy in the world that would not have envied the sight that greeted him every night when he walked out of the bathroom: sexy naked woman on the bed, knees bent, legs spread wide, one hand rolling a nipple between two fingers, the other hand circling her glistening clitoris. Jessica needed sex before she could settle into a good sleep. Luke always obliged her. During the five days of her menstrual cycle, she'd join him in the shower, but *never* did they go without it.

Until ...

"Sex. Fine. I said it. We haven't had it since the whole Fran thing. You've been wearing a full suit of armor to bed every night."

"A full suit of armor?" After hours of nothing but her side profile as she stared out the back window, because, yes, she was sitting in the back seat with Jones, Jessica relinquished a wide-eyed look in the rearview mirror at Luke. "Your definition of a full suit of armor is a tank top and panties?"

Years of practiced patience and complete self-control had given Dr. Jones the reputation of having an unbreakable focus—until Jessica Day. She could bring Hercules to his knees with words alone.

"Everything is relative, Jessica. So yes, going from masturbating in the nude on my bed to a tank top and panties, curled into fetal position with your eyes closed, would be equivalent to a full suit of armor."

With an easy nod, lips twisted, she turned back toward the window. "Interesting."

The steering wheel vibrated beneath his white-knuckled fists. His mother's keen observation skills would have him under interrogation within minutes of arriving if he didn't get things worked out in the next five minutes. No pressure.

A mile from their house he down shifted and pulled to the side of the road. Amber eyes met his in the mirror again.

"I'm going to let you drive the rest of the way." As sure as her naked body distracted him, he knew his GTO would erase whatever grudge she'd been holding.

Luke grinned as she opened the door, but it quickly faded when she hooked Jones's leash to his collar. "What are you doing?"

"Come, baby," she said, leading Jones along the side of the road.

"Jess ... I'm letting you drive my GTO."

"Pfft..." she kept walking "...letting me drive down a road that won't take it out of second gear is a fucking insult and you know it."

ASSHOLE. The good doctor didn't want to be called Jones. Well Jessica decided he wasn't worthy of the biblical name, Luke, either. Asshole seemed much more fitting as she walked the last mile to Felicity and Tom's house. She really hadn't been mad at him. Luke loved Fran at one time and she knew he loved too hard to just let all those feelings vanish. Four bottles of Heineken proved it. Jessica would never find complete closure while Matthew Green still drew air in his lungs, but Luke could find it with Fran.

However, the humming idle of the GTO crawling behind them ... *that* made her mad. The "full suit of armor" was a sign of respect, an understanding that Luke needed time to work through his feelings about the news of Fran. Sex was Jessica's drug of choice to drown out painful emotions, but it had always been temporary. She didn't want to be Luke's drug, even if he was hers. If Dr. I-don't-have-to-admit-I-have-human-emotions Jones wanted to psychoanalyze their sex life, then she had only two words: game on.

"Jessica!" Felicity called from the front porch.

Jessica held out her hand to block the setting sun. Jones bucked against his leash, going into his spastic mode. New people with high-pitched voices had him going berserk like a dog on speed. Her arm worked best in its socket so she released the leash about twenty yards from the porch and prayed Felicity was a dog person who didn't mind the occasional tackle and a lick down equivalent to a carwash.

"Jess?" Luke grabbed her arm before she reached the porch.

She turned, ripping her arm from his grasp. "Asshole."

Luke sighed. A look of defeat stole his beautiful features. "Please don't."

"Don't what?"

"Don't do this in front of my parents."

"Why can't we just be ourselves with your parents, huh? Why do we always need a plan or script?"

"We don't. I'm just saying—"

"Good." Jessica turned and marched to the porch. "Hi, Felicity." They embraced.

"Hi, honey. How's my boy treating you?"

"He's whining about not getting enough sex and he's jerking around my emotions for his car ... but other than that, I can't complain."

"Oh for God's sake," Luke mumbled, taking the last step to the porch.

Felicity released Jessica then gave Luke a firm, motherly glare. "Sounds like his dad. When Tom had that car he never let me drive it. Not. Once. And don't even get me started on the whole sex deprivation speech."

"My over-educated son should know better than to bring a bitter woman to spend the weekend with his mom." Tom pushed open the screen door.

Felicity turned, lifting onto her toes to give Tom a quick kiss. "You know I'm a peacemaker."

He hugged her. "Except when you're stirring the pot." Tom smacked her ass.

Luke rolled his eyes, proving even grown children get embarrassed with their parents' PDA.

"We have two other couples staying this weekend, so I have you both in the purple room. That is ... if you're still okay sleeping in the same bed?"

"We're fine, Mom." Luke slung both bags over his shoulder and grabbed Jessica's hand, dragging her toward the stairs.

"Dinner's in an hour, lovebirds. So get your kissing and making up done before then. Tom will take Jones for a walk."

Jessica squeezed Luke's hand so hard he grunted by the time they reached the purple room. Releasing both her and the bags, he shut the door. The pleading look of a truce or forgiveness he'd given her just moments earlier had been replaced with a look of rage. Other women would have cowered to such an intimidating glare, but not Jessica. It turned her on because truthfully she did need sex with Luke. She craved it more than food and some days more than air.

"Take off your clothes, now."

A smirk played along her lips. She loved it when Luke went all alpha on her. Even she'd been shocked how much she loved submitting to him. Some days it felt like a need, a confirmation that he was the one person she could trust with every part of her being. He promised surrendering to him would give her the greatest sense of control. And he was right, but not on that particular day.

When her clothes were nothing more than a pool of cotton on the floor, she stepped toward him, shoving him back on the bed. His eyes grew wide for a second before narrowing into dark pools of blue ink. He started to sit up as she straddled his legs.

She shook her head, shoving him back again. "You know I love every inch of your hard, lean, muscled flesh. And your mind ... God I love your mind. But you know what I've *come* to love most about you, Dr. Jones?"

He swallowed hard as she positioned her knees on either side of his head.

"Your mouth."

Luke dug his fingers into her hips, pulling her down to him.

"Fuck," she yelled as he parted her with one slow stroke of his tongue. Who was she kidding? It had been too long and she wasn't going to last long with his greedy tongue spearing into her then lapping over her clitoris. The goal was to take what she needed then leave him. Desperate. Blue-balled. Angry.

She was on top in a place of control, yet every ounce of it began to slip.

"Pinch your nipples," he said with each word vibrating against her hypersensitive sex that felt seconds from exploding.

"No." She shook her head. He wasn't in charge, she was. Her terms. Her control. It was his lesson, not hers.

He turned his head and bit the inside of her leg.

"Ow!"

"Pinch. Your. Fucking. Nipples."

Like a dog chasing a rabbit, all she could think about was the orgasm. It was so close yet just out of reach. He wasn't going to win, but as a trade for the release she needed so desperately, she cupped her breasts, pinching her nipples. It felt good but not enough to push her over the edge.

"Luke ..." She couldn't remember when his hands left her hips, but it didn't matter. She lowered to his face again, but he just kept kissing and nipping at her inner thigh. "Luke ..." Begging was not part of the plan. He would pay for making her beg—just as soon as he put his mouth back where she needed it. One more slow lick and she'd be there.

"Oh ... fuck ... fuck ... fuck ..." His eyes rolled back in his head.

"What the ..." she stilled, staring at him. Luke had *the* look, made *the* sound. Jessica looked over her shoulder.

"You did not—"

"Oh you bet your sexy ass I did. Now up you go." He lifted her off him and sat up, wadding the front of his cum-covered shirt before pulling it over his head and tucking himself back into his jeans. "I'll grab a clean shirt and give you a few minutes to ... finish up." He smirked while zipping his jeans.

Jessica's urge to make Luke bleed had been in remission until that moment. A broken nose and busted testicle seemed like the most fitting punishment.

"Oh..." he stopped at the door after shrugging on a clean shirt "...you have my permission to tell my mom that you're pissed at me because I wouldn't let you ride my face to the finish."

"Asshole."

"I adore you too." Luke shut the door.

CHAPTER TWENTY-ONE
KNIGHT

LILITH RESPECTED Jillian's wish to not talk about AJ, yet she knew if—*when*—he died she'd know. Even if Lilith and Dodge didn't say anything, Jillian knew Cage or AJ's parents would contact her. Missing two men who were still alive felt like a knife continuing to carve at the empty cavity that once housed her heart.

Luke. She imagined him with someone else by then, maybe even in love. He deserved that. The part of her that wanted that for him felt equally loving and masochistic.

AJ. No news was good news, unless he suffered. Jillian couldn't go there.

Radiation.

Seizures.

Migraines.

Memory loss.

It was too much—until she received a text that crippled her emotions to the point of questioning her own will to survive.

Sarge: *Fly to Portland and rent a car. Then wait for my instructions. But DO NOT come to my parents' house.*

"You look like you've seen a ghost," Jackson said as he climbed the last step, flinging his sweaty towel over his shoulder.

Jillian nodded, eyes fixed to her phone.

"Shit. Not another message."

She shook her head slowly.

"Then what?" He slipped her phone out from her hand. "No." He handed it back to her then brushed past her to the kitchen.

"I have to go," she whispered, feeling dazed and maybe a little in shock.

"No way. Need I remind you what happened the last time you made a trip to the West Coast?"

"He needs me."

"So do I." Jackson chugged back a glass of water.

"Then come with me."

Jackson shook his head.

"Because of Ryn?"

"Because I have students, and a house, and a life here now. Because we're not supposed to leave this state without notifying G.A.I.L, because—"

"Because you're in love."

"No." He glared at her, continuing the adamant shake of his head.

"I don't blame you for staying for her, but don't blame me for leaving for him."

"Not the same thing and you know—"

"You're right, it's not! You've been here with Ryn and I've been a fucking miserable mess for weeks, but you wouldn't know it because I've done what I do best—ignore the worst Goddamned hand of cards anyone has ever been dealt." She sucked in a shaky breath. "But I'm tired of missing him and wondering why he's there and I'm here."

Jackson sighed. "Fine, then call McGraw and if he approves your little trip then you have my blessing."

"I'm going and you're not going to say anything to McGraw," Jillian said each word with slow precision.

"You can't do this to me again."

Jillian drew her brows together. "Again?"

"Claire."

"Don't," she warned.

"You told me you were going to San Diego with Claire and I wasn't supposed to say anything to anyone."

"That's not—"

"What?" Jackson rested his hands on his hips and leaned forward. "Fair? Is that what you were going to say? Because you're right, it's not fair. It's not fair that you make me feel responsible for everybody's fucking life. It's not fair that I have to keep your secrets *and* keep you alive."

He was right and every cell in her brain knew it. A downside to being Jillian Knight was the tendency to ignore all reason. She did everything one-hundred percent or not at all. AJ was unfinished business.

"I absolve you of your brotherly duties because I'm going. I have to."

Jackson looked at the ceiling. "You're so fucking stupid."

Passionate. Jillian lived her life with an intensity born of deep passion. Jackson did too, he just refused to see their shared reflection in the mirror.

McGraw didn't stop Jillian from making her first trip to Portland. Jillian had no reason to believe he'd stop her from making a second trip. Although Jackson didn't like him, he still referred to McGraw as Jillian's other big brother. She retched a little every time Jackson made the comparison.

After landing in Portland, she rented a Jeep and texted AJ.

Done

Her nerves were frayed from the opposing friction of fear and anticipation over seeing him. She had no idea why he'd beckoned her and why it seemed to be such a secret. It didn't matter. *He* was the only one who mattered as she waited in a Subway parking lot just five miles from his parents' house.

Sarge: *One hour. 2 blocks north.*

"Calm the fuck down, Jillian." She rested her hand over her chest. "It's not like you're kidnapping him."

It had been too many weeks since she'd seen him. A lifetime ago, or so it felt after resigning herself to the fact that she would never see him again. She held her breath as a figure moved toward the Jeep, a dark shadow in the night.

He opened the door and slid in the gray leather seat. Jillian continued to hold her breath. He didn't even look at her.

"Go." The profile of the man beside her barely resembled the man she'd been with in Omaha. He'd lost weight, mostly muscle weight, and his cheekbones were more prominent against his slightly sunken eyes. No hair. No eyebrows. No eye lashes.

Her gaze lingered on the raised burn mark near his left temple. She clenched her hand to keep from reaching for him. Finally, she exhaled, turning on the headlights and shifting into drive.

"Where are we going?"

"Anywhere but here."

"Home?"

He shook his head.

Less than ten minutes later he was asleep. She rested her hand on his. He didn't move so she just drove. By three in the morning Jillian needed sleep. Somewhere in nowhere Idaho she pulled into the parking lot of a hotel and paid for a room. AJ still hadn't moved. Jillian found herself brushing her fingers over his wrist, feeling for a pulse. A weak beat, but nonetheless, a beat.

"AJ?" she whispered several times before he stirred to consciousness. "Let's go inside."

With groggy eyes he surveyed the area and nodded once. Jillian wrapped his arm around her shoulder, doing her best to steady him enough to make it to the room. He collapsed on the bed and just like that, he was out again. Jillian swallowed past the lump in her throat as she looked at the shell of a man that she used to know.

After pulling off his shoes, she tucked a pillow under his head and tried to move his legs so they both rested on the bed instead of hanging off the edge. Then she sank onto the bed next to his and closed her eyes, hoping when she opened them he'd look different—stronger, more alive.

A MOANING of a wounded animal woke Jillian several hours later. She shot up, disoriented and panicked until AJ came into sight. He coughed a few times then squinted his eyes open.

"Water," he said with a raspy voice.

Jillian filled a cup in the bathroom and handed it to him as he struggled to a sitting position on the bed. He took it down in three large swallows.

"More."

She nodded and refilled his cup. After drinking the second glassful, he let his eyes settle on her for the first time.

"You're stunning," he whispered, the dryness in his throat still evident.

Luke had told her everything was relative, so although she felt far from stunning, given her present company, she conceded to the stunning compliment.

"Thank you. You look like shit."

AJ worked hard for a small smile. It was barely detectable, but she saw it.

"God, I've missed you." He dropped his head back against the headboard.

"Well, I assumed from the nasty burns that they've been frying your brain, but that crazy statement just confirmed it."

Another hint of a smile. "Come here." He opened his arms.

Jillian stared at him.

"Don't act like you're afraid of breaking me. You've already done that ... more than once."

She wanted, *needed*, a smart-ass remark to give back to him, but seeing him that way broke something inside of her. So she curled up on his lap and rested her ear against his chest as he wrapped her in his arms.

"Jackson's screwing your housekeeper." She batted away a rebel tear.

AJ's chest vibrated with a soft chuckle. "Of course he is."

"She's beautiful and very nice. I can't believe you didn't snatch her up yourself."

He kissed the top of her head and another tear broke free, but she caught it before it fell to his chest. "I'm not into the pretty, nice girls. I kinda have a thing for evil temptresses who usually have a black eye or busted lip. Flawless beauty is overrated."

Jillian smiled, pressing her lips to his sternum. "You just said I'm stunning."

"I meant shocking. Your hair is a tangled mess, and you need a shower."

"Fuck you."

Another kiss on her head. "There's my girl."

"At least I have hair."

"Low blow."

She slid her hand over his crotch. "I don't think you're ready for a low blow. Maybe after I get some food in you."

"You're emasculating."

"So I've been told."

Her fingers drifted down his ribs that had become more prominent than his *half dozen*. "Aric James?"

"Hmm?"

"Are you running away?"

The already stagnant air in the room thickened in the silence.

"I'm taking a break."

"A break from what?"

AJ rested his cheek on the top of her head and squeezed her so tight she could barely breathe. "Death."

Jillian cursed her damn tears. Love hurt so much.

"I left a note next to my phone for my family. It said everything there is to say, then it ended in goodbye."

His thumb brushed her cheek, catching a few tears. Tears that belonged to him. Tears of pain ... his pain. She couldn't stop drowning in his pain.

"When I saw you parked along the side of the road, it was the first real breath I'd taken in over six weeks."

Every word pulled the knot in her stomach tighter.

"Greta had a Lascivio party."

Jillian loved the way his gentle laugh tickled her cheek. If he could take a break from death, so could she.

"I knew you and your brother would rob all innocence from Peaceful Woods."

"We're doing our best."

"I've taken you away from Lilith."

"Their daughter is coming to stay for a while. Maybe until I get home."

"So how long do I have you?"

The knot tightened even more.

"As long as you need me."

AJ NEEDED HER. How long he needed her was the question that had a grave answer. Forever. Unfortunately, AJ's forever had a finite number of days compared to most other people. He loved his parents and even the newfound friendship he'd made with Brooke—an amends of sorts. The only reprieve from thinking non-stop about Jillian came with a weekend visit from Cage. He loved that boy. He loved him so damn much.

His parents took him to his doctor appointments, fed him, washed his laundry, and encouraged him in his dark times that had become more frequent as the effects of the radiation began to set in. Yet he started to resent their presence in his life because it all came at a cost and Jillian was that cost.

"You're not eating enough." She gave him her best evil glare as he poked around at his plate of room service food: grilled salmon, broccoli, and a twice-baked potato. "You only ate a dry piece of toast and a hard-boiled egg for breakfast."

"You ordered everything on the menu."

Jillian shrugged as she slurped in a long piece of spaghetti. "You were asleep and I didn't want to wake you to see what you wanted."

"I haven't had an appetite worth shit for weeks."

"Clearly." She gave him the once-over look.

"Sorry." He frowned at his barely-touched plate of food. "I'm not a great dinner date yet."

"No worries." She held up one of the paper napkins. "It's not a real date anyway."

AJ shook his head. "You're impossible. I can't believe with all the meals we've shared that none of them have qualified as a date because of the stupid napkin not meeting your standards."

"Well, a girl's gotta have standards."

"You don't see how ridiculous it is that your napkin standards exceed your dress-code standards for getting the mail?"

She sucked in the last piece of pasta then licked her lips. "I'll have you know, I've been wearing more clothes lately to get the mail."

"Because it's colder outside. Right?"

A smirk stole her attempt to come across as a changed woman. "Maybe."

AJ went to stand then grabbed his head, eyes squeezed tight.

"You're in pain."

"No." His seething response contradicted the "no."

Jillian riffled through his backpack, the only thing he brought with him. "These?" She held up a prescription bottle.

He peeked through his squint. "Yes."

She handed him two and his water. "You only have four left. Maybe you should call your doctor's office and see if they can call in a refill."

AJ shook his head, swallowing the last of the water. "Something tells me when a cancer patient goes MIA, doctors don't continue to offer up drugs."

"You didn't finish treatment?"

"Two weeks left. Close enough."

"Jesus! You put in all that time and misery to quit two weeks before the finish."

"Finish?" He laughed through the pain. "When they, as you put it, 'fry my brain,' I'm not sure there is a finish."

"So now what?" Jillian moved their plates to the tray by the door.

"I don't know. What do you think?"

Disbelief echoed in her sarcastic laugh. "What do I think? I think I let you go, gave you back to your family so they could be with you for as long as you had left. I think my whole fucking life has been an epic tale of bad timing." Plunking down on the bed, she sighed. "I'm not going to lie. I wanted to use you. You triggered something in me and I couldn't think about anything else. I wanted to make you bleed and suffer. The need to conquer you consumed me. There was something so cathartic about the fight for control."

"But?"

Jillian shook her head. "But I'm not a monster anymore, even though I've done some things in my life that are unforgivable. I have this human side that still *feels,* and most of the time I hate those feelings that make me so vulnerable."

Luke would have been proud of those words and that realization kept her talking.

"When we met, I saw someone in you ... someone I hated." Someone she murdered. "But then I saw someone else and everything changed."

AJ held out his hand and Jillian took it, straddling his lap. "Who did you see?"

Brushing the pad of her thumb over his naked brow followed by the burn marks on his head, she shared a sad smile. "Me. Beneath your hardened exterior and need for self-preservation, I saw a painful vulnerability—one that you would never show. Some days when I look at you it feels like I'm seeing my reflection."

CHAPTER TWENTY-TWO

Jackson may have missed his calling. Playing music required one special gift, writing it encompassed a whole new level of talent. Of course, he could do both and made it look effortless. Playing meant he was in a jovial mood, composing happened only when he needed to completely forget about life. Ryn showed up unannounced on that particular forget-about-life day.

A knock at the door. Another knock. The chime of the doorbell.

Jackson played several measures, erased a few notes, added a sharp, and played it again.

A few more loud raps at the door.

"Hello?" Ryn cracked open the door with hesitation.

Jackson gritted his teeth. Something was off, maybe just one note, but that one wrong note ruined the whole piece.

"Hey."

He looked up with a slight squint.

Ryn stopped in her approach. "I knocked ... and rang the doorbell."

Jackson nodded once, pushing his taped glasses up his nose.

"I missed you yesterday."

Tuesday. Jackson chose not to be there when she cleaned their house. The women in his life had been playing him, using him. It was Karma, he couldn't deny it, but that didn't mean he would continue to take it up the backside. Jackson wasn't Jude, but the same blood coursed through his veins and nobody—especially not a woman— could jerk him around like a toy, to be played with then discarded on a whim.

"I didn't want to distract you." He looked back down at his composition book, changing a chord, possibly the offending one.

"You wouldn't have. Or maybe you would have, but only because I may have wanted you to."

Keeping his eyes trained on the music, he chuckled a soft breath of sarcasm. "Well, by all means ... whatever you want is all that fucking matters."

She drew in a breath and held it for a few seconds. "Um ... have I done something wrong?"

"Wrong? No, that couldn't possibly be. You're a woman and women can do no wrong. Isn't that correct?"

"Maybe I'll just go," she said with a small voice, backing up one slow step at a time.

"Sounds like the best idea I've heard all day."

"Why are you being such an asshole all of a sudden?"

"Asshole?" Jackson stood, sending the bench crashing behind him. "You think *I'm* being an asshole." He stalked toward her.

Ryn took another step back.

"I'm not being an asshole!"

The booming rage in his voice made her flinch. With her next step back she tripped over the leg of the chair, falling backwards.

"D-don't hit me ... p-please don't." She curled into a ball, covering her head with her arms.

The entire world gave out beneath him. Ryn on his floor, helpless and shaking—fearing *him*. Nothing had ever felt so gutting.

"Fuck ... Ryn." He bent down.

"No!" She tensed, her whole body tightening into a smaller ball as a sob escaped.

"It's okay." He hooked her waist with one arm. She screamed and flailed as he picked her up, trapping her arms with his as he sat on the couch.

"Let me go!"

"Shh ... I'm not going to hurt you."

Eventually she surrendered, falling limp in his arms with her face buried in his chest.

"You're right. I'm an asshole ... such a fucking asshole," he whispered in her ear. "But I swear to God, I'd never hurt you."

His sister was a caged animal with sensitive trigger points. Jackson should have known that a woman who survived an abusive marriage would have her own triggers and breaking points.

Asshole ... total asshole.

He held her tight, gliding a calming hand over her hair while whispering *sorry* to her over and over. After she stopped shaking, he cupped her red, tear-stained face and tilted it up to him.

"I am *so* fucking sorry."

Ryn sniffled, rolling her lips together. "I'm so embarrassed." She tried to shake her head in his grasp. "I can't believe I reacted like that. I guess ... I don't know ... I tripped so many times trying to get away from Preston, and when I was on the ground he ..." huge tears rolled down her cheeks as she bit her quivering lip.

"He hit you?"

She nodded.

"He kicked you?"

Another nod.

Jackson's brow tensed. "No one is ever going to make you feel that vulnerable again. I promise." Brushing his lips against hers, he waited for her to respond. After a few seconds she kissed him, slow at first then desperate as her hands clawed his shirt as if she couldn't get close enough.

He pulled back, leaving them both breathless. "Come on. Your training starts now."

"I don't think Jillian and I are the same size," Ryn said from the top of the stairs.

"Close enough. Come down here."

Ryn tugged at the borrowed exercise shorts that barely, and maybe didn't quite cover her ass. The sports bra proved to be a bit more flattering than her compression ones, but her abs were sad ... so very sad.

"Maybe we should do this tomorrow. I'll wear some yoga pants and a tank top."

"Get your ass down here."

On a deep sigh, she descended the stairs. As if the outfit wasn't embarrassing enough, she couldn't stop having flashbacks of her extreme reaction to Jackson's temper. She knew he wouldn't hurt her, but when she fell it triggered something so instinctual. Preston's voice echoed in her ears, his fist cracked against her cheek bone, and the toe to his shoe sent a piercing pain to her ribs. It had been years since a flashback felt so real and crippling.

"You're so much sexier than you think you are."

"I'm sorry." She wrung her hands together behind her back.

"Never apologize for being sexy."

Her lip curled as a warm blush crept up her neck. "About how I reacted earlier. I'm so embarrassed. I acted like a complete psychotic freak."

"It was all on me." He grabbed her hand and jerked her into his chest. "And trust me ... *you* are not a psychotic freak. I can guarantee Jillian has that title."

"Jillian? Really?"

Jackson nodded. The intensity in his expression radiated an unspoken pain. "It's completely justified. She hasn't always been this way. There are just some things in life that can only be erased by death. I don't want her to die, so I've accepted the crazy."

"I love the way you love her."

He nodded with a thoughtful pull to his brow. Ryn imagined being loved by Jackson would be an extraordinary gift.

"Let's do this, hot pants."

She rolled her eyes. Would he ever let her live down the panties in the fridge incident?

They started small. Jackson reinforced some things she'd already learned about preventing confrontation. Then he showed her some basic moves to strike the most effective body parts: eyes, nose, ears, neck, groin, knee, and legs.

"You're exerting too much energy with weak attempts," he said.

She was already gasping for air and had yet to land a single strike.

"It's hit or be hit. You may only have one chance so make it count. Got it?"

Ryn nodded. "But I don't really want to hurt you."

"If you can't make me bleed, knock the wind out of me, or make me buckle over in pain, then you're always going to be an easy target."

She kicked at his knee with the pressure of shoving open the back door to bring in the groceries.

"No."

Her heart pounded. The conserving energy thing wasn't going so well.

She went for his other knee. He easily avoided her strike.

"You're telling me with your eyes exactly what you're going to do."

She met his eyes then squinted. He pissed her off with his arrogance.

Smack!

"Oh shit! I'm so sorry."

He blotted the slow drip of blood from his nose with a smirk on his face.

"Better. Much better."

"But you're bleeding." Her face morphed into a tight wince.

"By choice." He grabbed a towel and pressed it to his nose.

"You let me do that on purpose?"

Jackson chuckled. "It's your first day. I'm not going to lie and give you false confidence, so yes, I let you make me bleed. We both needed to know that you could put some power behind your punch."

"You played me."

Another chuckle rumbled from his chest as he tossed the towel aside. "I'm getting mixed signals. Are you upset because you made me bleed or that I let you make me bleed?"

Her jaw unhinged then closed, but nothing came out. Why was she upset? Plopping down on the mat, she criss-crossed her legs and focused on catching her breath.

"You were mad at me when I showed up. Why?"

Looking to the ceiling, he drained a bottled water then licked a drip from his lip as his gaze locked with hers. "Jillian went to Portland for AJ. It's kind of complicated, but it wasn't the ... *safest* decision. I told her not to go but she did anyway. It's impossible to protect someone you love when they put themselves at risk halfway across the country."

"What's so dangerous about going to Portland?"

Jackson chewed the inside of his lip, focusing on her with a thoughtful stare. "Earthquakes ... volcanoes ..."

"Yeah, sure. I'm not buying that, but it still doesn't explain why you were so mad at me."

Jackson lifted his arms and pressed his palms to the side of his head while shaking it. A low grumble accompanied his frustration. The last time they were together the sex was good. Good? No. They'd had exceptional sex. She hadn't inspected the condom, but it seemed as though he came. If not, his acting skills were quite good. Ryn didn't care for that scenario. A guy faking it? For some reason that seemed so wrong. Sexist? Maybe.

"How do I explain this without sounding like a ..."

"A?"

He scrubbed his hands over his face, mumbling beneath them. "A girl."

That brought a curious smile to her face. "A girl?"

"Yes." His hands dropped to his sides as he leveled her with his gaze. "Random sex. The 'guy' thing. I was good at it … really good at it."

Those were not inspiring words.

"I never gave women a chance to be clingy or needy or even the opportunity to fall asleep next to me."

Jackson Knight had been a man whore. Ryn sort of knew that, but she sure didn't appreciate the reminders.

"I avoided biological clocks, second dates, family dinners, holding hands, and often names weren't even exchanged." He nodded. "I know … I was a real prick. But I'm not now, or at least I don't want to be. So when you kicked me out the other night it pissed me off. *I* don't get tossed to the curb like a rejected teddy bear, so when you did it, I realized how much of a clingy female I'd become. I found myself being the one who wanted to stay just to see your face in the morning. But you … well you were me or the old me—the hump 'em and dump 'em person. Anyway, I was mad about Jillian for leaving, rejecting my protection, and I decided to have some menstrual-cycle pity party like a fucking pussy and the anger you saw was really at myself. I was just deflecting it at you, and I shouldn't have. I'm sorry."

Her eyes grew with each point he tried to make, like air being pumped into her head, leaving it ready to explode.

"I'm not even sure where to begin. First, I did not kick you out or hump you and dump you. As I recall, you left."

"Two seconds after I got you off with my fingers shoved in your pussy and your nipple between my teeth, you said,

'So ... I'll see you Tuesday.' So, yeah. I'm not an idiot. You dismissed me."

Everything in Ryn's head spun, making her dizzy because nothing made sense. Pussy? Did couples really use that term with each other? She tested it out in her mind. ... *two fingers shoved in your pussy* versus ... *two fingers shoved in your vagina*. It could go either way.

"Would you look in the mirror? I'm sure it sounds like I'm beating this horse to death, but you. Are. A. God! In ten years you are still going to look like a god because men like you only get better with age. I, however, will look fifty: wrinkles, bags under my eyes, all of my skin suffering from loss of elasticity. I want you to be forty and me to be thirty, but it can't be that way. Thirty for me consisted of supervising slumber parties and shopping for training bras ... oh and trying not to upset my husband, who fucked every woman except me then beat the shit out of me for not working hard enough to keep him interested in me."

With a deep sigh, the kind that came after releasing a lifetime of guilt, Ryn pulled her brows together. "I try to eat well, I exercise regularly, and my bathroom vanity is covered in bottles of creams and lotions that have promised me the fountain of youth but have yet to deliver. I love ... *whatever* this is we've been doing. It's been such a vacation from reality. When I'm with you it's just ... indescribable. Our flirty banter, our pretend wedding with a Vera Wang dress and Ed Sheeran, and the things you say to me that make me feel sexy and desirable in a way I never imagined possible, it's ..." She shook her head.

"I agree." He stood, easing toward her with a caution he lacked when she arrived. "Except for one thing."

"You agree?" Ryn looked up as he laced his fingers through her hair, cupping her face.

"Yes. You do eat well and exercise. And I've seen your bathroom counter ... all those stupid creams are a waste of money because you can't improve on beauty like yours. The banter, our wedding, the things I say to you, the way I look at you, how fucking hard I get every time I touch you ... it's not pretend. It's not a game. It *is* reality. Okay, hot pants?"

Ryn rebounded from her dump of insecurities and giggled instead. "I'm never wearing underwear around you again."

Jackson quirked a brow. "Mmm ... that sounds like a *tasty* idea."

The hot flush of embarrassment she felt could have melted Saturn. Sure, she was forty but did that have to mean she was a prude? The woman behind the red face had led a sexually sheltered life coming from the school of boys having penises and girls having vaginas.

"I can't believe you just said that." She averted her gaze to the side even with his hands holding her face so close to his.

"I'm just being honest. I find myself constantly craving your pussy."

"Oh my God! Stop staying that." Wriggling out of his grasp, she fisted his shirt and buried her face in his chest.

Jackson kissed the top of her head as he chuckled. "What do you want me to say? I like licking—"

"Stop!"

Another devious chuckle. "Or eating—"

"No! No! No!"

"Do you prefer cunt to puss—"

"Vagina! It's a vagina, okay?" She stopped short of also emphasizing that it's not a meal or snack. Although, denying how much she enjoyed his tongue exploring her *vagina* would have been a lie.

Jackson's chuckle escalated into a full roaring laugh. "You want me to call your pussy a vagina? You think that's sexy?"

Ryn smiled, face still buried in his shirt. "I don't want you to call it anything. Please ... just let me die."

CHAPTER TWENTY-THREE

DAY

JESSICA HAD balls that were arguably bigger than most men's. However, they failed to meet the size requirement for sharing with his parents the riding-Luke's-face-just-shy-of-an-orgasm incident. He played her, used her for his own pleasure, then tossed her aside to prove a point—he was a worthy adversary.

"Hope you like fajitas, Jessica. I am in the mood for margaritas and guacamole tonight," Felicity said while filling the glasses, complete with sugar and salt rim garnish.

"I love Mexican."

Luke handed her a glass. The shit-eating grin needed to be wiped off the smug bastard's face. "Did you get everything *finished* up?"

Evil coursed through her veins as she cocked her head to the side while accepting the drink. "Did Luke tell you about Fran?"

Felicity and Tom jerked their heads in Luke's direction. The easy mood vanished, leaving an eerie silence and tension so tight it felt as if the floor could crack open and swallow them whole.

Jessica thought she'd seen every one of Luke's facial expressions. She was wrong. There wasn't a hint of adoration left. The icy look he gave her left her heart pounding in her throat.

"So ... you two have discussed Fran?" Felicity asked. Each word sounded cautious as if she, too, could feel the dangerous tension.

Luke swallowed, glaring at Jessica. She wanted to take back every word.

"We discussed how Fran and I met."

"Oh ..." Felicity's nervous smile hid something. Jessica didn't know what.

"I ... *we* found out last week that Fran needs a heart transplant."

Tom and Felicity nodded slowly.

"Jessica thinks I need to go visit her in Scottsdale."

What was going on? The three of them knew something ... something Jessica didn't.

The victim turned monster had been in some very uncomfortable situations in her life, but nothing quite like that moment. Nobody spoke, yet everyone looked at one person: Jessica.

Finally, Tom cleared his throat. "Shall we eat?" He might as well have said "at ease."

Felicity dumped a bag of corn chips into a bowl and handed it and the dish of guacamole to Tom as though the previous two minutes never happened. Except they had happened and Luke's lingering gaze filled with anger, disappointment, and pain reminded her that she had somehow epically fucked up.

"Have a seat," Luke said, devoid of all emotion.

She sat down. Jones plopped his big body on the floor behind her chair because he was a mama's boy.

"So did you get your place sold since moving in with Luke?" Felicity asked.

"I rented. Only wealthy or very old people own property in San Francisco."

"I anticipated starting work on my sailboat before cooler weather hit, but now I think it's just going to have to wait until spring. You still in on the project with me?" Tom asked.

"Of course." She glanced at Luke for confirmation that they would still be together in the spring. He gave her nothing.

"Lake has a boyfriend and he has family in San Francisco, so I think you'll be seeing your sister a lot more."

Luke nodded, dipping the same chip into the guacamole over and over without ever taking a bite.

"What are your plans for the holidays?"

Luke stayed in his zombie zone as if no one else at the table existed.

Jessica smiled at Tom. "My parents have invited us to their house for Thanksgiving, but we haven't really committed to anything yet."

Tom nodded, much like his son. She questioned if he even registered her answer to *his* question.

"Of course, my other boyfriend invited me for a sex-filled weekend on his private island off the coast of Italy."

All. Three. Nodded.

"Dammit, Jones!" Jessica stood, resting her palms on the table.

Three heads jerked up and the dog scampered off to the living room, certain he was in trouble. Old habit. Luke may have bought her a dog and named him Jones, but when she was pissed, Luke's name was still Jones. Actually, first name Dammit, last name, Jones.

"I didn't want to have it out right here in front of your parents, but it would seem they know more than I do so maybe this needs to be a group conversation. You know damn well that *I*, more than anyone else, believe the past should stay buried with the dead, but yours is not, so out with it. Francesca—I want every. Little. Detail."

Tom and Felicity frowned at Luke with pain in their eyes.

"Jessica, sweetie, he might not be ready to talk about this," Felicity said.

"Is that right, Luke? Because you said I could ask you *anything*, and now I want everything."

"Maybe we should give you two some privacy."

"Sit. Down."

Tom and Felicity didn't move. Jessica could be cutthroat —literally.

"I'd been drinking Heineken with my college roommate, Levi," Luke spoke in a grave tone. "We'd both had at least four or five too many. He told me about his friend back home who was screwing his roommate's fiancée. He asked my advice ... asked me what his friend should do if the roommate found out they were screwing around behind his back. I couldn't even think that night ... I was completely wasted. So I laughed and said he should put a bullet through both of their heads."

His parents watched him. Pain. The pain was palpable, and she still didn't know why.

"A week later I found Levi in the shower with blood and bits of his brain scattered on the wall, a gun next to his limp hand. In the note on the counter he said he wasn't worth going to jail over so he saved me a life sentence, and he chose the shower to keep the mess contained because of my obsession with cleanliness. Then he asked me to forgive Fran and raise his kid as my own."

Tom wrapped his arm around Felicity as silent sobs shook her body. But Luke ... he said every word without an ounce of emotion, eyes locked to Jessica's the whole time.

"Fran had his baby?" Jessica whispered.

Luke shook his head. "Nope. While he positioned his newly purchased forty-five at his temple, Fran was off having an abortion and then she planned on ending it with him because she still wanted to marry me. I've always wondered whose heart stopped first ... his or his baby's." He blinked slowly several times. "I think you can guess why Fran and I didn't work out. We both had blood on our hands."

"Luke," Jessica said but no other words came out.

"Anyway, I started college majoring in business. After my first year I switched to pre-med, inspired by my work as a firefighter. Psychiatry has been my own personal quest to figure out why, even in my plastered state, I thought death was a fair payback for cheating. And even more than that ... what makes a person give up absolutely everything because he broke some sort of bro code."

He stood and before completely unfolding himself from the chair, he kissed Jessica on the cheek. "That's everything, my love," he whispered over her skin before he turned and walked out of the dining room.

The slam of the front door felt like a book closing at the end of the final chapter.

"Luke made his peace with Francesca after Levi's funeral. It wasn't pretty, but it was final. Even though he doesn't blame her, she's been dead to him for years. If she dies, maybe he'll feel some sort of peace that Levi's been reunited with the woman he loved and the mother of his child. But Luke doesn't need to see her."

Jessica heard every word Felicity said, but she couldn't determine if they were words of wisdom or those of a mother trying to protect her child from any more pain.

LUKE STOOD at the end of the dock, squinting against the cool, numbing breeze as the sun set behind a scattering of clouds suspended in the orangish-purple sky. He missed Levi every damn day.

New bro code: save the bro, kill the ho.

Levi would have laughed at that. He had the best sense of humor. The guy actually giggled like a girl. Luke gave him shit about it, but secretly he loved watching Levi laugh. At the same time, he was a total idiot—missing half of his classes to watch *The Simpsons* and lift weights. Levi looked like an ironman. He claimed muscles and an accent was all it took to get the ladies. Fran certainly helped prove his point.

"That blood on your hands ..."

Luke sucked in a quick breath as Jessica's voice drew near.

"... it never disappears. At best, you might be like me and find someone who loves you so completely that they see past that blood to the naked, untainted flesh beneath it." She wrapped her arms around his waist, resting her cheek against his back.

He squeezed her hands. "I figured you'd be like everyone else and try to convince me that I'm not responsible for Levi's death."

"I suppose I should, but we both know I'm not like everyone else."

"Amen to that." He turned, holding her like the lifeline she was while releasing a long breath.

"Why didn't you just tell me all of that a long time ago?"

"I would have, had our relationship not started out as doctor/patient. You were my focus and I needed you to trust and respect me enough to let me help you. I felt like sharing the weakest moment ... the darkest time of my life would lessen my credibility as a psychiatrist."

"But you told me to ask you anything."

"I did."

"Why?"

"Because you trusting me as the man who adores you beyond words has become more important to me than your opinion of Dr. Jones."

"I think you overestimated my opinion of Dr. Jones."

"I think you eat men's egos for breakfast."

Jessica smiled, looking up at him for a few seconds before it reversed into a frown. "I was rude to your parents. I think I need to apologize."

"We were all rude to you."

She took his hand, pulling him toward the house. "I hadn't noticed."

"Of course not ... you were too busy planning your holiday getaway with your lover on his private island."

She whipped around. "So you *were* paying attention."

"I'm always paying attention ... but only half of the things you say to me deserve a response." He jerked his hand from hers then gave her a playful body check. She stumbled a few steps to the side.

"First one to the house gets to swim naked in the lake tonight," he said, sprinting to the house.

"Dammit, Jones! You did *not* just shove me."

He'd fallen hard for a fiery little woman, but he knew without looking back, she chased his ass with a huge grin on her face. Even if he didn't die with her, he'd die loving her.

Jessica apologized to Felicity and Tom. They both dismissed it, insisting they were the ones who needed to apologize. After the truce, they ate lukewarm fajitas and finished the rest of the melted margaritas and browned guacamole.

"Luke's jumping into the lake naked tonight. I think we all should."

Luke choked on the last ounce of his drink while his parents smiled, eyes wide.

"I—it was a joke." He cleared his throat.

"I'm in." Felicity looked at Tom.

He winked at her, white teeth peeking through his boyish smile. Jessica hoped decades and a slew of kids later that Luke would still look at her that way.

"Great! We're going to need blankets, a roaring fire in the back fire pit, and more alcohol." Jessica stood with a slight wobble to her tequila legs.

"I'll get the blankets and alcohol." Felicity eased out of her chair with Tom holding her steady at the hips.

"Luke and I will start the fire."

"No! No. No. No." Luke shook his head. "Did you not hear me? It was a joke. There will be no jumping in the freezing lake naked. I am not ... I *refuse* to get naked with my girlfriend *and* my parents. God ... just no."

"Come on, Son, live a little."

Luke glared at Tom. "As a doctor I should warn you of the dangers. You could go into cardiac arrest or—"

Tom laughed. "I hate to disappoint you, but this isn't my first skinny dip in the lake ... not even my first this week." He swatted Felicity on the ass. She blew him a kiss over her shoulder.

Luke remained glued to his chair at the table with his face buried in his hands.

"Oh my God!" Jessica giggled in Luke's ear. "I love your parents so much."

Luke looked up with a wrinkled, pleading look etched on his face. "Do you two jump in the lake naked with any of my siblings?"

Felicity tucked a six pack of beer between the pile of blankets. "No. But only because they've never suggested it."

He glared at Jessica.

"This is happening ... it was your idea. Don't make promises you can't keep. Now, up." She tugged his arm until he lumbered to standing.

Surrounded by the chirping and rustling creatures of the night, they made their way down the hill to the fire pit Tom stoked to life with more kindling.

"Who's going in first?" Felicity taunted her son with a sly grin.

"It should be Luke, but the stick in the mud is always the last one to join the party so ..." Jessica shimmied out of her jeans.

"Jess, don't ... please."

"Sorry." She giggled. "I lost all inhibition three drinks ago, Jonesy."

Top. Bra. Panties.

"Carpe diem!"

The air was cool in the lower fifties. The water—arctic.

Rising to the surface, she gasped only to be greeted by Tom and Felicity midair, holding hands. Boobs, balls, and bare booties.

"Ahh!" A creature from the deep attacked her. "Oh my God, Luke." She wrapped her arms around his neck. "I d-didn't s-see you j-jump i-in."

His bluish lips sucked on hers until their teeth chattered against each other. "F-fucking cold." Luke grinned, his whole body shivering.

"Ten, nine, eight, seven, six, five, four, three, two, one ... out!" Felicity yelled as she and Tom raced to the ladder on the dock.

Tom showed no signs of aging as he leapt up the ladder and helped Felicity out. Jessica and Luke quickly followed, all four staggering in a shivering race to the fire and blankets.

"H-here." Felicity tossed Luke and Jessica a huge blanket. "W-wool." She and Tom wrapped up together in the other blanket, plunking down in a chair by the fire.

As their bodies regained a bit of feeling, dodging hypothermia by mere seconds, Jessica started giggling. "We're completely naked, wrapped in a blanket together four feet from your parents who are also naked, wrapped in a blanket together."

Tom and Felicity shared her humor with big smiles while Luke rolled his eyes.

"My parents are pretty cool, but they would *never* do what we just did."

"Hear that, Luke. Jessica thinks we're cool." Tom smirked.

"Yeah, Dad. Jumping in balls first, practically two feet from my girlfriend's face ... that's real cool."

The cackling around the fire pit grew with each new

remark. Everyone had their own assessment of the sixty seconds of complete insanity. It may have been the cold water, the crisp fall air, the flicker of the flames, or the amazing company, but Jessica felt so alive. A weird feeling enveloped her for that small moment in time: normalcy.

"I love your son," Jessica said with a soft voice.

Three sets of eyes fell onto her as the only sound that remained was the flames whispering into the night. Luke hugged her tighter to his naked body. It wasn't sexual, it was natural, destined, perfect.

"He saved me from a dark place. He proved I'm worthy of love, physical touch, endearing words, and complete adoration." She interlaced her fingers with his over her belly. "My best friend and I were kidnapped before our senior year in high school."

"Jess ..." Luke whispered.

She shook her head. A quivering smile tugged at her lips. "It's okay." Her hands squeezed his. "I'm ... better now. I'm better because of you."

He leaned forward and kissed her neck.

"Claire, my friend ... she died. My innocence died that day too. To say I've had trust issues would be a monumental understatement. I've done some things that are truly unforgivable, even ... unimaginable. But your son never wavered, not even a blink. Luke's never looked at me as broken, even though I am. He's just loved all my pieces—even the ones that have made him bleed."

His parents had no reason to take her words literally and that was fine. They didn't need all the details. Her confession of where she'd been and how far she'd come segued to the most sincere thank you ever.

"I know he doesn't live in the ten-mile Jones radius with his own bed and breakfast. But thank you for letting him find his way in life ... thank you for letting him find his way to me."

The dam broke. Felicity didn't even try to wipe her tears, she just let them stream down her face.

Fate. It was a mysterious concept, an unknown destination, and often a heartbreaking journey. For the first time since Claire died, Jessica saw a glimpse of light beyond the cold, eternal darkness. She hoped it was a new day—the dawn of forever.

CHAPTER TWENTY-FOUR
KNIGHT

Jɪʟʟɪᴀɴ ᴀɴᴅ AJ ʜᴇᴀᴅᴇᴅ sᴏᴜᴛʜ, running from the colder weather while keeping a good state or two between them and the West Coast. AJ's body gained some strength, rebounding a bit since the radiation treatment. With that extra boost of strength came pain—debilitating, death-would-be-a-sweet-relief type of pain. Forty-eight hours after the last pain pills were taken, Jillian thought she would have to physically put him out of his misery for good. But she couldn't ... not to AJ.

"I'll be right back," she whispered to AJ as he thrashed in bed, releasing painful moans and grunts that broke Jillian —someone who was nearly impossible to break.

Grabbing her phone she stepped out of their hotel room into the hallway.

"If someone has a gun to your head, it serves you right for being so fucking far away from where I planted your ass."

"I'm sure you wish someone had a gun to my head, McGraw, but that's not why I'm calling. I need a favor."

"Sorry, sweetheart, I'm all out of favors."

"I'm sending you a photo of the label from a bottle of pain pills. I need refills ... unlimited refills at the nearest pharmacy."

"I'm not a doctor."

"You have the power to make the fucking sun stop shining. Pills. Lots of them. Now."

"I don't like how you talk to me."

"I didn't like how you fucked me."

The line went silent, but she knew he was still there.

"You're wasting your time. Just put your highly-decorated sergeant out of his misery."

"Time is all I have these days and you know that, asshole. There's a Walgreens on the corner. Fifteen minutes." Jillian pressed *End*.

As she opened the hotel room door, she heard a clattering of glass.

"What are you doing?"

AJ twisted the cap off a bottle from the minibar refrigerator and gulped it down then reached for another.

"Stop!" She grabbed it from him and shoved the rest of the bottles back in the refrigerator then slammed the door shut. "Twenty minutes. Give me twenty minutes and I'll have some more pain meds for you. Okay?"

AJ sat back on the edge of the bed and pressed the palms of his hands into his eyes. "Fuck!"

Her heart felt like it could explode into tiny pieces from witnessing him in so much pain. "Twenty minutes. Stay out of the minibar." She grabbed her purse and phone then raced out the door.

When she returned, AJ looked up at her from the bed, shaking and sweating.

"Here." She helped him sit up and handed him two pills and a glass of water.

"How did you get these?"

"You don't want to know."

AJ nodded and swallowed the pills.

"Maybe I should take you back."

The bloodshot glare from his tired eyes gave her real physical pain. She stared at the bottle of pills, contemplating how much longer she could go before needing to pop a few too.

"If you want to take me back..." he grimaced "...I understand. I know I'm asking for a lot. But if you're asking if *I* want to go back, the answer is no."

She gently pushed him back onto the pillow and crawled up beside him, resting her head on his arm, her hand over his heart. "Then we keep going." Where they were going, she didn't know.

"If you need to get back home—"

"Nope. I'm yours."

She stayed by his side as he rolled and turned, flinched and shook with torment until the pain medication took hold and pulled him under. After sliding out of bed, she grabbed her phone and settled into the other bed.

Jillian: U awake?

Jackson: Am now.

Jillian: Sorry. Just wanted to let U know I'm OK.

Jackson: Where are you?

Jillian: Utah.

Jackson: WTF?

Jillian: AJ wanted to leave, but he doesn't want to go back to Omaha.

Jackson: He's running.

She smiled.

Jillian: He's living.

Jackson: He's dying.

Jillian: Aren't we all? I need an escape, just while he sleeps. Make me lol.

Jackson: I've got nothing.

Jillian: BS – U always have something, Mr. Snuffleupagus.

Jackson: Ryn hits like a girl.

Jillian: I'll remedy that when I get home. Not funny tho – try again.

Jackson: She doesn't like pussy or cunt.

Jillian: I'm lol, but I don't know why. R U telling me she's not a lesbian?

Jackson: She doesn't like the terms. Vagina, just vagina.

Jillian: Sounds like a boner-killer or "erection-killer"

Jackson: You'd think, but my penis still likes her vagina.

Jillian: The fun buzz is wearing off. Enough about you and Ryn's genitals.

Jackson: Love you. Pissed as fuck that you left, but I still love you.

Jillian: Told U to make me lol not cry. <3 U 2! TTYL

"Pussy," she whispered to herself with a big smile.

"You're staring," AJ said with his eyes still closed.

"Just making sure you're still alive. Is that kind of gruesome?" She picked at the frayed knee of her jeans while sitting cross-legged on the bed beside him.

He peeked open one eye. "I wouldn't expect anything less from you."

"Do you think there's a manhunt for you?"

"You make me sound like a criminal."

"You did escape."

He pushed himself into a sitting position with a grimace and a low groan. "I did, out the front door."

"True. So are you hungry?"

"Not really, but I'm guessing you're going to make me eat."

Jillian leaned forward and kissed the corner of his mouth. "Yep." She popped the p. "Continental breakfast near the lobby. Maybe they'll have cloth napkins and it can be our first official date."

"You and your cloth napkins. I don't get it. You really don't think we've had an 'official' date because we haven't had cloth napkins?"

"How many times do I have to tell you? A girl's gotta have standards."

He eased out of bed wearing only half a grimace. It was progress. After a shower and packing up their minimal belongings, they ate breakfast sans cloth napkins and continued southeast, taking the byways through southeastern Utah into southwestern Colorado.

"Let's stop here."

"A brewery?"

"Food and beer. No beer for you. You have drugs."

"I'm actually feeling a little better today."

Jillian wrapped her arm around his waist as they walked through the deserted parking lot for a late afternoon lunch. "I noticed. You've been eyeing my boobs all day."

"Because you're not wearing a bra."

"The shirt has a built-in shelf bra."

"I see your nipples."

She laughed. "It's a little chilly today. What are you going to get? Bacon cheeseburger? Steak and fries?"

"Probably just a salad."

"Fuck the salad. You need some meat and potatoes."

AJ opened the door for her. "Maybe they have a good Tofurkey dog."

"Ooo ... wouldn't that be grand."

The waitress sat them near a large wall of windows with a picturesque view of the lush valley sprawling all the way to the majestic Rockies. Jillian ordered for both of them, a veggie burger and the house burger both with fries and *two* beers after AJ gave her an intense glare when she tried to order him an iced tea.

"Do you happen to have any cloth napkins?" AJ asked when the waitress brought their food.

"Sorry, sir." She shook her head.

Jillian sniggered. "Nice try, Sarge."

"She's not going to get a good tip."

"Absolutely not. Teach that bitch a lesson for not being more accommodating." Jillian squeezed ketchup and mustard onto her bun. "Don't roll your eyes at me. I'm not the one who asked her about the cloth napkins."

"True, but it wouldn't be an issue if it weren't for you."

"God ... this is to die for," she mumbled over a very unladylike mouthful before catching how inappropriate her words were. "Shit. That's not what I meant. I just meant that it's good or—"

"Stop." AJ trapped her feet between his under the table and leaned forward. "If you choose to die for a sandwich, then I'll respect that." He sat back and shrugged. "It's not a bad way to go. I'd much prefer it to this cancer shit in my fucking brain."

Wiping her mouth with the non-cloth napkin, she grinned. "I love you, Aric James."

He nodded with an intense look, the kind that made her feel his eyes everywhere, but most especially between her legs. Grasping his sandwich with both hands, he lifted it from the plate. Before taking a bite he slowly licked the sauce that had squeezed out along the edge.

How desperate was she to be envious of a cooked piece of meat? It had been a while since she'd had sex or even brought herself to orgasm. AJ took a big bite then slowly licked his lips. Thankfully Marvin Housby saved the day. Jillian giggled.

"What's so funny?"

Jillian felt herself blush which was a very rare occurrence for her. "I was getting..." she looked around the restaurant "...turned on by you looking at me and then your tongue lapping along your sandwich." Her laughter turned into an actual snort as she lost control of the moment. "But then it reminded me of Marvin Housby."

"Marvin?"

She nodded. "Greta told me he masturbates to the pictures on the ValuPak coupons, like the girls on the Hardee's ads."

AJ cleared his throat, blotting his napkin against his mouth to hide his own humor.

"You looked like one of those girls on the Hardee's commercial, and I looked at you like Marvin Housby and burger babes."

"You think I look like a girl?"

"No. Just the way you were tonguing your sandwich."

"I wasn't *tonguing* my sandwich."

The growly beast that sat across from her brought such life to an otherwise barren existence. The uniqueness of their love could never be compared to anything else. Luke had the best of her and she didn't want it back—not ever. But AJ filled her lungs with life after death, he gave her so much hope that there was in fact light beyond the darkness.

"What's the first thing you remember?"

"About what?" He dipped a French fry in ketchup.

"Your life."

All she wanted to do was crawl inside his head as he looked out the window past the mountains to many years ago. Just a glimpse, that's all she needed, a small piece of his innocence.

"I'm not sure. I think it's the first time my mom took me camping. My father had been deployed for almost a year and so we went camping with my aunt, uncle, and my two cousins in Northern California."

He smiled at the window. For a small moment in time he wasn't fighting the cancer or PTSD. It was just a boy and a memory so special he kept it safe for over forty years.

"It was in the fall like now, and cold, as in freeze-your-ass-off cold. I must have been three or four. We huddled around the smallest fire ever. If any of us breathed too hard it nearly snuffed it out. My mom made s'mores except she forgot the graham crackers so we just sandwiched burnt marshmallows between two pieces of milk chocolate. I went to bed with sticky hands but my mom didn't care. She still zipped me up in her mummy bag with her to keep me warm. When we arrived home my dad was waiting on the front porch."

Jillian—*Jessica*—knew how it felt to not know if or when her father would come home. Every time he walked through the door felt like Christmas.

They finished eating, letting his childhood memory linger in the air around them like a delicate bubble that neither wanted to pop. Eventually their waitress popped it for them.

"Can I interest either of you in dessert?"

They both shook their heads so she handed AJ the bill. "Your daughter has your smile."

AJ shot a lethal scowl at the back of her head as she continued on to another table.

"Lunch is on me, big daddy." Jillian grabbed the bill.

"No tip. Not one penny."

———

A PRIVATE CALL to an unreceptive and pissed off McGraw and thirty minutes later they were pulling into a parking lot of a sporting goods store.

"Did you forget your yoga mat?"

"Funny, big daddy, but you know I don't do yoga."

"If you call me that one more time—"

"Make it good ... really good. Maybe even a little sexually deviant."

AJ glared at her as she killed the engine. Big daddy's eyes slipped to her boobs again.

"Wait here."

"Why?"

"It's a surprise." After blowing him a quick kiss she shut the door and jogged to the entrance. Less than ten minutes later she and two employees pushed out carts overflowing with gear.

"What's all this?" AJ asked, stepping out of the Jeep as Jillian opened the back and loaded everything with the help of the store employees.

"I'm taking you camping."

"You're serious?"

She nodded her head, signaling for him to get back in the Jeep as she climbed into the driver's seat.

"How did you get all that stuff in such a short amount of time?"

"I offered to screw anyone who gathered my list in under five minutes. As you probably noticed it took closer to ten so I'm off the hook."

AJ frowned.

"I'm joking." She squeezed his leg. "I know a guy."

"A guy?"

"Yes."

"By any chance is he the same guy who's responsible for the pain medication?"

"Yes."

"A doctor?"

"Satan."

"You sold your soul to the Devil for me?"

With a slight head cock, she stared at the road, thinking about that assessment. "No. I'd say the Devil sold his soul to me."

Jillian felt AJ's gaze on her, but she kept her eyes trained ahead—to the future, a million miles away from her past.

"Grocery store?"

"Of course. But you can come in this time. We need grub for a few days."

Ice for the cooler and four bags of groceries later, they were on their way again. AJ started to drift to sleep just as they pulled into the parking area of a primitive campsite.

"Looks like we're the only ones here." Jillian smiled at AJ as she got out. "I'll set everything up. You just rest."

"I'm not sitting on my ass while you set everything up." He climbed out with slow, stiff movements.

"You should take a few pain pills anyway so they've kicked in by the time we get the tent set up."

"I'm fine."

His grumpy reply that she suspected to be a lie gained him an exaggerated eye roll straight to his face.

"Fine."

They set up the tent, an eight-person castle that allowed AJ to fully stand at the tallest part in the middle.

"S'mores?" Jillian called from outside the tent.

AJ grinned as he stepped out, seeing her roasting four marshmallows to a toasted-brown perfection over the low flame of their little camping stove. She had graham crackers and chocolate squares waiting on their plates. Pride beamed from her whole face as she pressed everything together and handed him his plate.

"And you thought I couldn't cook."

AJ shoved half of it into his mouth, leaving a mess of chocolate and marshmallow smeared along his lips.

"Good?" Jillian chuckled, taking a much smaller bite of hers.

"So good." Graham cracker crumbs shot out from his over-stuffed mouth.

"How can you even taste it with your mouth so jam-packed?"

After some lion-sized chews and a few big swallows he could talk without spitting all over her. "I can't remember the last thing that tasted this good."

Every smile felt like the last, like watching the finale to a fireworks display. Jillian captured each one, letting it make a slow burn into her memory.

"You're staring. My face is a mess, isn't it?" He brushed his fingers over his lips.

Jillian moved over to his lap. "I've met two-year-olds that eat neater than you." She ran her thumb along his bottom lip then sucked the tip of her thumb.

He grabbed her wrist and pulled her thumb from her lips back to his.

"You should take your pills," she whispered, feeling a sudden wave of nerves from the intimacy of his touch.

Leaning forward, he rested his forehead on her chest, his hands on her hips. "I'm not ready to stop feeling yet."

Drawing in a shaky breath, fighting a lifetime of emotions, she kissed the top of his head, pressing her palms to his cheeks.

He looked up at her. "Missing you hurt worse than anything they did to me."

Biting her lips together, she shook her head. "Loving you feels like torture."

"I'm sorry," he whispered.

"I'm not." She kissed him, welcoming every emotion: the pain, the breath of life, the uncertainty, the fear, the love. So. Much. Love.

"Aric James ... I need *us*."

He carried her into the tent and set her down, kneeling at her feet. Their eyes stayed locked the whole time. Jillian didn't even want to blink, fearing he'd vanish. Life always changed in that one. Single. Blink.

They undressed each other with a slow reverence, letting every touch, every look, every second ... every blink matter. With Luke every moment felt like the first, with AJ every moment felt like the last. As AJ moved inside her, she let it be *the* moment, because it was the only one she had.

"Jillian?" He kissed her neck, rocking his body against hers with agonizing patience.

"Yes," she whispered, feeling as if her body could float away.

"From this point forward..." he squeezed her breast

until she let out a small cry "...every breath I take belongs to you ... only you."

She wrapped her arms around his neck, holding him as close as possible to her. "I hate you ... I fucking hate you for leaving me." A strangled sob released into his neck while she continued to find her release. Her entire body wanted to let go of everything, everything except the beautifully broken man in her arms. How was she ever going to let him go?

"I hate me too." He fisted her hair with both hands and smashed his lips to hers as he released inside her.

CHAPTER TWENTY-FIVE

JACKSON DEMOLISHED any time record he had ever set running, and then tore through an abs, pushup, and pull-up workout like his whole body defied gravity. Living under the mercy of two women—one infuriating, one frustrating—paid a mental toll on his sanity, and the only way to keep everything in check was to make his body burn until his mind could no longer conjure a worthwhile thought.

Meredith Baker, his ten o'clock lesson arrived an hour early. Most of his students knew each other or were somehow connected because they'd all been referred to him by word of mouth. Meredith said she couldn't remember who gave her his name and it didn't matter how they "found each other" all that mattered is they were "together."

"Jackson." She batted her fake eyelashes.

"Mrs. Baker, you're early ... like an hour early." He shoved the last bite of his toast into his mouth as she wormed her way inside without being invited.

"Oh, am I?" The large-busted woman ran her fake nails through her wiry black hair and smiled, revealing red lipstick smudged along her slightly crooked white teeth.

His lungs begged for air as her toxic perfume diffused into the entryway. "Yes." He coughed. "It's only nine."

"Oh, silly me. I still haven't changed all my clocks since the time change."

"I see. Well, I haven't finished my breakfast and I still need to shower so maybe you could come back—"

"I don't mind waiting. Just pretend I'm not here." She adjusted her tight top that seemed to be in a wrestling match with her large breasts.

Jackson rolled his eyes behind her back then grabbed his last piece of toast while she surveyed the room as if she hadn't seen it numerous times before.

"It's odd that you don't have any personal pictures on the wall or fireplace mantel. Don't you think?"

He didn't respond. After all, she said to pretend she wasn't there.

"Did you hear me, Jackson?"

"I did, but I don't really have an answer for you."

"Where's Jillian?"

Jackson paused, mid-gulp of his Redbull. "What did you just say?"

"Your sister. I asked where she is."

"What does your husband do, Mrs. Baker?"

A nervous smile tugged at her thin lips as she ran her fingers over the top of the piano. "He ... he died."

"Oh? Sorry to hear that. When did he die?"

Fiddling with her earring, she cleared her throat. "Two years ago. It was a heart attack."

"You haven't remarried?"

Relief washed over her face when a knock at the door interrupted their conversation. Jackson kept his eyes on her until he opened the front door.

"Ryn."

She smiled but it quickly faded. "Hey, is everything okay. You look—"

"Everything's fine." He grinned, hoping she wouldn't see through it. "Come in."

"Thanks, I can't stay long I have an appointment in forty-five minutes. Oh ..." She stopped. "Sorry, I thought your first lesson was at ten."

"Crazy time change." Mrs. Baker offered her hand. "Meredith."

Ryn nodded, shaking her hand. "Ryn."

"Student? Friend?" Mrs. Baker questioned.

Jackson grabbed Ryn's arms and pushed her toward the bedroom. "She's nobody. Have a seat, Mrs. Baker. I'll be right out."

Ryn jerked out of his grasp the moment he shut his bedroom door behind them. "Nobody?"

"Shh ..." He reached for her but she stepped back.

"Are you screwing her?" She gritted her teeth.

"What? No, God no." Jackson tried to keep his voice low but still get his point across. "Would you just listen?"

Ryn folded her arms over her chest.

"I don't trust Mrs. Baker."

"Mrs. Baker?"

Jackson rolled his eyes. "Meredith."

"I'm not following."

"Just ... it's complicated. But if there's any chance that she's ..." he circled his finger in the cuckoo sign "...then I don't want her anywhere near you or knowing anything about you."

"You think she's stalking you?"

More like spying, he thought. The incredulity in her voice and expression held plenty of merit. It did sound crazy. But crazy was his life.

"At very least she's been lying to me, and until I figure out why, I can't trust her."

"Lying to you about what?"

Jackson sighed. He couldn't have that conversation with her, but the way she kept a safe distance from him led him to think he couldn't *not* have that conversation with her either.

"A couple weeks ago she told me about this great restaurant her husband took her to."

"So ..."

"So, today she told me her husband died two years ago."

Ryn shrugged. "He probably took her there while he was still alive."

Jackson rested his hands on his hips and leaned forward. "It was the Mexican restaurant we ate at last week."

"So ... oh shit."

Jackson nodded.

"That restaurant opened like ... two months ago."

"Exactly." He gave her a see-I'm-not-paranoid look.

She pursed her lips, brow drawn tight.

"I have to take a quick shower." He kissed her forehead. "Don't stress. I'll handle it."

Jackson hurried through his shower, mind reeling with the mystery of Mrs. Baker. What he didn't share with Ryn was Mrs. Baker's knowledge of Jillian ... specifically her name. It's not that it was a secret, he just instinctually felt protective of her so when students asked about her he simply referred to her as his sister—never Jillian.

"Aren't you worried about her being out there unsupervised, snooping through your personal stuff?"

Jackson dropped the towel from his waist. Ryn's gaze slipped straight to his cock then it made a lazy ascent back to his face. She blushed a little at the realization that he'd been watching her ogle him. He loved it.

"Done, hot pants?"

"Shut up." She moved to the window, finding a sudden fascination in the dirty pond out back. "Did you hear what I said about her going through your stuff?"

He pulled on his briefs and his jeans. "I did. She's not going to find anything." His phone and computer were in the bedroom. The Knights didn't exist beyond their address and a few online utility bills. There was nothing for Mrs. Baker to find, which made her presence in his life that much more disturbing.

"I'm always happy to see you, but if you didn't stop by to look at my cock, then to what do I owe this unexpected pleasure."

Ryn turned as he pulled on his T-shirt. "I talked to Maddie last night. I told her about Preston and the abuse."

"Good for you. How did she take it?"

Ryn frowned. "She didn't believe me. Preston beat me to it. Apparently two years ago he told her I went through a 'mentally' unstable time when she was younger. He even told her I tried to commit suicide by over-dosing on anti-depressants and when he tried to help me, I accused him of abusing me. He told her it was best to never mention it unless I brought it up to her."

Jackson pulled her into his arms.

"It gets worse. Now that she doesn't have to 'worry about my reaction' she's given me this ridiculous ultimatum that I know her father is behind."

"Which is?"

"She's refusing to see me or talk to me again until I drop the restraining order against Preston."

He held her back at arms' length. "But you're not going to, right?"

She shrugged. "She's my daughter, my only child. I can't just sever all ties with her."

"She thinks you're lying about her father. He has her so fucking brainwashed it won't matter what you do, she'll never believe you. But giving into this is going to put you in danger and it will be like admitting you were lying or over-reacting about the whole situation in the first place."

"It's ten o'clock." Mrs. Baker knocked at the bedroom door.

Ryn pulled her phone out of her pocket and checked the time. "I'm running late."

Jackson cradled her face. "Being an example of a strong woman is the best way to love your daughter."

She nodded, ever so slightly.

He kissed her until her body went limp in his grasp. "See you later, hot pants. Training, dinner, fucking." He smacked her ass.

She rubbed her hand over it like it stung, and he hoped it did. He wanted her thinking of him the rest of the day.

"Fucking?"

"Sorry. Sexual intercourse? Coitus? The union and rhythm of our genitals?"

"I-I've got to get out of here."

He loved pushing all her buttons, playing her with the ease of Black Beauty. Ryn reacted with her whole body and Jackson couldn't get enough.

GUNNER GREETED Ryn with a few sloppy kisses after her long day of crawling around on her knees cleaning other people's homes while hers collected a nice layer of dust. She packed her bag, what she assumed would need to be an overnight bag, then loaded her dog and his food in the back of her RAV4.

"Haven't seen you around much."

Ryn turned, an instant smile graced her face. "Drew. How have you been?"

He smiled that crooked smile that eased the stress from her asshole of an ex-husband and her young, naive daughter.

"I'm good, thank you." His expression sobered. "I know we don't have an official neighborhood watch, but I've noticed someone snooping around your place on more than one occasion. It's always been when you're not home and he never got that close to the house thanks to Gunner. I said something to him when he went through your mail the other day."

She fought to keep her panic hidden. "And?"

"He said he was your brother. When I told him your brother died, he told me to mind my own fucking business, got in his black Escalade, and I haven't seen him around since."

"Thank you." She gripped her keys.

"Do you know who it could have been?"

"Preston," she whispered.

"Your ex with a restraining order against him?"

"Copper blond hair mixed with a little gray, always in an expensive suit, gold Rolex?"

Drew nodded. "What's he want?"

"Me always on edge, looking over my shoulder, shunned by my own daughter, and completely miserable."

"What are you going to do about it?"

She took a deep breath. "I'm going to practice some self-defense, have dinner, and then ..." With a shrug she bit her lips together. Drew didn't need to know about the "fucking."

"Be safe. I'll keep an eye out and call the police if I see him again."

Ryn nodded. "Thanks, Drew."

Somehow her car made it to Jackson's, even if she couldn't remember a single turn or stoplight. The question was whether or not to say anything to Jackson about the information Drew shared. Their first meeting ended in Preston going to the hospital via an ambulance. She could only imagine what Jackson might try to do if he knew Preston had been snooping around her place. He had his own issues with his peculiar and suspect piano student.

"That's a big bag," Jackson smirked as she stepped inside the front door. "You moving in?"

"Oh ... um, no, it's just a change of clothes..." she stammered her words "...to wear to dinner."

He grabbed her bag and tossed it in his bedroom then kissed her so hard she questioned the whereabouts of her tonsils. "I'm just messing with you. My future wife can stay with me for as long as she wants. Forever would be ideal."

Her heart needed to know why he kept doing that. It was fun until she actually wanted him to mean every word. Even in that moment she shocked herself by thinking that. *Did* she want him to mean every word?

His smile faltered, perhaps because of the way her jaw hung to her feet. "Ready to kick my ass?"

Regaining control of her mandibular function, she nodded. Ryn assumed he'd teach her more moves, life-saving skills. Instead he had her demonstrate her pathetic endurance through a cardio and strength-training workout. People spent hundreds of dollars on fancy equipment and gym memberships and he brought her to his mercy with a jump rope and pull-up bar. Everything else didn't require anything: squats, pushups, dips, planks, burpees. The pinnacle of her embarrassment came when she couldn't even do one pull-up without him helping her by lifting up on her hips. Val would get an ass-chewing for letting Ryn think she was in good shape.

Sagging in the corner, sucking down water like oxygen, she watched him do one-arm pull-ups. Admiring his firm planes of muscles flex in waves along his back, arms, and legs, she became primed and so very ready for their post dinner plans. The chances of him feeling the same way after watching her die before his eyes seemed unlikely. Sweaty old lady nose-planting after seven pushups had to have been anti-climatic for his sex drive.

"Ready to shower, hot pants?" Jackson wiped his face and chest with a white towel.

"Just be honest with me. Am I your beard?"

He chuckled. "My beard?"

"Yes, as in you're gay but you don't want people to know so you have a woman with whom—"

"I know what the term beard means. You think I'm gay?"

"No. I think you could be having sex with women so hot even I'd consider a night of lesbian love if they offered. Instead you're with me and I'm certain I don't look like those fitness models after a workout. I can just feel how my hair surely resembles a drowned rat, and my face beams with heat so I know I must still be red even after twenty minutes of recovery."

Jackson hooked his towel around her neck and pulled her against him. "Are you done?"

Ryn gave it another moment of thought then nodded once.

"Good. So let's take my penis and your vagina upstairs and see what trouble they can get into in the shower."

Ryn rolled her eyes. "When you say it like that it sounds ridiculous."

"You think?" He lifted her over his shoulder and carried her upstairs. "In that case, maybe I'll just bury my cock so deep in your pussy you'll be tasting me every time you swallow. Better?"

"Yes, utterly poetic."

***

WITHHOLDING pleasure as a form of torture? Ryn found out the hard way it's a real thing. They monkey fucked in the shower in every position possible, stopping each time to find a new position a breath before Ryn climaxed. At first it seemed like a coincidence, after all he couldn't have known that she was about to orgasm.

Wrong.

By the fourth time she really began to suspect something, but before she could get the words out he whispered in her ear, buried balls deep from behind, "I'll let you come if you promise to never mention our age difference and always ... and I mean *always* act like the fucking goddess you are, making me barely worthy of even looking at you."

"Jackson ... please." She reached behind her head and clawed at his hair as he trapped her earlobe between his teeth.

"Tell me you're a fucking goddess," he growled, pumping into her a few more times just to keep her on the brink.

Sliding one hand from his hair she moved it toward her clitoris.

"No." He grabbed both of her hands and pressed them flat to the tile wall beneath his. "Say. It."

"Yes." She ground back against him.

"Yes what?"

"I'm ... I'm a goddess," she whispered.

He covered her clitoris with two fingers but didn't press down or move them a millimeter. "So close ... last chance." His hips rammed into her, pushing the slight ebb right back to the very edge.

"I'm a fucking goddess!" With the slip of his hand, she saw stars behind her eyes explode so bright she couldn't see anything else, but she felt absolutely *everything*.

"Damn right you are." He pulled out and guided her to sit on the bench in the corner. She happily sat down, her orgasm had turned her legs into Jell-O.

Jackson pumped himself a couple of times and then he spewed his *semen* all over her breasts—chin down, eyes hooded. Ryn stared at him wide eyed and then at her breasts dripping with water and *semen*. Admittedly, watching him grasping his *penis* turned her on more than she ever could have imagined. The unexpected mess left her confused. If his fascination with older women had anything to do with their experience, then she had to be a huge disappointment. He was clearly the more sexually experienced one in their relationship.

He continued to look at her breasts with pleasure and lust painted on his face. He seemed to wait for her to respond. Ryn had no idea what that response should be. She should have watched more porn over the years.

Mental note: Google semen on breasts.

What would a "fucking goddess" do? Gather it in her

hands and slurp it up? Smear it all over like lotion or an expensive moisturizer? Too weird.

"Clean up your mess ... now." She tipped her chin up and gave him a stern look while holding her breath. Breathing would have turned into laughing, at herself of course, because it took forty years for a man to jerk off on her breasts and when it finally happened she had no clue how to react. Her words were effortless even instinctual. She'd said the same thing to Maddie over the years about her bedroom.

Jackson raised a single brow, one side of his mouth curling into a sexy smile. Keeping his eyes locked to hers as if he could break her façade, he grabbed a bottle of shower gel and squirted it onto her breasts much like he did with his semen. Ryn gritted her teeth, holding strong. He smeared the soap over her chest, giving extra attention to her nipples. It felt good, too good, trying-to-make-her-break good.

Like the fucking goddess she was, Ryn held strong and made it out of the shower without begging for anything else, but just barely.

CHAPTER TWENTY-SIX

DAY

WATCHING Jessica sleep had become Luke's favorite part of every morning. He loved the way her lips twitched into a smile and each breath sounded like a sigh of contentment. Did she dream of him?

His heart rate increased as she stretched her naked body like a cat across the bed. When her eyes fluttered open he smiled a big, goofy clown smile, but he couldn't help it.

"I probably should be creeped out..." she yawned through her words "...that you're always standing in the doorway staring at me when I wake." Scooting to a sitting position, she wrapped a blanket around her shoulders. "But then I realize ... you're standing in a doorway—an exit—in case you have to flee from the monster, and that's the biggest downer ever."

Luke pushed off the door frame and moved to the bed. Without hesitation she pulled him back into bed and straddled his body.

"Stop calling the woman I love a monster."

She licked up his neck, another cat-like move.

"I'm sweaty."

"Mmm ... I see you went for a run without me again."

Luke palmed her bare ass, squeezing her tight glutes. "You slow me down."

She dug her teeth into his neck over his carotid and growled. "You're so full of shit. Just admit it ... I'm bad for your ego."

He chuckled. "Aside from your brother, I don't think there's a male ego in existence that stands a chance around you. You are a true man-eater."

"Did you take our baby with you?"

"About that ... it's possible Jones might not be coming home with us."

Jessica sat up. "Say what?"

"My mom said he slept in bed with them, wedged in the middle like the spot had his name on it."

"He'd sleep with us if you'd let him."

A true statement. Another truth they both knew but never discussed was the real reason Jones didn't sleep with them. It would have destroyed Jessica to snap out of a morning attack only to discover that her "baby" was dead from a broken neck because he brought her out of a deep sleep with a sloppy, wet kiss. Even before they moved in with Luke, Jones slept in his kennel. Jessica claimed it was because he wasn't completely housebroken yet—a half-truth.

"I don't love rolling in dog hair and turning over in the middle of the night to a wet nose in my face." Another half-truth.

"Well, they can't have my Jonesy. I don't care how cool they are." She grinned. "Because they are ... they are the absolute coolest people I have ever known."

"Please don't." Luke grimaced.

"What? How can you say that? Last night made it into

my top ten best memories of all time—maybe even the top five. I can't wait to tell Kelly."

"No. What happened last night … did *not* happen. Do you understand? Everyone drank way too much, and as far as I can or ever want to remember, we ate, sat by the fire, then went to bed."

"Sorry, babe. We both know the *only* memory from last night is the way the icy water sucked the air from our lungs, the adrenaline rush, and the way your dad wiggled his ass like a duck when he climbed out of the lake."

As he watched her giggle like a twelve-year-old, messy dark hair veiling her perfect breasts, amber eyes bursting with life, he felt the crushing reality of loving her so much. In that moment he knew all reason was gone and his instinct for self-preservation had vanished. He'd never survive her, not for one second.

She twisted his nipple, not like a doting lover, more like a frat brother asking for an ass whooping. Then she circled her tongue around it before pressing her lips to it. "So what's the plan for the day?" Hopping out of bed she swayed her sexy hips toward the bathroom.

"I'm thinking a scenic drive. If it warms up enough we could squeeze in a picnic somewhere. Oh, and my mom asked if we could find our way to Staples for printer ink."

Jessica peeked her head around the corner. "Staples?"

"Yeah, it's a little out of our way but—"

"No … I mean yes, we should definitely go to Staples. Is there anything else she needs from there? You know they have *everything*." She turned on the shower.

"Well, I don't know about *everything*." Luke chuckled to himself.

THE GTO GAME proved to be a fun way to toy with Luke. He thought he had control, crazy guy. Jessica specialized in control, specifically giving other people the illusion they had it. She always asked to drive. He always said no. Tactics she felt certain would guarantee her time in the driver's seat included physical manipulation, withholding sex, and blackmail with what had become a growing amount of information provided by Tom and Felicity.

Games had to be fun. Jessica grinned thinking of how much fun she would have with Luke ... right after they checked out Staples.

"I'll just run in and grab the cartridges."

"No. I mean ... maybe I should go too. Can you really trust me to not steal your car?"

Luke dangled the keys in front of her face.

"That's sweet." She batted her eye lashes. "I love that after all you've learned about me, you still think of me as an innocent damsel and not someone who could have this baby hot-wired and tearing down the road in under thirty seconds."

He frowned. "Get out."

Jessica skipped into Staples. Instantly her lungs filled with that smell she'd missed—the off gassing—it had been too long since she indulged in a good old office supply trip.

"Stinks in here, huh?"

She lifted her shoulders. "Depends on what you like."

"Well I don't know anyone who likes such a strong chemical smell."

Of course he did, he just didn't know it.

"Ink is this way. Oh, we won't need a basket. It's just two small boxes."

Jessica stared at the plastic basket she'd hooked over her arm. Two boxes? He surely had to be mistaken.

"I might need to grab a few essentials. I'll meet you back here at the register."

Luke quirked a brow. "A few essentials?"

"Did I stutter?" She traipsed off with her head held high. No one would make her feel guilty for having a slight office supply store addiction. After all, it had been months since she'd had a fix.

She may or may not have hid from him when she saw him looking for her. Mr. Antsy Pants wasted no time getting the ink. He probably didn't even take the time to compare Staple's compatible ink to the more expensive Canon ink.

Jones: *Where are you?"*
Jessica: *Bathroom. Thought I told U to wait upfront for me.*

Staples may or may not have turned her into a crazier version of her already insane self.

Jones: *Did you start?"*

Typical guy.

Jessica: *I use the restroom even when I'm not having my period!*
Jones: *O—K*

Peeking around an end display of the most dazzling assortment of spiral notebooks, she watched and waited for him to head back toward the front of the store.

Another deep inhale. There was no way of knowing how long it could take for her to splurge on another trip to Staples. She had to get as much of *everything* as she could. Ten minutes later ... possibly twenty—it was easy to lose track of time with so many distractions—she smiled at Luke as he spotted her walking toward him.

"You dropped something."

She looked behind her then bent down to grab the box that had fallen out of her overflowing basket.

"Powder-Free Disposable Nitrile Gloves?"

"Don't judge me, Jones." She brushed past him to the checkout.

Pink razors. Mouthwash. Three-pack Remote Controlled Pillar Candles. Retractable Pens. Sticky Tac. Post-it notes. Watermelon Bubblicious. Dragonfly Cotton Shower Cap ...

"I'll get the ink for your mom too." She motioned for him to set the two *Canon* ink cartridges on the counter.

His eyes flitted between her and her "essentials" the store clerk scanned and deposited into plastic bags. When he didn't say anything, she grabbed the boxes from him and handed them to the clerk.

"Two twenty-five thirty-nine."

Before Jessica could retrieve her money from her bag, Luke handed over his credit card.

"No, just wait I've got it."

By the time she found her wallet he'd already signed for the purchase. He grabbed the two bags of essentials and nodded for her to head toward the car. After they were both fastened in, he started the car and looked over at her. She kept her eyes trained ahead to the gray stone siding of the store.

"If you need me to be Dr. Jones for an emergency session I can do that for you."

"Two words ... argyle socks. So just put the car in gear and let's go."

They stopped by a deli and picked up sandwiches and

chips for their picnic. As they wormed their way through hills blanketed in trees, Jessica slipped her hand into her purse, retrieving her watermelon Bubblicious she snagged before the clerk could put it in the sack. Saliva flooded her mouth just from the smell after she unwrapped a piece. She popped it in her mouth and moaned with the first chew.

The party pooper shook his head in her peripheral vision.

"Open." She held a piece to his lips.

Luke shook his head.

"You have to."

Another shake.

"How are we going to swap gum in a few minutes if *you* don't have a piece?"

"We're not going—"

She shoved it in his mouth.

"You're going to make me drive off the road."

She grinned. "Then you should have let me drive. I'm an excellent driver."

"Okay, Rain Man." His response mumbled over the huge wad of gum.

"It's true. It's even possible that I was trained by a professional stuntman and former sprint car driver in the uh ... *art* of high-speed chasing."

Luke shot a quick sideways glance and several seconds later he shot her another with a look that fell somewhere between shock and horror. Jessica shrugged.

"I'm not sure I can marry you and not know *everything* about you."

"Only *if* you marry me will you ever know everything about me. Think of it as a wedding gift." She laughed, but it was a painful laugh. Nothing about G.A.I.L felt like a gift. It was a curse, one that not even death could destroy.

Only death would keep Luke from Jessica. One day he would marry her. One day he would know everything. Until then it didn't matter. A feeling deep in his gut told him her secrets were so much bigger than either one of them. He saw it in the way her eyes pleaded with him to trust her.

However, they had much bigger issues to deal with at the moment. The love of his life had a serious addiction to Staples, which resulted in him being force-fed watermelon bubblegum—the worst possible flavor.

"Right here." She pointed to a deserted scenic overlook.

He pulled into the gravel parking area.

"Did you bring a picnic blanket?" She peered at him over the frames of her glasses that sat low on her nose.

He slid his glasses down to mirror her serious look. "Yes. My mom gave me one."

She smirked. "It's probably the same one she and your dad wrapped around their wet naked bodies last night."

He wrinkled his nose.

"Time to swap." She leaned over and kissed him, running her tongue along the seam of his lips. "You suck at this," she mumbled against his mouth. Then she pushed her gum into his mouth.

"What are you—"

"Give me your gum." She teased his upper lip with the tip of her tongue, beckoning him to give it to her.

He shoved it in her mouth. The nasty watermelon taste almost ruined his favorite flavor—Jessica Day.

"You never swapped gum with a girl, did you?"

"Sorry." He shrugged as she sat back in her seat.

Jessica sighed. "The first time I swapped gum was with a girl in fourth grade."

Luke almost choked on his gum. "What?"

"Tina Reeves. She was "going with" a fifth grade boy. A rumor had been floating around that he was planning on French kissing Tina after school. She freaked out because she hadn't ever kissed a boy, let alone French kissed. So I offered to teach her."

Luke raised his usual skeptical brow. "You'd French kissed someone by the fourth grade?"

"No ... not until Tina."

Jessica's unpredictability never ceased to amaze him.

"But I'd seen it in the movies. It basically looked like two people trying to swap gum. Fifteen minutes in my bedroom with a Madonna CD and two pieces of grape Hubba Bubba later, Tina was quite the French kisser."

"How generous of you."

"Anything to help out a friend."

The woman before him had singlehandedly taken the life of a serial killer one unforgiving cut at a time. Even on their blind date when she bit him in the closet, she wasn't a killer. He never knew that Jessica. All she had ever wanted to be with him was the Hubba Bubba girl who liked skinny dipping, wet dog kisses, and apparently Staples. Luke knew he would spend the rest of his life, giving her that life—giving her back her innocence.

"I'm starving."

He nodded, not realizing how long he'd been staring at her. "Let's eat."

They spread out the blanket on a large boulder with a beautiful panoramic view of the lake.

"Which part of the blanket do you think hugged your dad's balls?"

"Probably two inches from the part that flossed his crack."

"Oh my God!" Her eyes grew wide. "I can't believe you said that. How very un-Jones of you." She laughed. "I fear I've tainted you."

They sat side by side on the rock with their legs dangling off the edge, sandwiches in hand. Jessica nudged his shoulder.

"Thank you."

"For what?"

"Skinny dipping, waiting by the register at Staples, swapping gum ... letting me experience life with you."

"The experience is mine."

With a furrowed brow, she looked up at him. "What are you experiencing?"

He leaned down and kissed the tip of her nose. "You. You're the greatest experience of my life."

She shoved a bite of sandwich into her mouth and mumbled over it like the well-mannered lady she'd never be. "That's just ... sad for you."

Luke watched her look out at the lake. He didn't miss the glassy tears that attempted to pool in her eyes. Would she ever feel worthy of true, heart-stopping, soul-shattering love? He hoped so because it's all he had to give her.

Her favorite doctor had been right: surrendering took as much strength as it did control. Every day she gave him a piece of her past in exchange for his future. As much as she wanted—needed—his love, accepting it took practice. A voice in her head kept reminding her to just "shut up and let him love you."

"The day will come that I don't want to kill Trigger, right?"

Luke sucked in a slow, deep breath. "I hope so. Maybe it will be the same day I care if Fran dies."

Jessica tilted her head, resting it on his arm. "You care. You just haven't let yourself feel it yet. Feelings are who we are ... actions are what we've become. I became a killer. I just have yet to feel bad about it. But I hope to God that someday I do. Killers don't feel remorse. If that day comes ... I'll finally be the woman you see. I've caught a glimpse of her in your eyes, and I can't help but envy her."

Luke twisted around and hopped off the boulder then offered his hand to her. "It's funny how we don't recognize our own reflections, but the one thing about them is they never lie."

Taking his hand she jumped down. "Dr. Jones, you should have majored in philosophy. On a more positive topic ... what's your theory on me driving back to your parents?"

"I don't have a theory, just a fact."

"Really? Enlighten me."

"You will not be driving my car."

She made a horn-like buzzing sound. "Wrong answer."

He folded the blanket and grabbed their empty bags then opened the trunk.

"Let *me* enlighten you. I'm going to strip, and ride your cock on the hood of your shiny red GTO, not giving a damn what passersby think until you—"

"Yeah all of that." He gestured to his arms full with the big blanket and the lunch bags. "Would you grab the first aid kit? I scraped my ankle on the rock over there."

She looked at the little box with the red cross on it. With a huff, she leaned into the trunk to reach it at the back, squirming until nearly three-fourths of her short stature was inside.

"Fuck!" She fell ... no she was *shoved* into the trunk and he closed it on her. He. Locked. Her. In. The. Trunk.

"As much as I like you riding my cock, and in spite of last night's bonding with my parents, I'm not an exhibitionist. And I just put a new coat of wax on her the other day so I'm not going to leave my ass print on the hood." He knocked twice on the trunk. "Hope you're not claustrophobic, but if you are, I'm pretty sure I just bought you some electric pillar candles in one of those sacks. They should take the edge off. Hold on tight, I'll go slow."

"Die. YOU. WILL. DIE!"

CHAPTER TWENTY-SEVEN

KNIGHT

1 Timothy 2:12

JILLIAN STARED at her phone as the sun peaked over the horizon. AJ struggled to get to sleep the previous night, refusing to take any pills until after they'd had sex—sex that felt like making love, sex that gave her so much heartache and guilt. Luke was gone, she tried to tell herself, but he really wasn't. Jessica died. Luke lived. Would it have been easier to move on had he died? Had Luke moved on? Had he *made love* to another? The ghost of the woman she once was couldn't bear the thought, but Jillian Knight wished him a life filled with a wife who embraced his quirks and maybe someday little Joneses tearing his orderly life apart in the best possible way. She hoped her four-legged baby would live out the rest of his life in a house full of people who understood him the way Jessica had.

To avoid waking AJ, she perched in a chair outside the tent, wrapped in a blanket, waiting for her one-bar wireless service to return an answer to her biblical verse search.

After churning in cyber circles the answer appeared on her screen.

"I do not permit a woman to teach or to assume authority over a man; she must be quiet."

"Fuck that," she whispered to herself. Her finger hovered over the forward button as she contemplated sending the message to Jackson.

"Jill—"

She clicked off the screen and unzipped the front of the tent.

"Goddammit! AJ?" He lost consciousness and his body began to wrench in muscle contractions. She dropped to her knees beside him, watching in horror. There was nothing else she could do. It took less than two minutes that seemed like an eternity, and then he went completely limp. Her lower lip quivered between her teeth as she pressed her fingers to his neck. Closing her eyes, she swallowed hard, finally feeling his pulse.

"I can barely keep myself alive ... I can't do this," she whispered, collapsing onto her side next to him.

After a few minutes he came to, focusing on her eyes with confusion in his.

"You had a seizure."

"Sorry."

Jillian huffed a small laugh. "You just up and left without anything, didn't you? What is this? Am I here just to watch you die?" The bitterness bled through her words.

"I was dying with them ... I'm living with you."

"Well, then it's a shitty way to live. You need some anti-seizure meds or something. I can't watch this every day."

"Take me back." The defeat in his voice hurt worse than watching his body lose control.

"I'm not taking you back." She crawled out of the tent, grabbed her phone, and walked toward the main road for privacy and better signal.

"I'm still getting texts."

McGraw's cynical laugh greeted her on the other end of the line. "Then let me bring you in. New identities, new location, maybe even a sex change. I always thought you should have been a guy."

"Is that why you buried your cock in my ass?"

"What the fuck do you want?" On the outside he'd perfected the tough-guy role, but Jillian—Jessica—always ignited the fuse on his patience.

"AJ needs his anti-seizure medication."

"Do you have a prescription?"

"No. He didn't bring any with him."

"You're dreaming, little girl. I'm flattered you think I'm God, but I'm not. I can't just thumb through a PDR and find him the right medication."

"Clearly you're an old fuck who hasn't been to the doctor recently. Welcome to the digital age where every-one's entire life, including their medical records, can be accessed online."

"You're asking me to break into the hospital's database?"

"I'm not asking. Message me with the pharmacy information."

JILLIAN AND AJ continued south with her drug dealer on speed dial. Each passing day AJ seemed to be doing better. Jillian would have been skeptical had AJ himself not acted a little shocked. He admitted the doctors said radiation was a wait and see situation. She insisted he still take his medications, if for no other reason than the fact that she'd repeatedly sold her soul to the Devil, or vice versa, to get them.

"You've been gone a while. How long is Jackson going to let you gallivant around the country with me?"

Jillian grinned, keeping her eyes trained to the miles of Texas highway before them. "I occasionally check in with my parole officer ... can you say the same? Besides, I told you Jackson's too busy courting your ex-cleaning lady."

"Courting?"

"Yes. He's decided it's time to marry and populate the world with little Knights. Pun intended."

"I think she's close to my age and maybe has a teenager or something. Shouldn't he be courting someone in their childbearing years?"

"I like Ryn and I should land my fist in your junk on her behalf for making her seem old and barren. Not to mention she's worked for you how many years? And you think she "maybe" has a child who FYI is twenty-one—a daughter."

"She was my cleaning lady, not my psychiatrist."

That hit so close to home.

"And honestly, I rarely saw her. Most people aren't home when their cleaning lady comes, and she only came twice a month. She actually did more odd jobs for me. I don't mind scrubbing toilets and running a vacuum, but laundry, dusting those stupid mini-blinds, light fixtures, and cleaning my fish tank..." she felt him glaring at the side of her head "...that's the stuff she did for me and it didn't require an exchange of personal information."

"I think when you ask someone to wash and fold your tighty-whities there really *should* be an exchange of personal information."

AJ shook his head. "It was more sheets and towels, occasionally my uniform or ironing some shirts."

"Good to know ... I thought she must have been pretty desperate for work. Anyway, I hope it works out. I'd love to be an aunt. I'd be the coolest aunt ever."

"Is that enough?"

"What do you mean?" She stole a quick, sideways glance.

"Don't you want to be a mom?"

"I feel like we've had this discussion."

"I feel like you're afraid to admit what you want, or maybe you're even afraid to want it at all."

"I don't want you to die. I'm not afraid to admit that. I want a romantic date with *cloth* napkins. I want to always be on top when we have sex."

The last part was a lie. Jillian realized her list of wants turned into her needs. Her deepest truth: she didn't want everything she needed or maybe she didn't want to *need* it. Needs were weaknesses.

"You'd be an amazing mother."

She guffawed. "How can you even say that with a straight face?"

"Your compassion equals your strength, and you're the strongest person I know."

"Well, it's a moot point. You can't have kids and I choose you."

"But—"

"I. Choose. You. And don't you dare talk about the fucking cancer. You're better ... we're better."

AJ sighed, gazing out his window. "We're better," he whispered.

IF HE LOVED HER, he'd let her go. AJ couldn't get that thought out of his damaged mind. Jillian loved him and she let him go with a simple *thank you*. He blamed his selfishness on the tumor ... by that point he blamed everything on the tumor. How much of her life could he steal and still feel like a man and not an inconsiderate bastard?

"How do you feel about ice cream?" She slowed, pulling into the dinky parking lot of an ice cream shop with a few picnic tables in front.

"I feel like you want some."

"I do."

That smile. When they first met he never imagined one day having a long list of traits he loved about Jillian Knight—quite the opposite. Life was nothing if not unimaginable. The woman was *real*. She never faked anything, not a single word, not a single smile. Every ounce of her being screamed, "Take me as I am."

Hence the selfishness. If life was short, then AJ's was less than a breath from ending, so he wanted to end it with something real.

"Let's get ice cream then." He smiled back at her.

"I hope they have dipped cones." She took his hand and pulled him toward the window.

"I'll have a twist cone dipped in chocolate." Her eyes beamed as if all her dreams just came true.

Who was this woman with the innocence of a young child dying to escape?

"Small vanilla in a cup."

"What?" She looked at him with wide eyes. "What he means is a hot caramel sundae with pecans."

"I do?" He looked down at her.

"You do." She pressed a kiss to his arm as he handed the lady a twenty.

They took their cool treats to the picnic table.

"We should stay here for the winter. I bet Omaha sucks in the winter."

"Can't be any worse than New York."

She paused with her dripping cone at her lips. A moment later she nodded. "True."

"Hurricane season is over. We should head to the Gulf and find a little shack to rent."

"Shack?"

"We don't need much."

He was looking at everything he needed.

"Don't worry, I'll do the laundry and dust the blinds."

"You clean?" AJ couldn't hold back his incredulous response.

"As needed. We might have to negotiate the definition of need. I have this feeling yours may be a bit more stringent than mine."

He nodded, taking a small bite of his ice cream. "Were your parents wealthy?"

"Why do you ask?"

"Work seems to be an option for you, not a necessity. You live in a nice house, drive a brand new Harley, drop a couple thousand dollars on camping equipment, and for that first week I'm pretty sure you paid for all the gas and the hotel room expenses. Unless you stole my credit card from my wallet."

Jillian licked her ice cream and chocolate covered lips. "Hmm ... I never thought about stealing your wallet. Total oversight on my part."

"I'm serious." AJ pushed his half-eaten sundae toward the middle of the table. His appetite was still off.

"They weren't wealthy, but they had money in savings, a house that was paid off, and pretty good life insurance."

"Well you're young and you should be putting that money in savings or investing it, not spending it on me."

"So you quit your job. Where are you getting the money?"

"Savings ... my house if it ever sells."

"You don't need to sell your house now."

"Jillian ..."

"What?" She shrugged, keeping her eyes on his ice cream that she decided to finish off.

"Look at me." He took the cup from her and held both of her hands, squeezing them until she surrendered her gaze to him. "I can't ... I *won't* pretend with you. I just want you *now* for as many days as I have. Because now—this moment—is all I have to give. It's yours. I'm yours. Please just let it be enough."

She looked at him without a single blink. Finally her head moved a fraction. It looked like a nod, a very small acquiescence. "You have ice cream on your nose."

AJ wiped his nose then looked at his hand. "Did I get it?"

"Nope."

He looked up just as a spoon filled with caramel and ice cream collided with his nose. Jillian's shoulders bounced as she bit her lips together and snorted a laugh.

"Funny?" He narrowed his eyes.

Cupping a hand over her mouth, she nodded.

"Stop." She tried to twist from his hold as he lunged over the table, locking her head between his hands while he rubbed his nose all over her face. She gave up the fight when his lips took hers.

Fate used his heart as a punching bag every time he touched her, a painful reminder that it could be the last touch, the last kiss.

"Aric James ..." she whispered over his lips.

"Shh ... *now*. Nothing else matters."

CHAPTER TWENTY-EIGHT

Lady Gaga blared through the speakers about her Nebraska guy as Ryn gripped the ballet barre. Her leg muscles ignited into a fiery burn under Val's drill sergeant orders. She welcomed the pain because her Nebraska guy was off. The. Charts.

"Coffee?" Val wiggled her brows at Ryn after the rest of the class left the building.

"I don't know I—"

"Sorry. It sounded like a question didn't it? I meant *we're going for coffee* because you owe me the latest scoop. I'm in a dating funk right now. I need to know there's life after divorce."

"Sorry, I'm on a tight schedule today."

"Just say it. You're going to have hot sex with that boy because he likes the taste of your sweat."

Ryn pushed on the front door and turned back. "Please don't call him a boy. I'm drowning in enough insecurity."

Val laughed. "Next week. I won't take no for an answer."

Ryn nodded and rushed out the door, digging through her purse for her keys as the cool fall breeze whipped her hair in her face.

"I love that my wife works hard to keep her figure."

She froze, feeling nothing but fear pounding against her chest. Preston's smug bastard face greeted her as she lifted her gaze. He wore his usual custom-tailored black suit, leaning against her car door with his ankles casually crossed as if he owned the world, as if he still owned her. Ryn held up her phone.

"You can't be here, so leave before I have you arrested."

"I want to apologize."

She narrowed her eyes. "Apologize? This better be about Maddie. How dare you lie to her and make her think I was ever crazy and suicidal."

He smirked. "I'm not apologizing for that. That's between you and Maddie. I'm here to apologize for your birthday. The whole passing out thing." He chuckled. "You know the funny thing about that ... the last thing I remember is that thug you brought putting his hand around the back of my neck and squeezing. He say anything about that to you?"

Ryn shook her head.

"I did some looking into him. It's like he didn't exist before moving to Omaha. Where did he say he's from?"

"He's none of your business." She reached for the door handle.

He didn't move. Instead, he bent down and whispered in her ear, "He's fucking what's mine so that makes him my business."

"I'm not yours."

He pushed off the door and slid on his shades. "Semantics, sweetheart. I'm just telling you something's not right about him so watch yourself."

***

Mrs. Baker reeked of all kinds of wrong. Jackson followed her home after her last lesson. She lived in a small split-level house surrounded by a jungle of weeds in a run-down neighborhood. Children's toys cluttered the front yard like she ran a daycare out of her home. Through his binoculars, he watched her get out of her car, go inside, and come back out fifteen minutes later wearing baggy ripped jeans and a flannel shirt—a fashion world away from the expensive clothes she wore to her lessons. But it wasn't her clothes that made his blood run toxic through his veins, it was her red hair. Had she been wearing a wig? Certain that at least on some level she could be a liability, he decided to plan her *removal*.

Fate, however, granted Meredith Baker a stay of execution when she missed her lesson to visit a friend in the hospital. Knowing she could be plotting his death, or even Jillian's, had him on edge the entire following week. Ryn fell victim to his nervous energy. All their lessons on self-defense turned into fuck fest on the mat. He fucked her hard and often, hoping the release would ease his impatience, but it didn't. It just left the woman he felt certain defined love in a constant state of confusion and physically exhausted to the point of avoiding him for days in between.

All of that was about to change as he lined the back of Woody with plastic. Jillian hated knives, but Jackson found them to be quite effective. He didn't enjoy the kill—that's how he slept at night. There was never any sort of high or adrenaline rush. It was a job. Remove the threat.

Unfortunately, Mrs. Baker was more than a threat. There was no way she worked alone, which meant he would have to drag the information from her. That's why he needed the knife. The quick neck snap was more his thing, but the threat of it rarely garnered much information. Evil people weren't afraid to die, but they didn't like pain.

From the garage he heard a car pull into the driveway. He slipped back into the house and grabbed his knife from the kitchen table. He had another lesson in an hour. There would be no time to waste on meaningless chitchat.

"Ryn." He tried to sound excited to see her as he strained to see if Mrs. Baker had pulled in too.

"I know you have a lesson, but I need to talk to you. Do you mind if I wait here until you're done?"

"Uh ... or I could meet you at your house?"

"Well I'm already here so ..." She looked at his hand. "You're holding a knife ... a scary-looking knife."

He looked at his hand as though he'd forgotten about it. "I am."

"You're not planning on killing anyone, are you?" She grinned.

"Ha. Well, now that you're here I'm not." Jackson gave her his sexy grin and winked while slipping it into his back pocket.

Ryn shook her head as she stepped inside. "Seriously. What are you doing with a knife?"

"I'm ... changing the batteries in a clock. It was easier than looking in Jillian's tool chest for a screwdriver."

"The tools belong to Jillian?"

"She likes working on cars and motorcycles. I like working on computers which don't require anything with the word Craftsman on it."

She pressed her finger to the taped center of his glasses

that were supposed to keep any spurting blood from getting in his eyes. "You're such a geek."

He grabbed her hand and bit her finger. "Watch it, hot pants."

The doorbell rang, the daunting reminder that Mrs. Baker would live to see another day.

"I'll wait downstairs. Maybe practice some pull-ups." She leaned up and pecked his lips before slipping around the corner.

"Mrs. Baker."

"Jackson." She beamed her flirty teeth-covered-in-lipstick grin at him as she stepped inside wearing expensive everything—right down to her Manolo Blahnik shoes.

He inspected her head to see if it was her real hair or if the red hair had been a wig. "You have a bug in your hair."

She rolled her eyes toward her brows as he yanked on a few strands of hair. The delayed "ouch" confirmed that it was a wig.

"Sorry." He smirked. "Got it." With a flick of his fingers he sent the nonexistent bug flying absolutely nowhere.

"That's fine." She eased her hand over her wig. "Is that Jillian's car in your driveway?"

"Why do you ask, Mrs. Baker?"

She took a seat at the piano. "Just curious I suppose. If it's not hers then you might have company."

"You're my company, Mrs. Baker." He slipped the knife under a magazine on the table and walked toward the piano giving her the you-should've-been-dead-by-now stare.

She averted her eyes. He grinned at the thought of how easily she would squeal like a pig, spewing out everything he needed to know before removing her from the equation. A necessary casualty.

"I'm not company. I'm your student."

Jackson sat in the chair next to the bench, resting his ankle on the opposing knee. "You are. So please..." he gestured "...let me hear your progress."

She played each song with perfection. Too much perfection. Mrs. Baker was his only student who practiced, although he suspected she knew how to play before taking lessons with him, in spite of claiming to be a novice. At the end of her thirty minutes he told her to have a good week—her last week of course.

After replacing the knife in its leather sheath in his drawer, he took a deep breath to expel the anxiety before going downstairs. If he didn't control his sexual urges with Ryn, he could scare the mother of his children away before he had a chance to implant them inside her.

RYN BRACED herself for the sexual hurricane that she knew would come tearing down the stairs at any moment. Jackson had ripped the zippers off two pairs of jeans, disintegrated four pairs of panties, and broken the clasp on her newest bra. She couldn't even complain about him being selfish because his first stop was always between her legs. Lips, tongue, teeth, and she was gone. Every. Time.

"I started my period." The words came out so fast it all sounded like one long word instead of four.

Jackson paused at the bottom of the stairs. "Jillian probably has something in her bathroom."

"No ... I just mean I or we can't ... you know."

He smirked then nodded, shoving his hands into his pockets, pulling the waist down to tease her with the wide band of his sexy briefs. "Is that what you needed to tell me?"

"No." She laughed at herself. It had probably sounded like that was her important news. "Preston was waiting by my car for me when I came out of barre class this morning."

"You need me to kill him? Done."

"No. Well, it's not a bad idea, but I'm certain that would guarantee I'd never see Maddie again or you for that matter because you'd be in prison."

The corners of his lips curled like he had the best secret ever. She trusted him, ninety-nine-point-nine percent. Yet that point-one percent held her heart captive in the hands of fear. Would she ever be completely free of that fear?

"I'm not happy that my ex-husband thinks you're his business, but after you sent him to the hospital on my birthday he's taken it upon himself to make you his business."

Jackson shrugged. "Then tell him to call me and we'll set up a *business* meeting, but until then he needs to stay the fuck away from you, or I'll be the first one to make contact and it won't be in the way of a phone call."

There it was—that point one percent.

"I can call the police if it becomes a bigger issue."

"I'm sure they'll slap him on the wrist. They might even take away his favorite toy for a month or so."

"Whatever, that's really not my point. My point is that Preston did some looking into your past and he said it's like you didn't even exist before Omaha. Don't you think that's kind of odd?"

"Yes. I think it's odd that your ex-husband is looking into my past."

Ryn tilted her head to the side, crossing her arms over her chest. "That's not what I mean."

Jackson narrowed his eyes a mere millimeter. That minuscule change in his expression, that may not have been anything more than a muscle twitch, left Ryn feeling guilty for bringing it up.

"So I haven't left my fingerprints all over my past. So what?"

Coughing out a sarcastic laugh, she gawked at him. "Fingerprints? What are you, a killer?"

"Do I look like a killer?" He smirked.

"I don't think killers have a certain look, personality maybe, but not a look."

"Well, if you think I have a killer personality then I'm going to take that as a compliment."

Ryn shook her head, unable to keep a straight face.

"What do you want to know?" He moved toward her with slow predatory strides that sent tingly goose bumps shooting up along her skin.

She retreated, the thick mats under her feet mixed with that look made it impossible to balance. Her back hit the wall, saving her from stumbling, but trapping her in his larger-than-life presence as he wet his lips.

"Do you want to know my favorite color? The first girl I kissed? How many comic books I owned? The longest book I've read?"

Gulp.

"Yes," she whispered, embarrassingly breathless.

He pressed his lips to her forehead. "Blue, like your eyes."

He kissed her right ear. "Stephanie Mills, third grade."

He kissed her left ear. "Three hundred and seventy-one. Batman was my favorite."

He kissed the hollow area in between her collarbone, circling his tongue around it. "The Bible."

"No way."

He nodded while unfastening his jeans.

Ryn swallowed hard, her body stiff. "M-My period."

Sucking her bottom lip into his mouth, he bit it with a chilling intensity as he stroked himself. "Don't worry. That's not where I'm going to put it."

CHAPTER TWENTY-NINE
DAY

Luke pulled into his parents' drive after taking the slower, nothing over thirty-five, less driven roads to ensure his precious cargo had a safe trip—in the trunk. To his surprise, she stayed quiet for the entire ride. Even when he got out, she didn't make a single noise. He considered opening the trunk to check on her, but his instincts told him to just stay away. It was nothing more than the silence before the storm.

"Hey, Luke. You two have a nice drive?" Tom asked, helping Felicity fold sheets in the living room.

"We did. It was a perfect day."

"Did you find a nice little place to buy and settle into when you move back here to get married and have lots of grandbabies for me?"

Tom rolled his eyes at his wife's question.

"We did not."

Felicity frowned.

"While I fully intend to marry Jessica and have a manageable number of children with her, I want it to be when the time is right."

"Not everyone can be like your mother and I were. Perfect timing on everything." Tom winked at Felicity.

"*I'm* in your wedding photos, sitting in the front row next to Aunt Beth. Brilliant timing, folks."

His parents shared their usual we-wouldn't-change-a-thing grins. If Luke were honest, he admired their decision to wait until they were ready to get married. They conceived him on their first date.

"Speaking of fate ... where is Jessica? Did she go upstairs?"

Luke smiled at his mom. "I think she's still in the car going through a few things she picked up on our outing."

"Oh, that reminds me. Did you remember my printer ink?"

"We did." He handed her the car keys. "They're in the trunk."

Felicity frowned as she snatched the keys while shaking her head. "Was it just too much for you to haul them inside?"

"Something like that."

As she brushed past him, Tom gave Luke a suspicious look.

Luke grimaced. "There's a pretty good chance I won't live to see the sunrise."

"You forgot her ink?"

"No. It's in the trunk—with Jessica."

IT BROKE Jessica's heart that her beloved would die soon, but there were certain acts of complete disrespect that were punishable only by death. Locking someone in a trunk was one of them. They'd had some good times together and for that, she was not only grateful but sympathetic enough to make sure his death would be quick with minimal suffering.

Had she been able to predict such an act of sheer evilness, she would have purchased batteries for her electric pillar candles. Instead, she waited in the dark, knees bent to one side, hands laced behind her head. She wore a dragonfly shower cap, blue nitrile gloves, and a mustache molded from Sticky Tac. On the inside of the trunk lid was a sticky note with sloppy I-wrote-it-in-the-dark handwriting that read:

I'm going to let Jones hump your $300 pillow and play tug of war w your socks when U R DEAD!

"Ahhh! Oh my gosh!" A woman's voice screeched.

Jessica felt like a vampire with the bright light frying her cornea—a deaf vampire thanks to the shrill pierce of Felicity's scream. Everything came into focus a little at a time. The note still stuck to the inside of the lid, the horrified, yet confused look on Felicity's face as she seemed to be reading it, and then the Holy Grail.

Jessica smiled as she sat up, pulling the mustache from her lip. "Hel-lo, Thelma." She snatched the dangling keys from Felicity's hand and hopped out. "Get in." She slammed the trunk and slid in the driver's seat. Yep. Just as she imagined: better than sex.

"Thelma?" Felicity questioned as she hesitantly got in the other side.

"Thelma and Louise. But don't worry, we won't drive it off a cliff or anything ... at least not today." Jessica tossed the gloves and shower cap in the backseat. "Buckle up. Once I start the engine we'll need to be spinning the tires out of here. Oh ... and keep an eye out the back window to say goodbye to Luke. In less than ten seconds he'll be on your porch having a heart attack or possibly a stroke."

"What's going on?"

Jessica loved that without knowing a single detail, Felicity buckled up. Of course the skinny-dipping mom would be all in. It was wrong for Jessica to have doubted her for a single moment. She moved the seat up, stomped on the clutch, and turned the key. The seductive rumble of the engine, finally under her control, made it hard to focus, but she needed to get out of there because the timer had started.

She backed out of the drive, shoved it into first, and waited, one hand white knuckled on the steering wheel, the other fisting the round black ball of the gear shift.

"There they are. Blow your boys a kiss, Felicity."

And she did because Felicity Jones was one. Cool. Chick.

Jessica tattooed the concrete with the back tires as she squealed out of the drive. She took a mental picture of Luke's reflection in the rearview mirror: slumped shoulders, hand over his chest, slightly bent at the waist, mouth agape.

Priceless.

"I think the joke is supposed to be on Luke, but then again, he sent me out to get the ink, knowing you were in the trunk. And you were wearing a shower cap, gloves, and a mustache so ... I'm confused."

"Let's just say your son would rather me ride in the trunk than sit in the driver's seat. No offense to you of course, but he may have control issues, and I'm usually not all judgmental that way because I like control too but—"

"So you didn't voluntarily get in the trunk? He drove home with you in there?"

"Correct. I'm not going to lie and when I say this I'm speaking to my partner in crime, Thelma, not Luke's mom."

Jessica grinned. "When he first shoved me in the trunk I didn't try to fight him. It caught me off guard, but I honestly thought he was trying to do something kinky with me."

Felicity laughed to the point of a girlish giggle. "So what did you do when you realized he was locking you inside?"

"Started plotting his death."

"Oh my goodness, he's his father through and through."

"Tom? No way." She shook her head.

Felicity nodded. "Yes, he is. Tom used to be a control freak when we first started dating. It didn't help that I was pregnant."

"Wait, you were pregnant when you *started* dating."

"Basically. Has Luke not told you that we conceived him on our first date?"

Jessica's jaw dropped then closed into a grin, eyes wide. "No."

"Yes. And now what I'm going to say is being said to Louise, not Luke's girlfriend."

"God, I love you. Go on." Louise laughed.

"Luke doesn't know this and I'm quite certain he wouldn't be treating this car like his most prized possession if he knew that his conception took place in this very back seat."

"Oh my God ... Oh my God ... Oh. My. God. Do you have any idea what you have given me?"

"No." Felicity shook her head. "I've given you nothing. Thelma told her partner in crime, Louise, about the first time she had sex."

"Aahh!" Jessica veered off the road onto the shoulder, coming to a stop. She couldn't focus on driving anymore. "Don't you dare try to silence me with some secrecy oath, especially since you just added the crème de la crème to the juiciest little secret I've ever known—you didn't just conceive Luke. You. Lost. Your. Virginity … in this very car. Luke's baby."

Dying. Jessica died a little inside. It would be the most painful secret *ever* to keep, and as much as she'd come to love his mom … she just couldn't guarantee that the day wouldn't come that she would need that ammunition to win a war.

"Seriously, we should like … bronze the back seat and never allow anyone to sit back there again."

Felicity looked over her shoulder and smiled as if she were replaying the memories in her mind. Jessica found it sweet and romantic. Luke would have had his head out the door hurling his last meal.

"Do you think about having children someday?"

The conversation took a whiplash turn.

Jillian pulled back onto the road. Running the GTO through the gears made her feel in control and eased her nerves.

"Sometimes. I didn't used to so much before I met Luke. And when I did, it was more like mourning something I would never have."

"You were his patient?"

Of course she didn't know for sure. Luke would never break that confidentiality … except with her parents. *Traitor.*

"I was. I'm not now. Well…" she shrugged "…not offi-cially. He's brilliant, he really is, but I'm an extra special, pardon my French, fucked-up case. I'm not sure anyone could 'cure' me. I want to believe I'm better, but I'm afraid I'm better *with* Luke, not necessarily *because* of him. He's even said it himself. If tomorrow he were to just disappear from my life, I wonder if the woman I've become with him would still exist, or if I would slip back to the woman I was before him."

"Can I ask who you were before him?"

Jessica huffed a small laugh. "I'd tell Thelma I was a monster, but I think that might frighten Luke's mom so I will tell her that I was simply a woman afraid of herself. A woman who longed for this exact moment in time, but never felt worthy of a future beyond work and physical exhaustion."

They continued to drive. Jessica knew Felicity needed to get back for the guests who were staying at their bed and breakfast, but Felicity never said a word. She let Jessica have her drive, her moment of quietude with the comfort of knowing she wasn't alone. Jessica loved the same thing about Luke. They could be together and feel the closeness without the need to fill the space with words. They could spend hours in bed or on the couch at night with her on her laptop studying and him reading or working on a crossword puzzle. Sometimes they'd share a flirty smile, but it was never awkward or boring.

Only in complete silence can the whisper of true love be heard.

Felicity rested her hand on Jessica's arm as they pulled into the drive over an hour after leaving Luke in a world of dismay. "My son is a smart boy."

Jessica stared at Felicity's hand on her arm. "I don't think his brain is responsible for us being together."

"That's why I said he's a smart boy. He's following his heart."

Jessica looked up at Felicity's loving smile. "Thank you," she whispered.

Luke and Tom were out back chopping wood. Jessica gazed out the window to determine if Luke was mad or if the pained expression on his face was from physical exertion.

"Tom's always smiling."

Felicity started cleaning potatoes for dinner. "Most of the time, yes."

"Chopping wood is not easy work, but Tom is sweating with a smile on his face."

"He loves working. If he ever stops that's how we'll know he's dead."

"Can I help you with dinner?"

"You could go ask Tom if he's grilling or if I'm broiling tonight."

Jessica could do that. It didn't require any preparation or actual cooking. "No problem. Of course I risk getting the *ax* for the grand theft auto."

"Send them my way. I've got your back, Louise."

Jillian walked around the side of the house. "Hey, baby boy," she rubbed Jones's ears after he ran to her, alerting the father-son-lumberjack duo of her arrival.

"Hey, Mario." Tom smiled or continued smiling.

"Tom Jones." She grinned, not yet risking a glance at Luke. "Felicity wants to know if it's grilling or broiling tonight."

He nodded and handed her his ax. "Here. I'll go talk with her. Don't kill each other."

She watched Tom walk toward the house then turned to face Luke. It was an eerily weird stare off. She wasn't mad at him anymore, but she also didn't feel remorseful for what she had done. His face seemed expressionless as well.

"I was going to let you drive her."

Jessica nodded. "I know ... that's the vibe I got from the trunk earlier."

"You know I just put new tires on her."

Another somber nod. "I know ... that's why I was a little surprised she didn't grip the driveway better."

"Did you let my mom drive too?"

"No, she didn't ask, and I didn't know when I'd get to drive her again so I was a little selfish." She pulled the insulated flannel shirt she'd grabbed from the garage around her body tighter as a cool gust of wind made her shiver.

Luke nodded with a slow inhale. "Smell that?"

She rolled her eyes up, nose scrunched. "Smoke?"

"My dad's up front grilling."

"O-kay ..."

Luke motioned toward the shed with his head. "We've got time for a quickie in the shed before dinner."

Both of their grins grew as they dropped their axes on the ground. Bodies and mouths crashed together while attempting to hobble as one to the shed without stumbling.

Once inside, they wrestled with each other's pants, not caring that they both were in flannel tops. The immediate need was for him to be inside her.

"Oh dear God ..." Her head fell back against the wall as he lifted her against it and thrust into her with one desperate move. He felt warm, and hard, and deliciously filling inside her. She made claim to his hair, using it for support as his hands dug into the muscled flesh of her ass moving her up and down.

"I adore you," he moaned into her neck as she closed her eyes.

Jessica rested her cheek on his head. "My God ... you give me *life*."

CHAPTER THIRTY

KNIGHT

IF MRS. BAKER didn't die soon, Ryn would leave Jackson. He felt certain of it. There was only so much nervous energy he could release in the form of sex before possibly scaring her off completely. She nearly died when he implied the intention of putting his dick in her mouth instead of her pussy—*vagina*—because she made the assumption he meant her ass, not her mouth.

When he told her to get on her knees, he saw relief wash over her face. He watched her mouth "thank God" to herself before happily accepting his cock. Although she sucked him like a champ, even swallowing every last drop, she expressed her preference to that over having it shot on her face or breasts. Jackson couldn't help but feel a jab of disappointment that her ass was off limits—in her words "forever." Nothing ruins a good blowjob quite like an anal sex ban.

Jackson: Where are you?
Jillian: Texas
Jackson: I have to remove someone.

Jillian: I'm on my way home. DON'T DO ANYTHING!
Jackson: Don't come home. It might not be safe for you here.
Jillian: Who? Why?
Jackson: One of my students.
Jillian: God you're sensitive about that damn piano.
Jackson: She knows your name. I never told her your name.
Jillian: Maybe one of your other students did.
Jackson: I always refer to you as my "sister." Period.
Jillian: It's not enough.
Jackson: I followed her. She wears a wig and dresses in expensive clothes, but lives in a shack and she lied about her husband being dead or maybe ever having one.
Jillian: Still not enough. I'm coming home.
Jackson: It will be too late.

His phone vibrated with a call. Sliding the mother of his unborn children from his chest, he slipped out of her bed. He'd taken her to dinner as an apology for his recent neurotic behavior. Ryn had thought it was a reward for the blowjob. That worked too.

Afterward he'd insisted on staying the night with her, which earned him the hairy eyeball. She couldn't imagine why he'd want to stay if they weren't going to have sex. The tears in her eyes didn't go unnoticed when he told her how lonely his body felt at night when it wasn't wrapped in hers.

As he stepped into the hall, Gunner greeted him with a stern look and low growl that said he'd be having his conversation with Jillian right there and not an inch farther.

"Yes?"

"McGraw's been supplying all of AJ's pharmaceutical needs. Do you need me to have him send you a mild sedative or maybe an antipsychotic?"

"I'm not paranoid." He was, but not all paranoid

people were crazy. "Meredith Baker is not who she says she is. She's a puppet, she has to be. I can't believe I didn't catch it sooner. She slips up all the time. I followed her to her house, practically riding her fucking bumper and she didn't notice me. Whoever hired her can't be much smarter, but if it's the same person who's been texting you, then they're managing to stay one step ahead and that makes me—"

"Nervous? Paranoid?"

"I'm not wrong about this."

"And if you are then you've committed murder without just cause. What if you didn't have G.A.I.L behind you, ready to swoop in and clean up your mess? Would you risk life in prison on her knowing my name and wearing a wig? For Christ's sake, do you know how many women would rather wear Gucci and look the part than have food on the table or a roof over their heads?"

Gunner stared at Jackson as if he had the same questions as Jillian.

"I can't just do nothing."

"For now you can. Besides if you kill her you'll never know who she's working for."

"I'd get it out of her first."

"How?"

Jackson clenched his teeth and narrowed his eyes at Gunner, who would not give him an inch of space past Ryn's bedroom door.

"I have my ways."

Jillian didn't have to say anything. He could feel her anger. It was thick in the painful silence between them.

"I'm coming home."

"I can handle this."

"With a fucking knife?"

"Jill?" Jackson heard AJ call her name in the background.

"It works." He winced as he said it. Just because Claire had died after being tortured with a knife didn't mean it still wasn't a very persuasive tactic.

"Where's Ryn?"

"In the bedroom."

"Go look at her perfect skin and imagine some heartless, soulless heathen making forty-four slashes into it based on some fucked-up assumption. Goodnight, Jackass."

"Jill—" He sighed. "Fuck," he whispered. "Women are stubborn."

Gunner tilted his head.

"Stick to humping pillows, buddy."

"Jackson?"

He turned just as Ryn cracked open the bedroom door, eyes squinted, blond hair matted, large white T-shirt barely covering her sexy legs.

"Are you ... talking to Gunner?"

"I, uh, am."

"It's after midnight."

"Yes. We never get to talk—man to ... man's best friend."

She nodded toward his phone fisted in his hand. "Gunner doesn't text."

He stepped back in the room, forcing her retreat to the bed. "I was talking to Jillian."

Ryn slid under the covers. Jackson followed, spooning her back to his chest.

"How's AJ?"

"Alive."

She grunted. "Thanks for that elaborate answer."

"They're in Texas."

"Texas?" Ryn turned in his arms as if he would have a different answer if she faced him.

"Yes. He wants her to help him die."

"He said that?"

Jackson smirked then rolled onto his back, tucking Ryn under his arm. "No. But that's what he's doing. She's too blind and kind to see it. And even if she suspects it, she's too stubborn to give up on him. Surrendering has never been easy for her."

"Are they coming home?"

He pursed his lips to the side and nodded. "Something tells me we'll be seeing her or *them* sooner rather than later."

"Jackson?"

"Hmm?"

"Can I tell you something and will you promise not to get mad or make me feel bad or irresponsible or reckless?"

"You're pregnant?"

"What?" She sat up resting on her elbow, giving him a scrunched-face expression. "I'm having my period."

He shrugged. "I wasn't convinced if that's what it was for sure since a few days ago you accused me of trying to 'break your vagina.'"

She jabbed him in the side with her fist. He chuckled.

"It's not funny. A few times I wondered if you were going to rip me straight up the middle in two. You've been weird ... even kind of angry. That's it ... it's felt like angry sex. Not even sex at times, more like just effing."

"Effing?"

"Yes, *fucking*," she whispered.

He roared a big laugh that only turned her face true crimson. "Why..." he tried to catch his breath through his laughter "...are you whispering? Are you worried about

Gunner hearing you or God? Because I'm quite certain that dog has already told me to back the fuck away from you in more than one language, and I know you haven't been to church in a while, but as far as I know, God can still read minds."

"Well excuse me, Mr. Vulgar, I didn't grow up using explicit language, and I had a baby before I had a chance to sow any wild oats and making a habit of using the F-word as an adjective and adverb to every single word in the English language. Don't people realize it starts to lose its effect after a while? It's like putting an explanation point at the end of every sentence.

'I'm going to wake the F up tomorrow and roll the F out of my effing bed, and take an effing hot shower before I effing eat an effing bowl of cereal. Then I'm going to get the F going to my first effing job, then meet my effing amazing boyfriend for an effing good lunch, and then if I'm done with my effing period we might F a few times until we're effing exhausted.'"

Jackson's body vibrated with laughter. "Am I the 'effing amazing boyfriend' in your little story?"

Ryn kissed along his chest, following the lines of ink. "Maybe."

"Maybe, huh? I can work with that. So before you went off on your effing tangent, what were you going to tell me?"

Ryn paused, resting her chin on his chest, looking up at him. "I miss my daughter. She's so stubborn, and naive, and some days even cruel. I see that, I really do. But she's this huge part of my heart and I can't be on the other side of this wall that she's built between us. Maddie's my child, I love her unconditionally. I would give my life for her, that will never change. So ... I'm dropping the restraining order. And if that puts me in danger, then so be it."

Her eyes filled with tears, but she never stopped looking at him.

"I'm sorry if you think that makes me a bad mom, or a terrible role model, or just a pathetically weak person in general. The day I chose not to get the abortion Preston wanted me to get was the day I chose my daughter. It was my unspoken vow that I would always choose her no matter what. *That* is the example I want to set for Maddie."

He brushed his thumb along her freckled cheek, catching her tears. She sniffled with a sad smile tugging at her mouth.

"If we're over. I get it. I'll always think of our time as a really long birthday celebration." Ryn shrugged. "You've always felt like a dream anyway."

He brought his other thumb up, brushing both of her tear-drenched cheeks at the same time. Ryn closed her eyes, biting her quivering lips together.

"Ryn Middleton ... do you love me?"

She swallowed through a small sob, squeezing her eyes tighter, setting more tears free. "Don't do this ... please."

"I'm sorry. I have to do this. I know Maddie owns so much of your heart, so much of your life. But the only way I can know if we're over is to ask you if you love me. Do you have enough of your heart left to give to me? Will you love our babies with as much of your heart and as fiercely as you love Maddie?"

Another sob.

"If you can answer yes, then we're never over. I've only loved three women in my life. The first gave me life, the second crowded me in the womb, and the third is a hot mess mere inches from my heart right now. And I hope ... I might even be praying right now that she says yes because I love her ... I love *you*, Ryn, so effing much."

Her sobs filled the room as her arms wrapped around his neck, her face buried in it as he held her to him.

"I didn't mean to fall in love with you."

Jackson smiled with her confession.

"But you just wouldn't leave my heart alone."

He chuckled. "I'll never leave your heart alone."

She drew in a shaky breath, bringing her head up to look at him. "I'm so scared."

His brows furrowed. "What are you scared of?"

"That I won't be able to give you everything you want."

"I just want everything you can give me."

"What if it's not enough?"

He smiled, bringing her mouth slowly to his. "It already is."

RELENTLESS THOUGHTS ROBBED Ryn of all sleep, so she eased off Jackson's chest and slipped out of bed.

She nodded her head to Gunner, who seemed more interested in standing guard at her bedroom door than having an early breakfast. She couldn't complain. He did exactly what he was trained to do.

"Come."

He rose to all fours and followed her downstairs. The sun wasn't even up yet, so she brewed her coffee and fed Gunner a few treats before wrapping up in a blanket on her favorite overstuffed chair with her laptop. Her social media was limited to Pinterest. Facebook and Twitter made Preston's unscrupulous lurking too easy so she stuck to pinning her dreams on boards.

She had a board for all the renovations she dreamed about doing to her house, none of which she could afford while helping Maddie with her college tuition. Her foodie board had tons of recipes she never made because cooking for one wasn't worth the time. Vacation boards, book boards, movies, music, poetry, quotes ... the only board missing was a Jackson board.

With an evil smile, she clicked the add board button.

Knight, she typed.

Over the next hour she proceeded to add pictures to her new board: Vera Wang wedding dresses, Ed Sheeran song lyrics, tattoos, and eventually she gathered the nerve to add a few photos of baby carriers and stylish pregnancy clothes.

Marriage? Babies? Is that what she said yes to?

Gunner jumped up and took his post at the bottom of the stairs like a security guard as Jackson made his way down. Ryn quickly closed her computer.

"I didn't know you were a morning person."

She smiled. "I'm not. I just couldn't sleep ... a lot on my mind." Her smile faded at him fully dressed. "You don't have to go. I made coffee and I'll make you breakfast."

He stopped a few feet in front of her chair with his thumbs hooked into his back pockets. "I need a run and a shower."

She nodded. "Can I make you dinner tonight?" Maybe something on her foodie board would actually come to fruition in her kitchen.

His lack of an immediate answer opened the door for doubt to creep into the mind of a woman who struggled to stay afloat in the pool of insanity. Perhaps he regretted something or everything. Setting her computer on the ottoman, she stood, keeping the blanket wrapped around her.

"If you think my cooking sucks maybe you should just

tell me now so I can yell at you, nurse my wounded ego for the day, and then we can make up later over takeout."

He inched his head slowly side to side, a dark look filled his eyes. Ryn recognized it. It was the same look that had led to the roughest sex of her life on several occasions the previous week. It made her heart race like chased prey.

He sucked in his bottom lip and dragged it through his teeth, closing the distance between them. With one firm tug he ripped the blanket from her body. Palming the back of her head he kissed her. Just as she suspected, it was hard, demanding, and bruising her lips as his tongue filled her mouth. His other hand grabbed her ass so hard she whimpered from the pain, but she was too turned on by his kiss to make any further objection.

The moan from deep in his throat coupled with the bruises forming on her ass beneath his fingers led her to believe she could end up on the sofa with his dick shoving her tampon a mile up her vagina. It's like he had an evil spirit possessing his body, and she wasn't sure what triggered its presence.

She whimpered into his mouth again and he released her.

He nodded, resting his forehead on hers, completely breathless. "Yes. Dinner. Tonight."

Ryn blinked, and blinked, and blinked some more as he walked out the door and to his car with a stiff gait, fists clenched.

Grimacing with a hiss of a breath, she rubbed her butt cheek. The wedding and babies were officially on a serious wait-and-see list.

CHAPTER THIRTY-ONE

AJ WANTED to go to Houston to meet up with an old air force buddy. When they arrived in town he didn't remember making that suggestion or any buddy of his who lived in Houston. Jillian died a little in that moment. The great big world felt suffocating, crushing, and a little too much to bear on her own.

She needed the grumpy, regimented, reads-the-paper-cover-to-cover-every-morning neighbor who gave her a sense of control—but he was lost in the mere shell of a man that sat across from her, picking at his salad.

She needed the brilliantly focused, paranoid but often right, possessive-and-protective-to-the-extreme brother who gave her the strength to fight back when life felt like a candy-stealing bully—but he was losing his own sanity between the man who wanted to be a husband and a father and the man who felt the need to kill in the name of keeping twins buried six feet under in San Francisco.

Jillian jumped from the clang of AJ's fork bouncing off the table and onto the floor. "I'll get you another fork."

"Jillian?" AJ rested both hands flat on the table, fingers spread, chin down, eyes closed.

"Are you okay?" She reached across the table and rested her hand on his.

His chest rose and fell in shallow breaths as he shook his head. He squeezed his eyes shut then opened them wide and squeezed them shut again.

"I can't ... I can't see very well."

She died a little more.

Swallowing past the lump in her throat, she gripped his hand and whispered, "Tell me what you want me to do." She hoped he didn't notice the tremble in her voice. "Do you want me to take you to the hospital?"

AJ shook his head, keeping his eyes closed, head bowed.

"I can get us a plane back to Portland. Maybe there's something your doctors can do."

Another slow head shake. "Take me back to the hotel."

She nodded, but after a moment, reality hit her. *He. Couldn't. See. Her.*

After pinning some cash under the napkin dispenser, she stood and walked around the table. She rested her hand on his shoulder as he slowly scooted his chair out and stood, bumping the edge of the table enough to knock over a water glass.

"Fuck."

"It's fine," she whispered again, knowing her voice would shatter into an avalanche of emotions if she said too much.

Taking his hand, she led him out of the restaurant and to the Jeep. They didn't speak on the way to the hotel. AJ rested his head against the window with his eyes closed. She hoped he slept and when he woke his vision would return.

No such luck.

When they arrived back at their hotel room, he sat on the edge of the bed. All she could do was sit across from him on the opposing bed, watching him stare blankly at the floor, occasionally blinking hard as if he could blink or shake away the blurriness—the impending darkness.

"It's time," his voice broke just above a whisper.

She looked at the clock on the nightstand and realized she forgot to give him his pain medication with dinner.

"Sorry, I forgot." Digging into her bag, she pulled out the bottle and set it on the nightstand then headed to the bathroom to get water.

When she returned she grabbed his hand to give him the water. He curled his fingers around it. The next few seconds happened in slow motion. As he brought the glass to his mouth she reached for the bottle. The cap was off and it was empty.

"No!" She whipped around knocking the glass from his hand. Shoving his head towards his knees, she dug her fingers into his mouth and began ripping out pills as he coughed. Losing his balance, he tumbled forward onto the floor.

"What are you doing?" she yelled, straddling his body while shoving his head to the side to retrieve the rest of the pills before he could swallow.

He continued to cough around her fingers digging into his mouth as he grabbed her wrists.

Content with the large scattering of expelled pills all over the floor, she collapsed onto him, banging his chest with her fists. "Why? Why? Why? I don't understand!"

His hands rested on her back as she continued to fist and claw at him. "I told you ... it's time."

She sat up, tears racing down her red, blotchy face. "It was time to take one pill. One. Fucking. Pill!" She grabbed the sides of his head and leaned forward resting her forehead on his. "Look at me," she whispered. "Please."

AJ opened his eyes. "I can barely see you." He closed them again. Down the side of his face a lone tear fell. His. Fucking. Tear.

THAT NIGHT he had another seizure and later vomited before falling to sleep. Jillian didn't sleep at all. She packed their suitcases and sent a text off to Jackson.

Jillian: *Be home tomorrow night.*
Jackson: *Alone?*
Jillian: *No.*
Jackson: *I'm fine. I don't need you to rush home.*
Jillian: *I need you.*
Jackson: *Safe travels.*

Then she called McGraw.

"It's two o'clock in the morning. West. Fucking. Coast. I'm changing my number," he grumbled.

"I need a private jet from Houston to Omaha tomorrow."

"He died?"

She gritted her teeth and blinked back the tears. "No, but he's losing his sight, and I'll need assistance from the hotel to the airport. Please don't act like you don't know where I'm staying. I spotted your guys following me yesterday."

"I have to keep an eye on you when you call me every other day asking for ridiculous favors."

"I'm done asking after this."

He laughed. "I'll believe it when I see it."

She had no emotion left, not even enough to yell at him and tell him how much she hated him ... how much he added to the ruination of her life.

"Text me the details when you get everything arranged." Letting her head fall back into the wall of the hallway outside of the hotel room, she pressed *End*, wishing more than anything she could press that same button on her emotions ... on her own life.

By eight o'clock her phone chimed with a text from McGraw, mapping out the times and details for their transfer back to Omaha.

"AJ?" She gently shook him, but it took her saying his name several more times and intense shaking to bring him out of sleep.

He peeled his eyes open.

She was afraid to ask, but she had to. "Can you see?"

He nodded once. "It comes and goes." He blinked hard.

She sighed. "We're leaving in an hour."

"Where?"

"Home."

AJ's expression tensed. "Portland."

"Omaha."

"Why?"

Jillian laughed. It was all she could do at that point. "Because you tried to overdose on pain pills right in front of me last night."

"So you're punishing me."

"Punishing you? Oh my God. It's not a punishment. I'm

not taking you back to your parents' and dropping you on their door step with a Post-It note that says, 'Blind and Suicidal.' I just want to go back to Omaha with you."

"It's not going to change anything."

"I know," she whispered. "Let's get you into the shower. Our ride will be here in less than an hour now."

"Our ride?" he asked as she helped him get out of bed.

"Yes. My drug dealer has arranged transportation to the airport and private jet."

"Priv—"

"And please don't ask me anything else about it because I can assure you in the scope of things right now, it *really* doesn't matter."

JILLIAN HELPED AJ to the hotel lobby fifteen minutes before their ride was supposed to be there.

"Sit here. I'm going to have the concierge send someone back up for our bags. I'll be right back."

AJ eased into the leather chair next to the lobby fountain.

She removed the hairband from her wrist and twisted her tangled blond locks into a messy bun then slipped on her sunglass. Her eyes were bloodshot and swollen from too many tears and no sleep.

"Good morning. How may I help you?"

Jillian handed the concierge her room keys. "Room 349. Jillian Knight. Could you have someone bring our bags down to the lobby, please?"

"Absolutely, Miss Knight."

"Thank you."

She turned and nearly ran into the gentleman in line behind her.

"Pardon me." He smiled with a nod and stepped around her as she looked down to retrieve her phone from her handbag.

"Jessica?"

For the first time in nearly a year ... she felt her heart. It beat just feet from her. "Luke," she breathed his name with the first true breath she'd taken in nearly a year. And when she looked up ... she saw her heart.

He looked just like she remembered—perfect. Except, all the blood had drained from his face. He eased his hand toward her head. She needed to stop him, she needed to flee, she needed to do something, but she couldn't. For a mere second in time she felt every cell in her body come to life.

Luke ever so slowly slid off her sunglasses. His mouth dropped open. He looked at a ghost. She stared at a mirage because out of the corner of her eye she saw several men in suits coming to take him away. The clock ticked no matter how much she wished to be frozen in time at that very moment. She'd dreamed of seeing him again since the day she last saw him at the cemetery. What do you say to the person who gave you *everything?*

Tick tock.

Two men grabbed his arms, but he still didn't take his eyes off her.

Say something, her mind screamed.

"Luke ... thank you." A flicker of a smile touched her lips as they pulled him toward the large revolving door.

Once he was outside she could see him yell her name as if something inside him awoke and he began to fight back, but it was too late. Two seconds later they had him stuffed into the back of a black SUV speeding away from the curb.

McGraw's men hadn't been following her because of her requests. They knew Dr. Luke Jones and Jessica Day were going to be in the same city at the same time ... and as if not even death could keep them apart ... they ended up at the same hotel, the same concierge desk, and then for one last time they shared the same breath of air—the same heartbeat.

In that moment she died. There were no more breaths to take.

"Miss Knight, we have to go." Two more suits pulled her toward the exit and another black SUV waiting at the curb.

"AJ—"

"Mr. Monaghan is already in the vehicle."

Luke. He loved her—adored her—and then he mourned her. But no longer. He would hate her forever.

Before they opened the door to the SUV, Jillian fisted the jacket of one of the suits. "You tell McGraw I'll bring him and everyone else involved to the gates of Hell if anything happens to Luke."

The young man swallowed hard and nodded. "I-I'll tell him."

He opened the back door and Jillian climbed in.

"Jillian?" AJ slid his hand across the seat in search of her.

She just stared at it ... stared at him.

AJ squeezed his eyes shut. "Where is she?" he yelled.

She grabbed his hand as the vehicle pulled away from the curb. "I'm here. I'm right here." Her other hand splayed against her heart, slowly clawing into a fist as she looked out the window, falling apart in silence.

"Where did you go?" AJ squeezed her hand.

"The restroom." Words struggled to move past the asphyxiating lump of emotions growing in her throat.

"Did you get our bags?"

She didn't know.

"We did," the suit in the front passenger seat assured.

They arrived at the airport, stopping a short distance from the steps to the private jet.

"I've got him. Just get the bags," Jillian instructed as she stepped out of the vehicle.

"Have you ever been on a private jet?" AJ asked as she led him up the steps.

"No." Every response came out on autopilot. Jillian Knight had never been on a private jet. AJ's distrust didn't go unnoticed by her. Why would he ask if she'd been on a private jet when she confessed her first time on a plane with him months earlier? Because he didn't trust her, that's why.

They settled into the leather seats of the exorbitantly expensive jet and within minutes they were in the air. It may have been an awful thought, but as they ascended into the clouds Jillian was thankful that AJ couldn't see her making the occasional wipe of her weepy, red eyes.

"What's wrong?" he asked as if he could read her mind.

"Nothing."

"You're crying."

"How—"

"I can feel your pain." AJ held out his hand.

She couldn't imagine having another man's arms around her. After seeing Luke it felt like cheating. Cheating on a man who thought she died. Cheating on a man who by all rights hated her. Cheating on a man who she would never see again.

AJ's hand hung in the air between them, so she took it and crawled up on his lap because she needed *someone* and in spite of everything that had just happened, she loved AJ and he loved her.

"Please tell me these tears aren't for me."

Jillian couldn't answer. She just sobbed into his chest because she needed to let go of the pain that was absolutely, unbearably, relentlessly *cutting* her to the depths of her soul.

CHAPTER THIRTY-TWO

THE DEMONS from Jackson's past continued to haunt him at every turn. If something didn't change, he would lose Ryn. She didn't have to say it. The marks on her body said it for her. Jillian had intimacy issues, not him. Yet since his sparring partner had been gone, there weren't enough miles of pavement to pound, enough pull-up reps, or enough jabs to the punching bag to give him the pain he needed. That realization haunted him as much as his past: Jackson Knight needed to feel pain.

"They don't hurt." Ryn pulled her jeans on over her thong that showed his fingers, bruises like tattoos on her ass from him two mornings earlier.

Sitting on the edge of the bed, he reached out and traced the bruises with a feather's touch. Then he gently took her wrists, inspecting the red marks he left minutes earlier from pinning them above her head.

Ryn pulled away to finish dressing. "I'm fine."

How could he make her understand? How could he tell her the people he'd looked up to most in life were liars, cheaters? How could he tell her years of using women for his own pleasure, a physical release devoid of all emotion, left him feeling incapable of having a normal relationship? How could he tell her he was conditioned to be a killer and he needed real physical pain to remind him of his own humanity?

Jillian's stalker and Mrs. Baker had triggered his instinct to defend, to protect, to *kill*. Without that pain he felt himself crawling out of his own skin while his mind incessantly churned out worst-case scenarios that gave him a constant feeling of paranoia.

Ryn bestowed a sense of peace amidst the chaos. When they were together he wanted to crawl inside her and drown in the feeling of peace forever. That desperation had led to him trying to get as physically close to her as possible. But nothing he did worked, it was never close enough ... the demons were still there.

Running from those demons left marks on the woman he loved. He was no better than Preston Iverson.

"I need some time."

She turned, buttoning up her shirt. "Time?"

He nodded, but he couldn't look at her. "You can't let people do this to you."

"Jackson, I said I'm fine."

"You're not fine!" He fisted the sheets beside him. "This!" He grabbed her wrist, turning it so they both could see the red marks. "This is not okay. This is not *fine*. It doesn't matter how many I love you's someone gives you or how many orgasms you have. You are a survivor of abuse so *this* can never be okay again."

She shook her head, tears welling in her eyes. "Don't do this. If you're done with me, then grow a pair and just say it. But don't hand me some you're-a-victim-it's-not-you-it's-me bullshit! You don't know what I've been through and how far I've come to get to this point in my life. Stop treating me like I don't know the difference between love and abuse. I'm not damaged goods. You have no right to jerk around with my emotions, telling me you love me one minute and two seconds later calling some timeout because you don't have what it takes to just tell me the truth."

"The truth?" He stood, feeling that simmering anger threatening to explode. "Jesus, Ryn! What I feel for you is so fucking incredible the word love just seems inadequate. I've never lied about my feelings for you. I'm not dumping you, or breaking up, or whatever the hell normal people do. I'm just fucked up right now and it's *because* I love you that I need to distance myself so I don't hurt you."

Her tears spilled over. "I don't understand."

Jackson sighed. "I know you don't." He closed his eyes for a few breaths. "And I can't explain it to you, and I know you can't understand that either."

She sniffed, wiping her fingers over her cheeks. He wanted to kiss every tear and tell her to just forget everything he just said, but he couldn't.

"So..." she shrugged "...that's it? I'm just supposed to leave and wait around for you on some leap of faith that tomorrow, next week, or months from now you're going to be less 'fucked up' and ready to make me the same promise you made the other night in my bed?"

"Yes," he whispered.

Ryn laughed, shaking her head. "Wow. That's pretty bold, even for you. You're asking a lot."

"Yes." His chin dipped toward his chest.

"I want to love you with that blind faith. I want to trust you with my heart ... I really do. But I'm not that woman anymore. I'm not the victim. I'm the 'fucking goddess' you told me to be, and she would never give everything in exchange for nothing. So if you can't tell me why you're so messed up right now ... if you can't trust me with that, then I can't wait for you."

Jackson nodded.

In spite of what she'd just said, Ryn waited for more because she had to believe there was in fact more. When he didn't say anything, she turned and walked to the door.

"Someday ... I'm going to give you everything."

She stopped with her back to him. "Sure, someday," she whispered before walking away.

He flinched as she shut the door behind her. That emotional dagger through the heart was a new experience for him. Jackson concluded the pain was more extreme than he ever imagined, so the sooner he could get his shit together, the sooner he could get the girl back.

After pulling on his pants, he grabbed his phone. Five missed calls from McGraw.

"Way to answer your fucking phone."

"Is it Jillian?" Jackson didn't have time for his shit.

"She and her nearly-dead boyfriend are on their way back to Omaha on my jet."

"*G.A.I.L.'s* jet. She already told me they were coming back. Why the five calls?"

McGraw laughed. Jackson could just see the look on the sick bastard's face. "Well, if you thought Matthew Green at that rest stop was the most insane coincidence ever, I think I can beat that one."

Jackson never thought Trigger being at the same rest stop as his sister was a coincidence, but he wasn't going to argue that point with McGraw.

"There was a medical conference in Houston—a psychiatric conference."

"Fuck," Jackson whispered.

"My men were on it. They were together for less than sixty seconds before they took him away."

"If you lay a—"

"Yeah, yeah ... some ridiculous gates-of-hell threat from your sister has already been relayed to me. I never thought you liked the guy."

"I don't like any guy who fucks my sister. It's a twin thing."

McGraw didn't respond.

"Where is he now?"

"In a secure location for debriefing."

"Debriefing?"

"We just want to know what they talked about."

"Then ask Jillian."

"Oh we will ... but we need to know if their stories match."

"And then what?"

McGraw laughed. "Don't act like you haven't been through all of this. We'll inform him that the lives of everyone he's ever cared about are all at stake if he so much as breathes her name again. Then we'll give him a little something to help him sleep while we deposit him safely back home. Now if you don't have any more questions, I have an appointment with the good doctor, but don't worry ... you'll be seeing me soon."

***

JACKSON TEXTED Jillian to let her know he'd pick them up from the airport, but she informed him McGraw had already made arrangements. He suspected it was for the best anyway. Jillian had to be running on some unbelievable, not-of-this-world strength reserve. She always managed to make it to him, but he was her safety net and when she finally fell, it was usually with barely a breath of life left in her.

She texted a request before landing.

Jillian: *I need U to clean AJ's place before we get there – EVERYTHING!*
Jackson: *OK*

The cleaning had nothing to do with mops and dust rags. She wanted everything removed that AJ could use to harm himself, right down to butter knives, forks, and chopsticks.

He watched from their kitchen window as the SUV pulled into AJ's driveway. A suited man got out and typed in the garage code. The SUV pulled in as the door shut back down. They weren't announcing their arrival to the neighborhood.

It was wrong on so many levels that he waited for her downstairs, hands taped, mouth guard in place. She needed to cry on his shoulder in a normal grieving way, but he knew she needed to make someone bleed more than anything. And the even more fucked-up part was his need to be that someone.

The door closed. He clenched his fists. Jillian didn't call for him, there was no need. She knew he was downstairs. A few minutes later she descended the stairs looking the part of death. He tossed her the tape. She wrapped her hands then slid in her mouth guard.

"Luke hates me."

Jackson nodded. He wouldn't lie to her.

"AJ is blind and suicidal."

Another nod. "Make me bleed."

THE PAIN. The blood. The fractured souls. They were the only reminders of the Knights' mortality. In Hell everyone was immortal.

Blood clots. Cuts fade. Pain evaporates. But the wounds in their souls would never heal. They would forever fester as reminders that they were bound to a past that could never be erased.

"You're angry." Jillian stared at the ceiling next to her brother.

The pools of sweat and splattering of blood kept them glued to the mat. The adhesion tugged like a Band Aid on their skin when they tried to move. Neither one could remember the final blow. At some point the pain numbed itself.

"You're unbelievable," Jackson said.

"Why do you say that?"

"This morning you saw the face that I know has haunted you. The one that hasn't allowed you to let go of Jessica. Then you had to bring your blind, sick neighbor home all the while pretending your world wasn't shattering all around you. And yet ... you're making an observation pertaining to *my* emotional state."

"I can't do anything about mine. We might as well work on you."

"I professed my love to Ryn two nights ago. She makes me feel ..."

"Feel what?"

"Everything. I feel everything with her. That's the problem. Every time I try to run from my past, I crash into her. I hurt her and she let me. I love her ... and I hurt her. I'm a killer, that's what I do. I hurt people."

"Jackson Knight is not a killer."

"I would have. If Ryn wouldn't have shown up, Mrs. Baker would be dead. Kill or be killed. It's all I know. It's always been so black and white ... I don't know what's in the middle."

"Knight. *We* are in the middle. As much as Jessica and Jude possessed a part of Sunny and Grant, Jillian and Jackson will forever carry the essence of their former selves. If Jessica wouldn't have watched her best friend die ... if she wouldn't have killed a man in cold blood, I don't know if Jillian would love AJ. But for you it's different. You'll stop crashing into Ryn when you stop running from your past. I think you're afraid to let Jude love her too."

"Jude didn't love anyone."

"He loved Jessica."

"That's different."

"Is it? Love is love. Sex was just one of many ways I expressed my love to Luke. I loved just being with him. I loved our runs, our dog walks, dinner on the pier, long drives, trips to Staples ... he complemented my life so completely. That was the bond I had with him. The passion —it was just *one* thing. Luke made me love him long before he ever made love to me. If given the chance, I think Jude would have loved Ryn."

She peeled herself from the mat and stumbled to an upright position with a bit of a dizzy sway. "I have to go see if AJ is awake yet, force feed him, divvy out the prescribed number of pills, and pray he doesn't start vomiting and convulsing on me again."

"God I hope he knows how lucky he really is."

"He has a brain tumor, he's blind, and I think he's losing part of his memory. It's probably accurate to say that 'lucky' is a bit of a stretch. But he loves me, he held me and wiped away my tears—the ones that belonged to Luke—when I think he knew they weren't really for him. And I know you think he called me to help him die, but I don't see it that way. He gave me his last look, and..." Jillian blinked away the onslaught of tears "...he's going to give me his last breath."

"Jill?"

She stopped with her back to him.

"I believe you. I believe that he loves you, but I still think you're wrong."

"About?"

"I don't think he's going to give you his last breath ... I think he's going to ask you to take it."

CHAPTER THIRTY-THREE

"DR. JONES, can you tell us what you and Ms. Day discussed in the lobby of the hotel?"

Jessica was alive.

Luke stared at the steel table beneath his propped up elbows. Nauseous. Confused. The effects of the sedative lingered like a hangover.

He'd been in Houston for three days. Charlie was supposed to meet him for the second half of the week. After coffee and an omelet with whole grain toast in his room, he left early for that day's seminar to drop a room key off at the concierge for Charlie. He was one of three people in line: a tall gentleman in a suit who looked a little familiar, perhaps another doctor he'd seen at the conference, and a woman at the front of the line. He couldn't see much of her except a pile of platinum blond hair when she'd make the occasional tilt of her head to the side while talking to the concierge.

"Dr. Jones? Our goal is to get you home as soon as possible, but we can't do that until you answer our questions.

"You're those people who trained her ... aren't you?"

The muscle in "Knox's" jaw ticked. Luke watched him,

knowing he would have to decipher the truth from his actions because his words, right down to his name which sounded made-up, gave nothing away.

"You know about us?" He smirked, but Luke didn't miss the three rapid blinks before he answered. "What did Ms. Day tell you about her training?"

"It's confidential."

"Well if you believe we—as you say—*trained* her, then I don't see what you could possibly tell me that I don't already know."

Once the shock of having seen a ghost wore off, the agony of how she looked settled into his chest, bringing to life a pain that felt as raw as the day he lost her. The image of her bloodshot eyes would haunt him forever. Her body sagged as much as the dark circles beneath those vacant eyes, like she hadn't slept in days. It was real. She stood before him, but there was no life inside of her.

"Are they all alive? Her parents? Jude?"

"Here's what you need to know, Dr. Jones. Jessica is alive. She's not being held against her will. And you will never see her again. If you want to continue breathing, then I suggest you acknowledge who holds the power. You need to answer my questions, and then we will return you to your life."

"You have my fucking life!" Luke slammed his fists on the table sending Knox's coffee off the edge.

Knox took a deep breath. His jaw muscles clenched again as he shook the hot coffee from his hand. "Unfortunate circumstances such as this one don't happen often, but when they do I usually give the *forgotten* a chance to go home. Ultimately my priority is protecting my own."

"She's not yours."

Knox smirked. "I can assure you ... I claimed her long before you did."

Luke lunged across the table. "You fucker!"

Everything went black.

Day

THE RESCUE SHELTER had told Luke the little black and white Great Dane was the runt of the litter and he probably would only grow to the size of a large Labrador retriever. At eighteen months he measured thirty-four inches in height, weighing in at just under one hundred and sixty pounds—so much more than he ever dreamed. That summed up his relationship with Jessica too.

The nearly two years since he'd met her felt like two seconds. His fear that she would settle into some sort of normalcy and the light that brought life to his existence would fade ... it didn't happen. Even with all his "studying," Jessica remained as unpredictable as the day they met. He had yet to wake up with her in his arms. The Qin dynasty remained separated from the Nomads. She seemed content with it more than he did. Jessica never imagined him, them, Jones, living together, holidays with family—a life. She never asked for a ring or a wedding, children, or a promise beyond today.

However, Luke wanted that—and he wanted it with her —but not until he could wake up with her in his arms. He wondered if her contentment would prevent that from ever happening. The progress they'd made with her past had by all accounts been remarkable. Separating Dr. Jones from Luke presented a challenge with certain topics, such as her past lovers or as she referred to them "victims." She doled the information out over many months. They both agreed it was one of the more difficult topics.

"Our kids are going to ride you like a horse, Jones." Jessica laughed as Jones greeted her at the door. Even in heels she wasn't that much taller.

Luke listened to her talk to said horse while he poured her a glass of wine in the kitchen. He loved those rare moments of hearing her talk about "our kids," as if it was a foregone conclusion. Then on cue, he heard one clack followed by a second as she kicked off her heels, letting them fly where they may. In their almost two years together she went from messy to a complete disaster, yet he still adored her beyond words.

"Mmm ..." She smiled as he handed her a glass of wine. After taking a sip, she lifted onto her toes and kissed him. That was the reason he too drank wine. It would forever remind him of how her tongue tasted sliding against his. "Therapy Thursday ... let's do this."

He smiled and followed her to the balcony with Jones right behind them. After a solid year of unofficial therapy three days a week, she requested her "sentence" be reduced. Luke said two days a week, she countered one ... so of course it ended up being one. Therapy Thursday.

"I think I'm ready to talk about the sex and blood."

"Oh?"

Of course most of their sessions had evolved around one or the other, but Luke needed more from her. He needed the missing pieces.

One: Why did she have such a controlling attitude about sex?

Two: What made a vegetarian feel empowered by the taste of blood?

She had seemed as perplexed as him by those questions for a long time. Luke believed her because he loved her and trusted her. Dr. Jones, with his unbiased mental clarity, held a bit more skepticism. Jessica hid something or suppressed it so deep as to try and convince herself it hadn't happened.

"So last night one of the students in my self-defense class pulled me aside after class to talk. Her boyfriend raped her, but it took her a long time to shed the guilt and acknowledge that it was, in fact, rape."

"Because he was her boyfriend?"

"No, because he made her orgasm."

Luke nodded, feeling uneasy about the direction of the conversation. Jessica had a way of disclosing her past with something that had recently triggered a memory.

"I know how she felt."

Luke tried to keep his voice even as he spoke through clenched teeth. "You were raped?"

Jessica stared at her wine and shrugged. "I'm not sure."

The reaction that stayed lodged in his throat was one of disbelief. How could she not be sure?

"It was three weeks after Claire died."

"Wait, you told me you lost your virginity when you were nineteen with the guy from the jazz club. You were seventeen when Claire died."

"Yes. I told you Pete claimed my hymen."

He set his wine down to prevent his death-hold from shattering the glass.

"One of the men who trained me took it upon himself to make sure I hadn't 'lost my edge' after Claire died. For the purpose of this story I'll call him Mick. Anyway, I didn't want to get out of bed or eat, let alone train for days afterward. All I wanted to do was plan Four's death. It consumed me. So my father sent me with Mick to a remote location, one of their training facilities that wasn't being used.

He pushed me hard for days. There wasn't a part of my body that didn't hurt. I could barely eat my face was so busted up, and one of my eyes had completely swelled shut. At first I didn't fight back. It felt like a punishment for being so stupid to go with Claire in the first place. But Mick taunted me ... he wanted me to make him bleed, and all I could think about was what a cathartic release it was for Four when he cut Claire. So I fought back and I made him bleed."

Luke cleared his throat, praying to God that Dr. Jones would take over because the thought of Jessica's father sending her off with some guy to get beat up, less than a month after her best friend was murdered, filled him with rage.

"How did that make you feel?"

She leaned her head against the back of the chair and closed her eyes. "Alive. It made me feel like a survivor."

He let the silence settle over them, knowing she would soon confess something that would gut him. Just the feeling alone made it hard to breathe.

"He asked me if Four raped Claire, which was weird because I thought surely my dad had given him all the details. When I told him no, he asked me if I thought I had what it took to keep from being raped."

Bile eased up Luke's throat.

"I said yes. Then he asked if I wanted to bet on it." Jessica shook her head. "I hated him so much. Mick always treated me like I was too young, weak, and naive. So I thought, fuck him, because I wasn't the only one who looked like shit. His face had caught my fists, elbows, knees, and feet on more than one occasion. I could hold my own.

Anyway, he bet me that I wouldn't be able to fight him off if he tried to fuck me. He didn't say rape, but it was implied. I asked what I got if I won. He said he'd take me back home instead of finishing our last few days of 'training,' because I would have proven myself to him."

"What was in it for him?" Luke asked.

Jessica locked her gaze to his. "He got to fuck me."

He drew in a slow breath.

"After I agreed, he said there was just one stipulation ... he wasn't going to tell me when it would happen. That night I stayed up until three o'clock in the morning, standing guard over my virginity. He slept six feet away in a sleeping bag on the concrete floor. Eventually, I let go ... I just couldn't hold on any longer. I awoke to a tapping on my foot. He stood over me, completely naked. It was the first time I'd ever seen a grown man naked. I couldn't move ... I could barely breathe as he just stood there stroking himself. I'd been expecting him to come after me—clothed with wild eyes. But that wasn't his game. He had a point to prove and it was that I was, in fact, young, weak, and naive. He asked if I was a virgin. I nodded. Then he said, "Run, bitch.""

"Jess ... you don't have to tell me—"

"I do." She gave him a sad smile. "It's time."

Luke nodded.

"So I ran, or at least I tried. He grabbed my ankle, and I fell face-first onto the concrete. It bloodied my nose and busted open one of the cuts on my lip. He pressed his naked body to my back then reached between us to shove down my pants."

Luke watched her stare into the sunset, but not a single tear formed in her eyes. She looked drained of all emotion.

"I was scared. I thought about my time waiting for Trigger to return and kill me, but not even then was I as scared as I was when Mick's cock pressed to my ass. I got it ... I really did. It's a different type of fear, and looking back perhaps I can understand a little why Claire's parents were so relieved that she hadn't been raped. It meant she didn't have *that* fear. It's paralyzing, especially for someone who hadn't *ever* experienced sex. As if the fear of the unknown mixed with the sheer weight of his body on mine wasn't enough, he slid his finger over my clit. As he rubbed me off, he asked me how it felt to be so fucking weak. I couldn't speak, let alone scream or beg for him to stop. It was this painful fear mixed with unwanted pleasure as I climaxed from his touch."

She took several big gulps of her wine then rubbed her lips together and looked at Luke. He didn't want her to look at him. He didn't want her to see the look of complete horror in his eyes.

"He smeared my arousal back ... all the way. Then he gave me one last out as he teased the head of his cock against my ass hole. He said, 'tell me your friend died because you were too fucking weak to save her and this all ends right now.'"

Luke clenched the arms of the chair, willing himself to not look away.

Jessica shrugged. "But I'm my father's daughter—stubborn to the point of my own demise. So I took a deep breath, braced myself, then I told him to go to hell."

"Jesus, Jessica ..." Luke flinched. He couldn't help it, even though he knew how it ended.

There was no possible way to react as anyone but the man who loved her. Dr. Jones was nowhere to be found, and Luke couldn't find any words that conveyed his ... shock? Anger? Disappointment?

She continued. "I don't think our humanity is on some

switch. I think it's more like candles on a cake. It takes a lot to blow them all out at once. I know Mick blew a few out that morning, and I think it allowed enough of my soul to stay hidden in the shadows to allow me to kill Four a few weeks later." She scrunched her nose. "Does that sound like an accurate assessment?"

Luke didn't have an accurate assessment. He didn't have any assessment. "Did you tell anyone?"

"No. That's why I could somewhat relate to my student. He'd pleasured me and I felt angry, but I also felt guilty. But for me it was more than that. I made a deal with the Devil and I lost, but we shook on it. And even when he gave me the chance to stop it, I didn't. So to this day I'm not sure how I feel about any of it."

"You were seventeen, Jessica. It's not about the plea-sure. It was at the very least statutory rape. Your first sexual experience was traumatic. Do you understand how much *that* itself may have affected your life?"

She shook her head. "Not really. Every part of my life has been extreme. It's been a world away from normal, even before what happened to Claire or any of my sexual experi-ences. The day Jude and I were enlisted into this "nonexis-tent" army of sorts was the day I became someone else. Jude was never raped, and he never watched his best friend die in front of him, but he's far from normal. He's a dysfunc-tional recluse who spends his evenings trolling for quick fucks then goes home to his stupid computer. How do you explain that?"

"I don't know enough about this "nonexistent" army, but as far as you and your brother are concerned, I think they stole your childhood innocence. I think you missed out on vital time in your teenage years. But they didn't steal your humanity. That's just a weak excuse for justifying immoral behavior."

Jessica frowned. His words may have carried an edge of accusation, but he didn't regret them.

"Come here." He pulled her onto his lap and cradled her face. "That stubbornness that you admit to? I think it prevents you from seeing the whole picture of your past. I think you'd rather die than consider yourself a victim. All you see is the monster inside, but that monster is something *you've* created to protect yourself from the pain. I think that's why you feel the need for revenge. You think it proves you're a monster and no longer the victim."

Tears filled her eyes. "Monsters are strong ... victims are weak."

"Oh, baby, that's where you're wrong. Monsters prey on others because they have no self-control ... they're the weak ones. And you're not just a victim, Jess, you're a survivor and there's no one stronger than a survivor."

With one blink of her tear-filled eyes, she released a little more of that pain that she'd been holding onto for so long.

"I did it to him too." Her lip quivered as much as her voice.

"Did what?"

"I got my revenge and maybe..." she sniffed "...maybe you're right. Because afterwards I didn't feel like the victim anymore."

Luke wiped her tears. "What did you do?"

"By ten the next morning Mick was being hauled out on a stretcher with a broken nose, two missing teeth, and a punctured lung from three fractured ribs. His biggest mistake has always been forgetting that he was only *one* of the men who trained me."

Luke gave her a slight nod of understanding. He didn't want to condone the behavior that he just told her was so counterproductive to her progress, but Mick deserved everything she gave him and so much more.

"What?" she asked as he continued to look at her, contemplating everything she'd just confessed.

"The blood?"

She nodded, brushing the pads of her fingers over her lips, a glassy look in her eyes. "Before they loaded Mick into the ambulance, he whispered, 'Come here,' through his weak breaths. I leaned down close to his face and he touched my lips with his bloodied finger. 'Taste that?' he asked. I slid the tip of my tongue over my bottom lip. 'That's power, sweetheart. And that power will keep you alive.'"

CHAPTER THIRTY-FOUR

KNIGHT

"Dr. Jones?"

Luke jerked from the strong ammonia infiltrating his nose.

"Welcome back."

It took a moment to adjust to the light as everything came back into focus. He began to move his hand to rub the back of his head that pulsed with pain, but metal gripped his wrists. Then an aching burn flared along his shoulders, and he realized his hands were cuffed behind the chair.

"I see the connection now between you and Ms. Day. You're both stubborn, impulsive, and have little regard for your well-being. It's touching really." Knox grinned from across the table, with the steam from a fresh cup of coffee spiraling into the air.

"You raped her."

Knox's smile faded. He motioned with his head and the three other men standing guard in the room exited.

"You're an educated man, Dr. Jones. I'm sure had you taken the time to remove your dick from the equation, you would have come to the only conclusion there is: Jessica

Day is certifiably insane. She should have been committed. But you wanted to keep her as your little pet instead. You thought as long as you had her on a leash she wouldn't be a threat to anyone."

Knox took a sip of his coffee then stood, pacing the room. "What do you know about her training and what we do here?"

"I know you take innocent children and train them to be killers."

"Killers?" Knox laughed. "Is that what Ms. Day told you? Or is that your own assessment? Because the whole purpose of what we do is to prevent innocent people from being killed. That's why you're no longer with your beloved. The day her parents were murdered, her name moved to the top of a list. Do you know what list that was?"

Luke glared at him.

"It was the Next List. As in, she was next on the list to be killed. That's where we came in to *save her life.*"

"Witness Protection?"

Knox smirked. "Sort of ... but more efficient. Members of our group don't have to jump through hoops and pray that a bullet doesn't land in their head before they reach the end. We protect our own at all cost, no questions asked."

"Who killed her parents?"

"Someone who realized her father was not who he claimed to be. People in the drug trafficking business tend to be a little unforgiving when they find out an undercover DEA agent has infiltrated their circle."

"If her parents were dead, why would they come after her?"

"Now you're asking me to think like a drug lord." Knox shrugged, lighting up a cigar. "I suppose it's like going to a buffet. Some people keep eating until they're full, others keep going until they feel they've gotten their money's worth. These kingpins always get their money's worth, and they have ferocious appetites."

Luke grimaced as he tried to roll his shoulders.

"Sorry, Dr. Jones. I'd let you go, but I can't trust you, and I'm not sure how many more of your attacks my patience can tolerate without actually killing you. And your absence in this world would get back to Ms. Day and her unpredictability would most likely bring about the apocalypse. Now, if you don't mind, it's time to tell me what the two of you discussed at the hotel."

Luke shook his head. "Nothing."

"Nothing?" Knox laughed. "You just saw the woman whose grave you visit every Saturday morning with your mammoth dog and a to-go cup of Samovar tea, yet you expect me to believe you said *nothing?*"

The metal cut into Luke's wrists as he glowered at Knox.

"Don't give me that look. You've been the biggest waste of man hours, but you and that dumb dog of yours have had an *angel* looking out for you per Ms. Day's request, or should I say per her *threat.*"

"I said nothing. She said ... thank you." His words mirrored the defeat in his heart. The only thing worse than losing her once was losing her twice. He'd had closure, but he would never have it again. Every day would be filled with worry and the permanent heartache of knowing that she looked broken and miserable and there was nothing he could do.

"Why did she say thank you if you didn't say anything?"

Luke's lip twitched into the hint of a smile. "'God gave you a gift of 86,400 seconds today. Have you used one of them to say thank you?' William Arthur Ward," he whispered.

Day

"This is the most ridiculous thing I have ever done," Luke declared.

Jessica giggled. "Really? More than skinny dipping with your parents?"

"That was insane. This is just *ridiculous*."

"I'd help, babe, but I have long, painted fingernails for the first time in nearly fifteen years and I don't want to chip them."

"Dammit, Jones ... hold still." Luke grumbled as he stood and slipped off his jacket. "Hold this, I'm going to have dog hair all over my suit."

"Maybe I should see if your dad can help. He's more patient with Jones than you are."

"There's no time. Besides, they've already been ushered to their seats."

Jones tilted his head at Jessica and she blew him a kiss. Luke rolled his eyes.

"He's a black and white dog. I don't see the point of dressing him in a goddamn black and white dog tuxedo." Luke lay down under Jones like a mechanic under a car, to button up the custom made dog tuxedo.

"Millie's wearing a dress, so Jones has to wear a tux. Besides this is Kelly's day and the bride gets whatever she wants."

"You mean it's *Gabe* and Kelly's day."

"Yeah, yeah that's what I meant."

Luke rolled out from under Jones and lumbered to standing, brushing off his pants and re-tucking his shirt.

"Thanks, man, for being such a fucking idiot." Gabe came into the room and smacked Luke on the back just as he slid his arm into his black jacket. "'I'm going to the rescue shelter to get Jess a dog. You should get one for Kelly.' Dumbest. Idea. Ever. The church is filled to capacity and my bride-to-be is having a breakdown because her four-legged bridesmaid's dress has shit on the back. Who the hell buys a dog a dress with a train on the back?"

Jessica grimaced, backing up toward the door. "Sounds like I'd better help defuse the bride."

Luke gave her a pointed look.

She shrugged. "Don't give me that look. That's why I had Jones's tux made without tails."

He rolled his eyes as she shut the door behind her.

"My apologies. Admittedly, the dogs were a moment of insanity. At least Millie fits in a kennel and doesn't shit logs the size of Redwoods."

Jones tilted his head at Luke.

"You know it's true." Luke narrowed his eyes at Jones.

Gabe laughed. "How did you end up with a dog that's bigger than your girlfriend?"

Luke chuckled. "So are you nervous?"

Gabe wiped his brow and showed Luke his sweaty fingers. "I'm scared shitless. Half of all marriages end in divorce. But I'm so fucking crazy about her and I want her to be mine in every way possible. I'm just as big a dog as Jones when it comes to her. I want to mark her—lay claim to her—so the whole world knows she's mine and I'm so fucking protective of her it's ludicrous."

"Please tell me those aren't your wedding vows."

Gabe laughed. "You have no room to make fun, man.

For the past two years I've watched you worship the ground Jessica walks on."

"Touché. Now get your ass to the altar."

MILLIE THE BULLDOG and her dress, minus the shat-on train, walked down the aisle with Jessica. Luke's heart ached as he and Jones watched her move with elegance and breathtaking beauty—flowing black hair over her sun-kissed shoulders and a floor-length strapless, champagne dress. He *absolutely* worshiped everything about her.

As if she could read his mind, her grin doubled when their eyes met. "I love you," she mouthed. He pressed his hand to his heart. It was ready to burst. He wanted it to be him standing closest to the altar and her meeting him there to start their forever. *Someday.*

There was a bride, some scripture, a poem, an exchange of vows, and a kiss, but all he saw was Jessica and all he heard was the beat of his heart. Gabe and Kelly walked down the aisle as husband and wife as the guests clapped and cheered. He and Jones met Jessica and Millie at the altar to walk out next.

"I can't breathe ... you're so beautiful," he whispered in her ear as he offered his arm.

"Luke ..." she shook her head.

Jessica dabbed her eyes as they exited the church. He wasn't trying to make her cry. It was just something that had to be said.

Luke's parents took the canines back to their house on the way to the reception lodge by the lake while Luke and Jessica drove the bride and groom in the GTO, tin cans, and a "Just Married" sign in the back window because

Luke wouldn't let them write anything on the actual window.

"I'm driving home," she whispered in his ear as he helped her out.

"Ahem, enough canoodling, you two. Help me out of the back. I think my groom is lost in the sea of my dress." Kelly laughed.

Luke helped her out and sure enough, there was a groom buried under a million layers of chiffon and tulle.

"That dress has got to go," Gabe declared as he crawled out of the backseat.

"Five hours, baby, and you can take it all off." Kelly fisted his lapels and kissed him.

"Enough canoodling, you two. Your guests await."

Kelly pushed away and elbowed Jessica with a grin as they made their way to the lodge. Toasts, dinner, cake, and dancing filled the late summer evening along the banks of Lake Tahoe. Luke stood on the sidelines with a cold beer, watching Jessica float around the room, throwing her head back in laughter as she talked with family and friends or danced like a young girl born of innocence and blooming with hope. Not another soul in the room would ever imagine that she carried a hundred lifetimes of pain inside those amber eyes.

"Luke ... dance with me!" She held out her hands from the edge of the dance floor.

He grinned and waited a few seconds, needing to let that image of her find its perfect spot in his memory. Then he set his beer on the table and weaved his way through the crowd to those open arms.

"I love you, babe." She threw her arms around his neck as he lifted her off the ground, kissing her like they were the only two people in the room.

Gasping for air as he eased her back to the floor, she stared at him with wide eyes. "Oh my God …"

"What?" He smirked, wiping her lipstick from his mouth.

Jessica leaned into him. "That kiss."

"What about it?"

She wet her lips and swallowed. "It's how you kiss me when you want me … *really* want me."

He hugged her to his body, swaying to the music. "I do *really* want you."

Her breath hitched. "Dr. Jones, you're *really* hard." She slid her hands down to his ass and curled her fingers.

"Fuck," he seethed while rocking into her with a jerk. "Don't do that," he warned in her ear. His parents were seated at a table twenty feet away. The last thing he needed was them watching him grind into Jessica on the dance floor, sporting the world's hardest erection.

A playful laugh vibrated from her chest. "Please, please, please tell me we're going to remedy this situation before we go back to your parents' house."

Luke was ready to remedy the "situation" right then and there. Watching his greatest adoration float around all day in that dress, with that smile, wetting those lips if he stared at her too long … it had been a slow burn of seduction. They *would not* be going back to his parents' place until the situation was remedied. He just wasn't certain of the specific details.

"Attention, everyone. The bride is going to toss her bouquet."

Jessica grinned. "In the bag."

Luke smiled. "You and me, sexy, in the lake, if you catch the bouquet."

"Oh, Jones … I love all your little wagers. But you

always try to squirm your way out of those lake promises." She blew him a kiss as she followed the throng of women to the other side of the dance floor.

"Jess, stand by me," Lake said, grabbing Jessica's hand. "I turn eighteen tomorrow and I've never caught a bouquet. Do you think it's my lucky night?"

Jessica smiled at Lake. "Yeah ... I think it will be."

Two of the groomsmen lifted Kelly into the air with her back to the mass of hopeful women.

"One. Two. Three!" Kelly tossed it over her head.

Luke smiled while shaking his head in complete disbelief. It was headed straight for Jessica. He imagined her taking out half the women to catch it, but it appeared fate had her back. However, at the last second, she shoved Lake right in front of her. Lake caught the bouquet with a huge grin, eyes wide with surprise. Jessica wrapped her arms around Lake and whispered something in her ear.

As Jessica made her way back to Luke, she shrugged and smiled. "Guess it wasn't in the stars for me tonight."

"I don't think there are enough stars in the sky to count how many times a day I fall in love with you all over again."

Lake sidled next to Luke, sliding her arm around his back. He hugged her to him.

"Here." She pulled one of the white roses from the bouquet and handed it to her brother. "It should have been Jess's, but she gave me an early birthday present. Marry her, Luke. Marry. Her." She reached up and kissed him on the cheek then hugged Jessica again before twirling off to the dance floor.

"Not even *close* to enough stars in the sky." Luke shook his head and tucked the rose behind Jessica's ear as he pressed his lips to hers. "Race you to the lake," he whispered over her lips, smiling so big his face hurt.

He backed slowly toward the door. Jessica remained statuesque, lips parted. Her whole face spelled shock. Luke nodded his head toward the exit. With a deep breath, a smile grew along her lips as her eyes gleamed with excitement.

The second he stepped outside he made a dash for the lake, knowing she would be not more than a breath behind him.

"Jones!" she squealed, chasing him down the tree-lined path to the lake.

Jacket, tie, shirt ... he tossed them to the wind. The adrenaline-fed insanity made him feel more alive than he ever imagined possible. He took a quick look over his shoulder as his legs continued to propel him forward. Long dark hair flowed behind his living dream. Her shoes tossed to the sand, and with each step she ran right out of her dress. Stopping at the water's edge, he slipped out of the rest of his clothes.

Jessica flew into his arms, sending him stumbling back into the cool water. It engulfed their tangled bodies beneath a star-studded sky—so many stars.

They emerged breathless, her body wrapped around his. "Luke ..." she rested her forehead against his. "Thank you."

"Thank you?"

She smiled. "William Arthur Ward. 'God gave you a gift of 86,400 seconds today. Have you used one of them to say thank you?'"

He closed his eyes as his heart swelled even more.

Never. Enough. Stars.

Knight

"THANK YOU? Okay then, Dr. Jones. That wasn't so hard, now was it?" Through a haze of smoke, Knox smirked around his cigar, taking another slow draw, a slight squint to his already beady, dark eyes. He looked at his watch. "If all goes well, we'll have you home by curfew."

"What about Jessica? She looked miserable ... not like a woman living of her own free will."

Snuffing the end of his cigar in the ashtray, Knox looked at Luke with a hint of pleasure in his eyes. "The guy she's been fucking is dying. Cancer ... a real bitch.

Luke closed his eyes. Numb.

"Now. You're going to wake up in your own bed tomorrow morning feeling much like you did when you arrived here—groggy and disoriented. That blow to your head earlier is going to give you one hell of a headache. I'd suggest taking something for it as soon as you wake. Once your mind stops spinning and the memories from today start to fall back into place, you're going to have the urge to tell someone—friends, family, the police. Don't. Everyone you tell dies. Any questions?"

Luke stared at the table. Someone brought Jessica back to life just to kill her in front of him. Another man. She was with another man—a man who was dying. The pain seeped into his chest like poison.

His body stiffened, rejecting Knox's condescending hand that landed on his shoulder.

"If it were me, I'd get drunk off my ass, stick my dick in as much pussy as possible, burn everything that bears her memory, and get on with my fucking life."

Knox opened the door and nodded. Two men stepped

in the room. One of them handed Knox a syringe. He pulled the cap off with his teeth then spit it on the floor.

"Are you ready to go home, Dr. Jones?"

"Why fake her death?" Luke continued to stare at the table as Knox held his head to the side with one arm while pressing the tip of the syringe to his neck with his other hand.

"Nobody looks for dead people."

Stick. Burn. Black.

CHAPTER THIRTY-FIVE

KNIGHT

THANKSGIVING WAS two days away and for the first time in her life Ryn had no plans. Her parents, not knowing about Jackson's it's-not-you-it's-me breakup, decided to take a cruise assuming Ryn would be with him since Maddie would be with Preston. Ryn dropped the restraining order and if her stubborn daughter would have answered her calls or listened to her messages, she'd have known that. Instead Ryn was on her way to clean AJ's house per Jillian's request and then Jillian and Jackson's place. She hadn't seen or spoken to Jackson since their breakup the previous week.

"Hi, Ryn." Jillian answered AJ's door.

She smiled, stepping inside while looking for AJ.

"He's sleeping."

Ryn nodded. "I'm afraid to even ask how he's doing."

Jillian sighed. "For the past week he's basically been sleeping. He has some short-term memory loss and vision issues. When we flew here from Houston I thought his vision was completely gone, but he's regained a bit a few times since. It's sporadic and unpredictable. I'm guessing swelling or the tumor. I don't know."

Ryn gave her a sad smile. "I'm so sorry. If there's anything I can do just name it."

"What you're doing today is great. The downside to his vision coming back sometimes is he sees how dirty things have gotten around here and apparently my cleaning is not up to his standards."

With a little chuckle, Ryn smiled. "Well, this I can do for you. Should I just avoid his bedroom?"

"No. The blinds are partially open, but he's really out of it so I wouldn't worry about waking him."

"Is his family coming for Thanksgiving?" Ryn hollered from the hall bathroom.

Jillian leaned against the doorway with her arms folded over her chest. "No." She scrunched her nose. "They don't know we're here. Nobody knows we're here except Jackson. I've even tried to keep my trekking back and forth to a minimum so the neighbors don't get too nosy. Jackson's been dropping off food. AJ doesn't want his family here ... he doesn't even want to be here, but I needed to come back for ... certain reasons."

"Why don't I make you both Thanksgiving dinner and bring it over? I'm sort of by myself this year and I love to cook so it would be no trouble."

Jillian lifted a single shoulder. "AJ's hardly eating anything, and what he does eat I have to force feed him—it's not pretty. And I don't eat meat so ..."

"But you eat, right?" Ryn couldn't help but smile at her own ridiculous eagerness.

Jillian laughed. "Yes, I eat."

"Great. I'll make a vegetarian Thanksgiving dinner, and then you'll have leftovers for a few days too."

"You don't have—"

Ryn shook her head. "I want to. Please?"

Jillian nodded. "Okay. Thank you."

After Ryn finished AJ's house, Jillian told her their front door was unlocked and Jackson may or may not be there. That meant Ryn may or may not have to clean their house for two hours with her heart in her throat.

"Hello?" she called as she peeked in the door.

No answer. She sighed and carried her supplies inside. Even without him there it was difficult to not feel his presence everywhere. With each room, she picked up speed, going from a small part of her hoping he'd show up to an overwhelming need to get out of there before he came home.

Releasing a sigh of victory as she wound up the vacuum hose, she turned toward the hall leading to the garage door.

"Hi."

Her heart wasted no time leaping into her throat. "Hi ... uh was my car in your way? I'm just leaving." She knew her car wasn't in his way, but her nervousness took over, grasping for anything to say that was random and impersonal like the weather or parking spots.

He shook his head.

"Great, then I'll just be going." Ryn grabbed as many of her supplies as possible to limit her trips back inside.

After loading her first armful of supplies in the back of her vehicle she turned. "Oh ..." She stopped inches from ramming into Jackson. "Thanks."

He handed her the vacuum and last bucket. "How have you been?" he asked after she shut the back door.

She bit the inside of her cheek. "I don't know how to

answer that. So I'll just say fine and leave because this is a little awkward." She tried to slip by him.

"Ryn?" He hooked just her pinkie finger with his finger and tugged it. That small touch stopped her heart.

"Please don't," she whispered, not wanting him to know the fragile shell of her heart could splinter into tiny pieces from his slightest touch.

"I miss you."

Ryn bit her tongue instead of screaming. Why did he say that? He missed her, so what?

"That's not my fault." She pulled from his grasp and even though it was just his finger, it took incredible strength to let go. Ryn hated herself for giving a man that much power over her again.

"What if we just went back to how things were before, except ... without the sex?"

On an uncontrolled laugh, she turned. "Friends? Are you taking another vow of celibacy or is this just your way of keeping me under your control so no one else can have me even if you don't want me?"

"Dammit!" He pushed her against the door, caging her in with his hands against the window.

She didn't move, not even a breath, as his came in huffs of angry hot air over her face. "Two weeks. Give me two weeks and it will be like this never happened." The muscles in his jaw pulsed.

"Just like that? Whatever it is that has you so 'fucked up' is just going to disappear in two weeks?"

Jackson stared at her with determination etched along his tensed brows, eyes narrowed as he nodded.

She turned, waiting for him to release her from his prison. Jackson let his hands drop to his sides. Ryn opened the door and climbed in the driver's seat.

"Two weeks," she said and shut the door.

DENIAL COMFORTED Jillian on the days that AJ slept eighteen to twenty hours. She convinced herself the body heals while sleeping and AJ's had a lot of healing to do.

"I'm tired." He yawned as she made him breakfast at eleven thirty.

"You just woke up twenty minutes ago." She slid him a plate with toast and butter. That was her specialty as long as the settings didn't get bumped on the toaster.

AJ looked down at the table and slowly moved his hands toward the plate.

"Can you see it?"

He blinked several times. "Yes, I can fucking see it!" AJ clenched his fists at the sides of his head.

Jillian took a step back. Her heart pounded against her chest. The rage hadn't reared its face for quite some time. The personality changes seemed to be non-existent since the radiation.

"AJ—"

"SHUT. UP!" He hammered his fist into the plate, cracking it into several large pieces.

Jillian flinched. His behavior frightened her the most because she knew no matter what he did, she wouldn't fight back.

He slammed his fist down again sending toast and pieces of plate flying.

"WHY..." *BANG* "...CAN'T..." *BANG* "...YOU..." *BANG BANG BANG* "...LEAVE ME THE FUCK..." *BANG* "...ALONE?"

The next bang came from the front door slamming against the wall like it had been knocked off its hinges.

Silent tears rolled down her face as Jackson stormed around the corner.

"Go home, Jill," he said, narrowing his eyes at AJ who stared at his bloodied fist covered in toast and embedded with bits of ceramic from the shattered plate.

The vacant look in AJ's eyes would haunt her, maybe forever.

"I'm not—"

"Jillian, I swear ... I will physically remove you from this house if you don't leave right now."

The need to wrap her arms around him and promise that everything would be okay remained locked inside the walls of fear. Fear that it wouldn't ever. Be. Okay. Again. Instead, she walked away.

***

THAT STRANGER HAD TAKEN A VACATION. AJ had hoped for good. But there he sat at the table, sweaty and bloodied with rage. His head jackhammered with pain as waves of nausea grew with intensity. He scooted his chair out, but before he could stand, his body buckled over his legs. He vomited the pills and water Jillian gave him when he woke up. The next round consisted of bile until all that remained were dry heaves, aching stomach muscles, and a burning throat.

A hand rested on his shoulder as his eyes watered with more pain. "What can I do for you, Sarge?"

AJ had an answer to that question, but he couldn't speak.

"Water?"

AJ nodded as Jackson handed him a towel.

The man who, by all rights, hated him, cleaned up his vomit and helped him to the bathroom.

"Do you want me to have Jillian come back over to help you shower?"

AJ shook his head.

"Okay. I'll be out here."

AJ nodded as Jackson shut the door. By the time he undressed and stepped into the hot shower, he could barely stand. Choosing to find the floor of the shower before it found him, he slid down the tile wall. Resting his head on his bent knees, he let the water wash away everything. He chased away the loneliness by feeling Jillian's hands on his head like a ghost. There would never be the right words to describe that touch. It brought him back from the deepest depths of pain and darkness. Would she ever know that? Would she ever know she loved him at his very worst? There was so much to say, but not enough time; there was never enough time.

By the time he toweled off and dressed, he needed another shower. Busting up his breakfast and blowing up at Jillian for absolutely no reason, expended his allotment of energy for the day.

"Do you need anything?" Jackson asked as AJ lumbered to his bed, collapsing into a partial sitting position at the head of it.

"Wwaor ..." AJ closed his eyes. Anger. Humiliation. Rock bottom.

"I'll get it."

Jackson returned with more water.

AJ wrapped both hands around the glass. He didn't trust his body. It seemed to be failing him.

"It's affecting your speech?"

AJ nodded.

"Did it just start?"

AJ nodded. "Y-es." He felt like a child trying to say his first word. And if life weren't already cruel enough, tears pricked his eyes because even his emotions were out of his control.

Jackson narrowed his eyes a bit. "Are you done?"

AJ stared at the glass of water still half-full.

"I'm not talking about the water."

He looked up. Jackson didn't blink or say another word. He didn't have to.

AJ nodded.

CHAPTER THIRTY-SIX

The droning whistle of the furnace ceased on the chilly November evening, leaving Jillian in silence. By the time Jackson texted her the all clear to go back to AJ's, he was already asleep again. She thanked her brother for cleaning up after AJ and staying with him while he showered. Then she thanked him for his patience, in spite of AJ's earlier outburst. Jackson kissed her on the head and left without saying much of anything. Perhaps there was nothing to say.

AJ needed her.

She would help him get better.

Luke belonged to Jessica.

He was her past and she died.

Everyone needed a mantra and that became hers. The bed creaked as she crawled in next to AJ and took his hand in hers. The need to feel the warmth of his body, the beat of his heart, the whisper of his breath ... it felt as vital as the air in her lungs, the blood in her veins. Seeing Luke, or what felt like a ghost of a life that no longer existed, only intensified her need to be in the arms of the man who gave her a second chance. AJ accepted the woman and the monster without explanation. Who does that?

"I love you, Aric James. You'll never know how much I needed you to come into my life when you did. You've given my existence a life again. This feeling in my chest feels like ..." she placed her other hand over her chest "...like a fucking heartbeat. I don't even know how that's possible, but it's there..." she rolled to the side and pressed her lips to his shoulder. "...and I need it."

He didn't move. Not a twitch. Nothing more than a slow breath and weak heartbeat. The lump in Jillian's throat thickened.

"I need *you*," she whispered as the first tear fell. "Until you asked me to come to Portland, I'd gone to all of Cage's games. I didn't tell you before now because I knew how much pain you'd feel just from the mention of his name. He's so damn talented and strong, but he needs his father. You *need* to be there to cheer him on, not just on the field but in life. Children need their parents ... even when they die, that need doesn't ever go away."

She closed her eyes and prayed. For years she questioned God's existence, most people in hell probably did. But maybe God saw how she'd loved another selflessly and would grant her one wish ... one answered prayer.

"Let me keep him ... even if I burn in hell later, just for now ... let me keep him."

GOD HAD DECIDED to at least give her request some thought, because Jillian awoke from the floor to the sound of AJ coughing. It wasn't a miracle healing, but ten hours after her request, he was still breathing. Or at least trying to breathe.

"Here." She knelt beside the bed holding a glass of water as he struggled to sit up a little bit.

He took a small sip and tried to clear his throat. "Tha-th-tha—" Closing his eyes, he shook his head and clenched his teeth.

"You're welcome." Jillian kissed his lips, resting her hands on his face. "I know this is hard for you right now, but it's going to get better." She nodded her head, waiting for him to open his eyes.

When he did, he shook his head. "N-no."

She resented the pleading look in his eyes. He covered her hands with his, pulling them to his chest as he tried to squeeze them.

"Mm-my r-re-real."

Pulling away, she stood and walked to the other side of the room, keeping her back to him. "Stop saying that. I don't want to be your fucking real. I want to be your goddamn future! Do you kn—" Her voice cracked from the pain in her chest "Do you know what I've endured to get to this point in my life?" She shook her head, brushing her fingers over her cheeks. "I *died* to be with you, and I know you don't understand that, but it's true. I gave up my last fucking breath to be here."

Jillian turned. And that new heart? It broke.

AJ looked at her through red eyes ... tears trailing down his face.

"Let me take you back to Portland. *Please.* I'll stay with you. I'll go to every appointment and hold your hand ... or prance around the room naked, or read you the boring newspaper. Just ... let me take you back and let me fight this with you."

AJ looked down at the floor for a few seconds that felt like an eternity as she waited for his answer. When he looked up ... he nodded.

***

JILLIAN PACKED AJ's bags while she waited for Jackson to get back from running a few errands. She hoped one of them was to Ryn's. It would be an awkward Thanksgiving dinner if they didn't at least call a couple hours truce. AJ had slept most of the day, but she hoped he would be awake for Thanksgiving dinner, even if he didn't eat anything.

"Jill?"

"In here," she called out the door of AJ's bedroom.

Not even a freight train could wake him when he was in his deep sleep.

Jackson stood in the doorway as she zipped up AJ's travel bag on the floor.

"Hey, did you get your errands ran?"

Jackson nodded.

"Please tell me you saw Ryn and made up."

"I messaged her."

"About dinner?"

He nodded.

"And everything is good?"

Another nod.

"Are we still eating here? I don't want to try to move AJ."

"Yes."

"What time?"

Jackson stared at her then looked at his watch. "Three hours."

"Perfect. I can do a load of my laundry, shower, and pack. Text me when she gets here with the food?"

A nod.

Jillian kissed a sleeping AJ on the forehead. "Love you," she whispered. "Don't look so grumpy." She pinched Jackson's cheeks as she squeezed by him. "It's Thanksgiving. I'm not cooking the meal. And AJ agreed to fight. It's a good day."

"A good day," Jackson repeated like he was testing out the words.

Jillian rolled her eyes. "I'll be back."

"Wear something nice."

She turned at the front door. "Really? You're in jeans."

"Ryn's dressing up. She doesn't want to be the only one."

Jillian shrugged. "Okay then."

She threw in a load of laundry to wash, then soaked in the tub, taking the time to shave all her neglected parts. After doing her hair and packing for their trip, she shrugged off her robe and slipped on a red shift dress and black heels. Just as she glided on her favorite red lip stick, her phone vibrated.

Jackson: *Dinner.*
Jillian: *Be right there.*
Jackson: *I love you, Jillian.*

His holiday sentimentality made her smile.

Jillian: *U2*

She slipped on a wrap and stepped out into the cool breeze. Ryn's car wasn't in AJ's driveway. Jackson must have let her park in the garage to haul in all the food. Soft music played in the background as she stepped inside. All the lights were off except for a soft glow that flickered from the dining room.

"Hello?"

No one answered.

She stopped at the entry to the room illuminated with candles everywhere. A table was set for two with the elegance of a five-star restaurant, a massive bouquet of roses in a large glass vase divided the two place settings at opposite ends. Jillian smiled.

Cloth napkins.

As she moved around the table to the setting behind the roses, her smile faded. The white napkin folded and held by a silver napkin ring had black ink—writing on it. She slowly eased into the chair, letting her wrap fall to the floor as she slid the napkin from the ring.

Jillian,

You look beautiful tonight—simply stunning as always. Please accept my sincerest apologies for missing our first official date. I had a chance to go and I took it.

"No ..." she sucked in a shaky breath as tears filled her eyes. "What have you done?" she whispered.

I don't know what's on the other side or even which direction I'm going, but I hope by the time you're reading this I'm sitting across from you, even if you can't see me.

She looked up at the empty chair across from her. "Aric James ..." she breathed his name as her tears stained the table cloth.

Some things in life you just know. I knew the day I laid eyes on you that the course of my life would change forever. I knew the first day you helped me through that migraine in the shower, that no one had ever touched me so deeply ... so completely. I knew the night you broke my nose that I hated you. It was also at the exact moment that I knew I loved you. Don't roll your eyes—it's the God's honest truth.

She sobbed and laughed a little through her tears.

And I knew the day I was diagnosed with cancer that I was going to die. What I didn't know was how desperately I would want to live. As we both saw, my body wouldn't cooperate with my mind. You deserve a life ... a real life. Not the pathetic excuse for existence that I had become.

The napkin shook in her trembling hands.

Time couldn't mend my body ... but you mended my soul. I'll leave knowing that I was the luckiest bastard alive because I was loved by you. And you, my beautiful girl ... you were loved by me.

~ Aric James Monaghan

ALSO BY JEWEL E ANN

Standalone Novels

Idle Bloom

Undeniably You

Naked Love

Only Trick

Perfectly Adequate

Look The Part

When Life Happened

A Place Without You

Jersey Six

Scarlet Stone

Not What I Expected

Jack & Jill Series

End of Day

Middle of Knight

Dawn of Forever

One (*standalone*)

Out of Love (*standalone*)

Holding You Series

Holding You

Releasing Me

Transcend Series

Transcend

Epoch

Fortuity (*standalone*)

The Life Series

The Life That Mattered

The Life You Stole

Receive a FREE book and stay informed of new releases, sales, and exclusive stories:

Mailing List

https://www.jeweleann.com/free-booksubscribe

ABOUT THE AUTHOR

Jewel is a free-spirited romance junkie with a quirky sense of humor.

With 10 years of flossing lectures under her belt, she took early retirement from her dental hygiene career to stay home with her three awesome boys and manage the family business.

After her best friend of nearly 30 years suggested a few books from the Contemporary Romance genre, Jewel was hooked. Devouring two and three books a week but still craving more, she decided to practice sustainable reading, AKA writing.

When she's not donning her cape and saving the planet one tree at a time, she enjoys yoga with friends, good food with family, rock climbing with her kids, watching How I Met Your Mother reruns, and of course...heart-wrenching, tear-jerking, panty-scorching novels.

www.jeweleann.com

www.ingramcontent.com/pod-product-compliance
Lightning Source LLC
Chambersburg PA
CBHW071741110726
47908CB00006B/1664